Aftermath

Also by Ann McMan

Dust
Hoosier Daddy
Festival Nurse
Backcast

The Jericho Series
Jericho
Aftermath
Goldenrod

Story Collections
Sidecar
Three (plus one)

Aftermath
— a Jericho novel —

Ann McMan

Bywater
BOOKS

Ann Arbor

Bywater Books

Copyright © 2012 Ann McMan

Print ISBN: 978-1-61294-131-8

Bywater Books First Edition: December 2017

Printed in the United States of America on acid-free paper.

Cover Design by Ann McMan, TreeHouse Studio

Aftermath was originally published in 2012 by Nuance Books, a division of Bedazzled Ink Publishing Company, Fairfield, California

Bywater Books
PO Box 3671
Ann Arbor MI 48106-3671
www.bywaterbooks.com

This novel is a work of fiction.

To the eye candy, from the author.

Introduction

The Greek philosopher Heraclitus (c. 504 B.C.) believed that the basis of reality was change and flux. "You cannot step twice into the same river," he wrote.

More than two thousand years later, British mathematician turned philosopher Alfred North Whitehead expanded on Heraclitus's supposition. "You cannot step into the same river once," he explained, "because there is no 'same river.'"

Change, he said, is the most fundamental aspect of reality—and continuity is the exception. And our own life experiences bear that out. With each passing moment, the present becomes the past. The beads of our lives are strung together like moments of change, and there is no time or space in which the patterns they create remain the same.

We cannot stop the river, and we cannot step into the same river twice.

Or once.

Aftermath is not so much a sequel to *Jericho*, as it is a look inside it—a peek at what happens between the pages, beneath the hood, and behind the curtain. It is the journal of my love affair with a small town, and the quirky people who live there. Writing it was a challenge for me because I know how much so many of you love *Jericho*. And in writing this book, I didn't want to disappoint you—any more than I wanted to offend or take advantage of you by churning out a flimsy rehash of the original story.

So *Aftermath* is not another *Jericho*. It shouldn't be, and it isn't. In the parlance of the Miller Analogies Test—*Jericho* is to *Aftermath* as Dodge City is to *Gunsmoke*.

I waded into the river, and it flowed around me. I paid attention. I took notes. And the story, as it was meant to do, went its own way.

—Ann McMan
Winston-Salem, N.C.

Foreword

David Jenkins

Last week on *Knot's Landing* . . . (Or what you need to know if you bought this book, but haven't yet read *Jericho*.)

Okay. They told me I had five hundred words to tell you everything you need to know about *Jericho*— the prequel to the book you're now holding. So, first, I'll give you a plot summary—then I'll quickly run through the list of major characters introduced in *Jericho*, so you'll have a shot at figuring out everyone who is anyone in *Aftermath*.

Here goes . . .

Syd Murphy's marriage to her philandering, rich husband is falling apart, so she leaves her home in Raleigh, N.C., and accepts an eighteen-month appointment as librarian in the tiny mountain town of Jericho, Virginia. In short order, she meets our resident Katharine Hepburn clone, Maddie Stevenson—the closeted local doctor who has recently returned to the community to take over her late father's medical practice. And, boy, did SHE ever bring some relationship baggage along. Maddie fights her immediate attraction to Syd because she thinks Syd is straight (duh . . . weren't we all at some point?)—and Syd struggles with how to understand her escalating desire to jump Maddie's bones. This prompts everyone to drink lots of wine. The two of them engage in this elaborate and annoyingly protracted dance around each other for about five hundred pages (until the publisher decides to print the final manuscript in, like, seven-point type to lower the overall page count). The two frustrated and wine-swilling heroines finally come to their senses and make their restrained version of mad whoopee during a dramatic hiatus in Los Angeles. Later, Maddie meets an adorable little boy named Henry on a flight back to Jericho from California—where she had been caring for her estranged mother, who was nearly killed by a centrifuge explosion in her medical lab. She ends up becoming Henry's foster parent after his soldier dad is deployed to Afghanistan, and his guardian grandmother suffers a stroke. Hey, don't look at me . . . I'm not the one who came up with this flimsy plot. Anyway . . . while in California, taking care of her mother, Maddie learns that the real reason her parents' marriage broke up a zillion years ago was because of her mother's discovery that Maddie's father was having a longtime, homosexual affair with his best friend—Maddie's beloved Uncle Art. Collective gasp. Of course, they hash things out while sharing a bottle or two of fine, California wine. MEANWHILE . . . the one constant in Maddie's life continues to be her dashing, erudite, and steadfast best friend, David—gay as a singing flight attendant, and proud of it. He, by the way, was instrumental in bringing the two heroines together through the careful manipulation of several bogus events where much hilarity, and even more wine drinking, ensued. Those tales, alone, make *Jericho* worth the price of a download, IMHO. Let's see . . . Oh! Maddie hires a savvy parish nurse who looks like a walking plot device, but who actually ends up being just a redhead—and not a red herring. Meanwhile, a lot of other creepy stuff starts happening when a local, ne'er-do-well, drug addict-cum-stalker develops a hankering for Syd and Lizzy (the new nurse)—and the town library gets burned down. What can I say? Bad stuff happens. People drink more wine. Time marches on. Roma Jean Freemantle trips over all kinds of crap. Maddie fixes a broken Xerox machine. Maddie and Syd eat lots of Crunchy Cheetos to deal with their sexual frustration. Tom Greene acts like an ass. Syd finally comes out to my sober and stalwart partner, Michael, after everyone in NINE counties has already figured out that she sings in the choir at the Lesbyterian Church. Her cheating husband shows up and tries to reconcile. Unfortunately for him, Maddie is way taller, and looks better in tight jeans—so that idea goes no place at, like, warp six. By the end of the book, the two heroines are living happily ever after on Maddie's ancestral farm with little Henry and Pete the dog. They spend their evenings like the iconic nerds they are—reading the unabridged *War and Peace*, and drinking TONS of wine. That's about it. Now you're up to speed and can launch right into *Aftermath*— immediately after you review this list of major players.

Jericho Dramatis Personæ

~~Hamlet~~
~~Prince of Denmark~~

Madeleine Stevenson (Maddie)
Annoyingly literal local doctor, private pilot, and resident hottie.

Margaret (Syd) Murphy
*High school music teacher (and formerly straight) town librarian—
now partner to Maddie.
Commonly mistaken for Sandra Dee.*

Henry Lawrence
*Six-and-a-half-year-old foster son to Maddie and Syd, while his father,
Cpl. James Lawrence, is deployed to Afghanistan.*

David Jenkins
*Social media guru, fashion arbiter, and lifetime best friend to Maddie.
Co-owner of Riverside Inn B&B,
and partner to Michael Robertson, world-class chef.*

Roma Jean Freemantle
*Perky local teenager with a propensity for falling down—
especially when Maddie is around.*

Curtis and Edna Freemantle

Roma Jean's parents, and owners of the local market. By the way, when you meet Curtis's mother in Aftermath, *be sure to call her "A-za-lee"— and not Azalea (like the shrub). Trust me on this one . . .*

Jessie Rayburn

Roma Jean's best friend.

Jeff Simon

Syd's cheating husband—pampered, rich son of Doris Simon.

Peggy Hawkes

Maddie's chatty clinic nurse, who is famous for her toxic lemon chess pies.

Byron Martin

*Sheriff of Jefferson County.
Think of him as Jericho's Andy Griffith . . . with less Brylcreem.*

Lizzy Mayes

*Maddie's nurse practitioner,
who is dating Syd's hunky brother, Tom Murphy.*

Janet and George Murphy

The awesome parents every gay person wishes they had. (Syd's parents don't show up in Aftermath, *but you need to know about them, anyway.)*

Tom Greene

*Annoying chief of the hospital ER, and perpetual thorn in Maddie's side.
Married to Muriel Greene.*

Gladys Pitzer

Twitchy local florist, and beleaguered mother of the late Beau Pitzer (meth addict, arsonist, and sometime stalker...it's a long story).

Dr. Celine Heller
*Maddie's formerly estranged, ultra-brainiac mother,
who lives in California and teaches in the med school at UCLA.*

Davis Stevenson, M.D.
Maddie's late father—former local physician in Jericho.

Arthur Leavitt, M.D.
Surrogate uncle, best friend (and more) to Maddie's father.

Phoebe Jenkins
*Former high school music teacher and director of local "symphony"
(don't even get me started on this one…).
My mother, and co-shopaholic.*

Hot Dude at Tire Store
If you could see him, you'd know why he's listed here.

Pete
Maddie's golden retriever (a hundred-pound lounge lizard).

Let the games begin!

"And he said, Go forth, and stand upon the mount before the Lord. And, behold, the Lord passed by, and a great and strong wind rent the mountains, and brake in pieces the rocks before the Lord; but the Lord was not in the wind: and after the wind an earthquake; but the Lord was not in the earthquake: And after the earthquake a fire; but the Lord was not in the fire: and after the fire a still small voice."

—1 Kings 19:11-13

Prologue

When the big one finally came, it wasn't like a thief in the night.

Nope. This one was arrogant enough to show up in broad daylight. And still, it managed to take everything it could carry from a score of families that had little to spare.

For weeks it had been predicted. It was all the evening news anchors could talk about. Night after night, wary residents slept with their weather radios on. And in the predawn hours, when the alerts would sound, they'd crawl from their beds, collect the kids and the pets, and head for their basements—if they were lucky enough to have basements. Others did the best they could and took refuge beneath their stairways, or in their smallest bathrooms or closets.

There were many close calls, but still, the big one never showed.

Not during the night, anyway.

Most mornings, during that three-week period, the bleary-eyed locals would get up and trudge off to their jobs. Over Styrofoam cups of coffee or cans of Mountain Dew, they'd talk about the magnitude of the storms that had rolled through the night before. How the wind blew the hood off Zeke Dawkins' old F150 and dropped it down right in the middle of Eunice Pollard's koi pond. Or how four inches of rain fell in thirty minutes and completely washed out Powerhouse Road, right near the county school. Or how golf ball-sized hail turned Deb Carlson's brand new Camaro into a thirty-five-thousand-dollar piece of Swiss cheese.

But life went on. Stories grew less dramatic. Weather radios sat idle. And soon, the good people of Jericho took all the dire forecasts of catastrophic weather with a hefty dose of salt.

At least they did until that Thursday morning, when everything changed.

Everything.

Chapter 1

So it looked like the school bus wasn't going to be able to make it.

Again.

Maddie looked at her watch.

It was 7:20. Peggy Hawkes had already called. After a ten-minute conversation about everything that had transpired in her life during the fifteen hours since they'd last seen each other, she told Maddie that she'd be late getting to the clinic. Powerhouse Road had washed out during last night's torrential downpour, and she'd have to take the long way in.

Of course, this also meant that the school bus wouldn't be running.

Syd was already gone, so Maddie would have to drop Henry off at school on her way in to work.

Again.

These storms were becoming a serious pain in the ass.

And she wasn't alone in feeling that way. People in the county were really starting to chafe under the cumulative weight of these monster weather systems that kept rolling through, night after night. It was clear that Mother Nature was on the rag about something—and everyone in the Southeastern United States was bearing the brunt of her wrath.

Syd had already packed Henry's lunch. His Transformers lunch box sat atop the kitchen table next to his favorite denim jacket and a handwritten note. Maddie picked it up.

She smiled and walked to the fridge. Maybe some yogurt would be good?

Or not.

She sighed and leaned her head against the massive door. All they had was Greek yogurt, and she hated Greek yogurt. She liked the fruity kind—the kind that didn't really taste like yogurt.

But those days were long gone. Syd had her own ideas about things. And just because—*one time*—Maddie had an insignificant test result that *hinted* at borderline high cholesterol, she now was consigned to endure life, subsisting on a diet of nuts, twigs, and lawn clippings.

She closed the fridge and looked around the kitchen.

There was a bowl containing some of those mini-bananas. She wrinkled up her nose. What were *those* about? They were just creepy—and too reminiscent of those mutant ears of baby corn that sometimes showed up in bad Chinese food.

She sighed.

It's not like a damn bowl of Fruity Pebbles once in a while would kill her.

She got an idea. She walked across the kitchen and called up the back stairs. "Hurry up, Henry! If we leave now, we can stop at Aunt Bea's and get a biscuit."

After a moment, she heard the sound of his little feet pounding down the big center hallway. He appeared at the top of the stairs with Pete in tow.

"We're not supposed to go there," he said. He started down the stairs.

"Use the handrail, buddy," Maddie reminded him. "And who says we're not supposed to go to Aunt Bea's?"

"Syd."

Maddie was confused. "When did Syd tell you that?"

Henry was now on the bottom step. He looked up at her. "This morning. She said you'd wanna stop there if you had to take me to school again."

Maddie rolled her eyes. Clearly, this was a damn conspiracy.

"Can I have a banana?" he asked.

She sighed. "Why not?" He ran across the kitchen toward the bowl of fruit. "Have *two*," she called after him.

"Can Pete have one?"

She thought about that. "How many are left?"

He counted. "Four."

She hesitated.

Nah. Too obvious.

"How about we give him a dog cookie, instead?"

Henry smiled. "Okay."

She walked to a large canister on the counter and got out a big Milk Bone. Then she turned and picked up Henry's lunch box and jacket. She opened the door to the porch. There was a low rumble of thunder in the distance.

Great.

"Come on, buddy. Let's boogie."

On her way out of the house, she wondered if Freemantle's had any more of those fried apple pies . . .

Syd shook her head. She didn't know who had the brilliant idea to start having these band rehearsals at seven-thirty in the morning, but, plainly, they were sadists who knew nothing about life in the country. Or about what it would be like to try and command the attention of thirty-two teenagers before breakfast.

Roma Jean had picked this semester to switch from the clarinet to the tuba, and she wasn't tall enough or coordinated enough to manage the damn thing. She kept hitting Jessie Rayburn on the back of the head with it when they practiced marching in formation. And that was only half the problem. Jessie played the marimba, and Roma Jean's tuba shouldn't have been anywhere *near* the percussion line.

Syd didn't know which noise was more annoying—Roma Jean's playing or Jessie's whining. Frankly, it was a toss-up. Even Fergus Wainright's saxophone—which was remarkably like the cry of a bull moose on the first day of spring—sounded good by comparison.

She'd had just about enough of this for one morning. Besides, she hated "Guantanamera." Why on earth had Phoebe Jenkins picked *this* to be the school band's signature tune?

She clapped her hands. Roma Jean kept playing. Well. Roma Jean kept doing what passed for playing. Syd stamped her foot—hard.

"Let's take five, okay?"

Outside, there was a boom of thunder that shook the building. The lights in the big gymnasium flickered. Syd could hear something hitting the roof—loudly. She looked up at the metal trusses.

Hail. It was hail.

There was more thunder. The lights flickered again. Then they went out.

Over the din of the hail, she heard something else. Something that made her heart skip a beat. It sounded vaguely familiar.

A train. It sounded like a train.

Shit.

Damn that dog.

He'd been outside for ten minutes now, calling for her and looking beneath every object large enough to conceal the fat papillon spaniel.

He knew her. He was sure that she was perched someplace, just out of sight, calmly watching him yell and stride around like a lunatic.

She probably had his fucking emery board with her.

He took another look at the sky. It was a freakish green color. *That couldn't be good.*

If she got wet, it would take most of the morning to comb out the tangles, and he didn't have time for that. The Inn was empty today, and they were having all the upstairs carpets steam-cleaned.

"Astrid! Where *are* you? Come on baby . . . come to Daddy."

Damn Michael for somehow managing to leave the kitchen door ajar when he left that morning for Wytheville. They had a big wedding party coming in early tomorrow, and he had insisted on getting to the farmer's market as soon as it opened.

Of course, he probably also insisted on hitting the Dunkin' Donuts, which was *always* open. That passion of his was starting to bear fruit, too. None of his clothes were fitting anymore. Last night, he'd worn a tan polo shirt—which was too tight—and his waistline looked exactly like one of those damn crullers.

They were going to have to have a serious talk about his diet.

And about how he kept leaving the damn doors open.

"Astrid!"

Where the hell was she? God, this dog was fucking stubborn. He should've named her after Maddie—they both had slabs of granite between their ears.

He walked further away from the house, along the crushed gravel path that led down toward the river. Sometimes she liked to sun herself near the big benches in the clearing.

He took another look at the sky. There wasn't any sun this morning. It was actually getting darker. And it looked like it was about to cut loose with . . . something. High in the trees, the leaves were shaking like torn pieces of paper. A gust of wind came out of no place and slammed into his back, nearly knocking him off his feet. A hard rain was falling now. The massive drops left comically-shaped wet spots all over his shirt. Something sharp stung his face. He noticed it piling up all around him and plucked a chunk of it off his shirt.

Hail. Jesus. *Huge* hail. He'd never seen it this big.

The wind was roaring now. The noise was making it hard to think. He began to panic.

"Astrid!"

He felt something brush against his leg. He looked down. Astrid sat, placidly staring up at him with an expression that seemed to say, "Where in the hell have *you* been?"

He snapped her up into his arms and turned back toward the Inn.

Then he saw it.

"Oh, my god."

One of his brand-new, fiberglass porch urns hit him dead-on and knocked him beneath one of the stone benches. His last thought, before he lost consciousness, was that he'd left the iron on.

Maddie took the gravel road that ran along Elk Creek, since Powerhouse Road had washed out. It took longer to reach the school going this way, but she really had no choice.

They topped the rise near the Cox barn, and big chunks of ice pelted the Jeep like stones. She knew she had to pull over, or the vehicle would be damaged beyond repair.

The wind picked up, and its roar was deafening. She didn't like the way the sky looked, either. It had turned an eerie, greenish color.

"Hang on, buddy," she said to Henry, who was strapped into the backseat. "We need to stop for a minute until this hail lightens up."

"Okay, Maddie," Henry replied. "It's really loud."

She nodded. "It sure is. But I think if we sit here for just a minute, we can ..." Something bounced off the hood and came to rest against the windshield. Maddie stared at it with amazement and confusion as it hovered there. It was a license plate. "2BAD4U" it proclaimed. Then, just as quickly, it was gone.

Ahead of the Jeep, she saw the leading edge of an enormous, swirling cloud of debris near the barn, headed straight toward them.

She unclipped her seatbelt and threw open her door.

"Henry. Unbuckle your seatbelt. Now!"

She reached the back door and grabbed Henry as he fumbled with the buckle. He tried to reach for his lunch box as Maddie pulled him out of the Jeep.

"Leave it. Just hang on to me as tight as you can."

She ran from the Jeep and headed for the deep ditch that ran alongside the road. She put Henry down, climbed on top of him, and grabbed hold of a large tree root that projected from the side of the ditch.

"Hold on, buddy. Just stay still, and we'll be okay."

Henry said something, but Maddie couldn't hear him over the roar of the storm. She hugged him tighter.

She felt things hitting her back and raining onto the ground all around them. The wind was like nothing she'd ever experienced before. Dirt, rain, and hail hit them from all sides. She held onto the exposed bit of tree root so hard she could feel the wood biting into her palm. She was afraid the slender handhold would snap, and they'd be pulled up into the maelstrom. The roaring went on and on. Something sharp struck her leg, and pain shot through her like she had been stabbed with a hot poker. Still she held on.

Then, just as quickly as it came, the noise abated, and the wind and rain stopped. She lay still on top of Henry for another full minute before she felt that it was safe to move.

Somewhere in the distance, she could hear a bird starting to sing. She raised her head and looked around them. The landscape had been completely transformed. Dirt and debris were scattered everyplace. The road ahead of them looked pockmarked—like it had been bombed. The Cox barn was gone, and so was her Jeep.

"Maddie? What was that?" Henry's small voice was muffled as he still lay beneath her.

She rolled into a sitting position. The pain in her leg was excruciating. A jagged piece of red metal lay in the ditch beside them. Her pant leg was stained with blood.

"I think that was a tornado, sport. But it's over now." She tried to sound calmer than she felt. She pulled him into a sitting position and ran her hands over his face and arms. "Are you okay? Did you get hurt anyplace?"

He shook his head. Then he looked around them.

"Maddie? Where is the Jeep?" He pointed across the road where they had parked. Nothing was left but a pile of mud and debris.

She pulled him against her side. "I think the storm took it."

He looked up at her with confusion. "Where did it take it?"

She pointed over the hill. "That way, I think. Toward the . . ."

Oh, Jesus Christ.

She closed her eyes.

The school. It was headed toward the school.

"Drop your instruments and get into the hallway. *Now!*"

Syd was frantic and doing her best to herd the students out of the dark gymnasium. She knew they had to move fast.

Someone was crying. *Jessie*, she thought.

The building started to shake.

"Run! As fast as you can—into the hallway. Now!"

She ran behind them, pushing at the stragglers.

Ahead, she saw Lila Freemantle, Roma Jean's cousin, struggling to haul her kettledrum along with her.

Syd reached her and took hold of it. She pulled it from her grasp and tossed it aside.

"No," Lila cried. "My parents rented that, and they'll be mad if it gets ruined."

"Lila. Leave it! Run! *Now!*"

Syd grabbed her by the arm and pulled her toward the exit door.

Two of the boys stood just inside the hallway that led to the main school building, holding the doors open for them. Syd pushed Lila through the door and turned back to make sure no one else was lagging behind. She thought she saw someone cowering next to the bleachers.

"Close these doors and get away from the glass. Lie down on the floor and cover your heads with your arms. Do it now!"

The boys looked at her reluctantly, then obeyed.

Syd turned and ran back across the floor toward the bleachers. She could feel the building shake. The floor seemed to be moving beneath her feet.

She reached the small figure, hunched over and struggling with something. It was Roma Jean. Even in the faint light, her red hair seemed to glow. She was whimpering.

Syd grabbed her by the arms. "Roma Jean. We have to run. We have to get out of here *now*."

Above them, the windows broke. Bits of glass and plaster dropped to the floor around them.

"I can't, Miss Murphy." Roma Jean sobbed. "I fell and got caught in my tuba. I can't stand up."

It seemed like the entire world was shaking. The roar of the wind was earsplitting. Syd could see things moving. Band instruments were sliding across the floor toward them.

Syd lifted the tuba away from Roma Jean's shoulders, then wrapped her arms around her from behind and dragged her toward the back of the bleachers.

Syd heard a loud boom as the roof blew off. A tidal wave of debris surrounded them as the walls collapsed.

Chapter 2

Michael was driving down U.S. 21 as fast as he could, which wasn't very fast. The road was too strewn with debris. Already, he'd had to stop twice to drag fallen tree limbs out of the way. The closer he got to Jericho, the worse it became. There were whole swaths of land that just looked . . . broken. Like some gargantuan rototiller had roared across it and churned up everything in its path.

That's it exactly, he thought as he crept along. *It's like the world got turned inside out.*

His anxiety increased with every click of the odometer. He tried David's cell phone number for the twentieth time. No answer. No answer at the Inn, either—just a busy signal. He knew that likely meant the phone lines were down.

Small wonder.

This storm damage was like nothing he'd ever seen before. Trees were twisted and snapped like matchsticks. And the oddest part of it was the way the road weaved in and out of the destruction. He was certain that from a birds-eye view, the terrain would look exactly like an unraveled garment. All he could think about were those hot summer months in South Carolina, when he'd worked second shift at the textile mill with his mother. When the humidity was really high—which it had been most of the time— the knitting machines would be prone to jam, and it could take half an hour to extract the tangled wads of fabric from the looms. Half an hour that they didn't make production, so they'd have to work a longer shift to make up the lost time. But the ripped and frayed yards of half-woven cloth that got yanked out and discarded looked *exactly* like this landscape: once tidy and regular patterns of color and texture that nature had transformed into a warped and unrecognizable mass of thread. No order. No harmony. No patterns that made sense anymore.

And it was going to take a lot longer than half an hour to set this to rights.

He tried David's phone again. No answer. He could feel himself starting to panic.

The National Weather Service in Blacksburg confirmed that Doppler radar indicated a tornado on the ground in Jericho near Highway 58. There were no eyewitness reports yet, and no indication of the breadth or scale of the damage. Rescue crews from several of the surrounding counties were on their way into the affected areas. Phone lines that were still operational were jammed with calls. It was impossible to get any emergency response agency to pick up.

His cell phone rang. He'd been clutching it so tightly that the vibration against his palm startled him, and he nearly dropped it. The Rover swerved as he fumbled with the phone to find the talk button.

"David?"

"No. Michael, it's Maddie."

Maddie. *Good.* Thank god.

"What the hell happened? Have you talked with David? I can't reach him. I keep calling, but it just rings and rings."

"Michael. Where are you?"

"I'm on 21, about four miles from town. Where are you? Where is David?"

"I haven't talked with David. I'm walking up Elk Creek, about half a mile past the Cox barn. Is there any way you can get here and pick us up?"

His mind was spinning. "*Us?* Why are you walking?"

"I have Henry with me. There was a tornado. We had to get out of the Jeep. Now I'm trying to get to the clinic."

"The Jeep?"

"Gone."

Jesus. "Have you been able to reach Syd?"

"No." For the first time, he could hear the strain in her voice. She sounded like she was making a real effort to remain calm.

Just ahead was the turnoff for Greenhouse Road. He could take that and cut over to Elk Creek—if the roads were passable.

"I can be there in about ten minutes . . . if the roads aren't blocked."

Over the hiss on the line he could hear her sigh. It was like the sound of air being let out of a balloon.

"Great," she said. "We'll keep walking toward town. Be careful. It's like a war zone up here."

"Okay."

"Michael?" she added.

"Yeah?"

"Try not to worry. We'll find them both."

He just nodded, finding it hard to speak, then realized she couldn't see him. "I know."

"See you in a few minutes."

The line went dead.

Pandemonium.

Mayhem, too.

Yeah. Byron shook his head. Pandemonium *and* mayhem. That about summed it up.

And those weren't two words that normally went together when talking about anything related to life in Jericho.

Not unless that time five years ago counted, when an eighteen-wheeler full of pigs collided with a tanker truck that had just pumped out sixty porta-johns at the fiddlers' convention in Galax.

Now *that* was pandemonium. The truck full of pigs overturned, and one-hundred-and-forty-five fat sows that were *en route* to Smithfield to become biscuit-sized slices of country ham got loose and hightailed it through the center of town, trailing an apocalyptic swath of human refuse in their wake. It took days to round them all up, and weeks to clean up the mess. And the stench had lingered for months.

But this? This was worse. *Lots* worse.

At least there were no reports of fatalities. Yet. Byron kept his fingers crossed.

But the worst damage was right through the center of town. Main Street was barely recognizable. Bricks and broken glass covered about every square inch. All the streetlights were down—most of them bent into unrecognizable shapes. Fire hydrants had been broken apart like snap beans, and water was pouring out over everything. A river of mud and sludge was rising over the mounds of debris that clogged the storm drains.

None of the buildings lining the tiny street looked unaffected. They were just damn lucky that the storm happened early, before most businesses were open.

The school was hardest hit—the gymnasium was completely demolished. He heard from Phoebe Jenkins that there had been a band practice early that morning, but most everyone had gotten to safety before the building got hit.

Only two people were still missing: Roma Jean Freemantle and Syd Murphy.

Byron felt his gut clench. He didn't want to be the one to face Dr. Stevenson if they didn't find her partner—and soon. He had no idea where Stevenson was. Reports said that her clinic had survived the storm. She was probably there. None of the phone lines were working in this area, and at least two of the nearby cell towers had been taken out.

He raised his radio and flicked the talk button.

"Tommy, where the fuck is that other backhoe? The goddamn rescue trucks can't get through this mess until we get some of this debris pushed off the street."

His radio beeped.

"Ten-four, Sheriff. I've got Mike Barnes en route."

"What's his 20?"

"About five miles south of town."

Byron shook his head. "Tell him to haul ass. We may have some people trapped in the school."

"Roger."

"Martin out." Byron clipped his radio to his belt and turned back toward the sound of a commotion coming from inside the grocery store. Two of his deputies were hauling out something that looked like most of a car bumper. It was bright red and had bits of paper and soggy pieces of what appeared to be lettuce plastered all over it.

"Any signs of people inside?" he called out to them.

"No sir," Travis Burns replied. "We found this stuck inside a freezer case."

Byron rolled his eyes. "Guys. Drop the fucking car bumper and keep looking for survivors. There might be *people* trapped underneath all these piles of shit, *capiche*? Use your goddamn heads."

The two deputies looked at each other sheepishly before carefully setting the car bumper down.

"Yes, sir," they said in unison.

"Jesus Christ," Byron muttered. He gestured toward the bank. "Halsey, this building looks stable. How about you two check it out?"

"Yes, sir."

"And don't forget to mark the front with spray paint to show you've been in there," he called after them as they started to climb over an upended Merita Bread van that was wedged up against the bank doors.

Someone tapped him on the shoulder. *Great*, he thought. *Another goddamn bystander wanting to ask if he'd seen their fucking dog.*

He turned around and found himself staring right into a pair of steely blue eyes.

Stevenson. And she didn't look happy. She looked . . . he wasn't really sure *how* she looked. Disheveled, for one thing. She had mud all over her clothes. And one side of her face was streaked with tiny scratches. She didn't look composed, that much was for sure. He guessed she'd heard about the gymnasium.

"Byron," she said. Her voice sounded flat. Unemotional. "What can you tell me about the school?"

He shrugged. It would be useless to lie to her. The fact that she was standing there in front of him and not out digging through the rubble with the rest of the county EMS teams, was proof enough of her level of distraction.

"Not much. The gym got hit. It's pretty much in ruins." He paused. "The band was in there practicing when the storm hit. Most of them got out."

She took a minute to absorb that. "Most?"

He nodded. "Two people are unaccounted for. Roma Jean Freemantle, and—"

"Syd?"

He nodded again. "I'm sorry, Maddie. I've got a crew over there searching."

She continued to stand there without speaking. He wasn't certain that she understood what he had said.

He took hold of her arm. "Maddie—"

She pulled free. "I've got to get over there." She looked around at the carnage that surrounded them.

"You can't. It's not safe. I've got that area sealed off."

She turned away from him and started to walk in the direction of the school. He noticed how unsteady on her feet she seemed. She was walking with a pronounced limp, and her right pant leg was torn and streaked with bloodstains.

He followed her and grabbed hold of her arm again. "Hold on, Maddie. I told you. No one can get in there. The rescue crews are searching the area, and they'll let us know as soon as they find them."

Maddie shook off his arm. "Fucking *try* and stop me, Byron."

"Maddie. Jesus Christ. Look at yourself. You can hardly walk. Let us do our jobs."

Her eyes were smoldering. But she seemed to calm down a little. "Fine. Then let me do *mine*. When they find them, they might be hurt, and I need to be there."

He sighed. There was no point in continuing to argue with her. "All right. But let me take you. I've got an ATV over there, and it'll be faster."

She nodded.

He looked around. "Davis," he called out to a young female deputy who was working with a volunteer fireman to shut off one of the waterspouts. "I'm taking Dr. Stevenson to the school. You're with me."

"Okay, Sheriff," Davis replied.

He turned back to Maddie. She had already limped halfway to the ATV.

As he followed her, he said a silent prayer that when they got to the school, Syd Murphy would be there—alive.

"What the hell happened?"

Michael was seated on the floor next to the low gurney where David lay holding an ice pack against the side of his head. Astrid was curled up beside him—snoring.

They were at Maddie's clinic, which had been converted into a makeshift emergency room. Lizzy Mayes, the county's itinerant nurse practitioner, and Peggy Hawkes, the long-winded nurse-cum-clinic-manager, were both there, tending to an unending stream of walk-ins and carry-ins. Several of the more serious cases had already been transferred by ambulance to the hospital in Wytheville.

David sighed. "I *told* you what happened. You're just not hearing me."

Michael shook his head. Clearly, David's head wound was worse than Lizzy had told him when he'd arrived forty-five minutes ago.

He had just picked up Maddie and Henry, and they were on their way to the clinic when his cell phone rang, and he heard David's voice. He had been beside himself with relief. David told him that he was fine, but shaken, and that the Inn had sustained heavy damages. He also told him what he knew about the school, and that no one had heard anything from Syd yet.

When Michael related the news to Maddie, she had insisted that he turn around and take her directly into town. David had also said that Isobel Sanchez was at the clinic, and she was helping out by watching the children of the people who had shown up needing treatment. So Michael had offered to bring Henry along with him after he dropped Maddie off near the entrance to town. Henry was now out back, playing kickball in the parking lot with Héctor, Gabriel, and half a dozen other children whose shell-shocked parents were inside trying to wrap themselves around the enormity of all that had just occurred—and all the ways their lives had suddenly changed.

He took hold of the ice pack so David could rest his arm.

"Honey," he said in the calmest tone he could muster. "You can't expect me to believe that a flying *car* destroyed the Inn."

David slapped his hand away.

"Don't patronize me. I'm not an imbecile, and I *know* what I saw. It was a fucking *car*—a bright red one—one of those jacked-up, steroid-infused street rods. You think I'd invent a ludicrous detail like *that*?"

"No. But I think you might have taken a bigger whack on the noggin than you realize."

David sighed. "Just who do you think you're talking to here? Who watched every damn episode of *Muscle Car* on Spike TV?"

Michael rolled his eyes. "That's not because of the *cars*. You just had the hots for that grease monkey, Rick Bacon."

"So? That doesn't mean that I didn't pick up a thing or two about those hopped-up breeder-mobiles. I sure as shit can recognize one when I *see* one—especially when the damn thing is *flying* through my fucking sun porch!"

Next to him on the gurney, Astrid stirred and lifted her head.

"Oh, *great*," David whined. "Now you woke Astrid up."

"*I* woke Astrid up?"

David gathered the fat dog into his arms. "Come here, baby. Daddy is sorry that Papa Mikey woke you up."

Michael sighed. What*ever*.

For right now, all that mattered was that David was safe, and that Maddie was on her way to find Syd.

Everything else could wait.

Chapter 3

The bleachers in Jefferson County High School were a long-standing bone of contention.

They had been installed way back in the summer of 1967, when the newly constructed school gymnasium was the county's pride and joy. The four telescoping wall units had been manufactured by the J.H. Pence Co. in Roanoke, and transported to the rural community of Jericho by railcar. Back in those days, gym bleachers were constructed out of boards harvested from old-growth Douglas fir trees—some of the hardest and hardiest wood available.

More than half a century of history was etched into the worn surfaces of those plank seats. Epic wins and losses, failed and fabled feats of sportsmanship, first loves, final betrayals, pomp, circumstance, rituals, and rites of passage—all played out on the polished gym floor below. It was even rumored that if a person was brave enough to crawl all the way under one of the fully extended units with a flashlight, they could find the governor's initials carved into the back of the riser nearest the scoreboard.

But times changed, and the exercise of team spirit was increasingly coupled with a greater demand for creature comforts. And the old bleachers were a source of continued aggravation to anyone who had to risk life and limb navigating them on crowded game nights. Disgruntled parents were always quick to point out that having to sit on them for more than ten minutes at a stretch was a bona fide pain in the ass.

Forty-plus years of hard use had taken their toll on the big units. Half of the top boards were warped, the center sections were beginning to sag, and one of the end components would only retract about two-thirds of the way.

People thought they needed to go. And they said so. Publicly. More than once, the need to replace the worn-out seating system topped the agenda at school board meetings.

But times were tight, and budgets were tighter. So when push came to shove, the precious few discretionary dollars that *were* available got channeled into things like funding the school's free lunch program or buying new microscopes for the science lab.

So the debate, and the complaints, continued with gusto until one fateful Thursday morning, when the monolithic monuments played their last—and most heroic—part in the history of a small town.

Light. There was a small sliver of light coming from someplace.

That had to be a good sign.

"Miss Murphy, I can't move my legs." Roma Jean was still beneath Syd. Or, at least, most of Roma Jean was still beneath Syd. She couldn't really see anything.

"I know, honey." Syd tried to sound as matter-of-fact as possible. In truth, she was terrified. "I'm on top of you, and I can't move, either."

In fact, it was far worse than that. Syd was wedged up against one of the iron support arms, beneath the front section of bleachers where she had pulled Roma Jean before the building collapsed. She could feel one of the big, floor-level rollers digging into her back. Her left leg was pinned below the knee by something heavy. Her foot was at an improbable angle. Every time Roma Jean tried to move, the pain was excruciating.

"Are you hurt anyplace?" she asked.

"I don't think so."

Beneath her, Roma Jean shifted. Syd thought she might pass out from the jolt of pain that surged up her leg.

"Try not to move, Roma Jean," she said, when she could speak again. "We don't want to risk bringing anything else down on top of us."

"I'm scared."

"I know you are, sweetheart. I am, too. But they'll find us. We just need to stay calm and wait until we hear them."

"How long will *that* take?"

Syd listened to the quiet all around them. It didn't sound like it was still raining, and she couldn't hear any wind.

"I hope not long. It sounds like the worst of the storm has passed."

"How will they know where to look for us?"

"They'll know because the others will tell them that we were still inside the gym when the storm hit."

Syd said a silent prayer that the rest of the kids had survived. She had no idea what had happened to the rest of the school building. Thinking about that made her feel nauseated, and she was already close to passing out from the pain surging up her leg. It was tingling now. If she didn't get it worked free soon, she'd . . . well. Better not to think about that right now. Besides, whatever was wrong, Maddie would find a way to fix it.

Maddie.

The storm had hit the school at about seven forty-five. Maddie would have been on the road with Henry by that time. Were they safe? Where were they now? *Dear god. Please let them be all right.*

"Miss Murphy? I have to go."

Roma Jean was starting to sound desperate. Syd needed to keep her calmed down. There was no way to predict how many more hours they would have to wait for a rescue team to reach them.

"I know how hard this is, and how scared you are. But we *have* to stay calm. They *will* find us. I promise you that."

"No, Miss Murphy," Roma Jean said with even greater desperation than before. "I mean I have to *go*. I can't hold it much longer."

Syd blinked, then fought to stifle a laugh. "You mean you have to pee?"

She could feel Roma Jean nod.

"Oh, honey. I'm sorry."

"I can't hold it."

"Then don't. It's okay. Go ahead and pee if you have to. Believe me, it won't make anything worse."

There was silence for a moment.

"I just did."

An acrid smell filled up their tiny space. Then Syd laughed.

And once she started laughing, she couldn't stop. Soon, Roma Jean joined her, and Syd could feel her small frame shaking beneath her. She didn't even mind that Roma Jean's movement caused her body to fill up with pain.

Soon, their small chorus of laughter spiraled its way up and out of the pile of debris that covered them and drifted out across the open air.

What the hell was that?

It sounded like . . . laughter? She listened again. Yeah. Laughter. That's exactly what it was. And it was coming from beneath the rubble on top of what once had been the south side of the gymnasium.

Charlie Davis looked around. "Sheriff Martin! Over here."

The sheriff was standing with Dr. Stevenson near the north side of the building, where most of the crew was sifting through the damage. They understood that two people were likely trapped near the bleachers when the building went down, but there were sets of bleachers on *both* sides of the gym. Since the north end appeared to have sustained less damage, the small crew decided to search there first. But Charlie had an instinct to try nosing around over on this side of the rubble, just in case.

Sheriff Martin quickly picked his way across the mounds of rubble and came to stand just beside her. Dr. Stevenson followed as quickly as she could. Charlie could see that she was having a difficult time walking.

"What did you hear, Charlie?"

She gestured toward the mammoth pile of blocks and twisted

metal that lay before them. "I swear I heard laughter coming from in there."

"Laughter?" Martin sounded dubious.

She bent down and picked up a crumpled license plate. *2BAD4U*, it read. "Yes, sir. Laughter." She held up the tag. "Isn't this Deb Carlson's?"

Byron nodded. "Looks like it."

Dr. Stevenson joined them. "What is it?" she asked, looking back and forth between them.

Up close, Charlie thought Dr. Stevenson looked pretty rough. She'd only seen her in person a couple of times before, and she remembered being impressed by her height and her good looks. Today, though, she didn't look so well put together. She was still really beautiful, but it was hard to reconcile the rumpled and mud-covered woman before her with the cool professional who always turned heads when she entered a room.

"Davis says she heard something like laughter coming from this area."

Stevenson's eyes met hers. *Damn. What an amazing shade of blue.*

"Is that right?" she asked.

Charlie nodded.

Dr. Stevenson looked at Sheriff Martin. "What are we waiting for, Byron? Let's make some noise."

Sheriff Martin shrugged. "Have at it."

She looked around, picked up a broken rod of metal, and limped to the edge of the rubble. Then she carefully tapped on anything that might conduct sound.

"Syd! Roma Jean!" she called out, over and over. "Can you hear us? Are you in there?"

She stopped and waited, rooted to the spot like a statue. She repeated the process for several minutes.

Beside her, Sheriff Martin sighed. "Maddie . . ."

She held up a hand to shush him and craned her neck toward the center of the pile. Then she sagged to the ground and rested on one knee.

She finally turned to them with clean lines running through the mud on her face.

"They're here," she said. "Alive."

The rescue crew of five men took the better part of three hours to uncover the section of bleachers that still stood, semierect, on top of Syd and Roma Jean.

It was the permanently extended part of the broken unit that had collapsed and was pressing on Syd's leg. Once the majority of the heavy pile of metal and masonry had been cleared away, the pressure eased up, and Syd could feel the tingling in her foot subside.

Maddie was there while the men worked to free them, constantly talking to Syd and Roma Jean and offering words of encouragement.

Syd felt the hand of hell loosen its grip the instant she heard Maddie's voice drifting down through the darkness. She didn't know which relief was greater: the certainty that she and Roma Jean were finally going to be freed from their dark prison or the dramatic proof positive that Maddie—and Henry—were both alive and safe.

"Hang on, you two." Maddie sounded closer now. "We can see the bleachers, so it won't be long now."

Maddie. It was hearing Maddie's voice. That was the greater relief.

Syd hadn't told Maddie about her foot yet, but now that they were close to being freed, she knew she had to.

"Be careful when you try to move the bleachers," Syd called up to her. "My left leg is pinned, and my foot is twisted around at a bad angle."

All movement above them ceased. More light was visible now. Syd could see shadows moving through it.

"How bad?" Maddie's voice sounded closer. And now it had *that* tone. Syd could tell that she had shifted into doctor mode.

"I think it might be broken."

There was momentary silence, and then Syd heard another voice. She thought it sounded like Byron Martin.

"Can you tell which end of the unit is on top of you?"

"The extended part—the side that never retracts. We ducked under it just before the building collapsed. Roma Jean is trapped beneath me."

"All right. Then we'll try to lift that section all at one time. Try not to move."

Syd laughed. "I think we can guarantee not to do that. Right, Roma Jean?"

"Yes, ma'am," Roma Jean said, in a small voice. "I promise not to move."

"Syd," Maddie's voice was back again, "I have some things here that I can use to stabilize your leg. So wait for me to get to you so I can turn it before you try to move."

Oh, honey, Syd thought. *I'd wait forever for you to get to me.*

"Okay, Syd," Byron said, after ten minutes that seemed like ten hours. "We've got some pry bars ready to lift this thing. Then we're going to prop it up so we can pull you and Roma Jean out."

She closed her eyes. *Thank god.* "Hang on, Roma Jean. We're almost free."

There was a loud, groaning noise. An explosion of light filled their tiny cavern as the wooden ceiling was lifted up. A cascade of dust surrounded them. It stung her eyes and piled up in the back of her throat. She coughed, and so did Roma Jean. The instant relief she experienced when the bleachers were lifted off her leg was so extreme, she thought she might pass out. When, finally, she felt a familiar set of hands touching her, she was grateful she hadn't.

Maddie gently ran her hands up and down Syd's arms and along her left leg.

"Stay still, okay?" Maddie's voice was very close now. She felt a soft touch on the back of her head. "We're going to have to straighten your leg out so I can stabilize your foot before we move you, and it's going to hurt."

Syd nodded. "Okay. Please hurry."

"I'll be as quick as I can. Roma Jean? You okay?"

"I'm okay," Roma Jean said. "I just want outta here."

"I know, honey. We'll have you up in just another minute, but just lie still until we move Syd, okay? Byron! Bring that stretcher over here and get ready to help me lift her."

Syd felt Maddie take hold of her left foot.

"Okay, honey. I want you to turn over onto your left side, but let me hold your foot. Don't try to move it. Got that?"

Syd nodded.

"All right. Go ahead and roll over."

Syd took a breath and turned her body so she was facing up. The pain was excruciating, but nothing like the white-hot sensation she experienced when Maddie gently placed one hand on her leg and pushed her foot beneath the steel support beam to free it. The pain was so intense it was surreal. She almost laughed—just because crying seemed like such an inadequate response. Tears mixed with the dust in her eyes.

When her dizziness abated, she could feel Maddie gently running her fingers over her foot and ankle, then up the sides of her leg and over her knee.

"That's my girl. My brave girl," Maddie whispered as she worked. "It should get a little better now. I think you might have some torn ligaments, but I can't feel any broken bones right now. We won't know for sure until we get some x-rays. But the pulse in your foot is good. Can you wiggle your toes for me?"

Syd was taking deep breaths, still struggling not to throw up. But she did her best to comply and moved her toes. It hurt like hell, but Maddie was right: The worst of the pain was receding. Already, it had retreated from the borderline of intolerable and settled back into the realm of merely excruciating.

Maddie attached the splints to the sides of her leg.

"All right. We're going to lift you to the stretcher now. Just let us do all the work, okay? Byron?"

She felt another pair of hands take hold of her shoulders, then she was on the stretcher, and Maddie's beautiful face was right above her. They were both fighting back tears.

Beside them, Roma Jean scrambled up into a sitting position. Charlie Davis helped her crawl up and out of their prison.

Syd took hold of Maddie's hand and squeezed it.

"Be sure to look at Roma Jean," she said quietly. "She fell. That's why I went back for her."

Maddie nodded and started to release her hand.

Syd gave it a short, reflexive tug. Maddie looked down at her. Syd opened her mouth to speak, but no words came out.

"I know." Maddie stroked the side of Syd's face. "Me, too."

Syd nodded and let go of her fingers.

Maddie decided to have Syd transported back to her clinic instead of to the hospital in Wytheville, rightly assuming that the ER was overwhelmed with cases, and Syd would be consigned to wait hours for treatment. Besides, she had everything she needed at the clinic to x-ray and cast Syd's foot herself, and afterward, she could remain on hand to relieve Lizzy and Peggy.

Syd had torn several medial ligaments, and Maddie suspected a corresponding malleolus fracture—although none showed up on the x-rays. This was the good news, and the bad news. Consequently, Syd was getting a cast below the knee on her left leg.

Henry had been ecstatic when Maddie arrived with Syd, and he begged to be allowed to stay in the room while Maddie applied the short, fiberglass cast to Syd's leg. Syd, who was equally thrilled to be reunited with Henry, did her best to disguise her discomfort so he wouldn't be too disturbed by the procedure.

It wasn't easy. More than once, she bit back expletives.

"Uncle David is here," he said to Syd, as he sat next to her on a small stool.

Syd fought a grimace. "He is?"

Henry nodded. "He has Astrid with him, too. They got hit by a big flowerpot."

Syd looked up at Maddie with a perplexed expression.

"One of his porch urns got picked up and thrown by the wind. He wasn't seriously hurt, but the impact did knock him out."

"The dog, too?" Syd asked with a raised eyebrow.

Maddie laughed. "I hope not. Astrid probably has half a dozen personal-injury lawyers on speed dial."

Syd rolled her eyes. "How bad was the damage to the Inn?"

"We're not sure. David told Michael it was pretty torn up."

Henry nodded energetically. "Uncle David said it got broke by a big red car."

Syd looked at him. "What did?"

"The house."

"David said the house got hit by a *car*?"

Henry nodded and looked at Maddie for corroboration.

Maddie shrugged. "That's what he told Michael. But you know his fondness for excessive statement."

Henry looked confused. "What's 'sessive statement mean, Maddie?"

Maddie was nearly finished wrapping Syd's leg with the damp purple fabric. "It means that sometimes Uncle David makes things sound more . . . unusual than they really are."

"He most certainly does *not*."

They all looked at the doorway of the small treatment room to see David, holding Astrid.

He turned his attention to Syd. "Hi ya, Goldilocks. Get to see the governor's initials while you were on your little field trip?"

Syd shook her head. "Nope. I shoulda sprung for the higher-priced tour. All I saw were some prehistoric Cheetos."

"Oh, really? Maybe you should've picked them up for later." He jerked his head toward Maddie. "You never know when they'll come in handy."

"That's true," Syd agreed.

She jumped when Maddie rapped on the side of the hardening cast—a tad too forcefully. "*Ouch*! Hey!"

"Oh, I'm sorry." Maddie gave her an innocent smile. "Were you saying something about needing Cheetos?"

Henry looked back and forth between them.

"I want some Cheetos, too, Maddie. Can we get some on the way home?"

David cleared his throat. "Speaking of homes. We appear to be without one. Any chance we can crash at your place until we can sort out the extent of the damage at the Inn?"

"Of course you can," Maddie said without hesitation. "And you can begin your tenure there by giving the rest of my family a ride home."

Syd opened her mouth to speak but Maddie shushed her.

"I'm probably going to be here for a good, long while, honey, and you need to go home and get this thing elevated." She rested a hand on the knee of Syd's unaffected leg. "I'll be home as soon as I can, I promise."

"Come on, Henry." David put Astrid down and cinched up her lead so she couldn't wander off. "Let's go find Michael and bring the car around back for Syd."

"Okay." Henry followed David out into the corridor.

"I'll be back for you in two shakes," David said to Syd. Then he left, closing the door behind him.

Syd looked at Maddie. "This whole thing is a nightmare."

Maddie sighed. "I know. But what else could I do? They're homeless."

Syd gave her a puzzled look, then rolled her eyes and socked her on the arm. "You're such a jerk."

Maddie laughed and took hold of her hand. They stared at each other. "You scared the shit out of me, you know that?"

Syd nodded and touched her forehead to Maddie's. "I know. I'm sorry about that. It all happened so fast. I had to go back for her."

Maddie drew back so she could kiss Syd on the forehead. "I know. I'm proud of you for that. We're damn lucky that all you ended up with are some torn ligaments."

"Yeah," Syd said, as she took hold of Maddie's face. "About that. At some point in the near future, we're going to have a *long* discussion."

"What about?" Maddie asked.

"Well. It might have something to do with your imprecise use of medical terminology."

"Oh really?" Maddie pulled away and looked at her. "In what way was I imprecise?"

"Do you really need to ask me that question?"

"Apparently."

Syd sighed. "Let's just say it might have something to do with an extremely misleading and inaccurate use of the phrase, 'it's going to hurt.'"

"Oh . . . that."

"Uh huh."

"I have a feeling I'm not going to like this discussion."

"I have a feeling you're going to *hate* it."

Maddie sighed. "Great."

Syd hefted her purple-clad leg. "How long do I have to wear this thing?"

"Six or seven weeks. Longer if you're not careful."

"Define 'careful' for me."

"In this case, 'careful' means you should refrain from giving in to any sudden impulses."

"Such as?"

"Use your imagination."

Syd narrowed her eyes. "You mean I can't use it to kick your ass?"

"Precisely."

Syd shook her head. "You lead a charmed life, Dr. Strangelove."

"I didn't used to, but I certainly won't disagree with you now."

Syd smiled at her. "Well, lucky for me, I already know how to get around on crutches."

"You do?"

Syd nodded. "I fractured my *other* leg when I was a junior in college."

"Really? You never told me that."

"I don't know that I want to tell you now, either."

"Oh . . . okay. Lemme guess." Maddie crossed her arms. "It must've involved a surfboard."

"No, brainiac. But it *was* a boating accident. I slipped on the deck of my father's little sailboat and smacked into the boom."

Maddie shook her head. "*The Perils of Pauline.*"

Syd spread her hands. "This is why I didn't want to tell you."

They heard two short blasts from a car horn.

"I think my ride is here. Wanna get me a set of leg irons?" Syd smirked. "Or are you gonna carry me outta here?"

Maddie raised an eyebrow. "Now *there's* an idea."

"Oh, no. No more heroic feats from you until you let Lizzy stitch up that leg."

"My leg is fine, Syd."

"I wish I could say the same for your pants."

Maddie looked down at her ripped and bloodied pant leg. "Yeah. I guess I should put on some clean scrubs before I see any more patients."

Syd nodded. "It's probably a good idea. And while you're at it, you might want to wash your face, too."

Maddie raised a hand to her cheek.

"Do I look that bad?"

"Afraid so. Want a rundown?"

Maddie nodded.

Syd crossed her arms and looked at her critically. "You're stressed, exhausted, filthy, and completely disheveled. I've never seen you look less professional."

"Jeez, don't hold back. Is there anything else?"

"Yeah. One more thing."

"I'm afraid to ask."

"You shouldn't be."

"No? What is it?"

Syd leaned toward her until their faces nearly touched. "You're still the most beautiful thing I've ever seen. And when I saw your muddy face above me at the high school, I fell in love with you all over again."

She kissed her. When they parted, Maddie seemed to have regained some of her customary smugness.

"The hell with it," she said.

Before Syd could protest, Maddie scooped her up into her arms.

"Are you nuts?" Syd asked in alarm. "What the hell are you doing?"

Maddie limped across the room with her.

"Curb service."

"What about your leg?"

"It won't get any worse now."

Syd realized that it was pointless to argue.

"Is this covered by my copay?" she asked.

"No. But I've got some ideas about how we can work that out."

"I'll just bet you do."

Syd opened the door, and Maddie carried her down the back hallway toward the waiting car.

Maddie and Lizzy worked tirelessly for the rest of the day, stitching up cuts, taping sprains, extracting shards of glass and splinters of wood from countless arms and legs, and listening to shocked and dazed storm survivors unreel a panoply of fantastic tales of near-epic destruction.

Six cases of more serious injuries had quickly been dispatched to the ER in Wytheville, and Tom Greene had already called Maddie four times in an angry panic, warning her not to send any more patients his way, then shifting gears and begging her to rush over and help triage the crush of wounded people clogging the hospital waiting rooms.

Maddie patiently assured Tom that she would make her way over to the hospital as soon as her own waiting room was under control.

Lizzy walked into the hallway when Maddie was on the phone with Tom—again—and waited for her to hang up.

"Look," Lizzy said. "If he really needs you over there, Peggy and I can try to manage things here."

Maddie sighed. "Tom already has enough cooks in his kitchen. The best we can do is continue to treat as many patients as possible here, and keep them out of his ER."

That seemed to make sense to Lizzy. She looked down at

Maddie's pant leg. "Why don't we duck into the supply closet for five minutes so I can dress that cut on your leg?"

Maddie looked at her with narrowed eyes. She noticed that Lizzy was carrying a laceration kit. "Did Syd call you?"

Lizzy took hold of her elbow and steered her toward the closet. "I'll never tell."

Once inside, Maddie perched on a stool and propped her leg up on a stack of boxes so Lizzy could have easier access to the jagged cut on the side of her calf.

Lizzy cut away part of Maddie's torn trouser leg and proceeded to debride the wound. "Yeah. You're going to need some stitches on this one."

Maddie watched her work. The small redhead looked more tired and disheveled than Maddie had ever seen her. Clearly, this day was taking an emotional toll on all of them.

"What was that racket I heard a few minutes ago?" she asked.

Lizzy chuckled. "You mean that crash that came from Room Two?"

Maddie nodded.

"I was stitching up a cut on Roma Jean Freemantle's arm, and she knocked over my suture tray."

Maddie rolled her eyes. "Why on earth did that happen?"

Lizzy swabbed Maddie's leg with Betadine. "You tell me. Charlie Davis ducked her head into the room to check on her, and Roma Jean jerked halfway out of her skin."

"Charlie Davis?"

Lizzy nodded. "That cute little deputy of Byron's."

"Charlie Davis?" Maddie asked again.

Lizzy looked up at her. "Right. *Charlie*. About so tall." She held up a gloved hand. "Blonde hair. Great smile." She winked at Maddie. "Plays for your team . . ."

"*My* team?" Maddie asked.

Lizzy looked at her with a raised eyebrow.

"Oh," Maddie said. "*That* team."

Lizzy shook her head and held up a syringe. "Need something to bite down on?"

"I think I can handle it."

Lizzy gave her the shot of Lidocaine. "Good. I don't think our patients would appreciate the sound of bloodcurdling screams emanating from the storage closet."

"Very funny."

"I do try."

Maddie closed her eyes. "This is sure one day for the record books."

"I know." Lizzy sat back for a moment to let the lidocaine take effect. "Thank god we haven't heard any reports of fatalities."

"That's for sure. And Tom didn't mention anything more dire than the types of injuries we've been seeing, either."

"More arrows in his quiver."

Maddie opened her eyes. "What do you mean?"

Lizzy shrugged. "Don't pay any attention to me. I'm just being selfish."

"About?"

"Dr. Greene has been making noises about cutting the funding for my position at the end of my contract."

Maddie jolted upright. "He *what?*"

Lizzy quickly took hold of her leg to prevent the dressings from falling to the floor.

"Hey, sit still. I don't wanna have to do this all over again."

"Sorry." Maddie relaxed. "What the hell are you talking about?"

Lizzy looked at her. "He didn't say anything to you?"

"No, of course not. This is the first I've heard anything about it."

Lizzy sighed. "He's such a sleazeball."

"You'll get no argument from me about that," Maddie said. "But what makes you say that in this particular context?"

Lizzy gently tapped the perimeter of the cut on Maddie's calf. "Is that numb yet?"

Maddie nodded.

Lizzy commenced making a row of tiny stitches. "He wants me to take a staff position at the hospital. I have no desire to return to that kind of nursing, and he knows it. But he thinks he has me over a barrel. If he pulls the funding for our parish nurse program, then I'll either have to sign on with him, or move someplace else to find work."

Maddie was fuming. "We'll see about that."

Lizzy glanced up at her. Her brown eyes looked tired. "Don't take this on like a hair shirt, okay? I know this clinic can't afford to pick up all of my salary, and I never expected this position to last forever. I'll figure something out."

Maddie's mind was racing. *Fucking Tom Greene.* That man was a perpetual thorn in her side.

She watched Lizzy continue to work. "What does *your* Tom say?"

Lizzy had been dating Syd's brother, Tom, for nearly a year now.

Lizzy smiled. "Tom says I should move to Blacksburg and find work there."

"And what do you think about that idea?"

Lizzy tied off her last knot and snipped the ends of the silk suture.

"I think it's too soon. Tom is a lot of fun, but he's got some growing up to do. And I'm not ready to leave Jericho. I feel at home here."

Maddie nodded. "Then let's just see what we can work out, okay? I've still got some cards to play where Tom Greene is concerned."

Lizzy applied polysporin to Maddie's wound and wrapped her leg with gauze.

"I just wish I could be more optimistic," Lizzy said. "But I've never felt comfortable around that man. Something about him just gives me the willies."

"He's a self-important jerk, but I think he's harmless."

"I wish I felt the same way."

"Has he ever done or said anything inappropriate?"

Lizzy thought about it for a moment. "No. But there's just something creepy about him." She shrugged. "Maybe it's his hands."

"His hands?"

Lizzy nodded. "Yeah. He's got those long, manicured nails."

"That's odd, but not really uncommon," Maddie said. "Lots of doctors are maniacal about their hands."

"I guess that's true." Lizzy finished wrapping Maddie's leg and collected her supplies. "Okay. You're all set. Although you might need to find another pair of pants."

Maddie looked down at her shredded pant leg. "You think?"

"Yeah. The beatnik look is a bit of a stretch for you."

Maddie stood up. "Thanks for doing this. Syd would've hung me out to dry if I showed up at home without having this taken care of."

Lizzy smiled at her. "No problem."

Maddie walked to a laundry bin and pulled out a pair of clean scrubs. "Give me two minutes to change into these, and I'll meet you back out on the front lines."

Lizzy nodded and reached for the doorknob.

"Lizzy?" Maddie touched her on the back of the arm.

Lizzy stopped and looked back at her.

"I promise I'll figure something out."

Lizzy smiled at her. "Thanks."

She opened the door and walked out, leaving Maddie alone in the closet.

Tom Greene.

Maddie pulled off her pants and stuffed them into a trash bag. Outside the room, she could hear Peggy telling someone that Dr. Stevenson would be right with them.

She sighed. *One crisis at a time.* She pulled on the scrubs and went back out to join Lizzy.

Chapter 4

When the sun came up the next day, it was clear that Jericho had fared better than anyone had reason to expect. Most of the serious property damage was confined to the main street in town, and to the school. The tornado was officially classified as an EF1—the first ever to touch down in the tiny mountain town. And although there were numerous swaths of destruction across the county that varied in intensity, there were no serious casualties—and no deaths.

The Riverside Inn had lost most of its roof and half of the big sun porch that ran along the back of the house. Several of the large white birch trees that lined its long driveway had been snapped and tossed around the property like confetti. Adjacent to the Inn, Michael and David's small bungalow had been all but destroyed when it was hit by an uprooted, one-hundred-year-old pin oak. Local construction crews were already spread so thin that repairs there would likely take weeks or months to complete.

Which meant that the boys would be keeping house with the girls for some time.

Michael graciously offered to look for an alternative place to live while they waited on repairs to be completed, but Maddie and Syd were unanimous in their rejection of that proposal. The farmhouse was more than spacious enough to accommodate them all, and having the extra sets of hands (and legs) available to help out during Syd's convalescence would be invaluable.

One of the front parlors was equipped with a queen-sized sofa bed, so they were able to create a makeshift bedroom for Syd on the ground floor of the house. David quickly nicknamed the space "Central Casting," and helped Maddie move many of Syd's personal belongings downstairs so she wouldn't feel too displaced while she was confined there.

Of course, Maddie elected to sleep downstairs with her, and David expressed enthusiastic support for that idea.

"At least I'll be able to get a good night's sleep now and then," he said.

"What are you talking about?" Maddie asked. They were upstairs, packing up books, videos, and lesson plans from a list that Syd had prepared.

David rapped on the wall that separated Maddie's bedroom from the guest suite next door.

"Hello? I don't want to go blind from having to listen to the two of you swinging from the roof trusses in here."

Maddie sighed. "I'll set aside how ludicrous and insane an insinuation that is, and just go straight to asking you to clarify how *hearing* something could make you go blind?"

David shrugged. "It's widely known that all *kinds* of things can result in blindness."

"David, how many times do I have to explain to you that when you temporarily lost your eyesight during my twelfth birthday party at the roller rink, it was because you fell and hit your head, not because you had just masturbated in the men's bathroom?"

He glowered at her. "You AMA types always toe the party line."

"I'm just trying to save you from continuing to cling to these petty delusions."

"What's that crack supposed to mean?"

She didn't reply.

He narrowed his eyes. "You're still trying to insist that I didn't see that damn Camaro, aren't you?"

"David . . ." she began.

He held up a hand. "I don't wanna hear it. Every other person in the county saw that fuel-injected demon from hell, and I don't hear you suggesting that *they're* all crazy."

"I haven't suggested that you're crazy."

"You haven't said that you believe me, either."

"Okay. All right." She sighed. "Against my better judgment, I'll admit that there *is* some evidence to suggest that the storm's debris field, which *happened* to contain Deb Carlson's car, caused part of the damage to the town. And, by the way, that *same* debris field also contained my Jeep. But I don't seem to be hearing any apocryphal news reports about *it* going on a similar, three-county rampage."

"There's nothing remarkable about that," David said.

"Why not?"

"Duh? You must be kidding me."

She thought about it. "No. I don't believe that I am."

He rolled his eyes. "Really, Cinderella. What self-respecting tornado would pick *your* boxy, uninspired Iacocca-mobile over a sexy, turbo-charged street rod?" He slowly shook his head. "Where's the market share in *that?*" He laid a hand on her shoulder. "You really need to get out more, or at least upgrade your satellite service."

She looked confused. "What does my satellite service have to do with this?"

"Nothing. But if you expect me to be the one to undertake *your* cultural education, I'm going to need prime-time access to something besides C-SPAN and the Weather Channel. This joint is about as cutting-edge as the Bates Motel."

She gave up and shoved the box she had been packing into his hands. "Shut up and carry this downstairs."

He took the box from her and glanced down at its contents. Then he reached into it and lifted out a VHS copy of *The Best of the Mary Tyler Moore Show.*

"I rest my case."

Maddie held up a hand. "I've got five fingers here—*one* of them is for you."

David headed for the back stairs, and she could hear him laughing all the way down to the kitchen.

In fact, David had been telling the truth about the real culprit behind much of the storm damage at the Inn.

And he wasn't alone in spinning a tall tale of devastation.

People said that God must have been gunning for Deb Carlson—or, at least, for her car. It wasn't enough that a hailstorm had transformed its spectacular crimson paint job into a mobile ad for Clearasil. No, the final indignity occurred when the tornado roared through the parking lot at Junior's body shop in Troutdale, and picked *her* pride and joy out from a lineup of other hail-damaged cars to be the one it chose to tango with.

Caught up in the maelstrom, Deb's Camaro blazed a path of destruction across three counties that went from the front page of the weekly paper right into the annals of history.

The storm tossed the car around like a tea bag—dropping it down, only to haul it right back up again. Rumor had it that Deb's car accounted for forty percent of the total storm damage sustained in Jericho alone. Farm Bureau claims adjusters who raised eyebrows at the epic reports were stunned when beleaguered homeowners produced actual pieces of the fire-engine red car as evidence.

Bert Townsend even had actual cell phone video of Deb's Camaro as it tore through the plate-glass window of Food Bonanza, and took out most of the fresh produce aisle.

Just as quickly, the car got sucked back out, and roared up Route 58 toward Mouth of Wilson, leaving a trail of broken glass, Vidalia onions, and Georgia peaches in its wake.

Bert later told a Roanoke-based TV crew that it was like the car had joined forces with the storm.

"It was like Elijah, hisself, was driving it," he said. "A real chariot of fire."

"How so?" the reporter asked.

Bert shrugged. "Well, the car kind of dropped down out of

nowhere, all gentle-like. And it was right-side up, too. Then it just turned itself around, and took off—headfirst—right through them plate-glass windows." He scratched his head. "It was in the store about two minutes before it come flying right back out. And dern if the lights wasn't on, too."

The reporter looked confused. "You mean the lights were on in the supermarket?"

Bert shook his head. "Nope. The car lights."

"The car headlights were on?"

Bert nodded. "At first, I thought that was mighty peculiar, too, but the storm knocked out the power in town, and it probably was pretty dark in there."

Deb's car made cameo appearances in at least six other locations across the area, before finally coming to rest across three center lanes at the Bixby Bowladrome on U.S. 21.

People who knew her joked that this would be the closest Deb would ever get to a perfect 300 bowling score. Her team from the glass factory, the Crystal Cougars, was better known for its prowess at picking up cans of Budweiser (and married men), than picking up spares on league night.

Rita Chriscoe, who ran the shoe rental and concession counter at Bixby's, agreed, but told a *Gazette* reporter that it would have been a better story if Deb had still owned her old car—the one she drove before she bought the Camaro with that settlement money from the carpal tunnel lawsuit.

"What kind of car was that?" the reporter asked.

Rita took a long drag off her cigarette. One of the only good things to come from all this damn storm damage was the fact that they could smoke inside the building again. With half of the roof missing, it wasn't like anyone would complain.

"It was one of them Oldsmobile Tornadoes," she said.

"Tornadoes?"

Rita nodded. The smoke from her cigarette wound up around her head like a halo. "A beauty, too. Dark blue. Eighteen-inch rims with spinners." Her eyes were dreamy. "Nice."

"What happened to the car?" the reporter asked.

Rita shook her head. She was scraping dried nacho cheese sauce off a rack of bowling balls that had the misfortune of being stored next to the snack counter when the storm hit.

"You know, it was the damnedest thing. That Tornado was parked over at Junior's right next to the Camaro." She lowered her voice. "Some of us think it was god's way of saying that GM shouldn't have stopped making Oldsmobiles."

The reporter nodded. "You mean like some kind of automotive natural selection?"

At first, Rita looked at him with a blank expression. Then she picked up another ball covered with orange-colored splatter. "Yes," she said with finality. "Just like that."

Tim Bixby even posted a photo of the bright red street rod on his Facebook page, with the caption, "Muscle Car Takes Bowling Alley By Storm." Then he convinced Bert Townsend to post his cell phone video on YouTube. Within three days, the story had gone viral, with more than two hundred twenty-four thousand people indicating that they "liked" the quirky, multimedia monument to Deb's misfortune.

The local Chevy dealer in Jefferson even talked about making the car the centerpiece of a storm recovery fundraising effort. Residents of the county who had sustained damages attributable to the marauding car were invited to submit photos that would become part of a permanent display in the dealership showroom.

Within six weeks of the tornado, all of the Chevy dealers in southwest Virginia and North Carolina had depleted their inventories of red Camaros.

At home in Jericho, Henry tried to talk Maddie into buying one of the now legendary cars to replace her Jeep, which had been destroyed by the storm. Maddie, horrified by this idea, took pains to explain to Henry that buying a car that looked like the one that had demolished part of Uncle David's bed and breakfast would be too painful a reminder for the distraught innkeeper.

Thank god.

Chapter 5

On Saturday morning, Maddie and David sat together at the kitchen table, drinking coffee.

Maddie was reviewing some notes Lizzy had made on patients she had seen at Mt. Rogers during her clinic hours on Wednesday night. There was no tornado damage at that altitude, but there were some minor injuries related to high winds and monsoon-like rain.

David was sorting through a large pile of mail he had retrieved from the post office the day before, and was busily ripping reply cards out of magazines. A tower of tiny cards rose up from the table. It was nearly as tall as Henry's box of Cheerios.

Something in one of the publications caught his eye.

"Yo, Cinderella?" he said. "Have you ever had any surgeries using transvaginal mesh?"

Maddie put down her coffee cup. "Excuse me?"

"If so, you could stand to make a *lot* of money in this big class action lawsuit." He held up a glossy, two-page ad in the copy of *In Style* magazine he was perusing.

She sighed. "Do you lie awake at night trying to invent new ways to make me insane?"

David looked offended. "Of *course* not. I'm just trying to help out."

"Help out? How, exactly?"

He flipped through a few more pages of the magazine. "Well,

now that you're really the only breadwinner in the family, I thought the extra income might come in handy."

"By suing the manufacturer of a product used to repair prolapsed uteri?"

He nodded enthusiastically.

She sighed. "I'd rather sell my eggs on eBay."

David looked her up and down. "Really? Think you have any left that haven't calcified?"

Henry walked into the room, cutting short Maddie's response.

"Maddie?" he asked. "When we talk to Daddy this week, can I show him my piece of the red car?"

Maddie looked at him in confusion. "What piece of the red car, Henry?"

David cleared his throat and started collecting his magazines and pile of postcards. "I have to get going. I need to have Astrid at the groomer's before nine."

"Wait a minute." Maddie held out a hand to stop him. She turned back to Henry. "What piece of the red car are you talking about, buddy?"

Henry looked back and forth between them. "The one that Uncle David gave me yesterday."

"Uncle David gave you a piece of the car?" she asked.

He nodded. "I can keep it, can't I, Maddie?"

Maddie sucked in a cheek and turned to David. "Care to elaborate?"

He shrugged. "The contractor found a tiny, *insignificant* piece of it beneath the rubble at the back wall of the Inn. I thought Henry would like it as a souvenir, so I brought it here for him."

"Tiny?" Maddie asked.

"Yes. Totally tiny."

"And insignificant?"

"Completely."

Maddie turned to Henry. "Where is it, sport?"

He pointed toward the yard. "It's outside behind the barn."

"Why is it outside, Henry?"

"Um." He looked at David, who was suddenly very interested in contemplating his thumbnail. "It's too big to fit in my bedroom."

"Really?" She looked back at David. "What piece of the car do we have, David?"

He shrugged. "It's an interior piece."

"An interior piece?"

"It *might* be part of the . . . dashboard."

"The *dashboard?*"

David was growing exasperated. "Is there an echo in here? Yes, the *dashboard*. Okay?"

Maddie sighed. "Henry? Would you do me a big favor and go and ask Syd if she's ready to have me help her with her bath?"

"Okay, Maddie." He ran off toward the front of the house.

"Walk, buddy!" Maddie called after him.

She faced David. "You gave Henry the dashboard of a car? Are you *insane?* This isn't a chop shop."

"Cool your jets, Cochise. It's not the whole dashboard, just the good part."

"What the hell does that mean? The *good* part?"

He sighed. "The part that has the steering wheel."

Maddie sagged in her chair. "Great."

"I wish you'd just relax once in a while. It might be fun to trick this thing out for him."

"David, I'm already having a hard enough time, convincing him that buying one of those absurd cars as a replacement for the Jeep would be too painful a reminder for *you*, and then you bring him the damn dashboard as a souvenir."

"Yeah . . . about that. Why not buy a Camaro?"

Maddie looked at him like he had just suggested that she dye her hair orange and have her tongue pierced. "You must be joking?"

"Oh come on, Cinderella. We both know that you flashed through puberty at warp six. Why not take a thoughtful pause and embrace all those developmental stages you skipped?"

"I don't need to buy a muscle car to reclaim the excesses of my lost youth. All I need to do is have a conversation with *you*."

David leaned forward in his chair. "Admit it. You know you'd look hot, roaring around in one of those things."

"I'd look ridiculous." Maddie picked up a file folder.

"See? This is what I'm talking about."

Maddie looked up at him over the rims of her glasses. "*What* is what you're talking about?"

"*This.* Your complete denial. It's so textbook."

"You're nuts."

"Am not."

"Are, too."

"No. Wait." He sifted through his pile of magazines until he found the one he was looking for. "There's an article about this phenomenon in here." He flipped through the magazine until he found the interview he was looking for and held it out to her. "See?"

Maddie glanced down at the flashy interview with Dr. Laars Pänz, the latest messiah of the self-help movement. "Oh come on, David. Not this dude again."

"Hey . . . don't knock him. I'll have you know that he was on *Conan* last week. *Conan.* The man's a guru. And a legend."

"The man's a fraud."

"You're just jealous."

"Why would I be jealous of someone who legally changed his first name to *Doctor*?"

David huffed. "Maybe because he's making a fortune on the talk show circuit, while you spend *your* days lancing boils."

"Whatever." Maddie returned her attention to her files.

David sighed. "Hey. What was Henry saying about seeing his dad?"

Maddie looked at him. "Didn't we tell you? We've been able to set up some Skype sessions for Henry and James. They can talk to each other about once a week now."

"That's great. Any idea about how much longer he'll be stuck in Afghanistan?"

Maddie shrugged. "We're hoping that he'll be included in this next round of troop reductions."

"And if he is? What will that mean about Henry?"

"We don't know."

They turned to see Syd standing in the doorway.

"Hi ya, Pegleg." David hopped up to pull out a chair for her.

"Good morning, husband." Syd made her way to the table and bent over to kiss the top of Maddie's head. "And good morning, wife."

Maddie wrapped an arm around her waist. "Hey, you smell good."

"Bathing does tend to yield such happy results."

Maddie looked up at her in surprise. "You already took a bath?"

Syd nodded. "I thought it was about time I figured it out." She lowered herself onto the chair David pulled out for her and handed him her crutches.

"To answer your question," Syd said. "We don't really know what will happen when James comes home."

"You've had him for a year and a half now," David said.

Syd nodded. "And James has been wonderful about that. There's no doubt about how grateful he is that Henry has been here with us."

"But," Maddie interjected, "Henry *is* his son, and we can't forget that."

"No matter how much we'd like to," Syd added.

Maddie took hold of her hand.

David shook his head. "I guess we all knew there was a chance it wouldn't last forever."

"Well . . . nothing's over yet," Maddie said. "And today is all we have. So let's just enjoy it and not get all maudlin, worrying about things we can't control."

David looked at her in surprise. "When the hell did you get so Zen-like?"

Maddie gave him one of her best deadpan expressions. "You're not the only one around here who watches *Conan*."

Henry raced back into the room. "Uncle David. Astrid just went poopie on the stairs again."

David held up his hand before Maddie could say anything. "I've got this." He stood up. "Come on, Henry. Let's clean it up and take her outside for a walk."

"Okay," Henry said. "Can I carry the poopie outside this time?"

They walked out of the room together.

Syd sighed. "That dog is a menace."

"I know."

"Henry is already getting too attached to her."

"I know that, too."

Syd looked at Maddie. "Just like we're too attached to Henry."

"How could we ever be *too* attached to him, honey?"

"You know what I mean."

Maddie nodded.

"What are we going to do if James takes him back?"

Maddie squeezed her hand. "James *will* take him back, Syd. We need to expect that. Henry is his son."

"I know."

"I know you know."

Syd sighed. "How is it possible for you to be so stoic about this?"

Maddie gave her a sad smile. "Because inside, I'm growing a tumor that could declare statehood."

Syd scooted forward and rested her head on Maddie's shoulder. "One day at a time, right?"

Maddie nodded. "One day at a time."

Astrid was taking her time, nosing along the base of the split-rail fence that separated the yard from the pasture behind the house. Pete had already lost interest in this pastime and trotted off to inspect the perimeter of the pond.

"Okay, Henry," David said. "Hurl it as far as you can, and make sure you throw it up in the air this time so it doesn't bounce off the fence and hit us."

Henry nodded. With great concentration, he flung the handful of tiny stools as high and as far as he could. They made an impressive arc over the top rung of the fence, splaying out against the bright blue sky like pieces of gravel.

Of course, the oversized work glove of Maddie's that he was wearing went sailing over the fence, too. Again.

David sighed.

"Stay here, buddy. I'll go get it."

Henry looked up at him. "Don't step in the cow poopie."

That had happened twice already, too.

"I won't."

David handed Henry Astrid's leash and climbed between the split rails and waded out into the high grass in search of Maddie's glove.

"Can I walk Astrid over to the barn so I can look at my steering wheel?" he asked.

"Sure," David said. "But don't let her pee on it again."

"I won't," Henry said. The two of them set off for the back side of the barn.

Henry loved it here. It was so different from living at Grandma's house.

Sometimes he missed playing with Jason and Tommy in the afternoons after he got home from school. Mrs. Manning would always let them go outside and play until suppertime. But Syd always made sure Henry did his homework first. That wasn't *so* bad, except on the days he had piano lessons. And now it wasn't like the wintertime, when it got dark so early. And sometimes, Gabriel and Héctor Sanchez came home with him and stayed until their mama came for them at suppertime.

He liked having Uncle David and Uncle Michael here. Uncle Michael made pizzas for him, and he baked really good cookies. And Uncle David always let him watch TV in the evenings before bed. He really liked that. Usually, Maddie wouldn't let him watch more than *one* show, and only after his bath. But Uncle David had put a TV in his bathroom upstairs, so if Henry took his bath in there, he could watch *two* shows every night.

Uncle David's favorite show was something called *The X Factor*.

He liked how Uncle David would yell funny things at the people while they were singing—usually about their clothes. Henry didn't think their songs were bad, but Uncle David said that this was what you were supposed to do during "boot camp." He didn't really know what that meant, either. Uncle David said that it was a lot like learning to play the piano. Henry didn't say anything to him, but he was really glad that Syd didn't yell at him while he was practicing. He was pretty sure that would make it harder to concentrate.

Astrid kept pulling on the leash like she had someplace to be. Henry was really hoping she would go poopie again. He wanted the chance to throw more of it over the fence.

Last time, he almost hit Before—the fat black and white cow with the yellow "B4" tag in her ear. B4 made a good target because she just stood there chewing grass and staring at him with those big, dark eyes. She was always by the fence up here behind the house, even though she lived at Mr. Baxter's farm. Henry really wanted to give B4 a better name, but Maddie said that probably wasn't a good idea, so that's why he just started calling her "Before."

Astrid stopped and sniffed around the woodpile. Henry held his breath and waited, hoping, but then she lifted up her head and moved on again.

Astrid was a funny dog. She wasn't like Pete at all. Pete ate *anything*—especially stuff he wasn't supposed to have. But Astrid would only eat really icky stuff. Uncle David called it "sweet-bread," and he cooked it for her every day. Henry really didn't understand that. It didn't look like bread and it sure didn't smell very sweet. Uncle Michael always complained about how it made the kitchen stink.

He wrinkled up his nose. It made her poopie stink really bad, too.

Hey!

He looked down. *Oh, boy!*

He looked back over his shoulder. "Uncle David!"

It was going to be a great morning.

◊ ◊ ◊

Jocelyn only had one more stop to make. She usually tried to wrap up this part of her day by eleven-thirty, so she'd have time to pull over for a smoke and a Pepsi before heading back into the post office to pick up her afternoon deliveries.

She checked the cellophane-wrapped pack that was propped up in the ashtray of her '57 Biscayne. *Damn.* Only four left. She'd have to hit the Quik Stop on her way back into town for another carton of Dorals. At the rate she and Deb were burning through them, they might as well buy stock in the damn tobacco company.

For the past couple of months, Jocelyn Painter and Deb Carlson had been working together, running a flag car business on the weekends. Most of their work came from the half-dozen manufactured home distributors on Highway 58. Those were usually short trips, an hour or two each way. But sometimes they got longer hauls—even the occasional overnight trip to Tennessee or West Virginia. And those trips were real cash cows—a dollar forty-five a mile, plus sixty-five dollars for the overnight, and fifteen dollars for each hour of down time. But ever since the tornado, Deb hadn't been able to help out as much. It wasn't that she didn't have a car to drive—she still had access to that old Oldsmobile she gave her mama when she got the Camaro.

She tapped the red and white steering wheel of her beloved Biscayne. Hell . . . *she* drove a classic car, and the thing still ran like a top. No, it wasn't that the Oldsmobile was too old. It was more that Deb just didn't have the heart for the work anymore. She said that when her Camaro got sucked up by that storm, it just blew the light right out of her—like a candle in the wind. In fact, she drove Jocelyn nuts playing that damn Elton John song over and over—only she called it, "Goodbye, Deborah's Rose."

It was pretty sad, really, but Jocelyn was a realist, and she believed that Deb had mourned long enough. It was springtime, after all. And mortgage rates were at all-time lows. That meant that tons of oversized loads of mobile American Dreams were just waiting to roll down the byways toward exotic and far-flung destinations. There was money to be made, and if Jocelyn was gonna be able to keep them both in Dorals, Deb would soon have to start pulling her weight again, or *Cougar's Flag Cars* would be nothing but a memory. Just like that damn Camaro.

She turned onto the long lane that led up to Dr. Stevenson's house. The trumpet creeper vines that covered most of the fence at the turnoff looked just about ready to burst into bloom. That seemed early for this time of the year, but it had been a lot warmer than usual. That's why they'd been having so many of those damn storms.

It looked like Dr. Stevenson's property had fared better than many parts of the county. Jocelyn didn't see too much wind damage as she followed the gravel lane along the creek that led up toward the outbuildings. She always liked it when she had a reason to ride all the way up to the big farmhouse. It was such a pretty and tidy place—no piles of trash or broken-down farm equipment parked all over the place. No junked cars or cast-off—*wait a minute . . .*

She saw what looked like the dashboard of a car propped up against the back side of the barn. She shook her head as she continued on toward the house. It was too bad. Sooner or later, everybody started collecting junk, but she was really sorry to see this place start going downhill. She really thought the cosmopolitan Dr. Stevenson was a class act, but maybe the locals were right, and you never could quite take the country out of the girl.

She stopped near the steps that led up to the wide front porch and shut off her engine.

Normally, she'd leave the mail in the box that faced the county road, but today was different. She looked down at the flat brown envelope that rested on the seat beside her. It had a cream-colored label that read *Law Offices of Graber, Helms & Hopper*. It was registered mail, and Jocelyn had to get a signature in order to deliver it. She had a pretty good idea what it contained, too. Just last week, she had delivered a similar piece of mail to Eunice Pollard. It was like an epidemic these days.

The big front door to the house opened, and a little boy came outside. A big yellow dog followed him. The dog saw her and ran down the steps with his tail wagging.

"Hey, Henry," Jocelyn called out as she made her way toward the steps, with Pete dancing around her feet.

"Hi, Miss Painter," he said. He was carrying a red coffee can.

"What are you up to?" she asked.

He pointed toward the pond. "I'm going to feed the catfish. Do you wanna come help?"

"Not today, sweetie," she said. "I have to deliver a letter to Miss Murphy. Is she at home?"

Henry nodded. "She's making brownies."

"Would you do me a favor and tell her that I'm here?"

He nodded. "Okay." He set his can down on the edge of the porch and ran back into the house. He returned less than a minute later. "She said to come on inside—they're in the kitchen."

"Thanks, Henry."

He picked up his red coffee can and ran off toward the pond with Pete in tow.

Jocelyn walked up the steps and opened the front door.

"Hello?" she called out, as she stepped inside.

"Hi, Jocelyn!" Syd's voice rang out from someplace. "We're in the kitchen. Come on back."

Jocelyn made her way down the wide center hallway toward the dining room. She could hear music playing. It was some kind of classical something—a piano thing. That reminded her of the concert they had at the high school last Christmas, when Dr. Stevenson's mother was here visiting. She played Christmas carols with the local symphony to help raise money for the rescue squad. Everybody said it was one of the best benefit concerts they'd ever had, but a lot of the people who showed up didn't give a flip about the county's 911 service. They just hadn't seen Dr. Heller since she left Jericho more than twenty years earlier, and they were dying to see how well she was holding up.

Pretty damn well, as it turned out.

Jocelyn had to agree. If Dr. Stevenson had inherited many of her mama's genes, then she was gonna be turning heads for many years to come.

She crossed the dining room and entered the kitchen. Syd was seated at a pine worktable, scraping thick batter from a large stoneware bowl into a rectangular pan. Her injured leg was propped up on a ladder-back chair. Dr. Stevenson was there, too, bent over some papers and file folders that were spread out across the kitchen table. They both looked up when she entered the room.

Syd smiled at her. "If you hang around for forty-five minutes, I can hook you up with one of the world's most decadent brownies."

Dr. Stevenson nodded. "She speaks the truth, Jocelyn. Pull up a chair, and I'll put on some fresh coffee."

As tempted as she was to accept, Jocelyn shook her head. She was on duty, and she couldn't mix business with pleasure.

"I wish I could, but I've got this registered letter that needs to be signed for. Then I have to get the receipt for it back in to the post office so Zeke can log it before he heads out for lunch."

She didn't mention the pit stop for more cigarettes. Quik Stop closed at noon on Saturdays, and they had the best price in town on cartons.

"Oh," Dr. Stevenson said. "That's too bad. We never get to see you, Jocelyn." She took off her glasses and stood up. "How's the flag car business going?"

Jocelyn shrugged. "It would be going a lot better if I could get Deb to come back to work."

Syd looked perplexed. "What's wrong with Deb?"

Jocelyn sighed and waved her hand. "It's all this business with her car. She just can't get over it, and hearing about it in the news every day and seeing those disaster relief posters all over town isn't helping."

Dr. Stevenson laughed, then sobered when Syd frowned at her. "I'm sorry, Jocelyn. I know it's not really funny." She looked at Syd. "But you have to admit that this whole marauding car thing really takes the edge off thinking about how catastrophic the aftermath of this tornado nightmare *could* have been."

Jocelyn thought again about "Deborah's Rose" and her own declining bank balance. "Tragic" didn't really seem like that much of an overstatement to her.

She nodded anyway. It was hard not to be agreeable when Dr. Stevenson was staring right at her with those deep blue eyes. She really did look like her mama.

Syd cleared her throat. "Still, we're *very* sorry about Deb's loss—aren't we, Maddie?"

Dr. Stevenson nodded apologetically. "We are." She picked up a pen from her pile of file folders. "Now, where do I need to sign?"

Jocelyn shook her head. "Actually, Dr. Stevenson, this is a letter for Syd."

"For me?" Syd was surprised.

"Yes, ma'am." Jocelyn walked over to her.

Syd reached out a hand to take the envelope from her. "I'm not expecting anything."

A flicker of something crossed Dr. Stevenson's face. "Aren't you?"

Syd's hand paused in midair. "Oh. Maybe I am." She looked at the label on the envelope. Then she looked at Dr. Stevenson and nodded.

Jocelyn didn't really know what to say, so she cleared her throat. "You just need to sign right here." She indicated the correct space on the NCR form.

Syd complied, and Jocelyn tore off the top copy of the receipt for her.

"I have to get going now." She really didn't want to be there when Syd opened the envelope. She had made the mistake of staying around when Eunice read *her* letter, and it didn't go well. She always did think that Lonnie Pollard was a poor choice for Eunice, who actually had been a really pretty girl in her younger days. Before that afternoon, Jocelyn had no idea that Lonnie had been dipping his wick into so many different pots.

She didn't know that Eunice could curse like that, either. All that abuse just flowed right out of her like she'd been saving it up for a lifetime. It was like somebody had pulled the stopper out of a bathtub drain.

She sure got an earful and an education on *that* delivery.

She stole another glance at Dr. Stevenson, who was just standing there quietly looking at Syd.

Yeah. It was time for her to go. "I'm sure I'll see you ladies around town. Have a nice afternoon."

She heard them each call out their thanks as she turned around and hightailed it back down the long hallway toward the front door.

"Are you going to open that?"

Maddie was still standing beside the table, watching Syd slowly turn the envelope over in her hands.

Syd looked up at her. "Yeah. I don't know what's the matter with me . . . I knew this was coming."

"Are you okay?"

Syd nodded. "It's funny. I mean, this is totally what I wanted . . . but it's hard not to feel a little sad."

Maddie didn't really know how to respond to that. She tried to push down an irrational surge of anxiety. Why wouldn't Syd feel sad? You didn't get a divorce decree every day. It made perfect sense—*didn't it?*

"Do you want to be alone?" she asked.

"No." Syd was adamant. "That's the last thing I want."

"Okay."

"Oh, this is just ridiculous." Syd ripped open the envelope and pulled out the sheaf of papers tucked inside it. Maddie watched her eyes grow wider as she read. "This *cannot* be happening." She flipped through the pages, and then tossed them down to the table with a look of disgust.

Maddie was more confused than ever. "What's wrong?"

Syd looked at her. "Well, it's not the decree."

"It isn't?"

Syd shook her head. "Nope."

"Well, then, what is it?"

"It's my official notification that Jeff has decided to contest the divorce."

Maddie's jaw dropped. "He *what?*"

Syd nodded. "Yeah. Nice of him to wait until it was within spitting distance of being finalized."

Maddie was amazed. "Why on earth would he do that?"

"I have *no* idea."

Maddie went to Syd. "May I look at the papers?"

"Be my guest." Syd held them up to her.

Maddie read through them as quickly as she could. "Sweetie, it says here that what he's contesting is the *grounds* for divorce. In other words, he's denying the charge of adultery."

"Oh, *that's* rich."

"Well, whatever it is, it means you'll now have to face him in court and prove your claim that he was unfaithful."

Syd sat back and glared at her. "You have *got* to be kidding me?"

Maddie showed her the relevant paragraph on the form. "Not so much."

"I so do not believe this." She sagged back against her chair. "His mother's fingerprints are all over this one. I so should've seen this coming. It was just too easy."

"What do you mean?"

"Doris Simon would never be able to sit back and let her precious son's reputation be tarnished by something like this."

"Something like what?" Maddie asked.

"Adultery. Of course she would have to clean up this little indiscretion for him."

"Honey, I really don't see how taking this into court could be understood as cleaning anything up. On the contrary, it would seem to draw more attention to it."

"Oh, trust me. Doris has no intention of seeing this go to court. Her goal is something else entirely."

"What might that be?"

Syd sighed and shook her head. "I wish I knew."

Maddie looked down again at the papers in her hands. "It says here that Jeff would be willing to consider mediation or counseling if you'd be willing to rethink your decision."

Syd looked incredulous. "A Glock to my head couldn't get me to rethink my decision."

Against her will, Maddie smiled. "I really love you."

"It's a good thing you do," Syd replied. "I think we're in for a bumpy ride."

"Of course." Maddie tossed the papers down onto the table. "I mean . . . it's been such a cakewalk so far."

Syd wrapped an arm around her waist and tugged her closer. "I don't know . . . at least it's never boring."

"You got that part right." Maddie hugged her and kissed the top of her head. She sighed and looked across the kitchen toward the back stairs, where Astrid sat growling and wrestling with some kind of elongated chew toy. The damn dog had already eviscerated most of Pete's tennis balls and half of Henry's shoes, so Maddie figured that she must have found a new prey.

While she watched, Astrid flipped the bright purple cylinder up into the air, and chased after it as it slid across the floor toward them.

Maddie's eyes grew wide, and she pushed back from Syd.

"Oh my god!" She pointed at the floor. "*Please* tell me that dog doesn't have what I think she has."

Syd followed her gaze, then gasped and gripped Maddie's upper arms. "Where in the hell did she get *that?*"

Maddie looked down at her. "I have a pretty good idea."

She released Syd and started toward the dog. But Astrid saw her coming, and it was clear that she wasn't ready to surrender her treasure just yet. Maddie lunged for the "toy," but, for once, the fat dog moved faster. Astrid scrambled to her feet and bolted toward the front of the house, skidding on the tile floor as she tried to run with her bobbing prize.

Maddie turned around and gave Syd a hopeless gaze. "*Please* tell me that I'm not about to go chasing after a dog with a dildo?"

Syd was laughing—so hard that tears were running down her cheeks.

Maddie sighed and walked toward the hallway. "Yuck it up, Goldilocks. Paybacks are hell."

Chapter 6

This was the most amazing bowl of shrimp and grits he'd ever eaten. Hands down.

And that was saying a lot, because he'd had the *best*—at least, until today.

The fried okra with capreze salad and jalapeño corn bread both were worth the price of admission, too.

He'd always heard that the food at Odell's Midway Café was good, but he'd never been able to make it over here. The little roadside restaurant was situated halfway between Jericho and Jefferson, and they didn't serve supper—just breakfast and lunch. And Michael was always too busy during the daytime to get out and scour the county back roads in search of local cuisine. But after he took his first bite of Wednesday's lunch special, he knew that he'd missed a lot. And he also knew that he wasn't leaving here until he shook the hand that cooked this incredible food.

He looked around the tiny place. The décor, if you could call it that, left a lot to be desired. There were four small tables with gingham oilcloth covers and mismatched chairs, and a row of booths along the front wall, upholstered with vinyl that had seen better days. The pale green linoleum floor was cracked and chipped, and half the sockets in the ceiling lights were missing bulbs. Presiding over it all was the inevitable portrait of Jesus at Gethsemane. It hung high over the short-order grill—warped and shiny with grease, and faded to the point that the Savior's hair looked almost neon in the fluorescent light.

Strangely, that sort of worked, too.

But the place was clean—squeaky clean. A blue and white certificate posted behind the cash register boasted a sanitation grade of 100.5. That was saying a lot for a backwoods greasy spoon that cooked everything it served on a griddle and a gas ring.

He lifted another spoonful of the spicy, fragrant grits. *Good god.* He'd swap his damn Bertazzoni range for a one-lunger hotplate if he could whip up something *this* good.

His server strolled by, carrying a sweating pitcher of sweet tea.

"You need more to drink, mister?" she asked.

He nodded. She was a pretty girl—sixteen or seventeen, he was guessing. She was tall and slender, with a beautiful coffee-colored complexion. When she reached out to refill his plastic tumbler, he noticed that she had a tattoo on the underside of her forearm.

"Nicorette?" he asked.

"It's my name," she explained.

"Really? That's unique."

"Yeah." She rolled her eyes and turned her arm over so he could get a better view of the tattoo. It was a beauty—lots of scrollwork and curlicues on the letters. "My mama *loves* to tell everyone how she had to quit smoking when she found out she was pregnant with me. She says she named me after her best friend."

Michael laughed.

"I don't really mind," Nicorette said. "It could've been a *lot* worse."

"How so?" he asked.

"See that girl over there?" She gestured toward the young woman behind the cash register who was busy restocking a tray of Beeman's gum. She lowered her voice to a whisper. "That's my cousin, Maybelline."

"I see your point."

They smiled at each other.

"I haven't seen you in here before," she said. "Are you from around here?"

"Not originally. But I've lived here for a few years now. I run the Riverside Inn near Jericho."

Nicorette's jaw dropped. "You *do*? We all heard about what happened to it in the tornado."

Michael held up a placating hand. "Well . . . some of those stories were pretty exaggerated."

Nicorette shook her head. "Well, they sure weren't exaggerated around here." She turned around and called out to her cousin. "Hey, May-Bell. Show this man the spoiler!"

Maybelline walked toward the kitchen area and pointed up at a bright red, fiberglass ornament that was tacked up over a swinging door like a lucky horseshoe.

"Mama found that the morning after the storm," Nicorette explained. "It was sticking out of the compost heap out back." She turned back toward him. "We cleaned it off real good before we brought it inside."

Michael just shook his head. "Is your mama here? I'd really like to talk with her about this food."

Nicorette looked at him with alarm. "Is it bad? Do you need me to get you something else?" She reached out to take his bowl.

"No!" He intercepted her hand and gave it a pat before releasing it. "No, honey. The food is *wonderful*. I want to ask her about who cooked it, and see if I could talk with them." He smiled at her. "I'm a chef, too, but I haven't had shrimp and grits this good since I left South Carolina."

Nicorette relaxed. "That's Mama and Aunt Evelyn. They do all the cooking. I'll go get her for you." She turned and walked back toward the kitchen, stopping to refill half a dozen glasses of tea on her way.

Michael stared at the flaming red memento from The Storm That Changed Everything. It hung up there on the wall, in a ludicrous face-off with Faded Jesus. It was a tossup, to guess which one of the two icons would persevere and lay claim to the most exalted place in the shared imaginations of this small community.

He looked again at the painting.

Nope. It was no contest.

As long as people in Jericho kept finding pieces of Deb Carlson's car, Jesus was going to remain stuck on his knees in Gethsemane for a good long time.

The door to the kitchen swung open, and a middle-aged woman, wearing a hairnet and a bright yellow apron, emerged. She was wiping her hands on a red-and-white striped towel.

Michael raised his hand and waved at her. She nodded at him and walked across the small restaurant toward his table, stopping along the way to greet other diners. She appeared to know everyone by name.

She stopped next to his table and looked down at him with a mixture of curiosity and suspicion. "I'm Nadine Odell."

She had a husky voice. Michael wondered if her "friendship" with Nicorette's namesake had been short-lived.

He got to his feet and held out his hand. "I'm Michael Robertson. I'm a professional chef, and I have to tell you that I've spent most of my adult life studying low-country cooking. And I have never, *ever* eaten food this good—anyplace."

Nadine stared at him for a moment before taking his hand. She smiled, and he saw where Nicorette got her good looks.

"Where are your people from?" she asked.

He pulled out a chair for her. "Aiken, South Carolina."

She nodded and sat down. "You go to culinary school?"

"Yes, ma'am," he said. "In Charleston."

She nodded again. "Well. I suppose they can teach you how to do some things."

He gestured toward his bowl of grits. "Not like this, they can't."

She sighed. "I never went to school to learn how to cook."

"Where'd you learn to do it, then?"

"My grandma, Harriet."

"She taught you?"

Nadine snorted. "Hell, no. I just paid attention. And when I got older and moved up here from Georgia, I tried to make things taste like I remembered." She shrugged. "Sometimes I get it right. Other times, not so much. But what I don't remember, Evelyn pretty much does."

"Evelyn?"

"My sister."

"So you both cook here?"

Nadine sighed. "Usually. But Evelyn hasn't been able to work much lately. Her mother-in-law is sick, and they've been taking care of her at home. I've had to cut back on our hours because I can't handle the place by myself six days a week."

Michael's mind was racing a mile a minute.

He had a fantastic idea. The universe had just served him up a super-sized plate of opportunity that was every bit as miraculous as the food that now sat on the table in front of him. He leaned forward in his chair.

"Nadine," he said. "Have you ever thought about taking on a partner?"

David balanced the flat box full of glass vases against his hip and knocked again on the aluminum screen door. He was sure that Gladys was at home. Her bilious green Reliant K was in the driveway, and the interior door to the house was standing wide open. He waited, but there was no sound of movement from inside.

He'd borrowed two dozen bud vases from Gladys several weeks ago, when they were getting the Inn ready for the big wedding event that never happened. Fortunately, the vases had been safely stashed away in an outside storage building, along with twenty-four rented tables and ninety-six folding chairs. The tornado never touched the unit, so he and Michael didn't have to worry about paying for *those* damages. Too bad they couldn't say the same for the six rented porta-johns that ended up strewn along the path that led down to the river. What a nightmare that cleanup was going to be.

He craned his neck toward the end of Gladys's tiny front porch.

Where the hell was she?

He noticed that her car was backed into its space, commando-style—like she wanted to be able to flee the scene in a hurry, should the need arise.

He thought about that one. Living all those years with that ne'er-do-well son of hers would certainly be enough incentive for that. It was hard to believe that it had been nearly two years since Beau died from complications related to his meth addiction—after his nightmarish attack on Syd and Lizzy, and his clumsy attempt to burn down the town library.

How much had all of their lives changed since then?

Most of them had managed to pick up the pieces and move on. Lizzy was now dating Syd's hunky brother, and she was well into the second year of her hugely successful tenure as the county's parish nurse. The only fly in the ointment for her was whether or not that lecherous old skinflint, Tom Greene—who controlled his weight in United Way dollars—would decide to renew the program funding at the end of Lizzy's grant.

Asshole. It was anybody's guess how that one would turn out.

And Syd? Well. Syd was Syd, and Syd was a survivor. *And* she had Maddie.

But Gladys? Gladys hadn't fared quite as well.

Nobody in the county held Gladys responsible for the things her son had done, but Gladys seemed unable to move beyond it all. She still kept her tiny flower shop open, but she didn't do much else. She didn't go to church anymore, and she didn't show up at any of the community events where she used to be a fixture. She just seemed to want to fade into the landscape.

David looked around. Even her tiny front yard—which at one time had been choked with an explosive array of colorful flowers—now contained only a few scraggly-looking foliage plants in cast-off containers.

He shook his head. It was really too bad.

He had just about decided to write her a note and leave the box on the floor next to her front door when he heard footsteps on the crushed gravel driveway. He turned toward the sound.

It was Gladys. She stood near the bumper of her K car and looked back at him with a sober expression.

"I was out back in the shed," she said, unapologetically. "I didn't hear you drive up."

He hefted the box of vases up so she could see it. "Hello, Gladys. I wanted to return these to you before any more time went by."

She nodded, but didn't say anything.

David continued to stand there. "Is there someplace in particular you'd like for me to leave these? I don't want to just set this box down here. It's kinda heavy."

Gladys waved a hand. "Follow me out back, and we'll put them in the shed." She turned around and walked off without waiting for him to follow.

He rolled his eyes, then picked his way down the steps and walked toward the back of the house. Gladys was already halfway to the shed, which really was like a freestanding garage. It had a big, rolling bay door that was partially pushed back, and there was an overhead light on inside. He could see shelves stacked high with flowerpots and pyramids of spongy, green blocks of Oasis. There were bags of soil and tins of plant fertilizer all over the place.

Gladys stood to the side when he entered the shed. Half of the space was set up as a man's workshop. There was an impressive-looking, rolling toolbox that was at least five feet high, and a banged-up auto creeper. Cans of motor oil and fuel injector cleaner were stacked on every surface. He also noticed a pretty raunchy-looking pinup calendar tacked to a support beam, and he wondered why Gladys had left that hanging there. David was no prude, but judging by the content of the photo, it was pretty clear that Beau's tastes ran to the exotic.

Whatever car Beau had been working on sat there, too— buried beneath a pile of grimy-looking canvas tarps.

Gladys gestured toward a big, beat-up table that sat on the opposite side of the space. It was shoved up against a side wall, beneath a dirty window that had several cracked panes. The surface of the table was littered with every imaginable kind of gardening tool, and about two dozen spools of florist's wire.

"Just put them down there," she said. "I'll deal with them later."

Judging by the look of things, David doubted that Gladys would be dealing with much of anything later. He followed orders and deposited the box where she had indicated. Then he turned around to face her.

Gladys stood wrapped in a beam of light that poured down from the naked bulb above her head. Her small frame cast comically large shadows across the canvas-covered car behind her. The yellow light made her skin look like parchment.

Part of the tarp was torn near the back bumper, and David could see a swath of bright red metal. It looked like it belonged to some kind of muscle car. He thought something about the lines of the car looked familiar, and he took a step toward it for a closer look.

"What car is this?" he asked.

She shrugged. "That's Beau's old Chevy. He never did get the dern thing running—even though he worked on it pretty much day and night."

"It doesn't run?" David asked. He walked to it and lifted up part of the tarp to get a closer look at it.

Gladys shook her head. "He towed it out to Junior's, but Junior said it would cost about twenty-five hundred dollars to fix what-ever was wrong with it. Beau was tryin' to save the money for it." She dropped her gaze to the floor. "I wish I'd a known *how* he was tryin' to save the money, I maybe could've helped him out some."

David looked at her. "None of that was your fault, Gladys. Beau had an addiction. He couldn't really control what he was doing."

"I don't know if that's true or not," she said. "He really could've hurt those two girls."

"But he didn't. That's what you have to remember. He didn't."

She looked at him with her small, sad eyes. "I just wish I knew how to make it up to them—up to everyone."

David laid a tentative hand on her shoulder. Through the thin fabric of her jacket, it felt like there was no flesh on top of the bone. "Gladys—believe me. No one blames you for what happened. And no one expects you to atone for it, either. It's *all* in the past." He gave her shoulder a squeeze. "You need to move on. Syd has. Lizzy has. The town has. It's time for you to try, too."

"I just wish I knew how."

David didn't know what else to say to her, so he didn't say anything. They stood there in silence, with his hand resting on her shoulder. After a minute, she looked up at him.

"Do you wanna see Beau's car?"

He nodded. "I'd really like that."

Together, they folded the canvas back to uncover it. What David saw took his breath away. Beneath all those grime-covered tarps sat a vintage, perfectly reconditioned, bright red, '68 Chevy Camaro.

He gazed at Gladys in amazement.

"If you're interested," he said, "I think I have an idea about something you can do that will benefit the entire community."

She gave him a surprised look. "What's that?"

"Let's just say that it involves this car, and about twenty-five hundred dollars."

"I don't have twenty-five hundred dollars," she said.

He smiled. "You leave that part to *me*." He ran his hand along the shallow trunk line of the car. "If we play our cards right, this little beauty can heal a whole slew of wounds, and bring an entire town back together again."

Gladys didn't seem to understand a word he was saying. She stared at him for so long that David was afraid she'd lapsed into some kind of trance. Then she nodded.

"Okay," she said, releasing the tarp. It dropped to the floor with a thud, and a cloud of dust rose up around it. "It's yours."

Chapter 7

The cab ride to the UVA Medical Center from the small, Charlottesville Airport took less than ten minutes. She was meeting with the ER Chief at noon, then heading straight back to the airport for the short return flight to Baltimore.

She asked the driver just to wait on her—she wouldn't be long.

Her decision to come here had been a last-minute thing, and she didn't normally operate that way. In, fact, she *never* operated that way. But this was different. A lot of things in her life were different now, and it was time to tie off some loose ends. Too much time had already been lost—by all of them.

In her view, enough was enough.

She knew that Maddie could argue—convincingly and with great eloquence—that this was none of her business. And she'd be right about that—to a point. But for too many years, she had allowed Maddie to call the shots in determining what roles they played in each other's lives. And she had paid a hefty price for that. Now? Now she had an opportunity to try and clean up part of a mess she had helped to create, or, at least, perpetuate. And she was going to try and do it—regardless of the fallout.

She didn't know what kind of reception to expect, but she didn't really care.

She made her way to Dr. Leavitt's private office, and was shown inside to wait on him. The receptionist assured her that he would only be a few more minutes. She had taken pains to arrange the appointment ahead of time, but she had used her assistant's name, to preserve her anonymity.

She didn't have to wait long. She was standing near a window that overlooked a grassy courtyard area of the medical campus when the door opened, and he entered.

"Miss Alvarez?" he said. "I'm sorry to have kept you waiting."

She turned around. "Hello, Art."

He stared at her for a moment without saying anything. She could tell that he was trying to make sense out of what he was seeing.

"Celine?" He looked and sounded confused—as if he couldn't take in who was standing before him.

She nodded. The years had been kind to him. He was grayer and a bit thicker through the middle, but still robust and handsome.

"How long has it been, now?" she asked. "Twenty years?"

"Nearly twenty-six," he said, in a quiet voice.

She nodded slowly. "I apologize for the subterfuge, but, frankly, I wasn't certain that you would consent to meet with me."

He slowly shook his head. "I'm sorry, Celine."

His apology just hung there in the air between them. He could have been apologizing for keeping her waiting, or for having an affair with her husband more than thirty years ago, or for climate change.

"I'm just so surprised to see you. Please." He gestured toward a chair. "Sit down."

She complied. Art sat down in a chair facing hers.

"I heard about your accident, of course. I'm so grateful that you survived, Celine. You look . . . wonderful."

"Thank you. That was a seminal experience for me, as I'm sure you can imagine."

He nodded.

"As tragic as those events were, Maddie and I managed to make use of them to find our way back to each other."

"I know that," he said. "And I'm happy for you both."

"Unfortunately, one of the casualties of that experience seems to be your relationship with Maddie, and I take responsibility for that. I'm sure you know that I told her about your . . . about you and Davis. But I don't know if you fully understand why I felt I had to do so."

He reached out to touch her on the arm, then quickly withdrew his hand. "You don't owe me any explanation for that, Celine."

"Yes I do, Art. You're important to Maddie, and I know how much you love her."

"That's always been true."

"I know it has. And she needs you, Art—especially now."

He sighed. "I got a letter from her last year. She wasn't exactly *angry*, but she was hurt and confused." He met her eyes. "I tried to contact her numerous times, but she said she wasn't ready to see me yet." He shrugged. "I didn't really know what to do, so I just gave up. I hoped that in time, she'd relent, and we'd be able to talk about things."

"Her father meant everything to her. Finding out that he withheld so much of who he really was from her was a devastating blow. It was like she lost him twice. I felt that I had to tell her the truth. She was shrewd enough to figure out that there were some missing pieces that explained why our marriage fell apart. And I didn't help matters by my delusional insistence that none of my life with Davis ever happened." She sighed. "I lay there for two days in that ICU ward, promising any god who was listening that if I got another chance to make things right with my daughter, I wouldn't waste it." She met his eyes. "So I didn't." She took hold of one of his hands. "And I don't think you should, either."

His eyes filled with tears.

"She needs you, Art. She needs us *both*."

He raised his free hand to wipe at his eyes. "I don't know what to do."

Celine smiled at him. "Seriously? You manage an ER in one of the best level III trauma centers in the country, and you don't know what to do about a stubborn internist who's acting like a first-year medical student?"

He gave her an embarrassed smile. "I guess you're right."

"I usually am."

He laughed. "God, Celine. I really have missed you."

"I've missed you, too." She stood up, and he followed suit.

"The past is the past, Art. Let's leave it there, where it belongs. What matters now is Maddie. I'd like for her to have a shot at being a better parent than I was."

He looked confused.

"I'll let *her* explain that one to you. We'll consider it an incentive." She glanced at her watch. "Now I have to go, or I'll need to refinance my house to pay the cab driver who's waiting on me."

"Where are you headed?" he asked.

"Back to Hopkins. I'm participating in a seminar at the Kimmel Center."

"May I walk you out?" For a second, he looked just like the shy resident she had first met more than thirty-five years ago.

She smiled at him. "I'd like that."

They started toward the door. "Celine?" He touched her arm to stop her.

She turned around.

"Davis really loved you," he said.

She stared at him for a moment. "I know. I loved him, too."

"For what it's worth, I'm eternally sorry for the way everything fell apart."

She nodded. "Me, too."

They left the office and headed for the bank of elevators at the end of the hall.

Two hundred miles away, Maddie walked into their makeshift, downstairs bedroom, and held out a rolled-up paper bag.

"Guess what I finally found?"

Syd was already in bed for the night, and lay propped up on pillows, reading. She lowered her book and studied the bag for a moment. "Your lost virtue?"

"Very funny." Maddie tossed the bag onto the bed. "I suppose I should be insulted that you'd think my virtue would fit into a bag this small."

"No," Syd smiled at her sweetly, "only the part you lost."

Maddie looked perplexed. "Is that a compliment?"

"Of course it is, darling. You're so damn cute when you're literal." She hauled the bag over and looked inside.

"Oh, good god. I can't believe you brought that thing in here." She smashed the bag closed and pushed it away in disgust.

"Well, what did you expect me to do with it?"

"I don't know. Bury it in the yard?"

"Now *there's* an idea. Imagine the fun anthropologists will have when they unearth *this* relic in about five hundred years."

"Well," Syd said thoughtfully. "If they're digging around here, it might be a nice break from all the Camaro parts they're certain to find."

"Who knows?" Maddie picked up the bag. "Maybe they'll think this is a piece of the car."

"You can't be serious."

"I'm dead serious." Maddie sat down on the edge of the bed. "It could easily have a direct relationship to *any* of those uber-trendy, midlife crisis cars."

"Like your Lexus?" Syd asked.

Maddie looked at her in disbelief.

"Oh, don't look so offended. You know it's true."

"Hey . . . if memory serves, *you're* the one who turned into a puddle of drool when you first saw my car."

Syd rolled her eyes. "That wasn't because of the *car*, you nimrod."

"It wasn't?"

"Of course not. It was because of *you*, inside the car."

Maddie squinted at her. "Wouldn't that seem to suggest the same thing?"

"What? That you bought the Lexus to ratchet up your waning hotness factor?"

Maddie crawled across the bed to hover just above her. "Are you suggesting that my hotness is waning?"

Syd took a moment to consider Maddie's hotness. It was pretty impressive—especially when viewed from a distance of about six inches.

"Nuh uh." She ran her hands up under Maddie's t-shirt. "We're not talking about tonight."

"We're not?" Maddie closed the distance and kissed her.

Syd moaned and pulled her down so Maddie was lying on top of her.

"Hey . . ." Maddie tried to lift herself back up, but Syd held her in place. "What about your foot?"

"Screw my foot," Syd muttered into her neck.

"Right idea—wrong body part."

"Come on, honey, you're brilliant." Syd kissed along her jaw. "Figure something out."

"I don't want to hurt you," Maddie whispered.

"This from the woman who 'stabilized' my damaged foot without anesthetic?" Syd used her hands to try and close the deal. Her strategy seemed to be working.

"That was different," Maddie managed to gasp. "It was an emergency."

Well. Her strategy *mostly* seemed to be working.

In desperation, she bit down on Maddie's ear. "Believe me, Dr. Strangelove. *This* is an emergency, too."

Maddie drew back and kissed her again—hard.

"You really wanna do this?" she whispered against her lips.

"Do you really have to ask?" Syd threaded her hands into Maddie's long hair and pulled her closer.

"Well, then," Maddie said, seductively. "I know just what we need."

"You do?" Syd was pretty far gone, but she still knew how to smell a rat.

"Sure." Maddie winked at her. "It's in the *bag*, baby."

Syd dropped her hands.

"You come anywhere near me with the contents of *that* bag, and you'll be trying to figure out how to maneuver around two broken body parts—mine and *yours*."

Maddie sighed. She grabbed the paper bag in question and gave it a good heave. It went flying across the room and landed with a thud behind a large, potted ficus tree.

She looked back at Syd. "Please remind me later that that's back there."

Syd pulled her close again. "What's in it for me?"

Maddie kissed her. "I'll do my best to come up with something."

Syd turned off the bedside lamp.

"Damn straight, Skippy."

"I need to discuss something with you, and I need for you to be serious."

David looked up from his laptop.

"I'm always serious."

Michael walked to the kitchen table and sat down. "Really?"

David nodded.

"What are you doing?"

David stared at him. The blue light from his laptop screen made his face look iridescent. "I'm working on the fundraising calendar."

Michael sighed. "I thought so."

"What's that supposed to mean?"

"Honey, we talked about this idea. Nobody in Jericho is going to buy those."

David snapped the laptop shut. "You're always so negative about any ideas I have."

"Only when they stand a good chance of violating about twenty-five Commonwealth obscenity laws."

"That's ridiculous. There's nothing wrong with this idea. It's an innocent fundraiser, designed to help out with the storm recovery effort."

They'd had this conversation before. Many times.

"Right. Having a bunch of beefy guys pose nude with cast-off car parts doesn't strike you as being the tiniest bit inappropriate for a general audience?"

David looked offended now. "No. It does *not*. And all the car parts will be strategically placed so the photos will be entirely PG. Bruno assured me that it would all be very tasteful."

"Bruno?"

David nodded.

Something about that name rang a bell. "Bruno Diaz, the porn star?"

"*Former* porn star. He's retired. Now he runs a photo studio and tanning salon—totally legit. We connected on LinkedIn. He's *very* committed to the artistic integrity of this project."

Michael shook his head. "David. Three quarters of the population of this county is Southern Baptist. Believe me when I tell you that they are not going to want to hang a pinup calendar called *The Full Monte Carlo* up on their refrigerators—no matter who it benefits."

David pouted. "You always rain on my parade."

Michael patted him on the arm. "Buck up, Fanny Brice. I've got something else for you to sink your teeth into. That's why I said I wanted to have a serious conversation."

"We're already having a serious conversation."

"No. I mean *really* serious."

David looked back at him with narrowed eyes. "Is this about that guy at the tire store?"

"What guy at the tire store?"

"Because I knew there was something about him I didn't trust."

"What are you talking about?"

"The way he looked at you when we were in there on Tuesday. He was totally checking out your stuff."

Michael was completely confused now. "What stuff?"

David waved his hand around in circles. "Your *stuff*—your package. I shoulda smelled a rat last week when you came home with that box of valve stems."

"I repeat: *What* are you talking about?"

"Like you'd even know what to *do* with a valve stem."

In frustration, Michael snapped his fingers in front of David's face. "Hello? Anybody home in there? I picked those up for *Maddie*."

David paused in his tirade. "For Maddie?" He still looked suspicious.

"Yes. For Maddie."

"What the hell is *she* going to do with them?"

Michael shrugged. "How should I know? Some lesbionic thing, no doubt."

"Oh. Well." David sat back against his chair and crossed his legs. "That sounds about right." He smiled. "So. You wanted to talk with me about something?"

Michael looked at him in wonder. "I honestly don't know why I haven't strangled you before now."

David jerked his head toward the front parlor, where Maddie and Syd had already retired for the night. "I'm afraid you'd have to get in line."

"*Why?*" Michael said with alarm. "What happened now?"

David sighed. "Well . . . it seems that Astrid found Barney."

Michael was confused. "Barney?"

"Yeah . . . Barney. You know . . . our little purple—"

"Oh, my god! You're not telling me that you brought *that* thing over here?"

David shrugged.

"I thought it disappeared more than a year ago. Where did you find it?"

"For your information, I didn't *find* it. It must've been in Astrid's toy box. It just came along when I packed up the rest of her stuff."

Michael covered his face with his hands. "David . . . they have a child living here."

"I *know* that."

"He lowered his hands. "Well start acting like it. If you don't, we'll both end up on an amber alert list."

"You don't think I already heard this same lecture—*twice*— earlier tonight from Dr. Kildare?"

Michael sighed. "We're going to have to find someplace else to stay."

"Why?" David looked distressed.

"Because you're supposed to be his surrogate uncle, not his Auntie Mame."

"Very funny."

"I'm not kidding, David. You need to dial it back."

David looked at him blankly. "I have no idea what you're talking about."

Michael sighed. "You know, it truly frightens me that you actually mean that."

"I'm good for Henry."

"In the sense that you sincerely care about him—yes, you are. But, honey," he laid a hand on David's leg, "Maddie and Syd have done an exceptional job for well over a year now, diverting attention from their lifestyle as it relates to fostering a child here. Let's do our part not to blow all that good effort to smithereens in less than a month."

David's brown eyes looked wounded. "I love Henry. I would never do anything to hurt him."

"I know that. I feel the same way. And it's up to us to protect him by not doing things that draw attention to his . . . eclectic home environment."

"So you're saying that I need to straighten up while we're living here?" He made air quotes with his fingers.

"No," Michael corrected. "I'm saying that you need to *grow up* while we're living here. It's not the same thing."

David sighed. "I'll try."

Michael patted his leg. "I know you will."

They sat there in silence for a moment. Somewhere inside the house a clock chimed.

"So, what was this other thing you wanted to talk with me about?" David asked. He started to pack up his laptop for the night.

"Oh, that." Michael smiled. "Remember how we always said we wanted to find a way to tap into the local food culture, so our business wouldn't have to rely so heavily on out-of-town traffic?"

David nodded.

"Well . . . I met a woman named Nadine Odell today, and I think she just might be the answer to our problem."

David paused, mid cord-wrap. "Nadine Odell?"

Michael nodded.

"Nicorette's mom?"

Michael's jaw fell open. "You know her?"

David rolled his eyes. "Duh. *Fabulous* tattoos."

Michael was bewildered. "How in the hell do you know her?"

David sighed. "Nicky plays clarinet in the school band. I play clarinet in Mamma's obscene parody of a symphony. Syd has me work with the kids once a month." He paused. "Any of this ring any bells for you, there, Inspector Clouseau?"

Michael shook his head. "I so do not believe this."

"Believe it. Unlike *you*, I have my finger on the pulse of this county."

Michael continued to look at him in amazement.

"Okay," David said with exaggerated patience. "Let me try and clarify all of this for you. Nicky's aunt Evelyn—Nadine's sister—is married to Curtis Freemantle's brother, Cletus. They live out near Troutdale in that apartment over the old Esso station—the one at the crossroads before you get to the turnoff for Ripshin Road? Cletus works at Junior's—you know . . . where the infamous Camaro was parked before that damn tornado slung it around like a Roman battle mace. And he's rumored to be the best dent man in five counties. He's the one who fixed the passenger door on the Rover last August, after that damn fatass B4 smacked into it at the low-water crossing. Cletus and Evelyn are taking care of Azalea—the Freemantle matriarch. Curtis says she's got Alzheimer's disease, but Edna says there's *nothing* wrong with her memory, she's just mean as a snake. I asked Maddie about that, but you know how *she* is. She won't give up shit. But at the Methodist church chicken supper, Peggy Hawkes was overheard telling Muriel Greene that Azalea might have some drug-induced dementia because she keeps mixing brand name and generic forms of the same drugs—insisting that they're *different*. This was right after Azalea threw that plate of slaw at Edna and started screaming that she was a whoring Jezebel. Azalea has *never* trusted Edna because her people were carpetbaggers who came to Virginia from Ohio after the War of Northern Aggression. That's why Cletus and Evelyn have to take care of her now. *Anyway* . . . Nadine's husband, Raymond Jackson, works as a dispatcher for one of the bigger Christmas tree farms over in Jefferson. He's the one who hired Carlos Sanchez. Nadine never took his name—she's always been independent like that. The Odell sisters have been running that little Midway Café for about five years now. Ever since the former owner, Travis Beeler, broke his neck after getting thrown from that mechanical bucking bull they used to have over at Bixby's. He was running around with Deb Carlson then, and lots of people say that's when her streak of bad luck started. Personally, I think that's when *Travis's* streak of bad luck started. He never should've taken up with her. Talk about your whoring Jezebels . . . that woman blows through men faster than a single-ply Kleenex."

"Stop." Michael held up both hands. "*Please.* I beg you to stop."

David raised an eyebrow. "What's the matter?"

Michael just shook his head. "I have *no* idea what I've been doing with my time."

David gave him a smug smile. "We each have our own special gifts, baby cakes."

Michael was in a daze. "I feel like I'm married to Rona Barrett."

"Rona Barrett?" David scoffed. "Puh-lease. With *that* hair helmet? I don't think so."

Michael rolled his eyes. "Okay, then . . . Billy Bush."

"That's more like it." David smiled at him. "So, you wanted to talk with me about working out some kind of reciprocal arrangement with the Odell sisters? I think that's a *great* idea. I've *always* wanted to get my mitts on that quaint little café. With a dash of imagination, some track lighting, a few potted plants, and a bolt of the right fabric—we can gay that joint right up. And it's *perfect* timing, since the Inn will be off-line for at least the next month or two."

Michael slowly got up from his chair. "I need a drink."

"Ooohhh," David cooed. "Me, too. Fix us a couple of mojitos—and I'll start working on the sketches."

Chapter 8

Maddie had finished seeing patients for the day and was in her office, transcribing some notes when her phone rang. She answered it without checking the caller I.D.

"This is Dr. Stevenson."

"This is Dr. Heller," the voice on the phone said.

Maddie smiled and sat back in her chair. "Well, hello, Mom. This is a nice surprise."

"Hello to you, too," Celine said. "I was hoping I could catch you before you left for the day."

Maddie laughed. "You know how that goes. If I don't get my notes entered before I leave, it's not going to happen."

"I remember," Celine said. "I was lucky if your father walked in the door before you were in your pajamas."

"I know. I try to be very diligent about making it home in time to have dinner with Henry." She smiled. "Syd would hand me my ass if I didn't."

Celine chuckled. "How is your whole extended-family arrangement working out?"

Maddie sighed. "Mostly okay. We've had a few . . . *infractions* . . . related to some of David's eccentricities."

"I can only imagine."

"Believe when I tell you that you probably can't."

"Oh, dear."

"Precisely."

"Well. I was wondering if you'd be able to provide accommodations for one more lodger—temporarily."

Maddie sat up. "Really? Of course. Where are you?"

"I'm in Baltimore—at Hopkins."

"You are? I didn't know you were coming East."

"It wasn't planned. The Kimmel Center is doing a seminar on neurodegeneration in Parkinson's disease, and one of their panel participants had to cancel at the last minute. They needed a toxicologist, and I needed an excuse to come and see my surrogate grandson."

Maddie smiled. "You don't need an excuse for that, Mom."

"I didn't want to presume—especially with Syd's injury. How is she, by the way?"

"Oh, she's about ready to run a half-marathon. Two more weeks, then we'll transition her to a soft-cast boot. I'm threatening to tie an anchor to her shirttail if she doesn't slow down."

"I'm anxious to see her. I actually had lunch with her uncle yesterday."

"Marsh?"

"Um hm. GSK was well-represented at the conference. It was good to see him. He's done very well."

Maddie smiled. "He had a great teacher."

Celine was quiet for a moment. "I had to fight an impulse to disagree with you."

"I'm glad you did."

"We learn by doing."

"That we do."

"Well," Celine changed the subject, "I should be able to shake free up here by early Friday afternoon. I can look into renting a car, or see what flights I can get into Roanoke."

Maddie thought about that. "I've got a better idea. How about you cash in some of those unused frequent flier miles on Stevenson Air, and let me come pick you up?"

"Oh, no. You *know* I hate riding in that thing."

"Mom," Maddie corrected. "You've *never* ridden in this

thing. Trust me. It's a far cry from that puddle jumper Dad had a hundred years ago. I'll even bring along some in-flight entertainment."

"I'm afraid to even ask what that means," Celine said.

"It means I'll bring Henry. He'll be ecstatic about seeing you, and the trip will thrill him."

"Oh, now that's just playing dirty, Maddoe."

"Come on . . . it's a short flight, and we can have you back here in time for a late supper." She paused for effect. "You don't want to miss *that*. Michael cooks, Henry accidentally feeds any vegetables he doesn't recognize to Pete, and David wears one of the two dozen dinner jackets the tornado chose not to take. In case you were curious, the puce one is his current favorite."

Celine laughed.

"What do you say?"

"How about you check this out with Syd, then let me know if, when, and where to meet you?"

Maddie smiled. "How about I do that and call you back in about ten seconds?"

"It's a deal."

"How long can you stay?"

"I'm thinking it will only be a few days—unless I can convince Laszlow to cover the last session of my toxicology seminar—then I might be able to extend my stay a bit."

"Really? By how much?"

"Maybe as long as a week or two. But I have to be back in California by the first of the month at the latest."

Maddie thought about that. "Can you take David with you?"

"Nice try."

"I'll call you right back."

"I'll be here."

They hung up.

Maddie sat there, holding the phone in her hand. It was surreal. She didn't possess enough fingers or toes to count off all the ways her life had changed in the last eighteen months. And they were *good* changes—frighteningly good. In fact, she felt like

God's spoiled child. She had Syd. She had Henry. And now, at long last, she had her mother. And that was perhaps the least anticipated but most surprising turnaround of them all.

She couldn't remember a time when she didn't miss her mother. It was like growing up without a limb—one she'd been born with, but lost somewhere along the way. And she never got over not having it. She was always keenly aware that it wasn't there—like an amputee who, years later, still felt a tingling where her leg used to be.

Life's great losses were like that. They piled up around her feet like dried leaves in the autumn. Every year they came, and every year, they took her by surprise. And every year, they filled her with the same faint traces of pain and sadness she always felt as the days grew shorter, and the warmth of summer faded into memory. But then, in the deepest part of winter, as she lay alone beneath a blanket of loneliness—if she closed her eyes extra tight, she could sense the coming of spring. It was always there, too. Every year. Waiting for her like a ribbon of hope that guided her through the longest night.

Well, Maddie and Celine's longest night had finally passed. And together, they had staggered into the sunlight like two sleepy prairie dogs. Now, although their interactions were earnest and affectionate, they were still careful of each other. And neither of them was entirely comfortable yet in this startling new landscape they had woken up to. It was still unfamiliar, and many aspects of it remained formless and unknown.

But, she thought as she lifted her phone and punched in the numbers to call home, *all the signs looked good.*

Syd answered on the first ring.

Very good.

Chapter 9

What should have been an ordinary Tuesday night at home was anything but.

They were having an early dinner, and it was taco night—Henry's favorite. David always complained about taco night because the hard shells tended to break, increasing the likelihood that tomato sauce would find its way onto his jacket. Of course, Maddie suggested that he could forgo the dinner jacket on Tuesday nights. But David was David, and David dressed for dinner.

This meant that conversation ping-ponged back and forth between reminding Henry (again) of why the Camaro dashboard wouldn't look nice on top of the piano and assuring David that Resolve really *could* get picante sauce stains out of wool.

The telephone rang, and Michael answered it.

"It's Joe Baxter," he said as he held out the phone to Maddie.

She got up and walked to the phone. No doubt the fat heifer, B4, had broken out again and wandered over to her pasture. Joe probably wanted to know if it was okay to come over and herd her home.

"Dr. Stevenson?" Joe said. He sounded out of breath. "You need to get over here right quick."

"What's the matter, Joe?" Maddie asked.

"Well, one of my bulls in the south pasture charged an old corncrib, and there was two people inside it."

"Did you call the EMTs?" Maddie glanced at her watch. She could be there in less than five minutes.

"No, ma'am. The EMTs can't do nothin' to help these folks out now. But I did call the sheriff," he added.

Maddie rolled her eyes and glanced at Syd, who was watching her with curiosity. The scene would be choked with deputies by the time she got over there.

"Okay, Joe. I'm on my way. Where should I meet you?"

"Meet me at the house. I'll take you out there on the ATV."

She nodded. "Be there in about five minutes. Make sure nobody touches anything, okay?"

She hung up and faced the table. "I have to run over to Joe's. It sounds like one of his bulls charged two people who were inside a corncrib, and they're . . ." She looked at Henry. "Unable to respond."

"Oh, no," Syd said with concern. "Do you know who they were?"

Maddie shook her head.

"'Tis the season for that," David said. "Bulls are pretty territorial this time of the year. I bet there were heifers around."

Michael agreed. "If it charged somebody, you can be sure it was protecting its turf."

"Probably." Maddie sighed.

David held up an index finger. "Did you say they were *inside* a corncrib?"

Maddie nodded.

"Interesting," he added. "I'm sure there's one heck of a story *there*."

"Sorry you agreed to be the county medical examiner, now, honey?" Syd asked.

"Getting there," Maddie replied. She ruffled Henry's hair and bent to kiss Syd. "I'll call you if it looks like I'm going to be late. Okay if I take your car?"

Syd nodded.

Maddie walked toward the back of the kitchen and grabbed her field bag off a high shelf near the door.

"See you later," she called out as she left.

David looked across the table at Syd with a raised eyebrow. "I'd pay good money to get the inside scoop on this one. I've got a feeling it's gonna be good and *juicy*."

"David," Syd said with a glance toward Henry. "It could all be perfectly innocent."

"You don't *seriously* believe that, do you?" he asked.

Michael glared at him. "Why are you always so determined to put a crude interpretation on everything?"

"Oh, come on." David picked up his taco. "And just what do *you* think they were up to in that nasty old corncrib? Starting a book club?" He took a bite, and his taco shell shattered. Large globs of ground meat and sauce dropped onto his shirt and rolled down the lapel of his puce jacket.

Henry giggled.

"Yep," Michael said with a smile. "*Good* and juicy."

By the time Maddie reached the ruins of the corncrib, the place was crawling with people. It looked like sheriff's deputies from three counties had converged on the scene. They were standing around in clusters, drinking coffee, and smoking cigarettes . . . waiting for her to arrive. She didn't see Byron Martin, but she knew him well enough to know that he would be none too pleased with the number of off-duty officers who had responded to Joe's call.

News in this county sure traveled fast.

She recognized Charlie Davis standing near the collapsed wall of the weather-beaten structure. She was nervously shifting her weight from one foot to the other. The low murmur of conversation that had been going on when Maddie arrived stopped as she approached the deputy.

"Hello, Doc," Charlie said, touching the brim of her hat. Maddie hadn't seen her since the day of the tornado.

"Hi, Charlie. Any I.D. on the victims?"

"Well . . ." She looked down at her shoes. "We're pretty sure the man is Lonnie Pollard."

Lonnie was the local insurance agent.

Maddie nodded. "And the other victim?"

She shrugged. "It's a woman. That's about all we can tell until we can—um—unhitch them."

Maddie raised an eyebrow. "*Unhitch* them?"

Charlie looked embarrassed. "Yes, ma'am."

"Okaaayyy," Maddie said. "Any idea how they got here?"

She nodded. "Yes, ma'am. We found a car parked about half a mile down the road there. It looks like Lonnie's—has a big Farm Bureau sticker on the bumper. It was locked."

"Is Sheriff Martin on his way?" she asked.

"Yes, ma'am."

"All right then," Maddie said. "Let's take a look inside, and see what we have."

Charlie stepped back and half turned away as Maddie carefully picked her way into what was left standing of the corncrib. One exterior wall had pretty much been demolished, but the other three sides were still intact. Beneath a fallen roof beam she could see the nude bodies of two people. The woman was face down, bent over a hay bale, and the man who lay prone on top of her did appear to be Eunice Pollard's estranged husband, Lonnie.

"Oh, good god," Maddie said as she approached the conjoined pair. She opened her bag and pulled on a pair of latex gloves. She knelt down next to them and felt each for a pulse, knowing she wouldn't find one. Lonnie had a massive head wound, likely sustained when one of the roof beams fell and hit him. There was blood on the edge of the thick board that lay across his shoulders. Beneath him, the woman appeared to have similar injuries. Both of their bodies were marked with what looked like dirty hoof prints.

She took Lonnie's temperature. All indications suggested that the couple had been dead for four to six hours. Apart from the obvious bull attack, there was no sign of misadventure.

Joe had found them when he was out riding along the fence at this side of the pasture, looking for B4—who, as Maddie predicted, had escaped again. The bull responsible for the attack was now locked in a paddock, waiting for animal control to arrive.

She looked around what was left of the tiny structure. A stack of clothing was visible beneath a pile of rubble near the door. She saw the strap of what looked like a red bag.

"Anybody check that bag over there for a wallet?" she asked.

Charlie shook her head as a deputy Maddie didn't know handed Charlie a pair of gloves. She pulled them on before stepping into the rubble and carefully uncovering the bag. Inside it was a matching red wallet, studded with rhinestones. She opened it and pulled out a driver's license.

She looked up at Maddie. "It's Myrtle Anne Nicks."

The other deputy snorted. "That figures."

Maddie looked at him. "Care to explain what you mean by that?"

He shrugged. "She's kind of famous for this kind of thing."

"What kind of thing?" Maddie asked.

He waved a hand to indicate the two crudely intertwined bodies. "Let's just say that Lonnie ain't her first back-door man."

"Jesus, Burns." Charlie elbowed the deputy in the side. "Wanna show a little respect?"

"For Myrtle Anne Nicks? You gotta be kidding. That woman could speak ten languages and not say 'no' in *any* of them."

"I *meant* for Dr. Stevenson," Charlie hissed.

"Hey," Maddie said. "Wanna stow the commentary and come help me turn them over?"

They looked at each other.

"Yes, ma'am," they said in unison.

"Do you want us to separate them first?" Charlie asked.

"Frankly," Maddie said, "I don't think we *can* until they come out of rigor."

"Talk about your hard-ons," Burns quipped. "Looks like ole cheatin' Lonnie finally found a way to stay up all night."

"Burns, you wanna put a fucking sock in it?" Byron Martin had arrived, and he didn't sound pleased.

Burns sobered up at once. "Yes, sir."

Byron jerked his head toward the pasture. "Go outside and call the damn funeral home, and tell the rest of those off-duty assholes that if I hear so much as a *snicker,* you'll all be spending the next month selling plastic poppies outside the Dollar General."

"Yes, sir." Burns looked at Maddie. "Sorry, Doc."

He backed out of the tiny space.

Byron shook his head. He walked toward the rubble and knelt next to Maddie. "What have we got?"

She sighed. "Two cases of blunt head trauma—his from this beam when the wall came down; hers from the bull. It looks like a pretty clear case of accidental death."

"Jesus." Byron looked down at the two bodies with disgust.

"Somebody's gotta tell Sonny," Davis said.

Sonny Nicks was Myrtle Anne's husband.

Myrtle Anne owned the local beauty parlor, Hairport '75. For the last couple of years, her son, Harold—who was an expert colorist and a huge Karen Black fan—had managed the salon.

"I know," Byron said. "I'll do it. Right after the Buford boys retrieve the bodies, and the county picks up that damn bull." He met Maddie's eyes. "I can't even *tell* you all the ways this is gonna blow this damn town apart." He shook his head. "A damn corn-crib in the fucking *spring.* What the hell were they thinking?"

"Well," Maddie said. "I guess there's no reason to put it off."

Byron sighed.

Together they rolled the fused couple over.

"Holy crap," Charlie said.

Myrtle Anne had a strange little smile on her face, but that wasn't the oddest part. In the center of her forehead was a round indentation—like the ring mark a wet beer can leaves on a coffee table.

Maddie ran her fingers over it. "It's a hoof print."

Byron shook his head. "Jesse Buford is gonna earn his keep on *this* one."

Once the excitement from the tornado died down, things in Jericho quickly got back to normal. Within a month and a half, the damage to Main Street had mostly been swept up or boarded over, and only the school still showed any signs of major disruption. It was business as usual.

And, predictably, nothing brought people out on a weeknight like a "viewing."

Thursday night at Buford Brothers Mortuary was one for the record books—a bona fide twofer. Nobody in town was going to miss out on *this* one. Buford's only had two reception rooms, and both viewings were taking place on the same night.

For the residents of a small Virginia town, this was like winning the lottery.

And tonight, every restaurant in Jericho was hopping. Over plates heaped full of country-style steak and creamed potatoes, people who had squeezed into their best church clothes speculated about how on earth the Bufords were going to keep the two families separated. Stories about how Myrtle Anne and Lonnie had been discovered in Joe Baxter's corncrib spread across the county faster than an outbreak of *e coli* at a church barbecue.

It was widely known that there was no love lost between Eunice Pollard and the Nicks family. In fact, there was no love lost between any of about two dozen county wives and the Nicks family.

People liked to say that Myrtle Anne loved her husband, and everybody else's, too.

A baker's dozen of Myrtle Anne's other "victims" were planning to attend the viewing *en masse*, in a show of support for Eunice, and everybody just referred to this contingent as "The Wives." Tom Buford had three rows of special chairs set up and roped off for The Wives at the back of Parlor One. They were in the same room with Lonnie, but were far enough away that nobody could question their disdain for his behavior.

Across the hall in Parlor Two, Harold Nicks had *no* chairs set up. He didn't want people hanging around and making a spectacle out of gawking at his mama. People said they heard that this was because Jesse Buford had to use an entire eight-ounce jar of mortician's wax to fill in the hoof print on Myrtle Anne's forehead. Some said it would've been easier to just not have the casket open, but Harold did his mama's last hairdo himself, and he wanted her to go out in style.

Nobody in town could backcomb hair better than Harold Nicks.

In fact, Sonny had always blamed Myrtle Anne for turning their son gay by taking him to work with her from the time he was a baby. He said the changeover probably happened because of all that exposure to activator and perm rods.

"That's what they do," Sonny said. "They shrink stuff up."

And it might have been true. When other boys wanted footballs and toy cars for Christmas, all Harold wanted were wigs and hot rollers.

Sonny just couldn't talk about it.

Parlor Two was choked with customers of Hairport '75. And it was a truly eclectic mix of people.

Harold cut and styled hair for a lot of men, too.

Sonny couldn't talk about that, either.

The vestibule that separated the two parlors at Buford's Mortuary was like a demilitarized zone. People who weren't particularly attached to either family found themselves milling around in the tiny space between the two rooms, not really knowing where to stand or who it was safe to talk to.

Depending upon where they stood, they could hear snatches of piped-in music emanating from each of the two viewing rooms. It was like a modified version of "Dueling Banjos"— except that Lonnie's soundtrack was of the more traditional "Old Rugged Cross" variety, and Myrtle Anne's was more . . . eclectic.

Harold said his mama loved the Dixie Chicks more than anything, and he was determined that her final farewell would feature the music she adored. Besides . . . Myrtle Anne wasn't much of a churchgoer.

Neither was Lonnie Pollard, come to that. But Eunice and The Wives felt like the music played at his wake was more of a testament to *their* tribulation than it was a monument to Lonnie's eternal reward.

In fact, some of the men clustered at the back of the DMZ near the water cooler speculated that, according to reports, ole Lonnie already *had* his eternal reward—in spades. There were rumors that the coroner had actually had to use a pry bar to separate him from Myrtle Anne.

Maddie and Syd arrived at Buford's early and paid their respects to Eunice—and to Sonny and Harold. Decorum required that they stay on for at *least* thirty minutes before they could leave. So they stood in the DMZ and chatted quietly and amiably with people who drifted back and forth between the two parlors.

Maddie was used to being sought out at events like this because she was the family physician to so many members of the small community, but also because her role as county medical examiner meant she was privy to the most lurid and discreet details of any unnatural death. And tonight, the room was full of people who hoped she might let an unknown tidbit slip if they asked her the right combination of questions.

Syd shook her head after the last interview ended, and the disappointed inquisitors moved on.

"You'd think by now they'd know that you aren't going to give anything up," she whispered.

Maddie smiled. "You can't really blame them for trying."

"Yes I can," Syd said. "My one good foot is killing me, and I want to get out of here so we can get some dinner."

"Why don't we go inside so you can sit down?" Maddie asked with concern.

Syd's eyes grew wide. "Are you nuts? I don't need any more associations than I already have with that group of jilted wives."

"I'd hardly call you jilted, Syd."

"You know what I mean," Syd whispered. "They ought to have t-shirts."

Maddie had to fight not to laugh. "Ten more minutes, then we can leave."

In Parlor Two, strains of "I Can Love You Better" could be heard, floating up over the din of conversation.

Maddie and Syd looked at each other.

"Okay," Maddie said. "Maybe *five* more minutes."

Just then, something cut loose in Parlor One. A low-pitched wailing started and slowly gained in intensity like an approaching police siren. There was a general commotion, and the sound of scuffling. They could hear chairs being knocked over.

Cries of "Eunice, no!" and "Somebody stop her!" filled the air.

Maddie managed to haul Syd to the side just as Eunice Pollard exploded from Parlor One, with half a dozen of The Wives in hot pursuit. They looked like the deranged offensive line from hell's football team as they roared across the DMZ toward Parlor Two. Eunice was clutching the urn containing Lonnie's ashes close to her ample chest, and screaming, "I'll give you a piece you'll never forget, you whoring bitch!" at the top of her lungs.

Most of the bystanders just stood there, too surprised to take action.

Several of Harold's "boys" tried to block Eunice, but she plowed through them like they were made of *papier-mâché*. Once The Wives crossed into enemy territory, their objective changed, too. They now appeared to be running block for Eunice, who was hell-bent on reaching what was left of Myrtle Anne.

"Whore! Bitch! *Cunt!*" Eunice shrieked as she fought her way to the front of the room.

Harold stood bravely in front of his mother's casket, watching his friends fall by the wayside as the demon woman approached. He seemed prepared to be Myrtle Anne's last defense against this final indignity.

He probably wished right then that he'd used that member-ship to Gold's Gym his daddy gave him last Christmas . . .

But it was too late now.

Eunice tossed him aside like a dried-up sponge roller.

"Here," she screamed, as she uncapped Lonnie's urn. "Have a mouthful of *this*, you cheap tramp!"

She upended the urn, and gray dust exploded into the air around the casket. It drifted across the room like a toxic cloud and sent people scrambling for cover—maniacally slapping at their hair and clothing as they fled to safety.

Stunned, Maddie took hold of Syd's arm.

"Let's get out of here," she hissed.

Syd looked up at her like she wasn't really seeing her. "Did that really just happen?"

Maddie nodded.

Syd shook her head. "And to think, I almost didn't come."

Maddie carefully steered her through the crowd toward the street door. Behind them, she heard someone comment that ole Lonnie always did like to spread it around.

Just as they reached the exit, the big door opened, and they found themselves standing face to face with two men in Army uniforms—officer's uniforms.

At first, they all stood there locked into a kind of awkward stand-off. The chaos raging in the background made the scene even more unreal. The soldiers looked confused, as if they were unable to make sense of the pandemonium going on behind Maddie and Syd.

Finally, one of the men spoke up. "Perhaps you can help us? We're looking for a Dr. Stevenson. A man at her residence told us we could find her here?"

Maddie was even more surprised. "I'm Dr. Stevenson. How may I help you?"

"I'm Captain Jacobs," he said. "And this is Lieutenant Wash-burn. We're from the Department of the Army."

Maddie and Syd exchanged nervous glances.

"I'm sorry to say that we have some unfortunate news about Corporal James Lawrence," the Captain said.

The only place open at eight-thirty on a Thursday night was Waffle House—or *Awful* House, as David liked to call it.

But that didn't really matter. Neither of them had much of an appetite.

Maddie ordered coffee, even though Syd told her it was a mistake and would likely keep her up all night.

Maddie just stared at her with that textbook raised eyebrow.

"You're right," Syd said. She faced their server. "Make that *two* coffees."

The server nodded and wandered off. It was a slow night at Awful House. Only two other tables had diners. Well. Only one table had diners. A *very* large man occupied a booth at the back of the tiny place. He appeared to be in an advanced stage of somnolence. His snores could occasionally be heard above the country music radio station playing in the background.

Syd was obsessively sorting the contents of a container loaded with artificial sweetener packets. Pink. Blue. Yellow. Pink. Blue. Yellow. Pink. Blue . . .

Maddie laid a hand on top of hers. "Honey?"

Syd sighed and pushed the container away.

"Once a librarian?" Maddie asked.

Syd shrugged. "I guess." She met Maddie's eyes. "What are we going to tell him?"

"The truth. What else can we tell him?"

"God. This is awful."

Maddie agreed. "It is. But at least he's *alive*, and he'll be coming home."

"I know. You're right—of course." Syd ran a hand through her short blonde hair. "How long is his convalescence likely to be?"

Maddie shrugged. "I honestly can't say. So much of it will depend upon him, and what kind of access to rehab he has. According to Captain Jacobs, he's lucky he didn't lose *both* of his legs."

Syd covered her face with her hands. "God. This damn war just needs to stop."

"No argument from me on that one," Maddie said.

"He's only twenty-five years old, for god's sake."

"I know that, honey."

"It's just so fucking pointless. The casualties aren't just the soldiers. They're mothers and fathers—wives and husbands. And they're *kids*, too." Her eyes met Maddie's again. "And this time, it's *our* kid."

Maddie nodded.

Their server brought over two steaming mugs of coffee. "You folks know what you want to eat?"

Syd gave Maddie a hopeless look.

"Sure," Maddie said. "How about a grilled cheese sandwich and a bowl of Bert's Chili?"

"Just one of each?" the server asked.

"Yes, please. We'll share."

"Cheese on the chili?"

"Why not?"

Maddie handed him the menus.

"Got it. Have that right up for you, Doc." He walked off.

"Doc?" Syd asked.

Maddie shrugged.

Syd shook her head. "I can't take you anywhere."

Maddie smiled at her. "On the contrary. *You* can take me everywhere."

They stared at each other.

"I love you," Syd said. "But that's not going to make me overlook all that cheese you just ordered."

Maddie laughed.

"I guess if there's any good news in all of this, it's that James is now out of Afghanistan."

"That's true," Maddie said. "And, hopefully, he'll make a full recovery and find a way to make a new life."

"With Henry," Syd added.

"With Henry," Maddie echoed.

"God. How are we going to give him up?" Syd closed her eyes. "Even thinking about it is like a kick in the gut."

"I know, honey. Believe me. I feel exactly the same way." She reached across the table and touched Syd's hand. "But we're not *there* yet. So let's try to take this one step and one day at a time."

Syd gazed across the small restaurant. Hanging on a narrow

strip of wall above the counter were framed and badly faded photos of various county landmarks. There was one photo of the high school band—taken the year they won the Southern States Championship in Chattanooga. Syd thought about her students, and how three-fourths of them had lost their instruments in the tornado. They weren't going to be competing in any festivals for a long time to come.

The casualties of *that* storm were far-reaching, too.

Next to the bleached-out band picture was a newer, brightly-colored photo of two men posing in the parking lot in front of the restaurant. Syd squinted at it. They were proudly holding up a red-rimmed car headlight—just like it was the winning catch at a bass tournament.

Oh, good god.

She looked back at Maddie, who was gazing at her with concern.

"I'm sorry to be so selfish," she said.

"Don't be," Maddie said. "I feel the same way."

"You just don't show it."

Maddie shrugged. "I grew up learning how not to."

Syd looked at her with all the love she felt. "How about we make a deal? How about we show each other everything?"

Maddie gave her a slow smile. "I thought we already did that—many times, if memory serves."

Syd rolled her eyes. "Sleaze."

"Hey." Maddie touched her hand. "We'll get through this. Together."

Syd nodded. "That's the one thing I'm sure of."

"And we'll always do what's best for Henry."

Syd sighed and slowly nodded her head. "I never thought I wanted kids. Now, I can't imagine my life without one." She hesitated. "Without *this* one."

"I know what you mean."

The server arrived with their food.

"Here you go, folks. I went ahead and split your chili into two smaller bowls." He smiled as he unloaded their food. "You get more cheese that way."

Maddie looked at Syd smugly and picked up her spoon. "Just what the doctor ordered."

Behind them, the sleeping man snorted—loudly.

They all looked at one another. The server shook his head. "I should charge him rent on that damn space." He wandered off.

Syd picked up her own spoon and pushed her mound of cheese around.

"I don't know who Bert is, but if he ate much of this, I'll bet he's now wearing a toe tag."

Maddie laughed. "It won't kill you."

Syd lifted a pyramid of the gelatinous orange goo out of her bowl. "Really?"

"Scout's honor." Maddie held up three fingers.

"Scout's honor?" Syd asked. "I thought you said you flunked the physical?"

"Well," Maddie ate a big spoonful of the chili-cheese, "now you know why."

"Thank god the rest of your advice is generally reliable."

At the back of the restaurant, the large man in the corner booth stretched and smiled. *Life was good.* He had another hour until his shift at the glass factory started. He was in a warm place away from his wife's bitching. He had a bottomless cup of fresh coffee. And he had two great-looking women to admire in between catnaps.

He couldn't think of a better way to liven up a dull Thursday night in Jericho.

Chapter 10

James Lawrence was the lucky one.

He had been the only soldier to survive the blast when the Humvee he was riding in hit a roadside IED near Kandahar. James was thrown from the vehicle, but his two companions died after the vehicle caught fire and exploded.

James was airlifted from the scene, and woke up thirty-six hours later in a post-op ward in Landstuhl, Germany. The attendants there told him three things: he had lost his left leg below the knee, he was on his way home, and he was no longer an active-duty soldier.

The rest he would figure out in due time.

He was transported from the U.S. Military Hospital in Landstuhl to Walter Reed National Military Medical Center in Bethesda, Maryland, where he would undergo post-operative care and rehabilitation for his transtibial amputation. He would be fitted for a permanent prosthetic leg once his wound was completely healed, but his regimen of therapy would begin almost immediately.

The speed of his recovery, his success in rehab, and the pace of his psychological adjustment to the injury would determine the length of his stay at Walter Reed. The physical therapist Maddie spoke with said that James would likely be there from eight to twelve weeks. After that, he would be discharged and allowed to return home. For the time being, home probably meant Kannapolis, where he would be close to his mother and have ready access to the VA Clinic in nearby Salisbury.

Before enlisting in the Army, James had been employed as an auto mechanic, and it was entirely possible that he could return to this line of work if he chose to do so. He was young and strong, and his doctors expected him to make a full recovery.

Maddie also talked directly with James and with his social worker at Walter Reed. They all agreed that it would be good for Henry to visit with his father in Maryland during his rehabilitation.

James wanted to see his son.

James also relied on Maddie and Syd to explain the nature of his injury to Henry, and to try and prepare him for the change he would see in his father's physical condition. Maddie sought professional advice for that, and she and Syd talked together with a field agent from the Wounded Warriors Project. They all agreed that they should take Henry to see James as soon as it was feasible. But first, they had to tell him about what had happened to his father.

Maddie and Syd wanted to keep their conversation with Henry on an even keel, so they decided that it would be important to talk with him under the most normal conditions they could muster. Henry gave them a perfect opportunity for this when he came home from school the next day with some pictures he had drawn of B4.

He spread them out on the kitchen table so Maddie and Syd could admire them.

In fact, they were pretty good drawings.

B4 was standing next to the barn with a mouthful of hay, and a large, wagon-wheel-like object was perched on her back.

Syd pointed to it. "What's that, honey?"

Henry looked at her with surprise. "That's my steering wheel."

"Oh," she said. "Of *course* it is."

Maddie chuckled.

"Can we show these pictures to Daddy when we talk to him this week?" he asked.

Maddie and Syd exchanged glances.

"Well, honey," Syd began. "We maybe can do better than that. Your daddy is actually coming home very soon."

Henry's eyes grew wide. "He *is*? Will he come here to live with us?"

Syd looked at Maddie, who took the nonverbal handoff.

"Sport, the reason that your daddy is coming home sooner than we thought is because there was an accident, and he got hurt. He's coming home so he can be in a hospital where they can take good care of him until he can be with you again."

Henry looked confused. "Is he at your hospital? Can we go see him?"

"No, honey. He's in an Army hospital near Washington, D.C. But, yes, we can go and see him in a little while, after he's had a chance to rest and get stronger."

"Can't he come here so you can take care of him?"

Maddie ran a hand through his dark hair. "I wish he could, Henry. But right now, your daddy needs special doctors who are soldiers, too. They will take very good care of him, and soon, he'll be able to go home."

"How did he get hurt?"

"There was an explosion, and the truck your daddy was riding in got blown up."

"Like the Camaro?" he asked.

"Well. No. Not exactly like that. This happened because the truck ran over a bomb along the roadside."

Henry looked confused. "Why would somebody blow up a car on purpose?"

Maddie shook her head. "I wish I could explain that to you, sport. But sometimes, when countries are at war, people do things that don't seem to make very much sense, and people get hurt."

"Is he gonna be okay?"

Maddie nodded. "Yes, he is. Your daddy is very lucky. But his left leg was badly hurt, so they had to take part of it off," she shifted in her seat to show Henry her own leg, "from here down."

Henry's eyes grew wide. "Did that hurt?"

"I'm sure it hurt a lot. But your daddy is very strong, and he had very good doctors taking care of him."

"Like you?" he asked.

"*Just* like her—only soldiers," Syd added. "And, honey, your daddy will get a substitute leg that will work almost as well as the one he lost in the accident."

"Can I see it?"

Syd nodded. "When his doctors tell us that it's okay for us to go and visit."

"When can we do that?"

"We're not sure, honey. But hopefully very soon."

"Can Gramma go, too?"

Syd looked at Maddie.

"I wish she could, Henry," Maddie said. "But Gramma needs special care, so she can't make long trips like this. When we go see your daddy, we're going to have to take an airplane."

Henry was excited now. "We're getting to take *two* trips in the airplane?"

He knew about the trip to Baltimore to pick up Celine.

Maddie nodded. "We sure are. But I think that when we go see your daddy, we might all ride on a big airplane, so Syd can go, too."

Henry looked at Syd's left leg, propped up in its purple cast. "You're just like daddy. I bet you will have a lot to talk about."

Maddie and Syd looked at each other.

He collected his drawings. "Can I go show these to Uncle David?"

Maddie nodded.

Henry started out of the kitchen at his customary breakneck speed. He seemed to do everything fast—especially growing up.

"Walk, buddy," Maddie called after him.

She looked back at Syd and sighed.

"From the mouths of babes," Syd said.

"No kidding," Maddie agreed. She reached a hand across the table, and Syd met her halfway.

"That went a lot better than it could have," Syd said.

"I know. We're lucky. He's a pretty resilient kid."

"I guess we don't suck too badly as surrogate parents."

Maddie smiled at her. "I don't think we suck at all."

Syd tightened her hold on Maddie's hand. "Why do I think that the hardest part of this is yet to come?"

"For him, or for us?"

Syd shrugged and met her eyes. "Yes?"

Maddie leaned across the table and kissed her. "I guess Henry isn't the only babe dispensing wisdom around here."

Chapter 11

"How do you want to handle this?"

Syd looked across the desk at her new attorney. Michelle Westin was a pretty woman. With her short, stylish hair and hazel eyes, she looked more like a twenty-something sorority sister than a hard-nosed trial lawyer. But Michael said she had the best reputation in southwest Virginia, and she was also licensed to practice in North Carolina. Syd was lucky just to get the appointment. They were meeting in her Wytheville satellite office, where she kept hours twice a month.

"I honestly don't know," Syd replied. "What are my options?"

Michelle lowered the stack of papers from Jeff's lawyers. "Essentially, you have three. One: you can reconcile."

Syd shook her head.

"Didn't think so," Michelle said. "Two: you can request mediation."

"What does that really mean?" Syd asked.

"It means that you both agree to sit down for an undetermined number of sessions with a third-party mediator who will try to help you resolve your differences amicably."

"I thought we had already done that."

Michelle nodded. "It seems that your husband has changed his mind."

Syd sighed. "What's the third option?"

Michelle sat back in her chair. "We face him in court before a judge, provide compelling evidence of his infidelity, and hope that you walk away with a divorce decree.”

Syd closed her eyes. When she opened them, Michelle was quietly watching her. She was slowly rotating a paper clip between her thumb and forefinger.

“Why is he doing this?” Syd asked. She really meant it as a rhetorical question.

Michelle shrugged. “You tell me.”

Syd looked at her in confusion. “What do you mean?”

“You were within weeks of a final decree, and he changed his mind. He must have had a reason. Have you had any contact with him?”

Syd shook her head. “No. None.”

“Has anything in your personal life changed? Anything he could have discovered and taken exception to?”

Syd didn’t like the direction this conversation was taking. “What I do with my personal life is none of his business.”

“Unfortunately, it *is* his business as long as you’re still his wife.”

Syd opened her mouth to say something, but thought better of it.

Michelle sighed. “Look, Syd. This is going to go a lot better if all the cards are on the table.”

“What’s that supposed to mean?”

Michelle seemed to shift gears. “You said that your husband is from a family of means. Is that correct?”

Syd nodded.

“And you also said that you signed a pre-nup agreement before your marriage—is that also accurate?”

“Yes.”

“Does your husband have any kind of trust fund?”

“Yes.” Syd grew uneasy as she got the drift of Michelle’s questions.

Michelle sighed. “I really don’t think it’s too hard to connect the dots here, do you?”

Syd felt embarrassed and vaguely light-headed. How could

she be so stupid? "But that's ridiculous. I'm not after his money. And even if I were, the pre-nup would take care of that, wouldn't it?"

"It doesn't matter what you're after, Syd. It only matters how the State of North Carolina chooses to divide what it regards as community property. And as for the pre-nup—I won't be able to make any kind of assessment there until I can see a copy of it. You didn't, by chance, bring one with you today, did you?"

Syd shook her head. "I don't even *have* one, as far as I'm aware."

"Then I'll have to request a copy from," she sifted through the pages of the letter, "Mr. Graber. Until then, we'll just have to plan for the worst and hope for the best."

"But this doesn't make any sense. Why would he suddenly decide to make an issue out of this? Why wouldn't he just ask me not to make any claim on his precious inheritance? I've *never* wanted his money."

Michelle watched her in silence for a moment. "As I said, something must have changed his mind." She continued to rotate the paper clip. "Any thoughts about what that might be?"

Syd stared back at her. She felt uncomfortable—like she'd just walked into a job interview with something stuck in her teeth. She began to get a sense of what it might be like to face this woman in a courtroom. It was clear that Michelle had something specific in mind.

Enough was enough.

"Why don't you just go ahead and ask me about whatever it is that's plainly dangling here between us?" she said.

Michelle seemed to dial back her aggressive stare. She dropped her paper clip. "I'm not your antagonist, Syd."

"Really? Then why do I feel like I'm turning on a spit over here?"

Michelle smiled. "Okay. Fair enough." She leaned forward in her chair. "Tell me about your relationship with Dr. Stevenson."

"With—" Syd began. "How do you know about that?"

"I'd venture to guess that the entire *county* knows about that, Syd."

Syd looked at her in amazement. "You don't seriously think that Jeff . . ."

"Wealthy family. Trust fund. Philandering husband defends his behavior by alleging that his wife left him for another woman." Michelle shrugged. "In *my* profession, we call that a blue plate special."

"That's *ridiculous*. I didn't even know Maddie when I left Jeff to move up here."

"Were there other women before Dr. Stevenson?"

Syd could feel herself blush. "Of *course* not."

"Can you prove that?"

Syd was speechless.

Silence fell between them like the curtain that drops between acts of an opera.

"Do you see now what we might be up against if we face him in court?" Michelle asked in a more congenial tone.

Syd nodded.

"I'm sorry to be so hard on you, but you need to know where this might all be headed."

Syd slowly shook her head. "I just don't get it. Why would he want to do this?"

"People do all kinds of things when they're hurt and angry. He may just want to stop you from ruining his reputation."

"How?" she asked. "By ruining *mine*?"

"No," Michelle said quietly. "Not yours."

Syd stared at her in disbelief.

Oh, my god.

"Are you going to tell me what she said?"

Maddie was watching Syd fold clothes. She was seated at the kitchen table, and tidy stacks of darks and lights stood tall around her like obelisks. Since the boys had moved in, laundry had taken on a whole new meaning. Just pairing socks was now an enterprise that required focus and concentration. Syd was adamant about taking on this role since her casted leg rendered her incapable of performing many other routine housekeeping tasks.

She pulled a pink and gray argyle sock from a pile of solids and held it up.

"Is this yours?" she asked, sweetly.

"Hardly," Maddie replied.

Syd tossed it back into the laundry basket on the floor next to her chair, where it became part of a growing pile.

"How is it possible for David to have so many socks without mates?"

Maddie shrugged. "I think that's a question for Carl Sagan."

"Well, next time we run into him, let's remember to ask."

Syd continued to sort socks.

Maddie watched her in silence for another minute. "Sweetheart?"

Syd looked up at her.

"Tell me about your meeting with Michelle Westin."

Syd took a deep breath, and expelled it slowly. "Do I have to?"

"You might as well. I came home early to find out, and eventually you'll run out of socks." She sighed. "You should also know that I'm determined to sit here until you do."

Syd pushed her jumbled pile of laundry away and turned to her. "How do you always do that?"

Maddie frowned. "How do I always do what?"

"How do you always make me forget what I'm pissed off about?"

"Oh, *that*," Maddie said. "I'm afraid I can't share that with you. You don't have the proper clearance."

"I don't?"

Maddie looked her over. "Nope. Not seeing it."

Syd leaned toward her. "Maybe you need to look closer?"

Maddie raised an eyebrow. "Is that an invitation?"

Syd bent forward and kissed her. "What do you think?"

Maddie sighed. "I think it's nearly three o'clock in the afternoon, and you're trying to distract me."

Syd looped her arms around Maddie's neck. "How am I doing?"

"Normally, you wouldn't have to ask me that question."

"I know." Syd kissed her again. "Why is today different?"

Maddie took hold of her arms and gently lowered them. "Because it's clear that we need to talk about whatever it is you're trying to avoid."

Syd leaned her forehead against Maddie's. "I know. I'm sorry to be such a pain in the ass."

"You're about the furthest thing in the world from being a pain in my ass."

"I wish that were true."

"It *is* true."

Syd sat back and looked at her sadly. "Not for long. Michelle thinks that Jeff is going to drag our relationship through the mud, alleging that it's my real motivation for seeking a divorce, and besmirch *your* reputation in the process."

Maddie was silent for a moment. "Is that all?"

Syd gave her an incredulous look. "Isn't that enough?"

Maddie shrugged. "I don't see how he could expect to gain anything by doing that."

"Darling, I think you're missing the part where Jeff publicly outs *you* as the other woman in this ludicrous little costume drama."

Maddie laughed. "Honey . . . this would hardly be breaking news. We've been living together for the better part of two years now."

Syd stared at her in amazement. "But surely you don't want something lurid like this being broadcast in the local media?"

"It wouldn't *be* in the local media, Syd. If this goes to trial, it'll be back in North Carolina. And, frankly, I don't give a rat's ass about who knows what, where you and I are concerned. We don't exactly hide the nature of our relationship right now, and I don't see any reason to have to start."

"What about your practice?"

Maddie shrugged. "My practice won't suffer much. And if it does, it does. We go on."

"And what about *my* job? Are you forgetting that I'm a public school teacher?"

"No." Maddie shook her head. "I'm not forgetting that. I'll admit that we might have to do some fancy footwork there."

"And what about Henry?"

"Henry will be just fine—as long as we keep a watchful eye on the contents of Astrid's toy box."

Syd laughed. "You're dramatically over-simplifying this."

"I know."

"But I love you for that."

"I know that, too."

Syd rolled her eyes. "You know . . . I'd really like to kick his cheating, pampered *ass* for this."

"Me, too," Maddie agreed. "But since we can't, we need to do the next best thing."

"What's that?"

Maddie smiled. "We let Michelle do it for us."

Syd sat quietly for a moment and then looped her arms back around Maddie's neck. "Wanna rethink my earlier offer?"

"Which offer was that?" Maddie ran her hands up along her back. "I can't really recall."

"Really?" Syd glanced at the wall clock in the kitchen. "I have about forty-five minutes to jog your memory."

Maddie kissed her. "You'd better work fast."

Syd smiled against her lips. "Fortunately, for you, I always do."

Chapter 12

Henry loved to fly.

Even though he couldn't really see out the front windows of the airplane, Maddie let him sit on the front seat beside her on the way to pick up Gramma C. She even got him a smaller pair of ear things so he could hear her better.

He liked taking off the best. Going that fast was really fun. He wondered if a car would do the same thing if it went fast enough. Maddie said that it wouldn't, but he really wasn't sure. He thought about the red Camaro. That *car* sure took off. And it flew all over the place. Lots of people saw it, too.

But Maddie was always right.

Maybe it was just a magic kind of car.

That had to be it.

Henry really wanted Maddie to buy a car like that, but she said they'd probably get another Jeep. He liked the old Jeep okay, but a flying car would really be cool.

Maybe Syd could get one.

Uncle David said that Syd's car was like a motorized hunk of limpa bread. Henry didn't really know what that meant, but Syd told him to give it up. She wasn't getting a new car until the wheels fell off her old one.

Uncle David told her that this probably wouldn't take very much longer.

They argued like that a lot. Maddie said it was like playing ping-pong with words instead of a ball and paddles.

He couldn't wait for his daddy to come live there with them. Maddie said they could go and visit him at the hospital soon. Henry had been working on pictures to send him to decorate his hospital room. Maddie said that Gramma C. had gone over to see his daddy yesterday.

Henry loved Gramma C. They always had fun when she came to visit.

Well . . . all except for those piano lessons.

Somebody was talking to Maddie on the radio.

"Cessna Four Two Nine Whiskey Papa, this is Potomac Center."

"This is Cessna Four Two Nine Whiskey Papa," Maddie answered. "Go ahead."

"Four Two Nine Whiskey Papa, Martin State Airport is twelve o'clock and fifteen miles. Expect a visual approach to runway three-three."

"Four Two Nine Whiskey Papa has Martin State in sight."

"Four Two Nine Whiskey Papa, contact Martin State Tower on one-two-one point three."

"Four Two Nine Whiskey Papa over to tower on one-two-one point three."

"Martin State Tower, Four Two Nine Whiskey Papa is with you for a visual to runway three-three."

"Four Two Nine Whiskey Papa cleared to land on runway three-three."

"Roger, clear to land runway three-three."

Maddie looked at Henry. "Okay, sport. Ready to help me set this thing down?"

Henry nodded enthusiastically. "Do you think Gramma C. is watching us?"

Maddie smiled at him. "I think so."

Henry sat back and grabbed hold of the sides of his seat like Maddie had told him to do during takeoffs and landings.

Henry felt a rumble when the landing gear went down. The airplane seemed to go faster, but he knew that it really was slowing down. Then he felt the tires touch the ground, and his seatbelt held him tighter against the seatback as Maddie put on the brakes. Out the windows, he could see the tops of buildings whizzing by.

"Four Two Nine Whiskey Papa, cleared to ramp," the voice on the radio said.

"Roger," Maddie said. "Four Two Nine Whiskey Papa to the ramp with you."

They turned off the runway and drove more slowly toward the building where they would pick up Gramma C. and get more gas for the ride back home.

Maddie parked the airplane and shut off the engines. A big man in a blue jumpsuit appeared next to the door on Henry's side of the airplane. He opened the tiny door.

"Hi there," he said. "I heard that your passenger here might need a hand getting out."

"Thanks," Maddie said. "I think he'd appreciate that." She helped Henry unhook his seatbelt. "You wanna hop out, sport?"

He nodded and let the man help him climb out onto the wing and then to the ground. Maddie followed him out, hopped down, and stood beside him. A big blue fuel truck pulled up next to the airplane.

Maddie took hold of Henry's hand. "Come on, sport. Let's go find Gramma."

"Okay, Maddie."

They walked toward the big glass building. Henry saw a tall woman standing near the doors.

"Gramma C.!" he yelled. He pulled his hand free and ran the rest of the way to greet her.

She smiled when she saw him coming and knelt down so she could hug him. Henry thought she smelled like those little oranges you always got at Christmas.

"Hello, little man," she said. "Thank you for coming to get me."

Maddie walked up to join them.

"Hello, Mom," she said. "I guess you can tell that your copilot was pretty anxious to greet you?"

"I noticed that," Gramma C. said. She stood up and hugged Maddie. "How about my pilot?"

Henry could see Maddie smile against the shoulder of Gramma C.'s green jacket. "The pilot was pretty anxious, too."

They stepped apart.

It was windy, and Maddie's long hair was blowing all around her face.

"Let's go inside," she said. "We can get something to drink while they refuel the plane."

Henry looked up at her. "Can I get root beer?"

"I don't know, sport."

"I like root beer, too," Gramma C. said.

Maddie looked at her in surprise. "You do?"

Gramma C. stared at her. "Of *course*. Do you think I exploded into adulthood like Athena from the head of Zeus?"

Maddie smiled at her. "I confess that the idea has occurred to me once or twice."

Gramma C. shook her head. "Well, I actually *did* have a childhood, and I loved root beer, too—just like Henry." She took hold of his hand. "Come on. Let's go and find some."

"Okay." Henry looked up at her. "Maddie likes coffee with *lots* of sugar. Syd yells at her about it."

Gramma C. nodded. "That's good. She should yell at her for that."

Maddie did that thing with her eyebrow.

They all walked into the building together.

On the flight back to Jefferson, Maddie and Celine talked in vague and nonspecific terms about Celine's visit to see James Lawrence. Henry was in the backseat of the airplane, playing with a puzzle Celine bought him in the gift shop at the FBO.

"It was a clean procedure with no complications," Celine said. "He has a good prognosis for a quick recovery. He's got some phantom limb sensation right now, but that should subside within another week or so. His attending is more concerned about evidence of PTSD related to the events surrounding the immediate aftermath of the injury."

Maddie looked at her mother. "I worried about that."

Celine nodded. "With good reason. It's a lot easier to address the physical aftereffects of combat than the emotional ones."

"What do they think about his ability to take on full-time parenting responsibilities?"

Celine looked apologetic. "I didn't feel that I could ask about that."

"I understand."

They rode along in silence for a few moments. Maddie understood that it would be better to wait until they were at home and safely out of Henry's earshot to pursue this topic, but she was having a hard time containing her curiosity—and anxiety. It was frustrating as hell. Like waiting on a set of lab results that she was ninety-nine percent certain would bear out the diagnosis she was already poised to make.

James would go home to Kannapolis, and he would take Henry with him. And that would be that.

She and Syd would find a way to go on. And maybe, if they were lucky, James would let them stay in Henry's life. Maybe he'd even consent to let them have him for weekend visits, or for part of his summer vacations.

That last thought made her insides twist. It reminded her of her own childhood in California with Celine, and all the holidays she had spent, roaring back and forth across the country in a desperate bid to spend time with her father in Virginia.

But that was a different time with different circumstances, and Maddie understood those dynamics now in a way she never did, growing up. Henry's life was far less complicated. He had a father who loved him, and now he had Maddie and Syd, too. And they would always be on hand to help James in any way they could.

They would always love Henry—even if they didn't see him every day.

She felt the nagging prick of a moroseness that was getting

harder to keep pushed down. She knew that Syd was struggling with the same thing. Each passing day carried them closer to the inevitable end of their time with Henry. It was a damn tell-tale heart, beating its staccato way out of the darkness of her subconscious and into broad daylight, where it could no longer be ignored. Sometimes the banging got so loud that she wanted to cover her ears with her hands to quiet it.

She felt a hand on her leg.

Celine was watching her with a worried expression.

Maddie rested a hand on top of her mother's and squeezed. "It's okay."

"It's really not," Celine said.

"No," Maddie agreed. "It isn't."

"I have faith in you," Celine said. "In *both* of you. You and Syd will find a way to make this work."

Maddie smiled at her. "We all will."

They flew along in silence, while Henry sat quietly in the back seat, intent on solving a puzzle of his own.

Chapter 13

Things were hopping at the Midway Café.

Since Michael had been on hand to help out in the kitchen, Nadine had consented to reopen the small restaurant for supper three nights a week, and business was booming. It wasn't long before word about the miraculous cuisine being served-up there spread to remote locations like Blacksburg, Roanoke, and Winston-Salem. Nadine's husband, Raymond, now spent half his time sprawled out across one of the back booths, swilling Diet Dr. Pepper and grousing about how much it was going to cost them to extend the parking lot. He was tired of people parking all over the grass out front. Nadine said he just needed to get his thumb out of his ass and order a truckload of gravel.

Nadine and David had even managed to hammer out an uneasy truce about "improvements" to the décor. All of the small tables now sported tablecloths—in plain white (Nadine won that round). And each table now had a simple clay pot with early spring hyacinths and curly willow tops (round two to David).

The menu was an eclectic mix of county standards and low-country specials. Michael was in awe of how Nadine could make even the simplest concoction vibrate with uniqueness. Sometimes it was as simple as adding Kellogg's Corn Flakes to the meat loaf and finishing it off with a ladle of wild mushroom gravy or glazing the country ham with Cheerwine. He paid attention, and he didn't ask a lot of questions. He learned that if he kept his peace, she'd sometimes volunteer little tidbits of information about the recipes.

"My grandma, Harriet, used to soak her cut-up chicken overnight in a bowl of buttermilk. She'd also throw three or four slices of fatback into the oil while she was frying it." Nadine laid another chicken leg into the hot iron skillet. "In my view, that fatback was always better tasting than the chicken."

"Why don't you cook it that way now?" Michael asked.

She mopped at her sweaty forehead with a thin, striped dish-towel that was nearly bleached white after many years of hard use. "Most of my customers already have one foot in the grave. I think it would be unchristian of me to hurry them along, don't you?"

"I don't know about that, Nadine. The closest I ever felt to the lord was the day I first tasted your banana pudding."

She slapped him with her hand towel. "Don't you blaspheme in my kitchen, boy."

"You know it's true."

She shrugged. "Walk your tall ass over there to the refrigerator and bring me that bowl of chicken thighs."

"Yes, ma'am."

Michael did what he was told. With Nadine, things worked better that way.

Michael also learned that Grandma Harriet made a damn fine hummus out of butter beans. "Of course, they didn't call it hummus in those days," Nadine explained. "It was just her Sunday bean spread, and she'd always make it in the hottest part of the summer, with the fresh beans that were left over from canning. I always hated it when I was a girl," she added. "But now, I realize that was just because I was sick to death of them from having to spend my school holidays shelling the damn things."

Michael suspected that Nadine's Sunday bean spread was a tad more exotic than grandmother Harriet's had ever been. For one thing, she seasoned hers with cumin and garlic. He talked her into trying it with some tahini and lemon juice, and the result was remarkable. They were now serving the modified hummus as a special appetizer, but Nadine insisted that they continue to call it bean spread.

"Nobody will eat it otherwise," she said. "And I don't want it collecting mold in my refrigerator."

Michael found it hard to disagree.

"Nadine, I want you to think about something," Michael said. He sat the big bowl of chicken thighs down on a table next to the stove.

She looked up at him. There were splatters of grease all over the lenses of her wire-framed glasses. Her brown eyes looked suspicious. "What is it?"

"With luck, the repairs on the Inn should be finished in another month or so."

Nadine started to transfer the chicken thighs from the bowl of buttermilk to a flat pan containing the seasoned breading mixture.

"I guess that means you'll be going back to work in your own kitchen, then," she said. Her tone was unreadable.

"Well . . . yes," he replied. "But I have an idea I want to run by you."

"What is it?" she asked again. Before he could reply, she added, "If it has anything to do with leaving your partner behind, you can forget about it." She dropped a couple of breaded pieces of chicken into the hot oil, and they started to sizzle. "You're just lucky I haven't taken a meat cleaver to that boy before now."

Michael smiled at her. "No. David goes where I go."

"Good thing." She clucked her tongue. "That boy gets on my last nerve."

Michael laughed. "Nadine, you have more last nerves than Carter's has little pills."

He could see her trying not to smile.

"What's this idea, then?" she asked.

He leaned his big frame against the counter and crossed his arms. "I was thinking that we might engage in a little *quid pro quo*."

She slapped him on the arm with her tongs. "Don't you be

suggesting any of that perverted stuff to me, boy. You know I don't cotton to any of that mess you white boys get up to."

"Hey!" Michael grabbed a towel and dabbed at the spot her tongs had left on his sleeve. "You just got grease all over my new jacket."

Nadine glared at him over the rims of her glasses. "I guess your boyfriend will just have to spot clean it, then, won't he?"

"Come on, Nadine. I know you like David."

"I might like him just fine," she said. "That doesn't mean I don't think the two of you are on a slippery road to perdition."

They'd had this conversation before.

"Are you quoting Grandma Harriet again?" he asked.

She shook her dark head. "Nope. Grandma Harriet took a more kindly view toward your kind."

"My *kind*?" he asked. "Why was that?"

"Maybe she was just the kind of Christian who didn't throw stones." She shrugged. "It also could be because she lived longer with Miss Rosa than she did with Granddaddy."

"Miss Rosa?"

Nadine nodded. "She played piano at the A.M.E. church in Denton. Grandma Harriet moved into Miss Rosa's apartment after Granddaddy died. They lived there together for more than thirty-five years. You never saw one of them without the other. When Grandma Harriet died, Miss Rosa only lasted a few weeks without her."

She used her tongs to turn over the chicken thighs. They were fried to a perfect, golden brown.

"That apartment didn't have but one bedroom," she added.

Michael smiled at her. "I guess that must mean we're in good company on the road to perdition."

Nadine nodded. "It don't much matter which road you're on, as long as you make the journey with someone you love."

Michael didn't reply, but he bumped Nadine's shoulder with his own.

She looked up at him with feigned impatience, but he knew her well enough now to understand that she was trying to downplay her uncharacteristically sentimental revelation.

"What was it you wanted to ask me about, boy?"

"Well," he said. "I was thinking that once my kitchen is back online, maybe you'd consent to come out to the Inn one night a week and cook with me there."

Nadine raised an eyebrow.

"And in return," he continued, "I'll keep helping out here one night a week."

She thought about it. "I might consider doing that. As long as I can do things my own way, and you won't bust a gusset if I slop something on your fancy-ass range."

He drew an imaginary "x" across his heart. "I promise."

She nodded. "Now quit your freeloading, and go get me a platter before these thighs turn into charcoal briquettes."

"Yes, ma'am," he said.

"And while you're at it, get the bean spread out and start filling up those small serving bowls." Nadine waved her tongs in the general direction of the refrigerator.

Michael walked to the beat-up Maytag and pulled out the big plastic container of seasoned butter beans.

"You know, Nadine . . . we need to think about renaming this appetizer."

"Don't you start with that hummus crap again. I told you nobody will buy it if we call it that."

"I wasn't thinking about calling it hummus," he said. "I was thinking we should name it for your grandma."

Nadine turned around and glared at him. The overhead light made solar flares on the lenses of her glasses. She looked like one of those neon-eyed space creatures from the Mos Eisley Cantina in *Star Wars*. And she could be just about as frightening, too.

"How about Harriet's Lasagna-Bean Spread?" he suggested.

It took Nadine a minute to get the reference. When she did, Michael was barely able to dodge the soggy towel she threw at him.

◊ ◊ ◊

Tonight's dinner at the café was special. Maddie and Syd were coming, and they were bringing Celine. Also present were David's mother, Phoebe, and the entire Freemantle clan.

Well. All of the Freemantles except Azalea, who still refused to break bread with Edna. And that was especially true on *this* day—the anniversary of the Battle of Cloyd's Mountain, where Union forces attacked and killed General Albert Jenkins, then burned the New River Bridge, just to add insult to injury.

Azalea didn't understand how David and Phoebe could tolerate sitting down to eat with a worthless Yankee whose people were responsible for killing their great, great uncle—no matter how good the damn fried chicken was.

She did, however, ask Curtis to drop her off a leg quarter and some broccoli slaw on his way home.

Celine had never eaten at Odell's. Her last visit to the small café had been decades ago, when Maddie was just a toddler. It was mostly a dive in those days, serving only hot dogs, barbecue, and an occasional case of food poisoning. But she was pretty sure of one thing: that *had* to be the same portrait of Jesus hanging over the short order grill. She remembered it because no matter where she sat in the tiny place, it seemed like his eyes followed her. She had said as much to Maddie's father on one of their last visits there, and he just laughed and told her she was paranoid because she was a Jew living in sin with a lapsed Presbyterian. But tonight was no different, and when a flamboyantly over-dressed David met them at the door and led them toward the café's "best" table, she was certain that the eyes of the Savior followed her as she made her way across the chipped linoleum floor.

David pulled out a chair for her with his customary flourish.

"Here you go, madam. It's the best seat in the house."

Celine looked around the tiny place. It was true. From this vantage point, she had an unobstructed view of most of the restaurant—including the short order grill.

She looked at David. "Would you mind terribly if I sat on that side of the table instead?"

He stood there, holding the chair with a perplexed look on his face. "You can sit wherever you like, Celine. But what's wrong with this seat?"

Maddie pushed behind him and claimed a chair that sat against the back wall. "It's the painting." She sat down and looked up at Celine. "Isn't it, Mom?"

Celine met her eyes. "I can't believe you remember that."

Syd laughed. "You're kidding me with this, right?" She eased herself down onto a chair next to Maddie and leaned her crutches against the back wall. She motioned for Henry to take the seat that David was offering. "She could probably tell you what you ate for breakfast nine years ago on Arbor Day."

Celine sighed. "It's true."

"What's Arbor Day, Syd?" Henry asked. He was already reaching for his water glass.

David looked at the painting, then back at Celine. "What about the painting?"

Celine shrugged. "It's the eyes."

"The eyes?" David asked.

Celine nodded. "They seem to follow you—like one of those trick portraits in the Agatha Christie novels."

Henry tugged at Syd's sleeve. "What's Arbor Day?"

"It's a holiday that encourages people to plant trees," she explained.

Henry seemed confused by the relationship between Arbor Day and the greasy painting hanging over the grill. "Did the pink man plant trees?"

"The pink man?" Syd asked. "Who is the pink man?"

Henry pointed to the portrait of Jesus.

Celine followed Henry's finger and looked more closely at the portrait, then laughed. He was right. The years had not been kind to the Savior's raiment. He looked like he was wearing a pink shawl.

David scowled. "I *so* did not know it would fade like that," he muttered.

"Fade?" Maddie asked.

David nodded.

"What did you do to it?"

"I tried to *clean* it. The damn thing was covered with more grease than the hot dog roller at Sheetz. So I took it down one day when Nadine was out arguing with Raymond about some gravel, and I sprayed it with Resolve. Big mistake."

Maddie narrowed her eyes. "You used Resolve to try to clean a painting?"

He nodded.

"David . . . Resolve is dry-cleaning solution."

He gave her a withering look. "I *know* what it is, thank you very much. For your information, I only used it on his *clothing*."

"Oh." Maddie chuckled. "Good plan."

David cut his eyes toward Henry. "You're just lucky we're in mixed company, missy."

Maddie looked around the tiny café. It was hopping. "You've certainly got that part right. What's going on here tonight? It looks like half of Jericho is here."

David shrugged. "If you ask Azalea, she'd tell you that it's because it's the anniversary of some Civil War battle."

Celine thought about that. "Cloyd's Mountain?"

Syd looked at her with surprise. "You remembered that?"

"Not really," Celine explained. "I just remember Azalea. I can't believe she's still fighting that war."

"What war?" Henry asked.

"The War of Northern Aggression," David said.

Henry looked confused. Maddie picked up her menu. "Don't worry about that, sport. Let's figure out what we're getting for supper."

"Okay, Maddie." He took hold of the menu and studied it. He was all business now. After a minute, he looked up at Celine. "Gramma, what's *chute-nay*?"

"Chutenay?" Celine asked.

Syd looked at Henry's menu to see what item he was asking about. She smiled at Celine. "He means chutney." She glanced back at the menu. "Apricot."

"Oh." Celine smiled and ran her hand over Henry's thick hair. It was amazing. He really did look like Maddie. "It's a special sauce with chunks of cooked fruit in it."

Henry wrinkled up his nose.

Syd sighed. "He won't eat chunks of anything."

Maddie laughed.

Syd glared at her. "And trust me, he comes by it honestly."

"Forget the chutney, sport," Maddie said. "Let's just get the fried chicken."

Henry brightened up at once. "I want a leg."

Maddie looked at Syd. "Hard to argue with that."

Syd rolled her eyes and looked at Celine.

Celine shrugged. "Don't blame me. She gets that from her father's side of the family."

David snorted.

They all jumped at the sound of a crash. Someone had knocked over a service tray, sending plates and glasses flying.

David sighed. "Excuse me. Duty calls."

He adjusted his bow tie and headed for the carnage. Nicorette was already there, and she and another young woman were busy helping someone to their feet.

Syd leaned forward to get a better look.

"Oh my god . . . is that Roma Jean?"

Maddie looked toward the pile of broken plates and dirty silverware.

"Yep. That's her." Maddie shook her head. "Some things never change."

"What do you mean?" Celine asked.

"She means that every time Roma Jean is within fifty feet of her," Syd said, "the poor thing ends up sprawled out across some section of floor."

Celine looked at her daughter. "Really?"

Maddie shrugged.

"I like Roma Jean," Henry volunteered.

"We know you do, sport," Syd said.

"We got to go for a ride in Charlie's police car. Charlie let me turn the blue lights on when we stopped at Aunt Bea's for a Coke."

Syd was confused. "When did you ride with Charlie?"

"After school on Friday," he explained. "I missed the bus," he added in a quiet voice.

"Henry . . ." Syd began.

"It wasn't my fault. Héctor took my lunch box, and I was trying to get it back."

Maddie was studying the small group of people who were busy clearing away the mess on the floor. "Isn't that Charlie over there next to Roma Jean?"

Syd followed her gaze. "It looks like her."

"Interesting."

"What's interesting?"

"This isn't the first time that Roma Jean's hit the deck when Charlie has been in the vicinity. The same thing happened after the tornado, when they pulled you both out of the rubble."

"Oh, really?"

Maddie was still staring at Roma Jean and Charlie.

Syd snapped her fingers in front of Maddie's face. "Hello?"

Maddie looked at her. "What?"

"Oh, please."

"What?" Maddie asked again.

"You're jealous."

"Am not."

"Are, too."

Celine laughed.

Maddie glowered at her. "*Not* helping, Mom."

"Sorry. It's just such a treat for me to see you acting like a teenager."

"A treat?" Maddie raised an eyebrow.

Celine nodded. "I missed a lot. Too much."

Maddie smiled at her. "We both did."

"Missed what?" David walked back up to the table. He was carrying a basket. "Here you go, buddy." He set it down in front of Henry. "Just out of the oven."

Henry leaned forward to peer into the basket. "What are these?"

"They're Nadine's famous cheese biscuits—made extra special by a hefty dose of red—" He stopped when he noticed Syd making rapid slashing motions across her throat.

"*Ix-nay on the epper-pay,*" she whispered.

David rolled his eyes.

"What are these red things, Uncle David?" Henry was holding one of the biscuits up for closer inspection.

David thought about it. "They're fairy sprinkles."

"Fairy sprinkles?" Maddie asked.

David shrugged. "Why not? Michael made them."

"Good cover." Maddie chuckled.

The bell over the door to the restaurant jingled. David sighed. "That's my cue. Back to work. Nick will be here in just a minute to take your orders." He started toward the door, then stopped dead in his tracks. He touched Celine on the shoulder. "Oh, god."

Celine looked across the tables of noisy diners toward the entrance, where a tall, white-haired man stood surveying the interior. It took a moment for her brain to process who was standing there. She felt a surge of adrenalin, and something else. Panic? Celine didn't normally panic, but she was pretty certain that this had to be what panic felt like.

The customer continued to look around the tiny place, lingering on the portrait of the pink man over the grill. When his eyes finally landed on Celine, he looked astonished. His agitation seemed to increase when he saw the rest of her party.

Celine looked at Maddie, who was watching her with concern.

"What is it, Mom?" she asked. "You look like you just saw a ghost."

"Close," Celine replied. She nodded toward the door.

Maddie followed her gaze.

"Oh, shit."

Syd saw him too. She laid a hand on Maddie's arm.

"Who is that man, Maddie?" Henry asked. He was busy picking the fairy sprinkles out of his biscuit.

"He's my—" she hesitated and looked at Celine.

"He's your Uncle Art."

After a moment, Maddie nodded. "Right. He's my Uncle Art."

"Why did he leave, then?" Henry asked. "Isn't he going to come and eat with us?"

Maddie looked back at the door. "He's gone."

Celine nodded. "This is your cue, Dr. Stevenson."

"What do you mean?"

"He came the first two hundred miles. I think you can walk the last fifty yards."

Maddie sighed. Then she pushed her chair back and stood up. "You're right."

They all watched her cross the restaurant and head outside toward the parking lot.

Henry looked up at David. "Are fairy sprinkles always this *hot*?"

David laughed. "Only if you're very lucky."

Syd slapped him on the arm.

"I'd sure like to be a fly on a cheap whitewall out there," he muttered.

"David?" Celine asked. "Why don't you go and find us another chair?"

"Isn't that overly optimistic?" he asked.

She shook her head. "Trust me, I'm a doctor."

"And a mother," Syd added.

Celine smiled at her.

"Whatever." David sighed and walked off to snag another chair.

The sun was setting, and it was reflecting off about two dozen windshields, so she nearly didn't see him standing there next to his battered, white station wagon. Art always drove old beater cars, and this one was no exception. Maddie remembered how her father used to rag on him about his "hooptys."

He was holding his keys, and the driver's side door was open. He was looking right at her as she crossed the parking lot. Raymond had spread so much gravel that it was like walking on a new swath of carpet with an extra-thick pad. Even the cars seemed to be sinking down into it. It made her progress toward him slower and more deliberate—like she was dragging her feet. Literally.

In fact, she wasn't. Once she had seen him standing inside the restaurant door and staring up at faded Jesus, she knew that everything would be okay. It felt like some cranky old machinery deep inside her had finally gotten unstuck and decided to start running smoothly again—just like that obstinate motor on Gladys Pitzer's prehistoric Electrolux. Maddie had broken that thing down and looked at it six ways from Sunday. She had repaired, replaced, and lubed nearly every moving part it had, and still the damn thing wouldn't run. Not until the morning she finally gave up and decided to tell Gladys that it was time to break down and head to Walmart for a new one. She was just about to load the old piece of junk into her Jeep when she had an impulse to try it one more time. Of course, it fired right up and damn near sucked all the tools off her workbench.

Deus ex machina. You just never knew.

But Art wasn't an ancient appliance—at least not in any nonliterary applications. She stopped in front of him.

He gave her a nervous-looking smile. "I really didn't know you'd be here, Maddoe. I feel like a stalker."

"'Here' as in Jericho, or 'here' as in Odell's?" she asked.

"Odell's," he replied. "I just got into town and wanted to grab a bite to eat." He looked over the parking lot full of cars. "When did this place become so *haute?*"

"Right about the time Nadine Odell acquired David as *maître d'.*"

Art looked confused. "*David* is working here?"

Maddie nodded. "Michael, too."

"I don't get it . . . is the Inn closed?"

"Temporarily," Maddie explained. "It was badly damaged in the tornado. They're both pitching in here while repairs are underway."

"Celine didn't mention that."

Suddenly his presence there was starting to make sense. "You talked with Mom?"

He nodded. "She came to see me."

Maddie was surprised. "She did? When?"

"Last week."

"I'm sorry," she apologized. "I didn't ask her to do that."

"I know that." He looked down at the keys in his hand. "We had quite a talk."

"I can only imagine."

"She told me that it was time for us to get past this—for me to get past my fear of seeing you."

"That sounds like her."

He smiled. "I thought so, too. She loves you a lot."

"I know. It's mutual."

"It wasn't always."

"No."

"I'm glad you two found your way back to each other."

She nodded. "So am I."

He seemed to hesitate. "I hope that we can find our way back to each other, too."

"Is that why you're here?"

He met her eyes. "Is that a serious question?"

She dropped her gaze. *Why am I acting like a petulant teenager?* She looked back up at him. "I'm sorry, Art. I don't mean to be so fractious."

The tension in his face seemed to ease a bit. "This reminds me of that time you and David decided to go joyriding on the tractor and took out all of the mailboxes on Silver Hill Road."

"Oh, god." Maddie raised a hand to her forehead.

"As I recall, the Turner clan was pretty nice about it, but Boyd Dickens made your daddy pay to have a stonemason come out there to restack those entrance pillars."

"That was *so* ridiculous. He practically lived in a mud hut. Why on earth did he have a driveway that looked like the entrance to South Fork Ranch?"

Art laughed.

"We actually did him a favor."

"Your father didn't quite see it that way."

"Well," Maddie agreed. "I guess he didn't."

"He'd be very proud of you, you know?"

Maddie sighed and looked away. Over the restaurant roof, a steady rush of hot air from the kitchen exhaust fan made the landscape behind it look blurry. It was strange. She knew the contours of Buck Mountain the way she knew the backs of her own hands, but right now, it was nothing more than a fuzzy mass of green and gray.

Art reached out a hand and touched her on the arm. "What is it?"

She looked back at him. "Why didn't he tell me? Why didn't *any* of you tell me?"

Art dropped his hand. "He didn't want to hurt you."

"Don't you think *this* hurts me?"

He nodded.

"I just don't understand it. I thought I knew him. I thought he trusted me."

"He *did* trust you."

"But not enough."

"Maddoe. It wasn't like that. It was a different time. You were a child—and he? He was conflicted about it. Always. He never really accepted it, and he certainly never was comfortable with it. His greatest fear was that you would find out."

"Even when he knew that I was gay, too?"

"Even then."

She shook her head. "It makes no sense to me."

Art sighed. "I know. But, Maddoe—the fact that you can't understand it doesn't make it less true. We all made what we thought were the best choices available to us in the middle of an untenable situation. Our actions may have been flawed, but we took them with the best intentions and the best information we had. And remember that we're talking about *our* realities and *our* limitations here—not yours. Your father was a very proud man, and he would never risk anything that he thought might change or jeopardize his relationship with you."

"What about you?"

"It wasn't *my* story to tell. And as much as I loved your father, you have to admit that he never had much of an input mode."

She stood there in front of him, speechless. He was right—about everything. And if she told herself the truth, what she felt more than anger or disappointment was *embarrassment*—embarrassment that she seemed to be the last person to figure it all out. Even David admitted that the thought had occurred to him on more than one occasion. And for Maddie, nothing was worse than being unable to connect the dots.

She looked at Art. "I'm sorry."

"Sorry?" He touched her arm again. "What on earth are *you* sorry about?"

"I was shocked and frustrated . . . embarrassed that I didn't know, and hadn't been able to figure it out." She laid a hand on top of his. "I didn't want you to see that. I didn't want *anyone* to see that."

"I can understand that."

"You can?"

He rolled his eyes. "Aren't we members of the same perverse fraternity?"

"I suppose so."

"You *know* so."

"Overachievers Anonymous?"

"That would be the one." He smiled. "The world's first thirty-six step program."

"Thirty-six?"

He shrugged. "Twelve-step programs are for amateurs."

She laughed.

"Maddie?" he asked.

She looked at him.

"I have no illusions. I know this doesn't fix everything."

"No," she agreed. "But at least it's a start."

He nodded. "And I'm grateful for that."

"I am, too." She smiled and touched his arm. "Why don't you come back inside and join us for some of the best fried chicken god ever made? And there's a little someone special you need to meet, too."

"A little someone?"

Maddie nodded. "Come on. It's a long story."

They turned away from Art's car, and slowly walked back across the parking lot toward the small café.

"Staring at that door won't make them reappear any faster."

Syd looked at Celine, who was watching her with an amused expression. "How can you be so certain that they'll both come back?"

"I know Art. And we both know Maddie." Celine took a sip from her iced tea and made a face. "Oh, lord. This is sweetened."

Syd laughed. "Of *course* it is. Have you forgotten where you are?"

"Apparently." Celine pushed the glass away like she'd just been served a glass of iced hemlock.

"Can we ask Nicorette to bring you something else?" Syd suggested.

"It's all right. I'll just drink water."

"You can have some of my milk, Gramma," Henry offered. He was patiently arranging his pile of fairy sprinkles into a picture of . . . something.

"That's all right, sweetheart. I'm happy with my water."

"Okay," he said.

"Henry, what are you making with all of those pep . . . *sprinkles?*" Syd asked.

He looked up at her. "It's the Camaro." His small voice had an almost reverent tone.

Syd sighed. "Of *course* it is." She rolled her eyes at Celine.

"You know you're going to end up having to buy one of those, don't you?"

"Why?" Syd replied. "We could pretty much build one with all the cast-off parts that keep turning up."

"True." Celine smiled. "But if you left that task up to Maddie, the end result would likely resemble a turbo-charged Hoover more than it would a muscle car."

"At least we might have a better shot at keeping up with all the dog hair."

Celine seemed amused by that. "Has Astrid really made that much of a difference?"

Syd shook her head. "Let's just put it this way. César Millan could add on to his beach house with the royalties he could earn off *this* dog."

Celine smiled. "Maddie did tell me about an episode where she added some . . . *color* . . . to your lives."

"Color?"

Celine glanced at Henry, then nodded.

Syd looked back and forth between Celine and Henry. Then enlightenment dawned. "*Color.*" She laughed. "Yes. You could say that. Well, as annoying as she can be, she certainly did find a creative way to defuse a tense situation."

"So I heard."

"Maddie now calls it our 'Purple Haze' episode."

"That seems like an odd signature tune for such a fussy little dog."

"You didn't get to see your daughter chasing her through the house. Trust me . . . it fits."

Celine smiled. "Tell me more about this letter."

Syd shrugged. "It's not all that complicated. For some unknown reason—*and* at, literally, the eleventh hour—Jeff has decided to contest the divorce."

"Any thoughts about why?"

"Oh, a few."

"Really? Care to share?"

"Well, if I were a betting woman, I'd say that his mother's manicured fingerprints are all over this."

"What makes you think that?"

Syd sighed. "Let's just say that Doris has always had definite ideas about what is and isn't in her son's best interest."

"Doris?"

"Yes . . . the dowager herself."

Celine was quiet for a moment. "Jeff is from Boston, isn't he?"

Syd nodded.

"Did you say that his mother's name is Doris?'

"That's right. Doris Simon, née Massena . . . I think."

"Massena?"

"I'm almost certain that's right. They were some preeminent Boston family. Made a fortune in medical supplies or pharmaceuticals . . . something like that."

"Or something like that," Celine echoed.

Syd raised an eyebrow. "You sound dubious."

"On the contrary. I'm fascinated."

"Why?"

Celine shrugged. "Let's just say that I went to boarding school with one Dorrie Massena from Boston, and I'm wondering if your dowager might be the same person."

"You're kidding?"

"Not so much. I lost touch with Dorrie during my college years. But from what I understand, she . . . eventually . . . married well—a stockbroker, I think."

"Did his name happen to be Howard Simon? Chinless? Thin lips? Wears his pants up under his armpits?"

"*That*, I cannot tell you. But I know she returned to Boston, and had only the one child."

Syd shook her head in amazement. "Our small worlds just keep getting smaller. First you know Uncle Marsh—now you know Jeff's mother."

"*Knew* Jeff's mother, you mean. If, in fact, she *is* Dee Dee."

"Dee Dee?"

Celine nodded. "An acronym for her unfortunate nickname at school. Children can be so cruel."

Syd smiled. "Why do I think I'm going to love this?"

Celine glanced at Henry, and then lowered her voice. "I should be horse-whipped for even mentioning it."

"Oh no you don't . . . You can't drop a bead like that and then retreat from it." Syd picked up her glass of iced tea. "Give it up."

Celine sighed. "Dee Dee was short for Dorrie the Douchebag."

Syd choked and spewed brown liquid halfway across the table. Alarmed, Celine handed her a napkin and patted her between the shoulder blades.

"Hey!" Henry cupped his small hands around his maze of sprinkles. "You got tea all over my Camaro."

Celine reached into the breadbasket and withdrew another biscuit. "Here you go, honey." She offered it to Henry. "Spare parts."

He took it gratefully and immediately started picking out all the red chunks of pepper.

Syd was still clearing her throat. "Douchebag?" she whispered.

"Oh, yes. Apparently, Massena wasn't the original family name. I gather they changed it when they relocated from Tennessee and acquired the Beacon Hill zip code."

"Tennessee?" Syd asked. "Doris is from Tennessee? What was their family name before?"

"Massengill."

Syd started to chuckle. Then laugh. Soon, her laughs turned into guffaws. They went on so long that other diners turned around in their seats to stare at her.

She fought to compose herself. "Oh, god."

Celine looked like she was trying not to smile. "There's no reason for you to know this, but in the old days, the S.E. Massengill Company had a pretty sketchy reputation. It's not hard to understand why a social climber like Dorrie's grandfather moved the family away and changed their name." She thought about it for a moment. "He did, however, remember to take his checkbook along. Dorrie always had the best of everything, and I gather that her proclivity for the finer things in life has continued. The Simons are a very old Boston family—related to the Peabodys, I think."

"That's right," Syd agreed. "Jeff said his great-great *somebody* was married to Nathaniel Hawthorne."

"Really? That's fascinating in its own right."

Syd shook her head in amazement. "So the lauded fortune of the great Doris M. Simon actually came from hawking vaginal tonics in the Volunteer State?"

"They were hardly sideshow barkers," Celine said, "but in general terms, that's an apt description of their rise to preeminence."

"Well, well. I wish I had known that in the years when it would have done me some good."

"You never know."

Syd laughed. "That's probably a good thing, too."

"Why?"

"I don't know if I could be trusted to keep information like this a secret. The temptation to take Doris down a few pegs might be entirely too great."

Celine just smiled and picked up her glass of sweet tea.

"I thought you hated that?" Syd asked.

Celine shrugged. "Sometimes, I like to throw caution to the wind."

Syd shook her head. "I see now that your daughter comes by it honestly."

"Believe me, Syd," Celine took a big sip from her glass. "You ain't seen nothin' yet."

Chapter 14

Charlie Davis was walking Roma Jean to her car. In fact, it really wasn't Roma Jean's car—it was her Uncle Cletus's old Caprice Classic. Cletus lent it to Roma Jean after her lime green '76 Chevy Vega was destroyed by the tornado.

The Freemantles *always* bought Chevys.

Of course, there was some argument about whether or not the tornado actually *was* responsible for the demise of the ancient car. Roma Jean's father insisted that the Vega was on borrowed time anyway, and that a bird strike or a direct hit in the right pothole would've been enough to total it. It already had a cracked engine block and leaked coolant like a sieve. It burned so much oil that Roma Jean had to drive around with a case of STP 10W-30 on its tiny backseat.

Still, when that steam table from the school cafeteria dropped from the sky and landed smack-dab on the roof of her car, Roma Jean found it hard not to see the romance in it all. She said her beloved Vega was *Gone With the Wind*—and she failed to understand how her daddy could laugh and suggest that she ought to just drive the steam table.

"It'll probably get better gas mileage, and it won't leak oil all over the driveway," he said.

But Uncle Cletus had stepped up and lent her his prized Caprice. Roma Jean didn't mind that one bit. It was a good ride—decked out with plush velour seats, opera windows, and a functioning eight-track deck mounted under the dashboard. She didn't much care for his music selection, and she spent hours on the Internet, trying to find out if there were any Kenny Chesney recordings available on eight-track.

As soon as she could save half the money, her daddy was going to help her buy one of the reclaimed, storm-damaged cars parked over at Junior's. She'd need it before the end of the summer, when she started classes at Wythe Community College.

Roma Jean wanted to be a librarian, like Miss Murphy. She still worked part-time at the small Jericho Public Library, and she hoped that by the time she got her degree, the library might be able to reopen for five days a week. She saw that as a more desirable career—and one she truly enjoyed—than her other options in the small mountain town. The one thing Roma Jean was sure of was that she wanted to stay in Jericho. That meant a lot fewer options for gainful employment, unless she thought about working in the glass factory, or growing old, punching a cash register at Food Bonanza. That's also why she was looking at colleges so close to home.

Once she finished the two-year associate's program at Wythe, she could transfer to Radford University as a sophomore. And Radford was the perfect distance from home—far enough away to give her the space she needed to explore some parts of her life that she couldn't really test out here in Jericho, but close enough that she could get back on weekends to see her family and keep her part-time job at the library.

Charlie had told her that there was a good "community" in Radford, but Roma Jean wasn't really sure what that meant, and was too embarrassed to ask for an explanation. She had a hard enough time forming complete sentences when Charlie was around. It would be impossible for her to ask for an explanation of all those code language terms that people seemed to use when they talked around something.

Roma Jean stopped next to the dark blue Caprice. She already had its enormous key in her hand, and she nervously turned it over and over as she stood there, staring down at the tops of Charlie's shoes.

"Thanks for walking me out," she said. "You really didn't have to."

"It was my pleasure," Charlie said. "Besides, I wanted to make sure you were okay after your fall inside."

Roma Jean could feel her face growing hot. "I'm sorry that I keep doing that."

"Don't be," Charlie replied. "I just don't want you to get hurt."

"I usually don't."

"Usually?" Charlie sounded amused.

Roma Jean forced herself to look up into Charlie's sky blue eyes. They were nearly as hypnotic as Dr. Stevenson's. *No,* she thought. *They are exactly as hypnotic.* She leaned against the car door to steady herself.

"I hate being such a dork."

"You're not a dork."

Roma Jean was startled. She didn't realize that she had said that aloud. This was going from bad to worse in a backpack.

"Then why do I always act like one?" she asked. It was meant as a rhetorical question, but Charlie seemed to consider it for a moment before she responded.

"I have a theory," she said. "I think you get scared and trip over things when you're . . . *nervous.*"

This was hardly breaking news. On the other hand, there was something about the way Charlie said the word "nervous" that worried her.

"What do you mean by 'nervous'?" she asked.

Charlie gave her a lopsided smile, and Roma Jean felt like she might pass out.

"You know," she said. "*Nervous.*"

Roma Jean suddenly felt like she was standing there in the middle of Odell's parking lot buck-naked. "Okay," she said, looking down at Charlie's feet again. "Maybe you're right. But there's nothing I can do about it."

"I'm not so sure about that," Charlie said. "I think I have an idea."

Roma Jean looked up. "You do?"

Charlie nodded. "I think that if you spent more time with me, you'd be less nervous. Less nervous equals less falling down. Make sense?"

Roma Jean shrugged.

"Oh, come on." Charlie gave her a playful nudge. "Why not at least try it?"

"I don't know what my parents would say." Roma Jean didn't know where her bravery was coming from. She didn't even know if Charlie meant "spend time with me" the way Roma Jean hoped she meant it. She really felt like a dork now.

But Charlie seemed unfazed. "I was thinking that maybe you could go to church with me tomorrow." She smiled. "I don't think they'd have a problem with that . . . do you?"

Roma Jean wasn't sure how she felt about that. Church? *Hey . . . wait a minute.* "Tomorrow is *Saturday*."

Charlie rolled her eyes. "I know. My grandma's church is having revival, and she'll never speak to me again if I don't show up for at least *one* meeting. I thought the Saturday one would be the tamest, and the shortest. Then, maybe, we could go get ice cream or something."

Roma Jean loved ice cream. But Charlie knew that. They had run into each other more than once at Foster's Dairy Bar in town.

"I guess I could ask Mama."

"Great." Charlie reached around her to open the car door, and Roma Jean nearly passed out from the scent of her hair. It smelled like wild cherries.

"The afternoon service starts at one o'clock, so how about I pick you up at your parents' house at a quarter of?"

Roma Jean just nodded. She climbed into the massive Chevy and plopped down with all the grace of a loon landing on a pile of wet reeds.

Charlie closed the car door. "Remember to wear your seatbelt."

Roma Jean fumbled around to find it—its clip had broken loose, and the thing was always tangled up someplace behind the big bench seat.

"Here you go." Charlie bent into the car and found it for her, then guided it over her shoulder and across her chest. The side of Charlie's hand brushed against her sweater, and Roma Jean felt hot tingles race up her arms and settle someplace behind her eyeballs. She held her breath until Charlie had snapped the belt into place and ducked back out of the car.

"I'll see you tomorrow?" Charlie asked.

Roma Jean just nodded. She turned the key, and Uncle Cletus's prize machine roared into life. It blew a cloud of thick gray smoke into the air, but once it settled down, it purred just like a housecat on a porch swing. She took hold of the thick stalk on the steering wheel and jogged the engine into reverse.

Tomorrow couldn't come soon enough.

Astrid yawned and stretched. Her painted red nails looked like leftover bits of Henry's fairy sprinkles.

Maddie shook her head. David had dropped the fat dog off about an hour ago, promising that he would retrieve her before the clinic closed for the day. He had errands to run, which likely meant that he was going by the Inn to check on the renovation. He'd had to stop taking Astrid out there because she'd already peed on the carpenter's compound miter saw twice. Maddie asked why he didn't just leave her at home, and David looked at her with disbelief.

"You're kidding me with this, right?"

Maddie looked at him impassively. "No, I don't think I am."

David sighed. "Well. I thought about it. But when I walked through the kitchen to leave, Syd was sitting at the table flipping through some international cookbook, looking at Korean cuisine."

Maddie sighed. "And your point would be?"

"Hello? Ever heard of *G-A-E-G-O-G-I?*"

"What the hell are you spelling?"

"Shhhh." David looked down at Astrid's plush dog bed. This was her travel bed, and it was in nearly pristine condition—

unlike her twenty or so other beds back at the farm—all of which had seen a lot of hard use.

Astrid spent a lot of time in bed.

"They eat D-O-G meat."

"*Who* does?" Maddie was really confused now.

"South Koreans." He rolled his eyes. "I really wish you would watch Nat Geo just once in a while."

"You're insane."

He shrugged. "I just can't take that chance. Syd hasn't been herself lately."

It was true. But Syd had a lot on her mind these days. They both did. There was the divorce, and their continuing uncertainty about what James Lawrence intended to do about Henry once he was released from rehab at Walter Reed.

"David, even if Syd does take leave of her senses and develops a ludicrous penchant for," she glanced down at Astrid, "*canine cuisine*—*your* dog would be the very last one at risk."

David looked offended. "What's that supposed to mean?"

On cue, Astrid rolled onto her back, exposing the innumerable rolls of fat on her belly and the bottoms of her hairy toes.

David stared at her a moment, then he looked up at Maddie. "I see your point."

"A breakthrough."

David rolled his eyes. "Don't let it go to your head, Cinderella." He looked around the area behind the reception desk. "Where's Lizzy? Doesn't she usually get nailed with these graveyard shifts?"

"She's up in Blacksburg today, hiking with Syd's brother."

"The *extremely* hot Mr. Murphy," David mused. "What a waste of some seriously fine raw material that is."

As usual, Maddie had no idea what he was talking about. "What is?"

"Duh. Tom dating a woman."

"I thought you liked Lizzy."

"I *do* like Lizzy."

"Then help me understand how his dating Lizzy is a waste."

David glanced at his watch. "I don't have enough time to explain that concept to you, Cinderella. And it certainly would require a PowerPoint presentation, at the very least."

"Well," Maddie shook her head, "it may end up being a good thing that her relationship with Tom Murphy is humming along."

"Why?" Now it was David's turn to look confused.

Maddie sighed. "Because Tom Greene is being irascible about continuing the funding for her position."

"You're kidding me?"

"No. Apparently, he has some other, more pressing, priorities."

"Pressing, my ass. What is *this* about? Some new kind of shakedown? What's he want this time? You to do a pole dance on his rec-room bar?"

"I honestly have no idea."

"Oh, come on. Don't be so naïve. You know he's just using this as a way to yank your chain."

"David, he's chief of the hospital ER *and* head of our local United Way. He can pretty much do whatever he wants."

David shook his head. "I *so* do not get you sometimes." He glanced at his watch again. "Okay . . . we'll talk more about this later." He walked toward the door. "I'll be back in a flash."

Maddie glanced at the clock above the door. David's flash had extended to nearly ninety minutes now. *It is unusually warm today. Maybe the construction workers all have their shirts off.* She looked around the empty room. *That could also explain why it's so slow in here today.*

Typically, these weekend clinic hours were among her busiest times of the week.

Maddie's nurse, Peggy, had left early to run an errand, so Maddie sat at her desk in the reception area. She heard the sound of a car roar into the front parking lot out front. It skidded to a halt, and she could hear gravel being slung in every direction. She stood up and started walking around Peggy's desk.

The door was thrown open, and two men entered. She was

pretty certain that the shorter one was Sonny Nicks. The other man was Bert Townsend, and he was more or less pulling Sonny into the clinic.

"Doc Stevenson," he said, in a panicked voice. "This man just got bit by a rattlesnake."

Rattlesnake? That was certainly uncommon—especially for this early in the season.

She hurried toward the pair. "Where is the bite, and when did this happen?"

"About twenty minutes ago," Bert said.

She noticed that Sonny looked a bit pale, but otherwise, seemed to be holding his own. He appeared to be breathing normally, and his eyes were alert. He was walking without assistance, but he was supporting his left arm.

"Can you walk a little bit further?" she asked Sonny.

He nodded.

Maddie led them down a short hallway toward one of her examination rooms. "Where were you bitten?"

"On the left hand," he replied. "I think it was a dry bite."

"Sit up here, and I'll help you lie back," she said. "What makes you think it was a dry bite?"

He shrugged. "I been bit before, and it weren't nothin' like this. This one ain't changin' color or swelling up too bad."

"Are you sure it was a rattler?"

"Yes, ma'am." He nodded. "Timber rattler."

Maddie was sure he'd be right. Sonny was an exterminator, and he sometimes dealt with the removal of venomous snakes when they turned up in people's backyards or inside their crawl spaces.

"How did this happen?" she asked.

"I was trying to catch it before it slid into an open cabinet. I didn't have my hook with me, so I just had to grab it by the tail. Dern thing reared back and tagged me, so I had to stomp it." He shook his head. "I hated to do that, but I pretty much had to 'cause of all the people around."

"Where were you?"

"Church."

"Church?" Maddie asked. She lifted Sonny's left arm and examined the wound. Sure enough, there were two puncture marks visible on the back side of his hand. There was some localized discoloration and swelling, but it didn't appear to have spread much beyond the site of the bite. She unclipped and removed his watch.

Bert nodded. "We was out to Bone Gap at the Full Gospel Tabernacle."

She looked up at him with a raised eyebrow.

"They're having revival services this week," he explained.

Maddie didn't like where this was headed.

"Care to tell me why there was a snake present?" She swabbed the bite area with Betadine, and then uncapped a black Sharpie to draw a circle around the leading edge of the swelling on Sonny's hand. She checked her watch and wrote the time down next to the black line across his wrist.

"Well," Bert said. "It was the damnedest thing. Nobody knew that preacher had brung a snake with him. Did you know that, Sonny?"

Sonny shook his head. "Nope. They do get up to some craziness out there from time to time, but this is the first I ever heard of any serpent handling."

"We all knew he was from someplace over in Tennessee," Bert added. "But nobody'd ever heard him preach before—much less seen his little helper."

Maddie had finished checking Sonny's vital signs. They were all normal. "Who is this man?"

"An evangelist." Bert shrugged. "Young feller. Name's Terry LeFevre."

"And he brought a timber rattlesnake into a building full of people?"

"No, ma'am," Bert said. "He brought two of 'em."

Maddie was now giving Sonny a basic neurologic exam. She lowered his leg back to the table. "Do I even want to ask what happened to the other one?"

Bert chuckled. "Ol' Azalea Freemantle did for that one."

"Azalea?"

Sonny nodded. "That other rattler was hightailin' it toward the choir loft, and Azalea saw it comin'. Next thing I knew, she pulled a snub nose .38 out of her knitting bag and capped the damn thing." He shook his head. "I never seen the like. She squeezed off one round and nailed it right between the eyes."

"Remind me never to get into another argument with her about the damn Civil War," Bert muttered.

"How on earth did the snakes get loose?" Maddie asked.

Sonny and Bert exchanged glances.

"It was an accident," Sonny explained. "The service was just gettin' goin', and we was all singin' the first hymn, 'He Set Me Free.' Most of the pews in the back was full, so some folks that come in late had to go up toward the altar to find seats."

"Nothin' unusual in that," Bert chimed in. "Only Nelda Rae Black and them Lear twins sit up in the amen corner. Now, *she's* the one who brought this preacher in, and them Lear twins . . . well. They just ain't right."

"Besides, it was hotter 'n hell's kitchen in there," Sonny said. "And most of us just wanted to be near the open doors at the back to catch some air."

Maddie checked the swelling on Sonny's hand and palpated his wrist and forearm for any signs of envenomation. Sonny just kept on talking.

"Anyway . . . it was Charlie Davis comin' in with that young Freemantle girl. You know . . . Azalea's granddaughter?" Sonny looked at Bert. "That one who's always fallin' over stuff. What's her name?"

"Roma Jean."

"Right. *Roma Jean*—Curtis and Edna's daughter."

Maddie was shocked. "Roma Jean Freemantle was there?"

Sonny nodded. He lowered his voice. "She's been seein' quite a bit of that Charlie Davis, if'n you know what I mean."

Maddie chose not to comment on that. "What happened?"

"Well," Bert took up the narrative. "She must a tripped over a power cord or somethin', 'cause as soon as they got to the front of the church, she was goin' ass over teakettle—right into a stack of speakers. There was a flat, wood box—kinda like a big ole dresser drawer—sittin' up on top of 'em all, and it went flyin'. Next thing you knew, Pastor LeFevre was hollerin', and everybody up front started stampedin' toward the back door."

"They wasn't just runnin', neither," Sonny added. "They was climbin' over them pews like the Marines takin' Omaha Beach."

Bert nodded in agreement. "That preacher didn't seem too worried, though. He just kept yellin' that people should 'heed the word' and 'follow signs.'"

"Hell," Sonny quipped, "the only damn signs them people cared about followin' were the ones that said 'exit.'"

Maddie sighed. There would be plenty of time to deal with all of this later. "Well, Sonny. It looks like you might be right. I think this is a dry bite, but I don't want to take any chances. I'm going to have the EMTs come and transport you to the hospital in Wytheville, so they can keep you under observation for the next eight hours or so."

"I don't need that." Sonny held up his hand. "You can see that the swelling ain't gettin' worse, and by now, it would be as big as a cow tongue if it had venom in it."

"I know, but you've been bitten before, and that makes you harder to treat if you do develop any serious effects. Besides, I've seen other people go home, thinking they're free and clear, only to turn up in the emergency room twelve hours later with acute neurological problems or internal bleeding."

Bert looked at Sonny. "I don't know, Son. That don't sound too good."

Sonny sighed. "Can't Bert just drive me over?"

Maddie shook her head. "Sorry. My clinic, my rules."

He sighed. "You're just like your daddy, you know that?" He chuckled. "Bossy."

She smiled at him. "So I've been told." She made a few notes on a small laptop computer. "Do you know when you last had a tetanus shot?"

He shook his head.

"Let's go ahead and give you one, just as a precautionary measure."

"Okay."

"Does he have to get it in his derriere?" Bert sounded hopeful.

Maddie chuckled. "Not this time, Bert." She walked to a small refrigerator to withdraw a Tdap syringe.

"Too bad."

Sonny rolled his eyes.

Maddie pushed up Sonny's sleeve and gave him the shot in his right arm.

"Now I'm going to call the EMTs to come and pick you up. Do you want to call Harold and have him meet you over there?"

Sonny nodded. "If I don't, and he hears about this some other way, there'll be hell to pay. I swanny—that boy gets more worked up than a sheep in a den of coyotes."

Maddie walked to a wall phone and dialed the number for the county rescue squad. She quickly brought the dispatcher up to speed on Sonny's situation and asked her to send a crew to transport him to the hospital. As soon as she hung up the phone, she heard the front door to the clinic open and close, and the rapid fall of footsteps. She was shocked when David rushed into the room.

"You'll never *believe* this, Cinderella," he exclaimed. "Oh . . . hey, Sonny," he added.

"David—" Maddie began.

"I was just at the hardware store, and Jocelyn Painter came in all in a swivet. *She* had just been to the post office, and Zeke Dawkins told her that he'd talked to Gertrude Baxter's sister, who said that Gertrude witnessed *all* of this firsthand." He took a breath. "Apparently, a tour bus full of snake handlers showed up and crashed the revival service out at Bone Gap."

Maddie tried again. "David . . . I'm with a patient. You can't just burst in here like this."

"They were on their way to Branson and had just stopped off for lunch at Shatley Springs. Jocelyn said they must've heard the music or something."

"David, I'm not kidding. You need to wait outside."

"Then, Azalea Freemantle saw them all coming in and started screaming something about a Yankee ambush. They say she stood up on her pew and started firing warning shots into the ceiling. Did you know that she carries a .410 Taurus Judge in her knitting bag? She told Cletus she got it to ward off carjackers—like there's any of *that* going on out in Troutdale . . ."

"David—"

"They call those things 'snake charmers,' but I don't think old Azalea much cares about capping reptiles. Not unless they're the two-footed kind—if you get my drift."

"David—"

"Jocelyn said all hell broke out when the tourists dropped their to-go bags of biscuits and their boxes of reptiles to run for cover. That's when all the rattlers got loose."

"David—"

"She said it was like watching YouTube videos of that soccer riot in Egypt."

"David—"

"That place is gonna need a shitload of new light fixtures."

"*David!*"

He paused in his volley of words to stare at her. "What?"

Maddie took a deep breath and gestured toward Sonny and Bert. "I'm with a *patient*."

"I *know*," he said. "Oh. Hey, Bert," he added.

"Can we talk about this later, please?" she asked.

He looked down at his feet. Astrid had wandered into the room behind him and was winding her way in and out of his legs.

"Does Daddy's fluffy little princess need to make wee wee?" he cooed.

They were all startled when they heard the clinic door open and slam shut—again.

Maddie closed her eyes. "What now?"

They heard the clack of shoe heels on the tile floor. Then the doorway to her examination room filled up with a large blonde man wearing khaki-colored Haggar slacks and a button-down white dress shirt. He was carrying what looked like an empty desk drawer, and he did *not* look happy.

His hair, however, looked fabulous.

"I'm Pastor Terry LeFevre," he announced in a booming voice. "And I'm here to bring the man who killed a servant of the Lord to justice."

"That's the preacher," Bert hissed to Maddie.

Sonny started to sit up, but Maddie laid a hand on his chest. "Stay put, Sonny." She looked at the evangelist. "I've got this."

LeFevre pointed a finger at Sonny. "Is this the man who dared to smite one of God's helpmates?"

Maddie walked around the table so she was standing between Sonny and the intruder. "This man is a patient, and you, Mr. LeFevre, are trespassing."

"That's *Pastor* to you, young lady. And as the Lord's ambassador, I am free to exercise my First Amendment right to spread the good news of God's Word anywhere."

"If you have a medical complaint, *Mr.* LeFevre, I'll be happy to tend you. Otherwise, I'm certain that a law-abiding citizen like you will respect my *Fifth* Amendment rights and leave this private property."

He stared at her. She stared back. Neither blinked.

"God's law trumps the laws of men," he offered.

"Really?" Maddie folded her arms. "Do you think our county sheriff would agree with your assessment?"

LeFevre was unfazed. "Even in a Communist-leaning Commonwealth like this, taking up serpents is only a Class 4 misdemeanor. I'll pay the two hundred dollars."

Sonny and Bert were looking back and forth between them like they were watching a ping-pong match.

Maddie pressed on. "Do you think the 'Communist' Commonwealth of Virginia will likewise dismiss the *felonies* of reckless endangerment and the unlawful transportation of dangerous wildlife?" She smiled at him. "Or did you remember to pack your permits?"

LeFevre seemed to waver. "There *was* no reckless endangerment until that young Sodomite fell into the speakers and knocked this box over." He held out his empty carrier. "Now I've lost two of my best rattlers."

Maddie had had enough. "Mr. LeFevre, I strongly suggest that you collect your umbrage and your righteous indignation and head for someplace more hospitable to your unique views."

He opened his mouth to reply.

"If you think you need help finding your way out of town," Maddie continued, "I'll be happy to ask Sheriff Martin to provide you with an escort."

LeFevre's face was turning purple. Then his countenance changed, and he dropped his gaze to the floor.

Astrid had wandered over to where he stood and emptied her bladder on the turned-up toe of his tasseled loafer.

"Well." David sighed. "Like a dog that returns to his vomit, likewise a fool repeats his folly.'"

LeFevre snapped his head up and stared at him. His gaze was anything but friendly.

"Proverbs 26:11," David added. He pointed a finger at his own chest. "I might be queer as a plaid rabbit, but I'm one Sodomite who *always* went to Sunday school."

The evangelist looked like he wanted to drop-kick David—and Astrid—back into the Old Testament. He opened his mouth to speak, but stopped short at the sound of an approaching siren.

He looked at Maddie. "I hope the Holy Spirit will enter your heart and open your eyes to the truth."

She smiled at him. "I hope so, myself."

He turned around and left the room. His shoe squished across the floor as he hurried toward the exit.

"Well," David said, "looks like the good pastor had to shake more than dust from his feet this time."

Bert erupted into laughter as Maddie shook her head, and walked to the back door to brief the EMTs about Sonny's condition.

Across town at Foster's Dairy Bar, Roma Jean looked out the big plate-glass window just in time to see the county EMT wagon speed by. It was headed out of town—probably toward the hospital.

She put her spoon down. Not even a big dish of Banana Bahama Mama could make her feel better. And Charlie had even asked Mrs. Foster to add wet nuts and extra sprinkles.

Banana Bahama Mama was her favorite.

"What's the matter?" Charlie asked.

She shrugged.

"Roma Jean?"

She looked up at Charlie. Big mistake. Charlie was leaning forward, and her eyes were as blue as the iridescent chips in the Formica top of their small table. She dropped her gaze.

"I'm such a klutz."

"We've been over this. You are *not* a klutz."

"That's easy for you to say. You aren't the one who knocked over a box full of poisonous snakes in a room full of people."

"Roma Jean . . ."

"I can't go anyplace."

"Roma Jean . . ."

"Last week at the 7-Eleven in Mt. Airy, I backed into the Slurpee machine when they were cleaning it out, and a big vat of Mango Melody syrup tipped over."

Charlie was trying not to laugh.

"It wasn't *funny*," Roma Jean said. "It spilled all over the battery kiosk, and the store manager yelled at me and told me to never come back."

"I'm sorry," Charlie apologized.

"They were having a big sale on triple A's, and all of the packages got soaked."

Charlie nodded.

"They were mostly twenty-four packs, too."

Charlie looked out the window.

"He was really mad. He said that nobody would buy batteries

with big red stains all over the wrappers. He said it looked like a sidewalk sale at a crime scene."

Charlie bit her lower lip.

"I really loved those Mango Slurpees, too."

"It's okay." Charlie reached across the table and laid a hand on top of Roma Jean's. "I'll take you to the 7-Eleven in Blacksburg."

Roma Jean stared at the tabletop. She had never noticed before how small Charlie's hands were. Small, and really warm.

"I don't know if my mama will let me go that far away."

"It's not much further away than Radford," Charlie said. "But we could always go to the one there."

Roma Jean looked at her. "You'd come see me in Radford?"

Charlie nodded. "If you wanted me to, I would."

Roma Jean dropped her gaze to the table again. She needed a safer topic, and fast. She waved a hand in frustration. "Why do they mess around with snakes at that church, anyway?"

"*They* don't. That evangelist was a stranger, and nobody knew he took up serpents."

"Well, you should go to the Methodist church instead. The only thing they ever take up there is the collection."

Charlie laughed. "I don't normally go to church there, Roma Jean. I only went this time because it meant a lot to my grandma."

Roma Jean picked up her spoon and jabbed at some of the multicolored sprinkles that trailed across the top of her sundae. "Well, she probably regrets that wish now."

"I doubt it. Grandma is pretty good at seeing past the unimportant stuff."

"You call *that* unimportant?"

"A crazy man with a box of snakes?" Charlie shrugged. "Yeah."

"But Sonny Nicks got bit."

"I know, but Sonny said it was probably a dry bite, and he'd be likely to know."

Roma Jean shook her head. "That whole thing just creeps me out."

"Me, too. But you gotta admit that seeing old Azalea pull that gun outta her bag was worth the whole experience."

Roma Jean rolled her eyes. "That's nothing. You should see her at the VFW turkey shoot. She wins nearly every year. Aunt Evelyn is always complaining because there are so many turkeys in the freezer she can't even fit a bag of okra in there."

"Couldn't they cook them up in the café?"

"Are you kidding? Nadine said she might as well stuff and bake the plastic bags they come in."

"Then why don't they give 'em away?"

"You mean like donate them someplace?" Roma Jean suggested. Charlie nodded.

"You don't know Gramma Azalea. She's persuaded that the federal government is gonna blockade Jericho. And that they'll need the food stores. She hoards kerosene, too, but Cletus won't let her keep that in the apartment."

Charlie laughed. "I don't suppose it would do any good to tell her that it would be kinda hard to blockade a land-locked town?"

"Yeah. You try to explain that to her."

"She *is* quite a character," Charlie agreed.

"She's nuts. Daddy says she's one brick shy of a load." Roma Jean fell quiet for a moment. "Sometimes I worry that I'm like her."

"What do you mean? Like her how?"

Roma Jean shrugged. "You know, not quite right."

"Oh, come on, Roma Jean." Charlie touched her hand again. "There's nothing wrong with you."

"Yes, there is." Roma Jean shifted on her seat, but she didn't pull her hand away. "I don't fit in. I never have."

Charlie just looked at her without speaking.

"I'm not like other girls," Roma Jean added. "And I won't ever be."

When Charlie didn't reply right away, Roma Jean knew she'd probably said too much. But she was tired of always feeling so anxious around Charlie, and she thought it was better just to get this over with. Charlie would realize that she was a freak, and that would be that. She wouldn't have to work so hard to avoid her any more, and maybe she'd be able to quit tripping over things, too.

"Roma Jean?" Charlie leaned across the table again.

Roma Jean just stared into her bowl. It was starting to look like Bahama Mama soup.

"Roma Jean. Please look at me."

Roma Jean looked up. Charlie had a strange little smile on her face. "I don't exactly fit in, either, but I *am* like a lot of other girls."

"What do you mean?"

"I mean that there are a lot of girls like us."

Roma Jean was confused. "Like us?"

Charlie nodded. "Girls who like girls."

Roma Jean could feel herself starting to panic. She pulled her hand away from Charlie's. "I can't talk about this."

"Why not?"

"Because it's—I just *can't*." She tucked her hands beneath her legs to keep them out of harm's way.

"Roma Jean, believe me—not talking about it doesn't make it not real. I know. I tried that for a lot of years."

Roma Jean could feel her heart pounding. *Why was Charlie doing this? Why did they have to talk about it?*

"What are you so afraid of?"

Roma Jean looked at her. Charlie was so pretty. She had smiling eyes, but right now they looked serious. *Everything*, she wanted to say to her. *I'm afraid of everything.* Instead, she just shrugged.

Charlie sighed. "Whenever you think you're ready, we can talk about this, okay?"

The little bell over the street door jingled. They both looked up in surprise and reflexively drew apart like they'd been caught red-handed at . . . something. Roma Jean stared in horror at who had just walked into the tiny ice cream shop.

It was Dr. Stevenson.

This was shaping up to be like a messed-up version of that George Clooney movie her mama loved so much . . . the one about that guy on the fishing boat.

She closed her eyes in mortification. *Somebody up there hates me.*

◊ ◊ ◊

Maddie noticed Charlie and Roma Jean right away.

She had decided to pop into Foster's on her way home for a quick bite of lunch since they served yogurt (which would satisfy Syd)—*and* she could get it with a topping of granola and sweet fruit (which would satisfy *her*). It was a win-win scenario. When it came to her diet, and what Syd chose to define as her "preteen palate," compromises like this one were few and far between.

Now that Sonny was safely en route to the hospital in Wytheville, she felt like she could allow herself this wicked indulgence. Besides, Foster's was next door to the recently reopened Food Bonanza, and Syd had asked Maddie to stop in and pick up some anchovy paste and sesame oil.

It was lucky for all of them that Food Bonanza didn't carry . . . what was that Korean dish David was spelling?

Mrs. Foster slapped a crimped paper boat that contained two hot dogs loaded with chili and slaw down onto the countertop. Maddie gazed at it wistfully. She thought about her bag of anchovy paste and wondered what manner of epicurean feast they'd have to try and trick Henry into eating tonight. It would be good for all of them when Syd's cast came off next week, and she could resume a more normal activity level. Maybe once she was less housebound she'd make fewer forays into the more exotic recesses of the cookbook shelf.

When her yogurt parfait was ready, Maddie picked it up and walked toward the table where Roma Jean sat with Charlie Davis. She didn't want to intrude, but she was anxious to make certain that both had recovered from their adventure at the revival service. She was also interested to hear their version of how events had unfolded once the rattlesnakes got loose.

And, although it annoyed her to admit it, her curiosity about the pair had been piqued by Sonny Nicks' covert suggestion that there was something more than friendship brewing between them.

They were both nicely dressed, and Maddie was surprised to see how much smaller Charlie looked in street clothes. Charlie was a local girl and a recent graduate of the Criminal Justice Training Academy in Bristol. She had come home to do her field training and, in Maddie's opinion, was one of the best recruits Byron had.

Charlie stood up when Maddie approached their table. "Hello, Dr. Stevenson." She started to extend her hand but noticed that both of Maddie's were full. She dropped her hand and tapped her fingers against the side of her trouser leg.

"Hello, Charlie," Maddie replied. "And hello, Roma Jean." She looked down at Roma Jean and her bowl of melted ice cream. "Is there something wrong with your sundae?"

Roma Jean shook her head. "No, ma'am. I'm just not very hungry."

"I don't imagine you are." Maddie smiled at her. "By accounts, it sounds like you two had a quite an ordeal."

"Not as bad as Sonny Nicks," Roma Jean said.

"That wasn't her fault," Charlie added. She looked at Roma Jean. "It was an accident. Nobody intended for those snakes to get loose."

"Sonny Nicks is an experienced animal trapper, and he's going to be just fine." Maddie set her parfait down on the tabletop. "But about that. Would you mind telling me just exactly what *did* happen out there? I didn't quite get the full story."

Charlie glanced nervously at Roma Jean, who dropped her eyes and stared at something floating in her dish. "Would you like to sit down with us?" she asked Maddie. She pushed out their extra chair.

"Sure, but only for a minute or two. I've got a hot dinner date with some kind of Korean dish I can't even pronounce."

Charlie nodded and reclaimed her seat. "At least you can eat your ice cream before it looks like Roma Jean's."

Maddie smiled as she sat down. "It's yogurt, and, for the record, it's the fat- and sugar-free variety and does *not* contain toppings of *any* kind." She looked back and forth between them.

"I want to make certain you're both clear about that so you can tell the same story if you're interrogated separately by Syd."

Roma Jean actually smiled at that. "Henry said she won't let you eat sweet stuff."

Maddie rolled her eyes. "Henry should have his own talk show."

"He kind of does."

"What do you mean?" Maddie ate a big spoonful of the parfait. It was delicious. Mrs. Foster made the granola herself, and it had big chunks of almond in it.

Roma Jean looked embarrassed, like she was afraid she'd said too much. She shrugged. "He likes to pretend he's Dr. Oz."

"Dr. *Oz?*"

Roma Jean nodded. "He likes to interview B4."

"Right." Maddie laughed. "It's widely known that Virginia *has* been struggling with a pandemic of bovine obesity."

"Well, she could always get a job, modeling for Chick-fil-A," Charlie said.

"That's true," Maddie said. "But until the protests die down, we'd have to hire a security detail to escort her to and from work."

Maddie tried not to smile when Charlie and Roma Jean looked at each other, then quickly averted their gazes.

"Is Sonny really going to be okay?" Charlie asked. "We were worried about him."

Maddie nodded. "I'm pretty certain that he won't develop any complications other than the bruising and swelling at the site of the bite, but he's going to spend the next eight to ten hours in the hospital as a precaution. He was very lucky."

"I'll say," Charlie added. "I've never seen anyone dare to stomp a rattler like that."

Roma Jean fidgeted in her seat. Maddie could tell that the conversation was making her uncomfortable. "I never should have gone there," she muttered.

Maddie took advantage of the opening. "Why *were* you there, Roma Jean?"

"I invited her. It's my grandma's church." Charlie rubbed her forehead. "Mrs. Black found that preacher. Nobody else knew who he was before today."

"Nelda Ray Black?" Maddie asked.

Charlie nodded. "He's supposed to be some relative of hers from Tennessee." She shook her head. "They're supposed to have services all week, but I don't think they will after what happened today."

"At least he doesn't have any more snakes," Roma Jean added.

"Well," Charlie poked her straw into what was left of her milkshake, "not unless he packed a few spares."

"Spares?" Maddie didn't like the sound of that.

"Yes, ma'am. Gramma said he was on a revival circuit—visiting churches all across the state."

Great. "Do you know where he was staying?"

Charlie shook her head. "He travels in one of those big motor coaches. It could be parked just about anyplace."

The bell over the front door jingled again. They all looked toward it. Byron Martin stood there, scanning the interior. He did not appear to be interested in ice cream. Maddie had wondered how long it would take the news to reach him. Not long, apparently.

Charlie sighed when Byron saw them and nodded at her. Then she stood up. "He wants to talk with me." She looked down at Roma Jean. "I'm sorry about this. I hope it won't take too long."

"It's okay," Roma Jean said. Maddie thought she sounded resigned. "I need to be getting home, anyway. I have to work tonight."

Charlie looked like she wanted to say something else, but Byron cleared his throat. She just took a deep breath and turned around to go and join him.

Maddie watched Roma Jean watch Charlie as she walked away.

"You know, Roma Jean," she said. "If you ever want to talk about anything . . ." She hesitated. She wanted to say, *you can always call Syd.* It wasn't her style to blunder into somebody else's business like this, but she already had one foot in the water, and now Roma Jean was looking at her with an alarmed expression.

"I mean about the incident today," she added. Roma Jean seemed to relax. "What *were* you doing out there?"

Roma Jean shrugged. "Charlie asked if I wanted to go with her to church."

Maddie raised an eyebrow.

"It wasn't like *that*," Roma Jean explained. "Her grandma goes there, and is always bugging her to come to services. She only went because of that."

"You mean to keep peace in the family?"

"I guess so." Roma Jean looked at Maddie. "She didn't know anything about those snakes, Dr. Stevenson. I promise."

Maddie nodded.

"Nobody knew about them until I tripped and knocked their box over. That's how they got loose."

"Did you see Mrs. Black?" Maddie asked.

Roma Jean nodded. "She was sitting right up front with the Lear twins."

"Did she seem surprised or upset when the snakes got loose?"

Roma Jean thought about that for a moment. "No, ma'am. She was pretty mad at Gramma Azalea for shooting one of them."

Maddie shook her head. "We're just lucky that no one got caught in the crossfire."

"Oh, you don't need to worry about that, Dr. Stevenson. Gramma never misses. Daddy says she could shoot a tick off a sleeping hound dog without waking it up."

"Jericho's own Little Sure Shot."

"What?" Roma Jean looked confused.

Maddie smiled at her. "Never mind." She finished her yogurt. "Do you need a ride home?"

"No, ma'am. I have Uncle Cletus's car."

"Well, I'd better be on my way, or Syd will have a posse out looking for me." She stood up. "Are you sure you're okay?"

Roma Jean glanced toward the door where Charlie was still deep in conversation with the sheriff. She looked back at Maddie. Her brown eyes looked almost amber today—*amber and terrified,* Maddie thought.

"I'm okay," she said in a small voice.

Maddie cursed herself for being so lousy at this sensitive chat stuff. She needed Syd.

"You know you can always talk to us . . . to Syd and me," she added. "To either of us—about anything."

Roma Jean nodded.

"You're only eighteen. You don't have to figure everything out all at once."

Roma Jean opened her mouth to say something. Maddie's cell phone started to ring. Maddie pulled it out of her pocket and glanced at the readout.

It was a text from Syd.

Where did you go for anchovy paste—the Black Sea?

She rolled her eyes and stuck it back into her pocket.

"I'm sorry. Syd's wondering where I am."

Roma Jean looked embarrassed. "I have to get going, too."

"You aren't going to wait on Charlie?" Maddie asked.

Roma Jean shook her head. "It looks like she's going to be a while, and I can't be late for work again."

Maddie gave her a quick pat on the shoulder. "All right. But remember what I said, okay?"

Roma Jean nodded and lowered her gaze.

"See you around, kiddo." Maddie turned away and started walking toward the entrance, where Charlie and Byron were still deep in conversation. Charlie was standing with her hands spread out, probably trying to show Byron the length of one of LeFevre's "helpers."

She nearly reached the pair when she heard a small voice behind her.

"Dr. Stevenson?"

It was Roma Jean. Maddie stopped and turned around.

"Maybe I will come out and talk with you and Syd sometime— if that's really okay?"

Roma Jean was such a pretty girl, with her shiny red hair and big brown eyes, and right now, she looked so grown up. *When did that happen?* Maddie smiled. *Maybe I don't totally suck at these sensitive chats after all.*

She couldn't wait to tell Syd.

"It's *totally* okay, Roma Jean. Anytime you want. Just stop by."

"Okay."

Byron called out to her.

Maddie sighed and closed her eyes before pulling her cell phone out of her pocket. Syd's whatever-in-the-hell-it-was would just have to wait a bit longer for its final ingredient.

Chapter 15

"I still can't believe we're doing this."

Syd was looking out the window at Lake Norman as they inched past it on their way to Charlotte. It was a warm day, and the lake was clogged with boats—probably accounting for the traffic slowdown through this pretty stretch of interstate that provided main channel views on both sides of the highway.

"Where are we, anyway?" she asked Maddie, who was busy drumming her fingers on the top of the steering wheel. They were driving Syd's Volvo. Part of their stated reason for making this trip was to shop—finally—for a new car to replace Maddie's Jeep.

"We're in Davidson," Maddie said. "The traffic always slows down through here."

Syd looked at her. "It does?"

Maddie sighed. "When the weather is nice, like today, there will invariably be a lot of boat traffic—and that means there'll be a pretty good chance that someone will be sunbathing near the highway . . . topless."

Syd dropped her chin to her chest. "Did you just say, *topless?*"

Maddie nodded.

"And you know this because . . ."

"Um," Maddie looked at her apologetically, "I've heard?"

"Nice try."

Maddie was smart enough to know that the better part of valor was keeping quiet.

"Oh, no you don't, kemosabe. You're not getting off the hook *that* easily."

They were at a dead stop now. Maddie threw up her hands. "How, exactly, did I get *on* the hook?"

"Beats me." Syd ran a hand through her short hair. "I happen to think you were born there."

Maddie didn't bother to disagree. "Sometimes it feels like it."

Syd leaned forward and craned her neck to try and see around the eighteen-wheeler stopped in front of them.

"Enjoying the view?" Maddie asked.

Syd sat back against her seat. "Shut up."

Maddie chuckled.

"I suppose *this* is why you're always so willing to make the supply runs to Charlotte?"

"Yes." Maddie nodded. "Precisely. It's widely known that topless sunbathers are out in droves during the winter solstice."

Syd gave her a withering look. "You don't *only* make supply runs in December."

"Now why ever would I choose to satisfy my prurient curiosity by driving all the way to Davidson when all I have to do is stay at home and watch *Manhandle* on any of David's thirty-two televisions?"

Syd thought about that. "Good point."

"I knew you'd listen to reason."

Syd laughed.

"Is this traffic ever going to start moving again?"

"Oh, sure," Maddie said. "It should loosen up once we get past this bottleneck."

"I don't understand why there are so many of those big auto trailers on the road."

Maddie shrugged. "Maybe it's a race weekend."

"Well they look like *piñatas* on wheels."

"Don't worry. They're probably all headed for Concord. They should peel off soon."

"I hope so." Syd looked at her watch. "I want to have time to relax and have a cocktail before we have to change and head out for the Blumenthal Center."

Celine was treating them both to a romantic, overnight getaway—complete with a room at the swanky, uptown Dunhill Hotel, and tickets to *Carmen* with Denyce Graves. She told them they needed to take advantage of having her on hand as a willing sitter for Henry. They had demurred at first, but Celine insisted, sealing the deal by saying she'd invited Art to come by and spend the evening getting to know Henry. It was hard to argue with that.

They had something else to celebrate, too. Maddie had removed Syd's cast earlier in the week, and the x-ray showed *no* signs of fracture. Syd was now in a walking boot, and, although she claimed it was hard to accessorize, she was beyond thrilled to consign the crutches to a hook on the barn wall. Of course, Maddie had been quick to point out that they could donate them to the Salvation Army. Syd agreed at once, and asked if the Salvation Army would likewise want to inherit any of the fourteen broken vacuum cleaners that now were clogging the only available access route to her car.

Maddie passed on that suggestion, so the crutches moved on, but the vacuum cleaners were still in residence. Maddie's progress on those was about as slow and deliberate as her progress through this infernal traffic jam.

Syd stared out her window again. Maddie was right: boats on the lake in this area were pretty much wall-to-wall. Then she thought she saw something on the bow of a big cigarette boat.

No way.

She looked more closely. *Well whattaya know.*

"Hooters!" she cried out.

Maddie glanced at her. "You can't possibly be hungry. We just had lunch ninety minutes ago."

"No." Syd pointed furiously at the water. "*Hooters*! Right there."

Maddie sighed. "I know you say they've got the best chicken wings, but, really, honey, we'll be in Charlotte within the hour, and we can get an appetizer with our cocktails."

"No. Really. *Hooters*! Right *there*!" Syd sputtered.

"Oh, great," Maddie said with excitement. "We're finally moving." She gunned the engine, and the Volvo surged forward.

"No! Slow down . . . you gotta see this. They're huge!"

"I know they are, honey. I heard those franchises really made a comeback in this part of the state—must be because of Brett Bodine."

"*Brett Bodine?*" Syd looked at her. "What the hell are you talking about?"

"NASCAR and Hooters." Maddie passed a long row of tractor-trailers, and the lake was no longer visible on Syd's side of the car. "Wasn't he their driver? I think he actually lives around here some-place."

Syd shook her head in amazement. "And people really trust you with their lives?"

Maddie gave her a perplexed look. "What?"

"Never mind." Syd leaned back against the seat and closed her eyes. "Just be gorgeous and drive."

Lu was pulling another double shift. Normally she didn't mind—the extra money was great, and she was saving up to add a War-Header exhaust package to her Softail Fat Boy.

Lu was a runner for the concierge. Her job was to get the guests whatever they wanted: show tickets, a take-out order of pad thai, a pack of Chiclets, or, occasionally, providing trans-portation arrangements for "professional" companions. Gigs like this one were great because the guests generally tipped *very* well, and The Dunhill was the best hotel in Charlotte.

At least, that's what The Dunhill told all the other hotels in Charlotte.

But Lu had no complaints. Except when she was working back-to-back double shifts.

She didn't often staff the front desk, but Denise was out sick again, and Tyrone needed help managing the crush of people scheduled to arrive ahead of the big weekend. She'd filled in here before. It wasn't really hard—she just had to be polite and kiss a lot of ass.

Tonight was no exception. It had been pretty slow so far, but most of the check-ins were expected to arrive within the next couple of hours.

She yawned and glanced at her watch. *Shit. Six more hours of this crap.*

Tyrone tapped her on the arm as he emerged from the small office behind the massive desk. "I'm ducking out for a smoke. Call me if anything comes up that you need help with, okay?"

She nodded. Before he could make his getaway, the big North Tryon Street entrance doors opened, and two women entered. The taller of the two was pulling a dark green roller bag.

Tyrone sighed and stuck his pack of cigarettes back into his jacket pocket.

Lu watched the two women make their way toward the desk. *Great day in the mornin'. Now what do we have here?*

She looked at Tyrone. The way he kept tapping his left foot indicated that he was jonesing for a smoke.

"Hey, buddy," she said. "I got this. Go on and take your break."

He gave her a grateful look. "You sure?"

She glanced back at the pair headed their way. *Oh, yeah . . . come to mama, girls.*

"Absolutely," she said. "Go have your smoke." He smiled and ducked out, heading for the service entrance. "Take your time!" she called after him.

She straightened her tie. *Holy shit, these two are fucking hot.*

The dark-haired woman smiled as she approached. She had unbelievable blue eyes. They glowed like Xenons on a dark stretch of highway.

"Hello," Lu said in her most professional voice. "Welcome to The Dunhill."

"Hi there," Blue Eyes said. *Christ, she had to be at least six feet tall.* "My name is Stevenson. We have a reservation for this evening."

"Of course. Let me pull that right up for you." Lu typed her name into the computer. "First name?"

"Madeleine."

Bingo. "Dr. Stevenson?"

Blue Eyes nodded.

"I have you right here. One night. Two queens. Nonsmoking."

The two women exchanged glances.

"Um." Tall Dr. Blue Eyes unfolded a piece of paper. "Our reservation was for one *king*."

You don't say? Lu had to fight not to wink at the pair. "I'm so sorry. Let me see if I can correct that for you." She scrolled through the list of available rooms. There weren't many. She looked up at the pair. "I'm very sorry, Doctor, but I'm afraid the only thing we have available is the double queen. But I'm sure that you and Miss—" She looked at the shorter, blonde woman, who was no slouch in the looks department either.

"Murphy," the companion chimed in. She was pretty sure the blonde already had her number. There was something about the way she was eyeing her. She obviously wasn't clueless like her partner, Tall Betty.

"Right. You and Miss Murphy will be *extremely* satisfied, and for the inconvenience, we are pleased to offer you a complementary full-service breakfast at our Harvest Moon Grille."

Dr. Blue Eyes smiled again. *Damn.* "I'm sure we'll be very comfortable."

Yeah . . . I'd sure like to see how you two get "comfortable."

"Your stay with us has already been taken care of by a Dr. Heller." Lu ran two key cards through the coder and placed them into an embossed folder. She penciled their room number on a slip of paper and tucked it inside the folder before sliding both across the countertop. "Your room is on the eighth floor. The elevators are beyond the stairway behind you. Turn right when you reach the eighth floor. Is there anything else I can help you with?" She smiled at the blonde. "Anything at all?"

The shorter woman chewed the inside of her cheek. "In fact, we do need directions to the Blumenthal Center. We have tickets to—"

"The opera?" Lu interjected.

Tall Betty nodded. "That's right." She looked down at her companion. "It's *Carmen*—a real treat."

Lu nodded. "Miss Graves is a guest here, too."

That got her companion's attention. "Really?"

Lu shrugged. "All the big ones stay here." She pointed toward the Tryon Street doors. "Take a right and walk approximately one block to the intersection of Tryon and East Fifth Street. The Blumenthal is across the street on the corner."

"Thanks." Tall Betty picked up the key cards. "Tell me. Why is the city so crowded tonight? It took us forever to get through the traffic jams."

Lu was incredulous. "It's Speed Street weekend. You know . . . *Stars, Cars, and Guitars?*"

Blondie looked confused. "Speed Street?"

Lu sighed. It was clear that Blondie and Tall Betty needed more help than she had thought.

"Speed Street is an Uptown festival that kicks off the Coca-Cola 600 Race in Charlotte." Both women stared back at her with matching blank looks. "Either of you two heard of NASCAR?"

"Oh, Jesus," Blondie muttered.

"Yeah," Lu replied. "He stays here, too."

That got a smile out of her.

"They're estimating the crowds at about four hundred thousand this year," Lu added. A thought occurred to her. "You *do* have dinner reservations someplace, right?"

They looked like deer in headlights.

Lu sighed. "You might as well give up on getting a table anyplace in this town tonight." She gestured across the lobby. "Even our restaurant is booked solid every night through Sunday."

Tall Betty exhaled. "Pizza?"

"Not so much," Lu replied. "Not unless you order it now and plan on eating at midnight. Of course, you can always try and grab something from one of the street vendors near the two live music stages."

"Music?" Blondie asked.

"Oh, yeah," Lu explained. "This year's lineup is great. They have Evelyn Champagne King, Halestorm, and Loverboy on the main stage."

"Wonderful." Blondie did *not* sound like she meant it.

"Lemme guess," Lu said. "Not your cup of tea?"

"Not so much."

"Well," Lu offered. "Why don't you two go on to the opera, then stop back in here when it's over. I'll call some of my contacts and see if I can't get you in someplace for a late supper."

Tall Betty looked impressed. "That's incredibly generous of you, and certainly beyond the call of duty."

"Not for The Dunhill." Lu leaned forward and lowered her voice. "We go *all* they way for our special guests."

Tall Betty looked surprised, but Blondie didn't. She cleared her throat. "Thanks for the offer. We'll think about it." She tugged on her companion's sleeve. "Come on, Maddie. We need to get dressed, or we'll be late."

"Right. Thanks, um . . . Lu?" Tall Betty was looking at her nametag.

"That's right . . . Lu." She took a Dunhill business card and jotted her name and cell phone number down on the back. "This is my direct line. Call me if you need anything at all."

She handed the card to Tall Betty, who stood there looking it over. "Your name is Lu Ferrigno?"

Behind her, Blondie chuckled.

"Yeah, yeah," Lu said. "I know. *The Incredible Hulk*, right?" She shook her head. "Some freaky-looking white dude who does infomercials. My parents thought it was funny . . . go figure."

"Is 'Lu' short for something?" Tall Betty asked.

Lu rolled her eyes. "Lucinda."

Tall Betty smiled. "Thanks, Lu." She waved a hand as they walked off toward the elevators.

Lu watched them go. *Oh, yeah,* she thought as she picked up the phone. *I know exactly where I'm sending the two of you.*

◊ ◊ ◊

As soon as the elevator doors closed, Syd jammed a finger into Maddie's chest. "Just what in the hell was *that* about?"

Maddie looked at her with a blank expression. "What do you mean?"

"Oh, come on! Don't tell me you missed any of that."

"Any of *what*?"

Syd shook her head. "How can you be so clueless? She was totally hitting on you." She paused in her tirade. "On *both* of us, probably."

Maddie looked alarmed. "Lu?"

Syd rolled her eyes. "Yes, *Lu* . . . short for Lucinda—or, in this case, *Lucifer*."

"Don't be ridiculous, Syd. She's just a kid."

"I've got news for you, Stretch. Lu Ferrigno may be many things, but 'kid' is not among them. Did you get a load of that tattoo on her wrist?"

"She had a tattoo?"

Syd looked at her with wonder. "Did you cut doctor class the day they talked about the benefits of empirical observation?"

Maddie sighed in frustration. "Now you're just being ridiculous. What possible significance does a tattoo have?"

"It was a band of concertina!"

"So?"

"Hello? It's kind of a butch hallmark."

"Oh, good lord. You're spending too much time with David."

"What*ever*. This whole trip is turning into a comedy of errors."

"No, it isn't."

Syd looked at her with a raised eyebrow.

"Okay," Maddie agreed. "The traffic sucked."

"You think?"

"And we had no idea that we were coming down here during *Speed Stick*—or whatever in the hell it's called."

Syd grunted.

"And maybe we got stuck in a room with two beds."

Syd growled.

"And it's likely that we'll never be able to set foot in a restaurant again."

Syd huffed.

Maddie glanced at the lighted control panel next to the steel doors. This had to be the slowest elevator on the planet—they still had four floors to go. She let go of the suitcase and pulled Syd into her arms.

"And if memory serves, we've got *lots* of experience, finding ways to have fun in hotels."

Syd wrapped her arms around Maddie's back. "You're lucky you're so goddamn irresistible."

Maddie kissed her on the neck. "I know."

Syd slapped her on the arm. "Jerk."

Maddie laughed and kissed her again. "Come on, shortstop. Let's go to the opera. There's *nothing* that a hot mezzo soprano singing 'The Habanera' can't fix."

Syd sighed and released her. "From your mouth to god's ear, kemosabe."

"What do you *mean* we don't have seats?"

Maddie took Syd by the elbows and pulled her back away from the Will Call window.

"I'm sorry, ma'am, but I can't find any record of this order, and the performance is sold out." The woman behind the glass was doing her best to be polite, but it was less than ten minutes to curtain, and there were still half a dozen people in line behind them.

"We've got a *confirmation* number." Syd waved their receipt around. "Right *here*."

Maddie pulled Syd to the side. "It's okay, honey," she whispered. "Sometimes these things just happen."

The overhead lights flicked off and on.

"I really am sorry, ma'am, but that's not a confirmation number we recognize, and I've got to help the other people in line." The ticket agent looked at Maddie for support.

"Come on, Syd. We'll figure this out later." She led Syd away from the line. "I'm sure there's a reasonable explanation."

"Oh, *sure* there is," Syd exclaimed. "We should've just bought tickets to the damn *race*."

"Honey . . ."

"I'm not kidding. We get out . . . what? Once in about *ten* months? And this is how it goes? *Seriously?*"

Maddie shrugged.

"And how can you be so fucking *calm* about everything?" Syd hissed.

"Sweetie, it won't do any good for both of us to freak out. Let's just go back to the hotel and try to enjoy what's left of our evening."

Syd sighed and looked up at her. "You're right . . . I'm sorry. I guess I've just had a bit of a hair trigger lately, and this isn't helping."

"No worries, honey." Maddie led her to one of the padded benches that were salted around the marble-floored lobby of the Belk Theatre. Most of the confirmed ticket holders were already inside. Only a few stragglers were still milling around, talking on cell phones or flipping through their programs. "Let's sit down here for a second and take some weight off your foot before we head back to the hotel."

"Okay." Syd sounded totally defeated. "I'm sorry I acted like a jerk." She plopped down onto the bench. "Should I go and apologize to the ticket person?"

Maddie glanced at the Will Call window, where the agent was already dealing with her next set of problems.

"I don't think so. She seems to have moved on just fine."

"This really sucks."

Maddie agreed. "It does."

Syd looked at her. "So what now? Domino's pizza and Pay Per View?"

"Nah." Maddie pulled out her cell phone and a tiny card. "I've got a better idea."

She punched in some numbers and waited until a husky voice

answered. "Hi, Lu? This is Dr. Stevenson and Miss Murphy. There was some kind of snafu, and the theatre lost our tickets." She looked at Syd. "Yeah, it does suck. Look—were you able to get us a dinner reservation anyplace?" She listened a moment. "You were? Great. Any chance you can move it up by a couple of hours?" She nodded at Syd. "Wonderful. We'll wait right here until you call us back. Thanks so much, Lu." She hung up.

"So?" Syd asked.

"So—she's fixing it for us—and calling us a cab."

"A cab?"

"Yeah. It sounds like this place—I think she said it's some kind of Irish pub—is across town near the Panthers stadium." She pointed at Syd's walking boot. "Too far for you to walk on that."

Syd sank back against the wall. "I don't really care *where* it is as long as they serve alcohol."

Maddie's phone rang. "Hold that thought. I think salvation is at hand."

Chapter 16

"Hartigan's?" The cab driver asked. He looked them up and down, not missing any detail of their glad rags. "You sure?"

Maddie looked down at her slip of paper. "Yes . . . that's the name. Near the football stadium? I think it's some kind of pub."

"Pub?" he repeated. "*Right.* It's some kind of pub, all right." He punched in some numbers on his meter. "Hop in."

Maddie helped Syd climb into the backseat of the cab, and the driver pulled away from the curb.

Tryon Street was teeming with people. They were everyplace—crowded into doorways, standing in groups on sidewalks, and clogging the side streets. Even inside the cab, they could hear the sound of country music blasting from one of the two open-air stages set up at opposite ends of the festival's Uptown venue.

"I wonder if they can hear that inside the hall?" Maddie asked.

Syd chuckled. "It would serve them right for losing our tickets."

"Now why would you wish such a misfortune on poor Denyce Graves?"

"I don't know. Maybe it would lend an air of authenticity to her performance?"

Maddie chuckled. "Right. Because bad covers of 'Dixie Chicken' mesh so well with Bizet."

"You never know." Syd thought about it. "Maybe we can ask her about it at breakfast."

"That's my girl. Delusional as ever."

Syd looked out the window at the crowd. "What in the world is on that guy's head?"

"Which guy?" Maddie leaned toward her to take a look.

Syd pointed to a man wearing a bright blue jumpsuit and a checkerboard cape.

"Oh, that's just Lug Nut," the driver volunteered. "He's the speedway mascot."

He blew the horn at a raucous group of jaywalkers. One of them yelled something unintelligible and gave him the finger.

"Oh, this should be *great* in another few hours," Maddie said. "I'm glad we're not walking."

Syd looked shocked. "Did that man in the Dale Jr. shirt just tell the driver to suck it?"

Maddie was surprised. "Dale Jr.?"

Syd pointed out the window. "Right *there.* The big dude with the even bigger number 88 across his . . . man boobs."

Maddie was staring at her in disbelief.

"What?" Syd asked.

"I'm just amazed that you know who number 88 is."

"I teach high school in Appalachia . . . ring any bells?"

"True."

"Junior is a *pussy*," their driver volunteered.

Maddie glanced up at him with surprise, but Syd just stifled a laugh. "You're just lucky I didn't smack you earlier for those condescending comments about Brett Bodine."

"Brett Bodine?"

"Back in the traffic jam—when I was . . . *preoccupied* . . . with hooters."

Up in the front seat, the cab driver chuckled.

Maddie rolled her eyes. "Oh, come on, Syd. Charlotte is supposed to be a foodie's paradise. Why are you so obsessed with missing out on a basket of indifferent chicken wings?"

Syd smiled and patted her hand. "You're adorable, but you're one fry short of a happy meal—you know that?"

"Don't worry, ma'am," the driver chimed in. "I hear they have *great* wings at Hartigan's."

"Thanks," Maddie squinted at the I.D. card attached to his visor, "Eddie."

"Breasts, too," he muttered. Then he snorted, like he'd said something funny.

Maddie gave Syd a perplexed look, but she just shrugged. "What else is good at this pub, Eddie?"

Eddie waved a hand. "You know, I ain't never really been there." He blew his horn again and swerved around a minivan that was double-parked next to the Oscar Mayer Weinermobile. "But I know some folks like to go there for the . . . entertainment."

"Entertainment?" Syd asked. "They have live music or something?"

He looked at her in the rearview mirror. "Or something. Right."

Maddie was starting to have second thoughts about this. She gave Syd a nervous look. "Those hot dogs back there actually didn't look half bad. Maybe we should just head back to the hotel?"

"Oh, come on." Syd punched her on the arm. "Where's your sense of adventure?"

"She's right," the driver chimed in. He glanced back at Maddie. "Besides, once you get past the smell, you pretty much got it licked."

It was clear to her that Eddie was enjoying this a bit *too* much. Maddie narrowed her eyes. She might be one fry short of a set— or whatever that aphorism was—but she knew how to smell a rat.

She pulled out her cell phone to Google Hartigan's Pub, just as the driver made a sharp right turn and jolted to a stop in front of a low, industrial-looking brick building. Behind it, the imposing Bank of America Stadium filled up the horizon.

"Here you go, ladies," Eddie said. "Hartigan's."

Syd looked at a large poster taped inside the front window. "What's pudding wrestling?" she asked.

Eddie cleared his throat.

Maddie sat back against her seat. "Okay. Back to the hotel."

"No." Syd took hold of her arm. "Come on. It'll be fun, and I'm *starving*."

Maddie demurred.

Syd cranked it up. "*Pleeeeaaassseeee?*"

Maddie sighed and unhooked her seatbelt. "I know I'll live to regret this." She looked up at Eddie. "How much do we owe you?"

"Nine-fifteen," he said. "Try the sweet potato fries."

Maddie handed him a ten and a five. "I thought you said you'd never been here before."

"Maybe once or twice." He shrugged. "Their cages have poles—you don't find that much anymore."

Syd was laughing now. "Oh, god. *This* I gotta see." She grabbed Maddie by the hand. "Come on, Cinderella. This is your wake-up call."

"Howdy, ladies." The waitress slapped a couple of menus down on their table. "My name's Josette, and I come bearing about twenty offers to buy you two a round of drinks."

"Really?" Syd looked around. Half a dozen women at other tables raised glasses and winked at her. "But we only just sat down."

Josette shrugged. "This crowd ain't used to seeing such finery on gals who ain't packin'—if you get my drift."

"Oh." Syd looked down at her black dress and single strand of pearls. "I guess we are kinda overdressed for a bar."

"You think?" Josette gave a husky laugh that turned into a cough. "You created quite a stir when you walked in. Dorinda up there behind the bar swore you were with the ABC Board."

"Really?" Maddie asked.

Josette jerked a finger toward the neon exit sign near the restrooms. "You didn't notice a couple carloads of coeds bust their gussets heading for the back door?"

Maddie looked around the crowded place. Most of the patrons *were* women—extraordinarily robust-looking women, although there were a few men here and there. But the couples were decidedly homogenous. The music drifting up from the club downstairs was deafening, and completely drowned out the volume coming from the flat panel TVs mounted near the bar. Since it looked like the TVs were tuned to live coverage of the Speed Street festival, she considered that a blessing.

She looked back at Josette. "We're not with the alcohol board."

"No shit, Mulder," Josette replied. "Can I get you and Scully something to drink?"

"What are the options?" Maddie asked.

Josette took a deep breath and shifted her weight. "We have all the usual stuff. You name it, we probably have it."

"Do you have a wine list?" Maddie asked.

"Well," Josette began with what seemed like exaggerated patience, "this ain't my normal night, but the last time I saw it, it was propping up a leg on that table in the corner."

Maddie turned around to look, but Syd kicked her on the shin. "Just bring us a couple of Newcastles."

Josette nodded and walked off.

Maddie rubbed her leg. "Why the hell did you do that?"

"Look around," Syd hissed. "How many people do you see swilling wine?"

"None," Maddie agreed. "But for your information, I wasn't planning to swill it either."

"Honey," Syd said. "Just try to relax and go with the flow, here."

"The flow?"

Syd nodded. "And for tonight, the flow looks more like beer than wine."

Maddie scooted forward on her chair. "That's not *all* the flow in this joint looks like. Are you getting a load of this crowd?"

"Oh, yeah. Not exactly like one of your AMA conventions, is it?"

"Nuh uh."

Syd gaped at her. "Oh, come on, sweetie. Don't tell me you've never been in a gay bar before?"

Maddie looked offended. "Of *course* I have. I went to a gay bar in grad school."

Syd laughed out loud. "You sound like Mitt Romney saying, 'I paid taxes once.'"

Maddie glowered at her.

Josette reappeared and deposited two ice-cold bottles of Newcastle Brown Ale.

"You beauties know what you want to eat?" She pulled a small pad and a stub of pencil that was dented with teeth marks from the front pocket of her denim shirt.

"Wings and sweet potato fries."

Syd looked at Maddie with surprise.

"Well?" Maddie shrugged. "When in Rome."

"Regular, hot, or nuclear?" Josette asked.

Maddie looked at Syd, then back at Josette. "How many are in an order?"

"Ten."

"Okay. One order of each."

"Got it." Josette walked off.

"Extra ranch dressing!" Maddie called after her.

"Are you nuts?" Syd asked.

"Nope." Maddie took a big swig of her beer. "*You're* the one who's been jonesing for wings all day."

Syd shook her head. "You're so clueless."

"Why do you keep saying that?"

"Never mind." Syd looked around the bar. "After we eat, do you wanna go downstairs and check out the action?"

Maddie looked at her like she had two heads. "About as much as I'd like to have a root canal."

"Come on. I keep watching the people coming and going from down there. Admit it. It would be a blast."

"No way."

"Why not?"

Maddie let out a long, slow breath. The sound of loud, raucous laughter near the bar distracted her. "There." She gestured toward the sound. "Check *that* out."

"What?" Syd turned in her seat to follow Maddie's gaze. A couple of drag queens were standing near the bar, getting glasses of wine. One of them was wearing a skin-tight pink leotard and a black satin bustier. Her platinum blonde, Perma-Tease wig was large enough to have its own zip code. The hand that held her wineglass was dotted with Heliotrope, glamor-length nails.

She turned back to face Maddie. "The drag queen?"

Maddie nodded.

Syd sighed and picked up her Newcastle. "Please don't disappoint me by suggesting that you're offended by drag queens."

"Of *course* not," Maddie said in a huff. "I'm offended that she thinks purple nail polish goes with those tights."

Syd choked on her beer and sent brown liquid flying across the table. Maddie leapt to her feet to avoid the spray, and knocked her chair over. Patrons at nearby tables laughed, and some even applauded. The drag queen at the bar looked at them and promptly dropped her wineglass when she saw Maddie.

"Jesus Christ, Mandy!" her companion yelled. "You got that cheap chardonnay all over my fucking Jimmy Choo's."

A chorus of cheers sounded all around.

Time stood still as Maddie stared back at the queen.

Oh. Good. God. This is so *not happening.*

Syd sat dabbing at her clothes with her napkin. She looked up at Maddie. "What on earth is the matter with you? You look like you're going to pass out."

Josette appeared at their table to help Maddie set up her chair. "Everything okay over here?" She handed Syd a damp cloth. "You need another beer, honey?"

"No. Thanks, Josette. I'm fine now."

Maddie dropped down onto her chair like a sack of bricks. "I need something stronger," she said to Josette.

"Sure thing, hon." She laid a palm against Maddie's forehead. "You okay? You don't look so hot."

"I'll be fine," Maddie said in a flat voice. "I just need a drink."

"Anything in particular?"

Maddie looked up at her. "Pick the one thing you'd *never*

serve—even to the person you loathe most in the world, and bring me a *double*."

"You got it, baby." Josette winked at her and walked off.

Syd leaned across the table. "What the hell is the matter with you?"

Maddie gave her a hopeless look. "Oh, god . . . That drag queen?"

Syd nodded.

"It's Tom Greene."

"*What?*" Syd jerked around in her chair.

"Stop it!" Maddie reached across the table and grabbed her by the arm. "Don't turn around . . . *he'll see you.*"

Syd pulled her arm free. "It's a little late for that, don't you think?" She looked back at the bar area. "She's gone."

"You mean *he's* gone—and, good."

"Are you *sure* it was Tom? I mean . . . come on . . . What are the odds?"

Maddie raised a shaky hand to her forehead. "I'd say about a zillion to one. But, yes, I'm sure. He recognized me, too."

"Oh, my *fucking* god."

"Exactly. We need to get out of here."

"Wait a minute. Why do *we* need to get out of here?"

"Are you kidding me?"

"No," Syd said, more calmly. "I'm *not* kidding. Think about it."

"Think about *what?*"

Syd rolled her eyes. "Honey . . . there's about a thousand ways you can leverage this little revelation."

Maddie sat back and slowly shook her head. "Do I *know* you? What are you suggesting? *Blackmail?*"

Syd nodded with enthusiasm.

"Absolutely *not.*"

"Maddie—"

"Are you *crazy?* Or do you suddenly have an irrational hankering for the oatmeal they serve at Red Onion State Prison?"

Josette reappeared with Maddie's drink. It was an eerie, lime-green color. It had a plastic swizzle stick in the shape of a small Tasmanian devil sticking out of it.

"Don't say I didn't warn you," she said as she set it down in front of Maddie.

Syd laid a hand on the server's arm. "Can I ask you a question, Josette?"

"Sure, hon. Shoot."

"That drag queen who dropped the glass of wine . . . Do you know her?"

"That's Amanda Playwith." Josette rolled her eyes. "I've seen her here a few times, but you girls gotta understand—this ain't my normal night. The drag shows are usually on Saturdays."

"Drag shows?" Maddie asked.

Josette nodded. "They had to switch nights this week because the pudding pool sprung a leak when one of the girls forgot to take off her butch collar." She glanced at her watch. "Your food will be up in just another minute or two. You should be done in plenty of time to catch the show, if you want to hang around."

"Thanks, Josette." Syd smiled at her.

Maddie waited until Josette walked off, then turned back to Syd. "*Amanda Playwith?*"

Syd chuckled. "You have to give him points for originality."

"I feel like I should be looking around for giant seed pods."

"Oh, gimme a break. How often does the universe drop something like this into your lap?"

"Thankfully, not very often." Maddie pulled out her cell phone.

"What are you doing?"

"Calling us a cab. We'll get Josette to pack our food up so we can take it with us."

"No way, kemosabe." Syd snapped the phone out of Maddie's hand. "I refuse to look this gift horse in the mouth." She pushed back her chair and stood up.

"What the hell are you doing?" Maddie felt a surge of anxiety. She'd seen this look in Syd's eyes before, and it was never good news.

"Finish your drink. I'll be back in a flash . . . no pun intended." Syd turned on her heel and took off across the restaurant.

"Syd, *no*," Maddie hissed after her. "Syd!"

Maddie sank back against her seat and watched Syd disappear down the stairs that led to the club below the restaurant.

"Fuck," she said aloud.

The club area beneath the restaurant was a blaze of Technicolor tundra. Syd was certain that the hammering noise from the sub-woofer would jar her fillings loose. She thought she recognized the song—a dance remix of an old Gloria Gaynor standard. The dark and the blinding flashes from strobe lights made it hard for her to get her bearings, so she decided to stake out a spot and wait for her eyes to adapt to the light.

There were men in drag all over the place. The last time Syd had seen so many fantastic heads of hair was on her ninth birthday, when her mother walked her past a flooded wig shop on Allegheny Avenue. The night before, they'd had a monstrous storm that dropped more than five inches of rain in two hours, and most of Baltimore County was under water. But Syd had a violin recital at Immaculate Conception School, and her mother was determined to get her there. Syd remembered walking down that long block lined with wigs, resting on their faceless, Styrofoam heads. They were stacked up on every flat surface, drying in the morning sun. For an impressionable nine-year-old, there was something truly creepy about the spectacle. In her mind, it coalesced with an episode of *Outer Limits* that her brother had persuaded her to watch one Friday night when their parents weren't at home. She'd had nightmares for weeks, and she always regarded "the wig incident" as one of her earliest Fellini moments.

She felt some of those same emotions pushing their way to the surface as she looked around the interior of the nightclub. But *these* wigs weren't attached to disembodied heads with no faces. They were parts of ensembles that vibrated with color and life. They were like sensational exclamation points at the ends of run-on fashion sentences.

Her eyes were adjusting to the light. It was easier now to make out details of the various examples of couture on display. Finally, she saw Tom—*Amanda*—lurking next to a short, portly-looking guy wearing black leather biker garb that was accented with a lot of chains. Someone bumped into her.

"Sorry," a gravelly voice said.

Syd looked up at . . . *her.* "It's okay," she said. Then she had an epiphany. She touched the man—who was a dead ringer for Tammy Faye Bakker—on the arm. "Excuse me for asking, but do you happen to know that guy over there with Amanda Playwith?" Tammy Faye looked across the room and squinted. No small feat with that much mascara.

"Oh, sure," she said. "That's Buster. They usually come together."

"Buster?" Syd asked.

"Buster Cherry. Mandy's better half."

"*Better half?*" Syd was dumbfounded. She looked at Buster more closely. *Oh, Jesus, Mary, and Winston Churchill on a cracker— that's Muriel Greene.*

"Thanks." She looked at her companion again. "I'm sorry. I don't know your name."

"Crystal Titz," she said, presenting a meaty hand. Syd gave it a warm squeeze. Crystal smelled like she had been dipped in a vat of Shalimar. "Tell me something, Sandra Dee." She looked Syd up and down. "What's a tasty morsel like you doing down here all by your lonesome? I'd think you'd find the upstairs crowd more to your liking tonight. Unless," she added with a nod toward Tom and Muriel, "you're looking to take a walk on the wild side?"

"Oh . . . no. Really. I'm not here alone," Syd explained. "My girlfriend is upstairs. I just saw Amanda there, and thought I recognized her from someplace else."

"You want me to introduce you?" Crystal offered.

"No . . . that's okay. I don't think Amanda would be very happy to see me, and I don't want to make a scene or ruin her . . . *their* . . . evening. It was just such a shock to see her so . . . dressed up."

"Right. I get it." Crystal waved a bejeweled hand. "Okay doll face. Enjoy the freak show." She started to walk off, but Syd stopped her.

"Can I ask you something?" she said.

"Sure, doll." Crystal hovered there, towering over her on three-inch heels.

"Do I *really* look like Sandra Dee?"

"Honey." Crystal rolled her eyes. "Seriously?" She patted Syd on the shoulder. "All you're missing is a beach ball, a crooner, and a bottle of pills."

Syd sighed. "Thanks a lot."

"Hang on a minute, doll face. In this crowd, I can't give you a higher compliment than that."

Syd smiled at her. "I guess that's something."

"Trust me." Crystal straightened Syd's strand of pearls. "Your girlfriend is one lucky prom queen."

"I hope so." Syd shook her head. "I don't think she's very happy with me at the moment."

"Why not?"

Syd held up Maddie's cell phone. "I came down here to sneak a photo of Amanda, but now it doesn't feel like the right thing to do."

Crystal looked down at the cell phone, then back at Syd.

"Well," she said, taking the phone out of her hand, "it's like Sister Mary Ignatius always taught us—sins of *o*-mission are only half as bad as sins of *co*-mission"

Before Syd could reply, Crystal turned to Tom and Muriel and snapped off half a dozen frames. With the ambient light show going on all around them, no one even noticed the camera flashes. When she finished, she handed the phone back to Syd.

"Tell your girlfriend that these are compliments of Crystal Titz—a.k.a. Larry Kozlowski."

Syd was dumfounded, but Crystal was now watching something going on over her shoulder.

"Don't look now, doll face," she whispered. "Here comes Katharine Hepburn."

Syd turned around, expecting to see another drag queen, but instead saw Maddie threading her way through the crowd toward them. "No." She turned back to face Crystal. "That's my . . ." But she was alone.

Crystal had disappeared into the crowd.

Maddie had now reached her side.

"Come on, honey," she urged. "Let's get out of here." She looked around. "I've already had my boobs pinched *three* times." She looked down at her chest. "Do these really look fake?"

Syd stared at her with wonder. "This has to be the *best* date I've ever had."

Maddie gave her a shy smile. "Really?"

"Yeah." Syd leaned forward and kissed her on the cheek. "Really."

"Good, 'cause it ain't over yet." Maddie winked at her and squeezed her hand. "You wanna go back upstairs and eat some wings?"

Syd handed Maddie her cell phone. "More than anything."

Back at the Dunhill, Syd and Maddie relaxed in a pair of oversized white hotel robes. When they finally got back from Hartigan's—a ten-minute cab ride that ended up taking more than forty-five minutes because of all the street revelers—they decided that a hot, soaking bath in the lavish, *en suite* garden tub was just what they needed. Everything was perfect, except for the fact that the bottle of wine they'd ordered an hour ago still had not materialized. Maddie was about ready to get dressed and go downstairs to retrieve it herself.

"Let me give room service another call." She picked up the phone and punched in the numbers. "Hello," she said when the call was answered. "I'm in room 814, and I'm curious about when our wine order might be here?"

There was a loud knock at the door.

"Oh, never mind," Maddie said into the phone. "I think it just arrived. Thank you." She hung up.

"Well, finally," Syd said with a yawn. "Maybe we should just tell them to forget about it."

Maddie was already halfway to the door.

"No way. After the day we've had, we deserve to have *one* thing go right."

Maddie opened the door, expecting to see a room service attendant, and was surprised to be staring into the smiling face of Lu Ferrigno.

"Hi there," Lu said. She held a tray containing a bottle of Courtney Benham Vin d'Eliza and two glasses. "Sorry for the delay on this. Things are still pretty nuts downstairs."

It was clear to Maddie that Lu wasn't missing much of her ensemble. She resisted an impulse to pull the robe tighter across her chest.

"Hello, Lu," she said. "This seems a little beyond the call of duty for you." She stepped back so Lu could enter their room.

"Oh, not at all." Lu stepped inside and waved at Syd, who was busy rearranging herself on one of the two queen-sized beds. "We perform all kinds of special services for our guests here at The Dunhill."

"No doubt," Syd muttered from the bed.

Maddie shot her a dirty look.

Lu walked to a small table and deposited her tray. "I'm actually going off duty, but I volunteered to run this up here so I could check in on you two and see how the rest of your evening went. Did you have a good time at the pub?"

Maddie deliberated about how to respond. "It was certainly . . . educational."

Lu nodded with enthusiasm. "They usually have a pretty good crowd on Friday nights. Lots of out-of-towners."

Syd laughed. "You can say that again."

Maddie glared at her.

"Well?" She shrugged. "Am I wrong?"

Maddie ignored her. "Thanks for bringing this up, Lu." She looked over the items on the tray. "Is there a ticket for me to sign?"

"Oh, no, Dr. Stevenson." Lu gave her a bright smile. "This one is on the house."

Maddie was surprised. "Why?"

"We like to treat our special guests like family."

There was something about the way Lu said "family" that made Maddie uncomfortable. She glanced at Syd for help.

"Oh, don't look at me, Miss Jean Brodie," she said. "I'm just sitting here minding my own business."

Maddie rolled her eyes. She turned back toward Lu, who was busy staring at something fascinating on the front of her robe. Maddie glanced down to discover that her neckline had gaped open, revealing a tad too much real estate. She sighed and cinched it closed.

"Thanks, Lu," she said. "You've been more than helpful."

Lu gave no indication that she was eager to leave. "Would you like me to open that for you?"

"No thanks," Maddie said. "I can handle it."

"It's really no trouble."

"I appreciate the offer, but I can take care of it."

"I have my own opener right here." Lu held up a shiny black bar tool with an orange Harley-Davidson logo on it.

"Thank you. But I travel with one of my own."

Lu looked impressed. "Big wine drinkers, huh?"

"Some people seem to think so."

"Guess I sent you to the wrong kind of place, then—didn't I?"

"I wouldn't say that," Maddie said. "The wings were great."

"Hot *and* spicy," Lu agreed. "Just the way I like 'em."

Syd chuckled.

"And you can't ever eat just *one*," Lu added.

Maddie chewed the inside of her cheek. "Thanks again, Lu. But it's late, and you're off duty. We don't want to take up any more of your time."

"Oh, don't worry about me, Dr. Stevenson. I can go all night."

"I'm sure you can, Lu. But I'm older and more worn down, and right now, I just want to relax with a glass of wine and then fall into bed."

Lu glanced behind Maddie at Syd. She leaned toward Maddie and lowered her voice. "Can't say I blame you for that."

Maddie was pretty certain that she must have reacquired that French fry missing from her Happy Meal, because none of what Lu appeared to be angling for was lost on her. And her threshold for being amused by it was starting to diminish. She opened her mouth to say as much when she heard movement behind her.

Syd climbed off the bed and walked to stand beside her. She was barefoot, and her head barely reached Maddie's collarbone. The white robe she was wearing looked cavernous on her. It drooped off one shoulder in a very provocative way.

"You're a sharp young woman, Lu," Syd said. Maddie was startled when she felt Syd's fingers stroking up and down her arm. "And I'm sure you understand how much I want to be alone with this tall drink of water." Syd slapped Maddie on the butt.

Maddie jumped, startled.

Lu looked back and forth between them.

"Oh. Sure." She cleared her throat. "Yeah. I get it." She backed toward the door. "You've got my numbers. Just let me know if you need anything."

"Oh, trust me, Lu," Syd ran her hand inside the folds of Maddie's robe, "I have everything I need right *here*."

Lu backed into a suitcase stand and nearly knocked it over. She righted it and quickly reached the door.

"I hope you enjoy the rest of your stay," she said over her shoulder. She was already halfway out the door.

"I am *sure* we will," Syd replied in her sweetest voice. "Oh, and Lu?"

Lu turned back toward them.

"Let us know if anyone complains about the noise, okay?" She dropped her voice to a whisper and tipped her head toward Maddie. "She's a screamer."

Lu opened her mouth to say something, but no sound came out. She nodded at Syd with a glazed expression, retreated to the safety of the corridor, and closed the door behind her.

Maddie drew back and looked at Syd with wonder. "Are you *nuts*? What the hell was that little performance about?"

Syd looked around the room. "Do you see Lu in here?"

"Of course not."

"I rest my case."

Maddie was exasperated. "Honey . . . She now thinks that *I'm* some kind of nymph, and that you're the female equivalent of Larry Flynt."

Syd rolled her eyes. "I'd hardly go that far."

"You know what I mean."

"Why do you always have to overstate everything?"

"I won't dignify an overstated question like that with a response."

Syd stood in front of her with her hands on her hips. "Explain to me why you care so much about what a twenty-something, baby butch thinks about your sainted reputation?"

"Syd. She's just a kid."

Syd jerked a hand toward the door. "Lu? *Kid?*"

Maddie nodded.

"You really need to take two reality pills and call me in the morning."

"What's that supposed to mean?"

"Do you honestly have no clue that Little Lulu was up here to audition for a starring role in tonight's Dunhill *ménage à trois*?"

"I think she was being overly friendly, but I wouldn't say there was anything demonstrably inappropriate about her appearance here."

Syd shook her head. "Honey, you'd say that even if she had offered to shuck off her polyester pants and do a lap dance on your face."

Maddie took a deep breath. "Now you're just being ridiculous."

"*I'm* being ridiculous?" Syd pointed a finger at her own chest.

Maddie nodded. "I'd say so, yes."

"Why?"

"Because Lu wasn't wearing polyester pants. They were a cotton blend."

Syd dropped her chin to her chest. "You are *so* spending too much time with David."

"That may be true, but it's entirely due to events outside my control."

"Well, maybe you should try concentrating on events that are *within* your control."

Maddie raised an eyebrow. "Such as?"

Syd sighed. "You really make me crazy."

"Isn't that my job?"

"Nope." Syd grabbed the front of her robe and tugged her forward. "Your job is to *drive* me crazy."

Maddie gave her a crooked smile. "Isn't that the same thing?"

"Nuh uh."

"Care to explain the difference?"

Syd sighed. "You medical types are all about empirical verification."

"Well," Maddie backed her toward the bed, "results *do* need to be repeatable to have integrity."

Syd grabbed Maddie's posterior with both hands. "I think I can ensure enough redundancy to satisfy your need for a consistent outcome."

Maddie pushed her down onto the bed. "Talk is cheap."

"What a coincidence . . ." Syd shifted a hand around and manipulated some very sensitive territory. "So am I."

Maddie jerked about a foot into the air. "Holy shit!"

"Like that?" Syd asked.

Maddie gasped.

"Then you'll love *this*." Syd added some creative improvisation to her ministrations.

"You're . . . not . . . wasting . . . any . . . time . . ." Maddie panted against Syd's ear.

Syd bit down on Maddie's bare shoulder. "I think we've already wasted enough time . . . don't you?"

Maddie pushed up on her forearms to grant Syd better access. "Good *god*, baby."

Syd kissed her way up Maddie's long neck. "You're so damn beautiful."

"Too much," Maddie gasped.

Syd reached Maddie's lips. "Too much?" she whispered against them.

"Talking." Maddie gave her an incendiary kiss. "Too much *talking*."

She got no argument from Syd, who happily applied herself to another form of oral argument.

Darryl huffed his way back down the long corridor. If they ever stayed here again, he was going to ask for a room closer to the goddamn ice machine.

Not that staying here again would be very likely. Shit. This damn room on the eighth floor was costing him three hundred smackers. Three hundred fucking bucks just so they could be in the middle of Uptown for Speed Weekend.

Goddamn loan sharks. They probably tripled their rates for this weekend.

But his wife got off on how impressive it was to stay at the "best" hotel in Charlotte. He didn't really care. He just hoped that this year's race would be better than last year's. Last year after six hundred damn miles, that cooter, Junior, ran out of gas on the final fucking lap.

Asshole.

Darryl stopped to indulge in a coughing fit.

About a quarter of the ice cubes in his bucket broke free and dropped out as he stood there next to a wall-mounted fire extinguisher, hacking away. He cleared his throat and kicked the loose cubes off to the side before continuing on his way.

He needed a cigarette, but, of course, their room was on one of the candy-ass nonsmoking floors. What kind of crap was *that*—a hotel in damn Charlotte with nonsmoking rooms?

He shook his head.

So far, this trip really sucked.

"*Sweet Jesus!*" Somebody yelled. It was a woman's voice, and she sounded anything but unhappy.

Darryl stopped dead in his tracks and backed up a step. *What the hell?* The sound was coming from behind one of the big wooden doors. He looked up and down the hallway. When he was sure that no one else was in sight, he leaned closer to the door.

"Sid . . . oh, *god*, baby . . ."

Darryl chuckled. At least *somebody* was having a good time.

Another muttered "Oh, god," was followed by a loud, piercing cry. Startled, Darryl jerked back from the door and lost a few more cubes. At this rate, he'd be out of fucking ice before he got back to the room.

"*Sid!*" the woman shrieked again, then fell silent.

Darryl was impressed. *Somebody sure as hell parted the beef curtains.*

He stood there outside room 814, eavesdropping for another full minute, but things inside had quieted down. He was tempted to tap on the door and give this Sid dude a high five.

Smiling, he hitched his ice bucket up closer to his chest and continued on his way.

Maybe staying here wasn't such a bad idea after all.

Chapter 17

Celine was sitting at the big kitchen table, reviewing abstracts of bioresearch papers submitted by her graduate students. So far, most of them were pretty tired retreads of pop-culture topics. She tossed another one onto the "come and see me about this" stack. It was the third proposal dealing with an exploration of the root causes of childhood obesity.

She glanced down at the title of the next abstract in her pile: *Anesthesia Management During Pneumonectomy.*

Okay. This one might have some potential.

She was halfway through the first page when she realized that someone had entered the kitchen and was standing just behind her.

"Do you need something, sweetheart?" she asked, without turning around. She assumed it was Henry.

"Well . . . um . . ." It was David.

Celine turned in her seat to look at him. He was standing near the door to the dining room and holding several sheets of white paper.

"You're busy," he said. "I don't want to bother you."

"No. It's fine. I needed a break from this." She gestured toward her own stack of papers. "Most of these would make better sleep aids than research topics. What do you need?"

"Well . . ." David cleared his throat. "I wanted to ask if you were, maybe . . . sort of . . . *fluent*—in German?"

"German?"

He nodded.

She took off her reading glasses. "Reading it, or writing it?"

"Yes," he said.

She smiled. "I can read and write it fairly well, but my spoken accent leaves a lot to be desired."

He walked to the table and sat down on a chair beside her.

"It's like this. I've been working on this fundraising project—you know . . . for the storm recovery effort?" He ran a hand through his thick, dark hair. "And part of it involves translating some German . . . *prose.*" He sighed. "I've tried to use some of the reference books in Maddie's library, and some of the online resources that are available. You know . . . things like Google Translator? But, trust me, that one's about as useful as a diet crouton."

"Google Translator?" Celine was unfamiliar with the service.

"Oh, yeah." David exhaled and waved a hand in frustration. "I mean, if all you want is to figure out how to ask something like 'where's the bathroom?' in Farsi—it might be just the thing. But it's next to worthless for a literary endeavor like this one."

"A literary endeavor?" she asked.

"Right. A literary endeavor." He reordered the papers in his hands. "So . . . for example. What might be some German words for . . . um . . . *rooster?*"

"Rooster?"

He nodded. "May I borrow this?" He picked up one of her red pens and held it poised above his top sheet of paper.

"Well," Celine sat back against her chair, "it kind of depends on the context of the sentence. How is the word being used?"

He thought about that. "As a noun?"

"I gathered that much. What is the context of the sentence? Is the term being used literally or euphemistically?"

He looked distressed.

"David, I don't think 'rooster' has a direct equivalent in German."

He glanced down at his papers.

Celine was beginning to get an idea about where this was

going. "Why don't you just show me what you're working on, and we'll take it from there?"

He demurred. "I'm not really sure . . ."

"Oh, for heaven's sake, David." Celine snagged his top sheet of paper. "You're worse than my first-year med students."

She put on her glasses and read over the short translation.

It's hard tail thumped painfully, like Tobi knelt before it. Rolf groaned. As a Tobi, Rolf rooster pushed it into the hot damp depth of its mouth, geknebelt onto its Massivität.

She reread it several times, then blinked and looked up at David.

"Rolf rooster?" she asked, in her driest, most professorial voice.

David looked like he wanted to sink beneath the tile floor of the kitchen.

"This is what you have so far?" she asked.

David nodded.

Celine sighed and held out a hand. "Let me see the original text."

Dumbly, David handed it over.

Geschichte von Rolf und Tobi
Zwei heiße Bauerjungen erste Fahrt im Zug.

Kapital 24

Sein harter Schwanz pochte schmerzhaft, wie Tobi knealt vor ihm. Rolf stöhnte. Als Tobi schob Rolf Hahn in die heiße feuchte Tiefen seines Mundes, geknebelt er auf seiner Massivität. Als, der Zug.

"I'm not even going to *ask* where you got this," she said, after she finished reading it.

He shrugged. "It's German . . . um . . . fan fiction."

"Fan fiction?"

David nodded. "It's posted for free on the Internet. I contacted the author of this series—a guy named Wilhelm Wotan—and he gave me permission to use it. Unfortunately, Wilhelm doesn't write in English very well, so I'm on my own with the translation." He sighed. "It's supposed to be the hottest series going across the pond."

Celine looked at him over the rims of her glasses. "It's a *series?*"

David gave her an energetic nod.

She looked back down at the paper in her hands. "This is really appalling."

David's face fell. "I didn't mean to offend you . . ."

"Oh, no . . . not your *idea*. I mean *this*." She pointed at a line of text on the page. "Kapital 24?"

David shook his head.

"Chapter 24. This . . . *prose work* actually has twenty-four chapters?" She shook her head. "*That's* what I find appalling."

She held out a hand. "May I?"

David handed her the red pen.

Celine quickly worked on top of David's haphazard translation. The only sound in the room was the scratch of her pen across the paper. When she finished, she held up the page.

"It's not perfect, but I think you can at least get the gist of the story."

David reached out to take it from her, and she pulled it back and held up an index finger. "If you ever tell *anyone* that I helped you with this, I will deny it until my dying day, *and* I will cut you out of my will so fast it will make your best bow tie spin like a top."

David sat, staring at her. "I'm in your will?"

Celine rolled her eyes and handed him the paper.

The Story of Rolf and Tobi
Two hot farm boys' first ride on a train.

Chapter 24

David looked up at her with excitement.

"My, god. This is *fantastic*, Celine."

He reread it.

"Wow," he said. "This Wotan dude really *can* write. I knew this was a brilliant idea. Move over Armistead Maupin. Here come the Huns."

"I don't think I'd go quite that far," Celine began.

"No . . . you're wrong. This is Bavarian *gold*."

"David . . ."

"We're going to have to talk international distribution rights."

"David . . ."

"And film rights, too." He scratched his chin. "I wonder if Jake Gyllenhaall is looking for another crossover hit?"

"David—seriously. You're going to have to find another ghost translator. I'm heading back to L.A. next week."

His face fell. "Next week?"

She nodded.

He lowered his papers to the table and looked at her with a wounded expression. "But who will I get to help me with this project?"

Celine smiled at him. He sounded exactly the way he had when he was seven years old, and she'd had to tell him that he couldn't come over to play with Barbies because Maddie had the mumps.

"You have an excellent resource right at your fingertips."

"Who?"

Celine raised an eyebrow.

"Maddie?"

Celine nodded.

"Fer-get-it. No way. Nuh uh. Not in this *life*."

"Why not?"

"With all due respect . . . are you *nuts?* I might as well ask that snake-handling preacher." He paused to consider what he'd just said. "On the other hand . . . with his big hair and tasseled loafers, even *he* would be likelier to help me out than she would."

Celine shook her head. "David, you underestimate her."

"I don't think so. As soon as Henry entered her life, she morphed into some kind of twisted, Goody Proctor clone."

"She just wants to be a good parent."

"She's already an *exceptional* parent. Somebody just needs to tell her that she doesn't have to turn this joint into a mini-version of Jonestown to do it."

Celine gave him a sad smile. "Well, her tenure as a doting parent is probably going to be short-lived."

David looked alarmed. "What do you mean?"

"I went to see James Lawrence last week. He wants his son back."

Her words hung in the air like a dark cloud.

"Did you tell Maddie this?"

"I didn't have to," Celine said, in a quiet voice. "She already knows."

Henry stood next to the split-rail fence behind the barn, feeding plugs of wild garlic to Before. He'd collected a pretty good mound of the stinky bulbs, and had them piled up in an old, white paint bucket.

Pete came trotting over at one point to see what he was up to, but as soon as he got within a foot of Henry's stash, he turned up his nose and headed back to the porch. The late afternoon sun was hitting the front of the house now, and Pete seemed anxious to return to his favorite spot atop an old rug on the glider. He had a great view of the pond from there, and he could be quick to respond if any unwelcome critters showed up for a drink.

Maddie had explained that even when it looked like Pete was napping, he was really still on the job, watching over them all.

Henry knew that Gramma C. would be unhappy with how his

hands smelled. They were pretty stinky right now. When he rubbed his nose a minute ago, the odor was so strong it nearly made his eyes water.

Maddie had told him that it wasn't good to feed garlic or onions to Before. But when Henry asked her why, Maddie just looked out across the pasture and said that Joe Baxter probably wouldn't want it. Henry didn't understand why Mr. Baxter wouldn't want his cows to eat something they liked so much. At least, Before really seemed to enjoy it. She'd already eaten almost half the garlic bulbs in his bucket.

She liked Starlight peppermints, too. And Maddie let him keep a bag of the red-and-white-striped hard candies in an old coffee can in the barn. He thought it might be nice to give a few of those to Before after she finished her garlic.

She sure was taking her time. As she chomped away, long, hollow stalks from the plants stuck out from both sides of her mouth. She looked just like one of those old men who were always sitting around in the back booth at Aunt Bea's. Only her whiskers were stained green, instead of yellow from too much coffee and cigarettes.

Daddy smoked, too. And he had a beard now, but his was dark, so you couldn't see any stains on it. But maybe that was just because of the computer picture. Henry got to see him every week on the big screen in Maddie's office, and it was just like watching a TV show. There were always other people walking around behind him and lots of bright lights making big white spots on the screen.

He hadn't seen Daddy's new leg yet, but Daddy said it was working okay, and he was getting used to walking around with it. He said that in another week, he'd be well enough for Henry to come and see him at the hospital.

Then it wouldn't be very long until he could come home.

Henry was excited about that. There were so many things he wanted to show his daddy, and he couldn't wait for him to meet Pete and Before. Now that Daddy was out of the Army, Henry was sure that he would want to stay on the farm with Maddie and Syd, too. They could all live together here. They even had one more empty bedroom upstairs. And he knew that Daddy would love Uncle David and Uncle Michael as much as he did.

Henry liked this time of day. It was starting to stay light longer, and he could be outside for a while now after supper—as long as he had his homework done. Syd always made sure of that. And she always knew if he tried to sneak outside before it was finished. Uncle David said she had eyes in the back of her head. Henry wasn't positive about what that meant, but he knew it had something to do with how you could never get away with anything. He knew better than to try, but Uncle David seemed to think that he could get away with things if he was really careful and didn't leave tracks.

Like that time Astrid ate all of those hard-boiled eggs that Uncle Michael had sitting out for a big batch of potato salad he was going to make. Astrid had a *big* accident on the porch right after that, and Uncle David gave her a rear-end bath in the kitchen sink because it had a sprayer he could use to rinse off all the soap. He made Henry *promise* not to tell Syd, and he didn't, either. But she figured it out when she tried to use the sink later that night, and the water wouldn't drain out. She found clumps of hair and . . . other stuff . . . in the drain. He had never seen her get that mad before. But even then, she didn't yell at him.

But Uncle David never tried to wash Astrid in the kitchen sink again, either.

Before was down to the last few clumps of garlic in his bucket. Henry was about to go to the barn for the can of peppermint candies when he heard the kitchen door open and close. He looked around the corner of the building and saw Uncle David headed his way. Henry guessed that meant that Uncle David had finished his own homework.

All day, Uncle David had been shut up in Maddie's study, working on some kind of special project. He said it was something he was doing to help raise money for the sad woman who owned the red Camaro before it got broken up in the tornado. Henry just hoped this project didn't mean that he would lose his own part of the famous car. He loved his steering wheel. And even though he wasn't allowed to bring it inside the house, he went out behind the barn and dusted it off every day. He couldn't wait to show it to his daddy. His daddy knew everything about fixing cars, and Henry was positive that someday his daddy would find a way to hook his steering wheel up to another car that would go really fast.

As long as Uncle David didn't try to do anything else with it first.

Henry didn't want to be selfish, but he didn't want to lose his steering wheel, either.

Even though Maddie didn't really like it all that much.

Uncle David was walking right toward him now, and he was carrying two cups of something.

"Hey, sport," he called out. "Want some lemonade?"

Gramma C. made great lemonade. It was way sweeter than Syd's, which always made his face pucker up when he drank it.

He wasn't allowed to have sodas.

Henry put his bucket down and reached out to take the cup from Uncle David.

"Did you finish your homework?" he asked.

Uncle David looked confused. Then he seemed to understand what Henry was asking about. "Yes, I did. Your gramma helped me figure some things out."

"She's really smart," Henry agreed. "Just like Maddie."

Uncle David made a face when he looked down at Henry's bucket.

"What are you feeding her?" he asked, gesturing at Before.

"Garlic plants," Henry said. "She really likes them."

Uncle David waved a hand back and forth in front of his face. "Apparently."

"Astrid likes them, too."

Uncle David looked at him with a worried expression, and Henry giggled. Then Uncle David messed up his hair. Henry ducked and tried not to spill his lemonade.

"You're teasing me, aren't you?" Uncle David asked.

Henry just laughed.

"You're just like your . . . just like *Maddie*," he said.

Henry didn't mind that one bit. He hoped he'd grow up to be tall like Maddie, too.

Uncle David looked at Before, who had finished her garlic and was now licking her lips with her fat cow tongue. She belched. It didn't smell very good.

Uncle David scrunched up his face and waved his hand back and forth some more. "Oh, *that's* nice."

"Do you wanna help me feed her some peppermints?" Henry asked.

"Believe me when I tell you this, Henry," he said. "No amount of peppermint will help her now."

"But she really likes them."

Uncle David nodded. "I know, sport. And Astrid likes hard-boiled eggs. But you don't see me feeding those to her, do you?"

Henry thought about Syd and the kitchen sink.

"No."

"Come on inside," he said. "Let's see if we can't get you . . . fumigated, before Maddie and Syd get back from Charlotte."

Henry was excited about that. Well. Not the cleaning up part. But it would be fun when they got home.

Uncle Michael was going to make pizzas, and they were all going to watch baseball. Henry loved baseball, and so did Maddie and Syd. Maddie was a Phillies fan, and Syd liked the Orioles. Uncle David said they were perfect for each other because both of their teams sucked. Syd just stuck out her tongue at him, and Maddie told him that he didn't have the character it took to back a losing team. Uncle David just sighed and said it was lucky for them that all those players looked so good in white pants.

The sound of a car horn made them both jump and turn around.

Syd's Volvo was coming up the lane. Pete saw it, too, and he jumped off the glider and started galloping toward the car. Syd smiled and waved at them from the passenger window.

Henry handed his empty lemonade cup to Uncle David and took off, running as fast as he could to try and beat Pete to the car.

Michael was getting ready to put the first of their two pizzas into the oven.

Tonight, he'd made one with sundried tomatoes, garlic, and vegetarian sausage, and another with fresh basil, goat cheese, and crispy prosciutto. Fortunately for all of them, Henry wasn't fussy when it came to pizza—if it was baked with enough sauce and cheese, he'd eat just about any kind of topping.

Syd, Maddie, Henry, and Celine were all in the front parlor, watching the Yankees get their butts smacked by the Orioles.

David wandered back to the kitchen to get another glass of wine. He told Michael that the game was an abomination, and it was too painful for him to keep watching.

"I didn't know you were such a Yankees fan," Michael said.

David shot him a withering gaze.

"I hate baseball with a passion, and you know that."

"Then what's so painful to watch?" Michael slid both pizzas into the wall oven and set the timer.

David gave a dramatic sigh. "They're playing in Baltimore, so Jeter is wearing his *gray* uniform, which does nothing to showcase his . . . *attributes*."

Michael shook his head. "However will you bear the disappointment?"

"Beats me. He really needs to take that road uni up a bit in the crotch." David held up the bottle of Meandro. "This stuff is pretty tasty. How many more bottles of it do we have?"

"You'll have to ask Maddie. She brought that back from Charlotte."

"*Really?*" David looked more closely at the label on the bottle of wine. "It must be a good one, then." He picked up his glass and filled it to the rim. "How many minutes until the pizza is ready?"

Michael glanced at the timer. "About twelve."

"Well . . ." David leaned against the center island. "I guess I can hang out here and keep you company then." He took a big swallow of the wine.

"I appreciate the condescension."

"Always do the least you can do."

"And while we're on that subject," Michael said. "Why did you take all those vases back to Gladys? We're just going to need to borrow them again."

Next week was the grand reopening of the Riverside Inn, and they were hosting a huge open house to celebrate. Everyone was invited. Nadine was helping Michael prepare the food, and David was in charge of planning a ceremony to commemorate the Inn's—and the town's—return to near normalcy. It had been a long haul, but now it was time to celebrate how far they all had come.

David shrugged. "I needed an excuse to go and check on her. And if we have to borrow them again, it gives me another reason to go out there. Besides," he picked up a stray bit of cheese and popped it into his mouth, "Gladys is helping me out with something special."

That couldn't be good news.

"You and *Gladys* are collaborating on something?" Michael asked.

"Yes, Doubting Thomas. Is that so hard to imagine?"

"David." Michael sighed. "A cure for cancer is hard to imagine. Oprah without a Wacoal is hard to imagine. You colluding with Gladys on *anything* is *impossible* to imagine."

David gave him the finger.

Michael rolled his eyes. "Will you go and grab that big serving tray and bring it over here so we can carry everything up to the parlor?"

David took another big swig from his wineglass and topped it off again before setting it down. "Don't touch this."

"Oh, don't worry." Michael held up both hands. "I heard your backwash all the way over here."

David turned toward the big sideboard that dominated the back wall of the kitchen and stopped dead in his tracks. "Oh my god!"

"What is it?" Michael looked up from the utensil drawer.

"You have to come over here and see this. It's just so precious."

"What is?"

David pointed toward the corner of the room, where Astrid reposed on her "kitchen" bed. This model was upholstered in tan cashmere with chocolate piping and ornamented with an embossed gold crown.

Michael walked over to take a closer look.

Astrid was asleep with her head propped up on her curled front paws, and her multiple chins spilled over the sides of her legs like a furry waterfall.

"She looks like an angel," David whispered.

"She looks like Winston Churchill after a three-day bender," Michael replied.

David frowned at him. "Where is my cell phone?" He was patting the pockets of his pants. "I want to take a picture of her."

Michael turned back toward the island. "How should I know?"

"Then where is *your* cell phone?"

Michael shrugged. "Probably upstairs on the dresser."

David sighed and looked around the kitchen. "I'll use Cinderella's instead." He tiptoed over to a table beside the porch door and picked up Maddie's cell phone. He walked around and took several photos of the snoring dog from multiple vantage points.

"These will make wonderful holiday cards," he said.

"Sure they will—once you Photoshop out that puddle of drool."

David stood up and walked to where Michael stood. "You're always so critical of any ideas I have." He held up the phone. "Just look at these images." He scrolled through them. "Any one of these would make . . ."

He stared at the phone with his jaw hanging open.

Michael looked up at him. "What?"

David was still staring down at Maddie's phone.

"What?" Michael asked again. When David still didn't reply, he sighed and grabbed the phone. "What on earth is the matter with you?" He looked at the photo. "Oh. My. Loving. God."

David grabbed it back. "Let's see if there are any more." He quickly scrolled through Maddie's photo album. There were half a dozen photos of a blonde-haired drag queen wearing a ludicrous pink bodysuit and black bustier.

"I *so* do not believe I'm seeing this," David murmured as he flipped back and forth through the images.

Michael chuckled. "Well. I guess we know where the girls spent their night on the town."

David looked up at him. "*Tell* me you recognize him."

"Who?"

David held up the phone like it was Exhibit A in a murder trial. "*Him.* The ugly man in the Ethel Merman wig."

Michael rolled his eyes. "No. I can't say I do. Why? Do you know him?"

"Duh . . . look again. It's Tom Greene."

"Tom Greene?"

"Yes." David pointed to a close-up of one of the images. "Tom Greene? Short? Self-important, pencil dick? Receding hairline? Runs the local hospital like Tony Soprano? Ring any bells?"

Michael peered at the image on the tiny screen. "Jesus god . . . is that really Tom?"

"Yes, it's really Tom. I'd recognize those ungodly fingernails anyplace. I *knew* there was something up that day I ran into him at Rite Aid."

"What are you talking about?"

"*Hello?* He was buying Yum-Yum Yellow nail polish. He tried to hide it beneath a twelve-pack of Clorets, but I saw it all right."

Michael sighed. "David. That could have been for Muriel."

"Muriel?" David flipped through a couple of images, and then held up the phone again. "You mean the King of Queens here?"

Michael took the phone from him. To be sure, there *was* something vaguely familiar about the butch in the leather vest who was huddled with Tom behind a barstool.

"I so do not believe this . . ."

"You and me both, bucko." David took the phone away from him. "This is the mother lode."

"What are you talking about?"

"What do you think I'm talking about?"

"I have *no* idea, but I do know enough to know that whenever you get *that* look in your eyes, it isn't good news for somebody."

"Damn straight." David was busy doing something with the phone.

"Wait a minute. What are you doing?"

"A little something called insurance."

"Insurance against what?" came a voice from the doorway. "And what are you doing with my phone?"

It was Maddie.

David wagged her phone back and forth. "Care to explain how you came by these terribly . . . *eclectic* photos of your nemesis, Dr. Greene?"

Maddie walked across the kitchen and snapped the phone out of his hand. "What are you talking about?" Her eyes grew wide as she scrolled through the images. "Oh, my *god.*"

David smiled at her. "Took the words right out of my mouth."

Maddie looked incredulous. "I had *no* idea these were here."

"Oh, really? Think it was some mysterious act of cyber-spontaneous generation?"

Maddie shook her head. "Syd must've taken these when she went downstairs."

"Downstairs? Just where in the hell were you two staying—the Moulin Rouge?"

Maddie looked at him with smoldering blue eyes. "Will you shut up? The only place we could get into for dinner was a pub that turned out to be a lesbian bar, and it happened to be drag night." She held up the phone. "We were as flummoxed then as you are now when we saw Tom there in his . . . cocktail attire."

"You call that cocktail attire? He looks like Moll Flanders on crack."

Maddie was systematically selecting, and then deleting the images. "David. You cannot mention a word about this to anyone."

"What? Are you *nuts?*"

"No. I mean it. You keep your mouth shut about this."

"But . . ."

"But *nothing*. Not one word. *Ever.*"

She continued to delete images. "If you do, I'll deny everything, *and* tell your mother about that time you wore her long-line girdle to the snack bar at that truck stop on I-81."

The oven timer dinged.

Michael chuckled.

David turned pale.

Maddie glared at him.

"I think we understand each other," she said.

David dropped his shoulders and went to get the serving tray.

"And while we're at it. Explain to me why are there five pictures of Winston Churchill on my phone?"

Across the room on her cashmere bed, Astrid snorted twice and rolled over onto her back.

"Oh. Never mind." Maddie put the phone into her pocket. "Let's eat some pizza."

Maddie and Syd decided to spend the seventh inning stretch outside on the front porch. It was a beautiful night, and not too cool. The moon was full, and its reflection on the pond made it look almost like daylight. They could see Pete nosing around the perimeter of the pond, probably hoping to scoop up any remnants of the pellets Henry would have been certain to drop earlier in the day when he was down there feeding the catfish.

Maddie took advantage of their few minutes alone and quickly brought Syd up to speed on what had unfolded earlier in the kitchen, including her decision to delete the incriminating images of Tom Greene from her phone.

"Well, thank god for that," Syd said. "Can you even imagine what David might have done if you hadn't walked in on him when you did?"

Maddie stifled a laugh. "If only you knew the number of times in my life I've heard *exactly* that same combination of words."

"I'll take your word for it."

"This time, it seems like the odds were in our favor."

Syd nodded. "You're right about that."

"But," Maddie nudged her on the arm, "you need to tell me why you took all those photos of Tom and Muriel. When I came down into that club area to get you, you really seemed to have had a change of heart."

"Oh, I *did*," Syd explained. "But by the time I thought better of it, I'd already met Crystal, and *she* grabbed the phone from me and took the photos."

"Crystal?"

Syd nodded. "Crystal Titz."

Maddie rolled her eyes.

"I think she said her real name was Larry Kozlowski. But, apparently, she knew Amanda and Buster, and was only too happy to oblige."

"I can only imagine."

"I honestly think it's to your credit that you really *can't* imagine it."

"True."

"Tom and Muriel." Syd sighed. "I still can't get over it." She looked up at Maddie. "They must be terrified about seeing us there."

"Don't you mean they must be terrified about *us* seeing *them* there?"

Syd nodded. "This kind of thing only happens in soap operas."

"Well." Maddie shifted her weight and leaned over to rest her arms on the porch railing, "I confess that I haven't seen a soap opera since David made me watch *General Hospital* in junior high, but I don't remember very many story lines about ER chiefs getting their jollies by dressing up like Lana Turner."

"You're being entirely too charitable."

Maddie looked up at her. "I am?"

"I'd say so. Tom looked more like Tim Curry than Lana Turner."

"Tim Curry had dark hair."

Syd smacked her on the arm. "Do you always have to be so literal?"

Maddie laughed and rubbed her bicep. "I really wish you'd quit swatting me. You're going to start leaving marks."

"Oh? Worried about how you'll look in the swimsuit competition, Miss Virginia?"

"Okay . . . now I *know* it's time for David to move back to the Inn."

"Hush. That'll happen soon enough, and Henry will be devastated."

Maddie didn't make any reply. She seemed fixated on something off in the distance. Syd tried to follow her gaze, but didn't see anything remarkable.

"What is it?" she asked.

Maddie shrugged. "It's nothing."

"It's not nothing. It's never nothing with you."

Maddie shrugged again.

"Come on . . . tell me what you were thinking about."

"It's no secret. I was thinking about Henry." They were silent for a moment. Syd moved closer and leaned against Maddie.

"I didn't tell you earlier, but I got an e-mail from James."

Syd was surprised. "When?"

"About an hour after we got home. He's going to be discharged in two weeks."

"Two weeks?" Syd drew back. "I thought he had at least another month of rehab?"

"Apparently, they think he's ready to be discharged, or will be ready in two weeks."

Syd backed up and dropped into one of the big Adirondack chairs. "I don't know what to feel."

Maddie straightened and turned around. "I know what you mean."

Syd raised her eyes to Maddie. The white light from the moon behind her made her features impossible to make out. She looked like a shadow of herself. "What are we going to do?"

"Do?" Maddie's voice sounded remote—like she was standing halfway across the yard, instead of two steps away.

Syd waved a hand in frustration. "He's going to take him."

"Yes."

"*Yes?* Is that all you can say?"

"What do you *want* me to say, Syd? We've known this was coming, and now it's here."

"I *want* you to say that this is as hard for you as it is for me."

Maddie's frustration seemed to boil over. "Of *course* it's as hard for me. I'm not made out of iron, you know."

"Then maybe you could act like it once in a while."

"What's that supposed to mean?"

Syd held up both hands. "*Stop.* Let's just stop . . . right now. This isn't helping either of us."

Maddie rubbed a hand across her eyes and nodded. "I'm sorry. I didn't mean to snap at you."

"I know."

Maddie fell into the chair beside her. It was the most inelegant maneuver Syd had ever seen her make.

They sat in silence. From inside the house, they could hear the faint murmur of the TV in the front room. Off in the distance, Pete grew tired of looking for fish food and took off barking at some kind of intruder.

"We need to get back inside," Maddie finally said. "They'll be coming out to get us."

"In another minute, okay?" Syd took hold of Maddie's hand. "You know something? This is exactly like that very first night I came out here. We sat in these same two chairs and struggled with finding the right things to say."

"I remember." Maddie squeezed her fingers. "I wasn't struggling with what to say, though. I was struggling with how to keep myself from jumping your bones."

Syd looked at her. Her features were clearer now. She thought she could even make out the blue of her eyes. "Oh, come on."

"Cross my heart. I knew I was a goner as soon as your tight little butt hit the seat of that very chair."

"Too bad we had to waste all that wine."

"What wine?"

"The wine that Pete sloshed all over my slacks."

"Oh . . . *that* wine." Maddie laughed. "That wasn't a waste— that was a noble sacrifice."

"How so?"

"It got you out of your clothes, didn't it?"

"And into yours, if memory serves."

"You know, I never washed that sweatshirt."

Syd looked at her in surprise. "You're kidding?"

"Nope. I didn't want to. It smelled like you."

Syd lifted Maddie's hand and kissed it. "You really do have a soft center, don't you?"

"Yeah," Maddie replied, in a sultry voice. "I'm told it's located someplace just south of the chewy nougat."

Syd dropped her hand. "Pervert."

"You started it."

Syd gave her a good once-over. "I think I finished it, too."

"You'll get no argument from me about that. I won't be able to cross my legs for at least a week."

Syd laughed and sat back against the high back of her chair. "God, what a day. I wonder what the hell else can go wrong?"

Her cell phone vibrated, and she jumped about a foot into the air.

"What on earth is the matter?" Maddie asked, with alarm.

Syd dug the phone out of her jacket pocket and held it up. "My phone." She peered down at its bright blue screen.

"Who is it?" Maddie asked.

"It's not a call. It's a text message." Syd took a moment to read it, then slapped the phone face down onto the wide arm of her chair. "Oh, I *so* do not believe this," she said with disgust.

"What is it?"

Syd looked at her. "It's Doris. She's coming through Jericho tomorrow, and she wants to see me."

"Doris?" Maddie asked. "Doris Simon?"

"That's the one. My ex-mother-in-law."

Maddie was incredulous. "What on earth does *she* want?"

Syd threw up her hands. "God only knows? I can only assume it has something to do with the divorce."

"Is Jeff going to be with her?"

Syd thought Maddie sounded a bit wary.

"She didn't mention him, so I doubt it."

"Where does she want to meet you?"

Syd shrugged. "She said something about lunch, so I guess it's up to me to pick a venue."

Maddie was silent for a moment. "So you're going to do it?"

Syd looked at her. "Do you think I shouldn't?"

"I honestly have no idea. What do you think?"

Syd stood up. "I think I want to see if we have another bottle of Meandro that David hasn't found yet."

Maddie stood up, too. "And then what?"

Syd took hold of her hand and led her toward the big front door. "Then we see if you can find another creative way to get my pants off."

Maddie just smiled and followed her inside.

Celine looked up when Syd and Maddie reentered the parlor. The baseball game was in full swing again, but Henry was sound asleep. He was stretched out across a sofa cushion with his dark head on Celine's lap.

"He didn't want to go up to bed until you came back inside," she said. "Michael and David gave up about fifteen minutes ago."

"I'm sorry, Mom." Maddie walked over to her. "Let me take him on up." She knelt down and carefully picked Henry up. He was wearing only one shoe, and the bright green sock on his other foot was hanging halfway off, too—making his foot look elongated like an elf's. Henry didn't wake up as Maddie carried him toward the stairs. He just tucked his head beneath her chin and snuggled in closer.

"I'll be back after I get him down," she said over her shoulder as she walked out of the room.

Syd picked up Henry's discarded shoe and sat down on the sofa next to Celine. She set her cell phone down on the cushion beside her.

The sole of Henry's shoe looked worn on one side. Syd shook her head. He was going through them faster than they could buy them. Plus she couldn't keep him from wading out into the shallow end of the pond with them on—no matter how many times they told him to stay out of the water. This pair was covered with splotchy stains. They really needed to be thrown away. But they were his favorites, and she couldn't find any more Spiderman shoes in his size.

"Is everything okay with you two?"

Syd looked up in surprise. She had almost forgotten that Celine was sitting there.

"I'm sorry, Celine. We stayed out on the porch too long."

"Well, you didn't miss much in here. David was so distracted that he couldn't sit still. Finally, Michael told him to go to bed. He followed along in short order."

"What's the score?"

Celine smiled at her. "Do you really want to know?"

Syd looked down at the shoe in her hand. "Not really."

"I didn't think so."

Syd angled her body toward Celine. "Did Maddie tell you that she heard from James today?"

Celine looked surprised. "James Lawrence?"

Syd nodded.

"No."

"Well, she did. And, apparently, he's going to be released from Walter Reed in two weeks."

Celine didn't reply right away. "That seems awfully soon," she said in a quiet voice. "I would've expected him to be in rehab for at least another month or so."

Syd shrugged. "I guess we all should be pleased that he's making such good progress."

Celine was silent until Syd looked at her.

"But you're not?" she asked.

Syd shook her head. Then she threw up her hands. "I mean, of *course* I want him to do well. And of course I want him to be released from the hospital—if he's ready. But this means . . ."

Celine laid a hand on her leg. "This means he'll take Henry."

Syd nodded again.

"Does Maddie know anything else about his plans—where he intends to live or how he plans to manage financially?"

"I don't think so."

Celine squeezed her leg. "Try not to worry any more than you have to right now. There is still a lot to be worked out before any of this happens."

"I know."

Syd put Henry's shoe back down and picked up her cell phone. She turned it over and over between her hands. She gave a bitter-sounding laugh. "And as if things weren't bad enough, I get a text message from Jeff's mother telling me that she's coming through town tomorrow."

Celine was surprised. "Dorrie is coming here?"

"Not here as in *here*, but here as in Jericho. She wants to meet me for lunch."

"That's . . . interesting."

"Isn't it? I can only guess what she wants to talk about."

"Is she coming by herself?"

Syd shrugged. "I honestly have no idea."

"Are you going to meet her?" Celine's tone sounded neutral.

"I suppose so." Syd slouched into the sofa cushions. "Who was that ancient king who took all the small doses of poison to build up an immunity?"

Celine smiled at her. "Mithridates?"

"That's the one." Syd closed her eyes. "He was my role model when I was married to Jeff."

"Was it really that bad?"

"You have no idea."

"So, as your new mother-in-law, I shouldn't be concerned until I see you sneaking small shots of theriac?"

Syd opened one eye and looked at her. "I don't think you need to worry."

"Where do you intend to meet her for lunch?"

"I don't know . . . probably the café."

"Will Maddie go with you?"

Syd shook her head. "I doubt it. She works in Wytheville tomorrow. I wouldn't ask her to, in any case."

"Why not?"

"This is my mess, and I want to be the one to clean it up."

Celine was silent.

"Do you disagree?"

Celine shook her head. "It's not my place either to agree or disagree. Besides . . . knowing Dorrie, I think you'd be better served by taking along a two-by-four instead of a bodyguard."

Syd laughed.

"What's so funny?" Maddie stood in the doorway. She glanced from the two of them to the TV screen. "It looks like the Yankees lost."

"They did?" Syd looked at the television, where talking heads were recapping the game. "At least something went right this evening."

Maddie looked confused.

"Don't worry." Syd sat up and patted the sofa cushion to indicate that Maddie should come and join them.

Maddie obeyed and sat down to watch the replays. "How did you two miss the end of the game? A ninth inning grand slam is a pretty dramatic finish."

"From your mouth to god's ear," Syd said.

Maddie glanced at her. "Did I miss something else?"

"No, honey." Syd leaned her head against Maddie's shoulder. "I'm just thinking about *other* kinds of end games."

◊ ◊ ◊

Upstairs in their room, David was busy doing something on his laptop.

Michael had already finished in the bathroom and was turning back the bed. "Are you about ready to turn in? I'm beat."

David didn't look up from the screen. "Just another minute—I'll be right there."

"Can't it wait until morning?"

"Nope."

"What are you doing, anyway?"

"You might say that I'm managing our investments."

Michael sighed. "At eleven o'clock at night?"

David waved a hand. "Time waits for no man." He chuckled. "Or woman."

"What the hell are you talking about?"

"You wouldn't understand."

"Now *there's* a piece of late-breaking news."

David hit the return key with a flourish. "Done."

Michael climbed beneath the covers. "Great. Now can we go to bed?"

David snapped his laptop closed and stood up. "Yes, my furry prince, everything is in hand." He looked at Michael and twirled an imaginary moustache. "Or will be shortly, if you remembered to floss . . ."

Michael just sighed and turned off the bedside light.

Outside their window, the full moon continued along its slow, but determined path across the night sky.

Chapter 18

"You don't see a ducktail spoiler like that every day."

David was startled by the comment coming from just behind his right shoulder. He fought an impulse to check his hair before he turned around.

It was Jocelyn Painter.

"Now that there's a beaut," she said. "A '68, isn't it?"

David nodded. They both were looking at Gladys's sporty street rod. Junior had it up on a lift in his center garage bay, but it was still pretty hard to miss.

"I swanny. Those factory inserts on that stock hood look ten times better than any of those repro cowl induction vents most people think they have to have on these muscle cars."

David had *no* idea what she was talking about. "Yeah. That's just what I was thinking."

He flicked the ash off the end of his cigarette. He'd been trying to quit, during the time they'd been living with Maddie and Syd, but sometimes the urge for a smoke was overwhelming. Like right now. It was hard to be around all this gritty, manly stuff and not want to fire one up.

Jocelyn was outside having a cigarette, too. They stood together on the small, marked-off section of concrete that was designated as safe for smokers.

"It's good to see you, Jocelyn. What brings you out here so early on a Monday morning?"

It was barely nine o'clock.

She turned around and gestured at her ancient Chevy. It was parked out front next to a sagging phone booth that was nearly as old as the car. "Damn Biscayne blew a bulb in the right taillight, and Junior's is the only place I can get 'em in a hurry."

David nodded. "How are things going? I saw that Fleetwood Homes was advertising free delivery right now."

She took a long drag off her cigarette. "I wish I could say that things were going good. I rode shotgun on the sale of six Coronado Ultras just this month alone, and could've done twice as many if only Deb had been able to work."

"Deb still in mourning, then?" David asked. "I'm sorry to hear that."

Jocelyn slowly swung her head back and forth. "Every time I think she's about ready to turn a corner, another damn piece of that car turns up someplace. Then she sinks right back down into a pit of despair. I swear . . . that damn thing has more lives than a busload of alley cats."

David patted her on the shoulder. "Keep the faith, Jocelyn. Sometimes things have a way of working out."

She took a final drag on her cigarette and dropped it so she could pulverize it with the toe of her boot.

"I hope you're right. Oops . . . there's Junior with my bulb. I gotta scoot—the new Cabela's catalogs are out today, and I'm gonna have to make half a dozen trips back into town just to haul 'em all."

David waved goodbye as she hurried toward her car, and reminded her to be sure and bring Deb to the open house next week.

Junior was already kneeling at the back of the Biscayne, removing the red glass cover from her taillight. He held up his hand to let David know he'd just be another five minutes.

David decided that was long enough to enjoy another smoke.

He stood there for a few minutes, enjoying the warmer temperature. He didn't even need a jacket this morning. It was clear that it was going to be an early summer. The wild Shasta bushes that lined the fence across the road from Junior's were already loaded with constellations of fluffy, white flowers.

He thought he saw Cletus Freemantle drive by in his old

blue, Chevy pickup. There was somebody slumped down in the passenger seat, but David couldn't make out who it was. Maybe Azalea? Junior said that Cletus was off today because he had to take his mother into Wytheville for something.

David snorted. *Probably to Walmart for more ammo.*

Another car roared in and rolled to a stop.

Great.

At the rate *this* was going, he'd be better off just to leave the damn check under that dust-covered pyramid of empty oilcans in Junior's "office."

He watched a late-model silver Mercedes back into a parking space out front. Then he got a good look at who was driving it.

He smiled and ground out his cigarette.

Oh, yeah. This can totally work.

He pulled his cell phone out of his pocket and spooled up his photo album. Then he headed toward the somewhat portly woman who had just climbed out of the big sedan.

She looked a lot less formidable without the chains and leather vest.

"Hi there, Muriel," he called out. "Fancy meeting you here."

Lizzy hung up the phone and turned around to face Maddie. "Well, that has to be about the strangest conversation I've ever had."

"What do you mean?"

Maddie was restocking the supply cabinet in the hallway that led to the clinic's examination rooms.

"It was Tom Greene." Lizzy sat down on a nearby stool. "Just when I think I know what to expect from that man, he shifts gears and comes at me from some entirely new direction."

"What's his angle this time?" Maddie asked. "He want you to rent a naughty nurse costume and serve drinks at the Masonic Lodge?"

Lizzy blinked. "No, but I have to say that's about the most appalling idea I've ever heard."

Maddie shrugged. "I've known Tom a long time."

"Well, I think this one will surprise even you."

Maddie closed the cabinet door and crossed her arms. "What did he want?"

Lizzy raised her brown eyes to Maddie's. "He was calling to say that he'd had a change of heart, and he's decided to extend the funding for my position for another two years."

"What?" Maddie dropped her arms. "That's incredible."

"Tell me about it."

Maddie shook her head. "I'm nearly speechless. What do you think happened to change his mind?"

"I have no earthly idea."

Maddie thought about it. There was no way this was because of *them*—unless Tom was just running scared after their encounter in Charlotte.

No. That wouldn't be enough to scare him . . . *straight*—unless he knew about the photographs, of course. But that couldn't be it. Syd wasn't the one who took them. Besides, she had deleted all those images last night after David found them. *Unless . . .*

She was starting to get a sick feeling.

Lizzy was looking at her strangely. "Are you okay? I thought you'd be happy about this."

"Oh, god, no. I *am* happy about this. Ecstatic, in fact." She smiled at Lizzy. "Are you going to get this in writing?"

Lizzy looked at her with disbelief. "Of *course* I am. I don't trust that man as far as I could throw him. I'm going by the hospital after work to pick up the contract."

"Wise woman."

Peggy Hawkes stuck her head around the corner. "Doc Stevenson? Your eleven-thirty just canceled."

Maddie glanced at her watch. "Wasn't that our last appointment this morning?"

Peggy nodded. "But Roma Jean Freemantle is here, and she's complaining about her elbow."

"Her *elbow*?"

Peggy rolled her eyes.

Maddie looked at Lizzy. "Why don't you go ahead and take

an early lunch? You can get a jump start on getting that contract signed."

"Contract?" Peggy asked.

Lizzy smiled at her. "Tom Greene just renewed my funding for two more years."

Peggy clapped her hands together in excitement. "Maybe we'll get that wedding after all."

Lizzy stared at her with an open mouth. "Wedding?"

Peggy nodded with excitement.

Maddie cleared her throat.

"I'm glad you're happy about this, Peggy," Lizzy said. "But there is no wedding on my immediate horizon."

"Oh, you girls always say that. And as soon as those young men pop that question, you're all doe-eyed and dreaming."

"Not all of us," Maddie quipped.

"*You* don't count." Peggy corrected her. "But I think I'll have to do something nice for Tom and Muriel."

"I think that's a *fine* idea, Peggy," Maddie agreed. She smiled sweetly at her nurse and decided to indulge an evil impulse. "Why don't you bake them a lemon chess pie?"

Peggy bobbed her head like the plastic poodle that was a fixture in the back window of her Buick.

"That's *just* what I was thinking."

"Kismet," Maddie muttered. Peggy's pies were legendary in the county—as things to avoid like the plague. She couldn't think of a nicer way to repay Tom Greene for being such an iconic asshole.

"On that . . . *happy* . . . note," Lizzy said, "I think I'll go sign the contract while there's still time."

"You do that," Maddie said. "Peggy, please bring Roma Jean back, and tell her I'll be right with her."

Peggy nodded and headed back to the waiting room.

"Elbow?" Lizzy asked.

Maddie shrugged.

"Uh huh." Lizzy grabbed her bag out of a locker and walked toward the back door of the clinic. "Good luck, Dr. Phil."

Maddie watched her leave—half hoping she wasn't right.

Syd ducked into Freemantle's market on her way to meet Doris at the Midway Café.

Henry needed a new battery for his PlayStation controller, which actually meant that *David* needed a new battery for Henry's PlayStation controller. Normally, this was something they'd have to pick up at Walmart, but Edna had told Syd in church on Sunday that she had to keep them in stock for Azalea, who was addicted to *Grand Theft Auto*.

Edna explained that Evelyn actually bought the unit so she could play her *Just Dance 3* exercise game—but Cletus quickly co-opted the thing and added a slew of the more questionable titles. He pointed out that nobody was better at capping hookers than Azalea.

"It's like she's on some kind of religious crusade," he told Edna.

Edna was unimpressed and even less surprised, but she ordered the batteries just the same.

"That'll be six twenty-three." Edna slid the plastic package across the counter. "Do you want a bag?"

Syd shook her head. "No, thanks, Edna. I'll take it just like this." She gave Edna a ten-dollar bill.

"Are you in a hurry to get someplace?" Edna opened the cash drawer and withdrew Syd's change.

"I'm meeting someone for lunch at the Café," Syd explained. "But I've got a few minutes."

Edna closed the cash drawer and took a quick look around the interior of the small market.

"I've been wanting to ask you about something," she said, in a low voice. "But I don't want to embarrass you or get too personal."

Syd was intrigued. She'd known Edna Freemantle for nearly three years—ever since the day she arrived in Jericho to open the town's fledgling public library. The Freemantles were like her surrogate Virginia family.

"You can ask me anything. I hope you know that by now."

Edna nodded. "But this is different, and I don't want to offend you by making any wrong assumptions."

Syd really had no idea where this was going, but she wanted to try and put Edna at ease. "Whatever it is, just say it. I promise that you won't offend me."

Edna looked dubious.

"I promise," she repeated.

Edna nodded, but she wouldn't meet Syd's eyes. "I, um . . . I think it's possible that Roma Jean might be like *you*."

"Like me?" Syd still didn't get it. "You mean, because she wants to be a librarian?"

"No . . ." Edna looked up at her. Her gray eyes were dark with worry. "Like you. Like you and Dr. Stevenson."

"*Oh.*" Syd felt like an idiot. "Oh, god . . . I'm sorry, Edna. I didn't know what you meant."

Edna slowly nodded, but didn't say anything.

Syd felt like she had five seconds to come up with the right thing to say. Why did Edna pick *now* to have this conversation— now when she was fifteen minutes away from having to meet Doris?

"What makes you think that Roma Jean is . . . like me?" she asked.

Edna shook her head. "It's just a feeling I have–that I've always had, really. And she's been spending a lot of time with Charlie Davis, and everybody knows about her. Nelda Rae said that's why Charlie went away to school. She got in trouble a couple of times for . . . well . . . you know."

"Don't you like Charlie?" Syd asked.

Edna shrugged. "She seems like a nice girl."

"Do you think she's bad for Roma Jean?"

"I don't know. I don't want Roma Jean to get into something that might not be right for her. What if she goes too far with Charlie and then can't get out of it?"

Syd nodded. "I agree that Roma Jean is young. But she's a *good* girl, and she has a good head on her shoulders. You gave her that . . . you and Curtis. And I don't think she'd ever do *anything* that she didn't think was right for her. And we both know how much she loves her family."

"But what if it's just something that she can't control?"

"What if it is? She's a teenager, Edna. The next few years for her are going to be all about figuring these things out—whether that involves Charlie Davis or not."

Edna looked down at the countertop. "I just don't know if I can support her in this."

"You don't really have to support her in *this*. You just have to support her—like you've always done. And trust her enough to believe that she'll make the choices that she thinks are best for her."

"What if she makes the wrong choices?"

"Then she'll be the one who lives with them—just like we all do."

Edna sighed. "Curtis won't talk about it."

"Have you said anything to Roma Jean?"

Edna looked horrified. "No. I can't do that. What if I'm wrong?"

"It's okay." Syd touched her hand. "Let this evolve in the way it's going to go. She's a grown-up now. Even if you wanted to, you couldn't change who she is—and she's *wonderful*. Roma Jean is one of the kindest-hearted and sweetest young women I've ever known. You should be very proud of the job you've done raising her."

"I am."

"Then try to concentrate on that, and give her the trust and respect she's learned to expect from you. I don't think she'll disappoint you."

"I wanted grandchildren . . ."

Syd smiled. "So did *my* parents." She held up the PlayStation battery. "You see how that turned out."

Syd could tell that Edna was embarrassed and trying not to smile.

"I guess I need to let you get on to your lunch date," she said. "Thanks for talking to me."

"We can talk *any* time, Edna. I mean that."

Edna nodded.

Syd squeezed her hand. "Try not to worry."

"I'll try," Edna said.

Syd turned toward the door.

"Say hello to your little boy for me," Edna called out.

My little boy? Syd felt her throat grow thick.

"I will," she promised.

She waved goodbye to Edna and walked out to her car.

"How does that feel?"

Maddie was holding Roma Jean's arm and gently rotating her elbow.

"Not too bad," Roma Jean replied.

"Does it hurt at all?"

"Maybe a little."

"Tell me again how you injured it," Maddie said.

"I was shelving some books at the library, and I ran into the corner of the circulation desk."

"And when did this happen?"

"Saturday."

"Has it gotten worse since then?" Maddie was looking for any obvious signs of bruising or swelling, but didn't see anything worrisome.

"Not really." Roma Jean hesitated. "Charlie wanted me to come over and see you right away, but I told her it wasn't that bad."

Maddie sat back on her stool. "Charlie was with you when it happened?"

Roma Jean nodded.

"Well, I don't really see signs of any serious injury, but I want you to take it easy on this arm for a few days. No lifting or straining, okay? And take some ibuprofen for any pain or minor swelling that might show up." Maddie made some notes on Roma Jean's chart. "And call me right away if it starts feeling worse."

"Okay."

Maddie stood up, but Roma Jean remained seated on the examination table.

"Was there something else you wanted today?" Maddie asked. She was terrified that Roma Jean would say yes. Roma Jean nodded.

Shit.

"What is it?"

Roma Jean shrugged.

"Roma Jean?"

"It's about Charlie."

"Oh." Maddie sat back down on her stool. She had a feeling that this was going to be a long conversation. She stole a quick look at the clock above Roma Jean's head and wondered how Syd was faring with Doris. She watched Roma Jean fiddle with the hem of her blouse.

"What about Charlie?" she asked.

"She was helping me on Saturday."

"Okay." Maddie was pretty sure she knew where this was heading. But she also knew that Roma Jean needed to get there on her own.

"She stayed until closing time so she could help me lock up." She looked up at Maddie. "She likes to walk me to my car—it's kinda creepy out back. I don't really feel safe out there since the fire."

Maddie nodded. Beau Pitzer's failed attempt to burn down the tiny library had damaged a lot more than the books inside the building. His rampage had nearly cost Syd and Lizzy their lives.

"I can understand that, Roma Jean. But Beau won't hurt anyone again."

"I know. That's what Charlie says, too."

"She's right."

Roma Jean nodded. "I guess so."

"Is that what you wanted to talk with me about—your feelings about being alone at the library?"

Roma Jean shook her head.

Maddie decided to take the plunge. "Is it something else about Charlie?"

Roma Jean nodded.

Maddie could see tears forming in the corners of her eyes. "Do you want to tell me what it is?" she asked, in a quiet voice.

Roma Jean sat there, biting her bottom lip. Then she took a deep breath and let it fly. "I was trying to do the deadbolt on the back door, and it wasn't working because the door swells up whenever it rains, and you can't force it—because I already tried that and broke the key off in the lock twice—and Charlie was standing there beside me and kept saying that I should let her try, and she finally just tried to take the keys out of my hand—but I was so nervous that I dropped them, and we both bent over at the same time to pick them up and hit our heads together—and when I reached out to touch her head to be sure she was okay, she kissed me."

Maddie sat there for a moment, mentally trying to punctuate all Roma Jean had just said. "Could you repeat that last part, please?"

Roma Jean looked at her. "The part about hitting our heads?"

"No," Maddie corrected. "The part after that."

Roma Jean looked down at her shoes. "She kissed me."

"That's what I thought you said."

Roma Jean was blushing, and her face was beet red. "I didn't want that to happen. I tried really hard not to do it."

"It doesn't sound to me like you did anything."

"*But I did*," she said. "I didn't stop her. I didn't want to."

"And that scares you?" Maddie asked.

Roma Jean nodded. "I never wanted this to happen. I didn't want to be like that."

"Like what?"

"Like Charlie. Like . . . like *you* and Miss Murphy." Tears rolled down her cheeks. "I *can't* be . . . my parents won't ever accept it. If they find out, I won't be able to live at home anymore . . . I'll have to move away, and I don't have anyplace to go." She wiped at her eyes. "I graduate from high school next Sunday, and I don't want to be alone, Dr. Stevenson. I don't want to be a freak."

Maddie picked up a box of Kleenex and held it out to Roma Jean. "Do you think Charlie is a freak?"

Roma Jean blew her nose. "No . . ."

"Do you think I'm a freak? Or Syd?"

Roma Jean shook her head.

"Then why would you say such a thing about yourself?"

Roma Jean bit her lip. "Because I've *always* been different. I never liked boys—no matter how hard I tried." She wiped at her eyes. "I even went on a date with the Lear twins, but I was just miserable the whole time."

"You went out with the Lear twins?"

Roma Jean nodded.

"*Both* of them? At the same time?"

Roma Jean nodded again. "They do everything together." She shrugged her narrow shoulders. "I figured if I couldn't make it work with two boys, there wasn't much hope for me with one." She rolled her eyes. "I was sure right about that. It was a big-time slobber fest . . . really gross."

Maddie tried hard not to laugh.

"Roma Jean, can you tell me how you felt during that encounter with Charlie?"

"It *hurt.*"

Maddie looked at her with alarm.

"No . . . it *really* hurt. Her chin hit the top of my head right here." She pointed at a spot above her right eyebrow.

"No . . . that's not what I meant."

"It isn't?"

Maddie shook her head.

"You mean when she kissed me, don't you?"

Maddie nodded.

Roma Jean looked away. "I really liked it. It wasn't like being with the Lear twins at all. She was soft, and she smelled so nice . . . like those really good cherry cordials they sell at CVS."

"Did it scare you?"

"Not at first. It just felt . . ."

"It just felt—what?" Maddie asked.

Roma Jean looked at her. "Good. It just felt good."

"Roma Jean. There are a lot of things in life that feel good, and not all of them are. That's why it's important for you to take your time and be really sure."

"Do you think Charlie is bad for me?" Roma Jean was looking at Maddie with a panicked expression.

"No. That's not what I'm saying at all. I'm saying that there's a difference between things that feel good, and things that feel *right*."

"How did you know it was right with Miss Murphy?"

Maddie was unprepared for that question. But, in all fairness, she could hardly refuse to answer. "To be truthful, I didn't know at first. And like you, I tried to fight against it."

"Why?"

"It was complicated. I had just returned here to live, and Syd was trying to deal with the breakup of her marriage. I didn't want to complicate her life any more than it already was, and I wasn't even sure if she felt the same way about me as I knew I was beginning to feel about her."

"But you two seem so perfect for each other."

Maddie smiled at that. "I hope we are. But it could just as easily have gone another way. And that's why it's so important to take your time and not rush into anything you're not really certain about."

"Did you always know?"

"Did I always know what?"

"That you were . . . that you liked girls."

"Oh." Maddie thought about how to answer her, and how much it was appropriate to share. "I guess I probably started to figure it out when I was about your age—although I never really acted on anything until I was well into college."

Roma Jean seemed surprised by her answer. "What did your parents say?"

"Well, they didn't really 'say' anything."

"Why not?"

"I never really talked with my father—not directly, anyway. It was just kind of understood between us, and we never discussed it in specific terms. But I never doubted his support for me, and I know that he *knew*, but just chose not to talk about it with me. And I think that might be a pretty typical reaction for many folks—especially in a small community like ours."

"What about your mom?"

Maddie sighed. "Explaining my relationship with my mother would take more time than either of us has right now. Let me just assure you that any problems I ever had with her were unrelated to her discovery of my sexual orientation. Fortunately, we now are on the road to a much happier and healthier bond. And remember that my mother is a scientist who lived most of her adult life in California. She generally takes a much more academic view of things."

Maddie could tell that Roma Jean really didn't know what that meant.

"She pretty much takes things in stride," she added.

"But she likes Syd?"

Maddie smiled. "She loves Syd. But it's also true that I had another partner before Syd who she didn't like very much."

Roma Jean shook her head. "I don't think Mama likes Charlie."

"Why do you say that?"

"She never wants me to spend time with her. She never really says much, but I can tell by her reactions when Charlie calls or comes over that she thinks it's not good for me."

"Have you thought about asking her what she thinks?"

Roma Jean looked horrified. "No. I'd *never* do that."

"Okay." Maddie backed off from that suggestion.

"Do *you* think Charlie is bad for me?"

"Roma Jean. It only really matters what you think. But to answer your question—no, I don't think Charlie is bad for you . . . or for anyone. Charlie seems like a fine person to me—honest and hard-working. And I know that Sheriff Martin thinks very highly of her. It took a lot of guts for her to put herself through police training, and then come back here to live. I think she's an admirable young woman."

"I think so, too."

"Do you want to keep seeing Charlie?"

Roma Jean nodded.

"Do you think you can trust Charlie to give you the time you need, and not to force anything that you might not be ready for?"

Roma Jean nodded again. "She knew I was pretty freaked out. She apologized over and over for . . . what happened."

"That's good. It's important for Charlie to respect you—and your process. No one should ever push you into anything that you don't freely choose."

"I know."

Maddie smiled at her. "Then as long as you remember that, you won't have any problems."

"Okay."

"Do you have other people you can talk with?"

Roma Jean looked at her. "You mean about *this*?"

Maddie nodded.

"Not really. Well . . . maybe Jessie. But nobody else."

"My best advice for you is to find some people you can trust—friends who can offer you support while you try to work your way through the harder parts of this process. Can you do that? Do you know of any places where you might go for support?"

"Charlie said there were some groups in Wytheville and Radford."

"Maybe you could try visiting one of those, then—when you think you might be ready."

"Okay."

"There are also some wonderful books on this topic that you might consider—if you find things like that helpful. I know they were to me. Just being able to read about the experiences of other women—and men—who were struggling to navigate many of the same personal and family issues made me feel less alone. Less isolated."

Roma Jean seemed interested in that idea. "How would I find out about those?"

"For starters, I'd say that your former librarian would be an excellent resource."

"You mean, ask Miss Murphy?"

Maddie nodded. "If you feel comfortable with that. I'm sure she'd be honored to help you out with a reading list."

Roma Jean got to her feet. "Thanks for talking with me, Dr. Stevenson."

Maddie stood up, too. "Roma Jean. I'm your doctor, but I'm also your friend. I hope you know that you can talk with me anytime—Syd, too."

Roma Jean looked close to tears again. "I know."

Maddie stepped forward and pulled Roma Jean into a hug. Roma Jean grabbed on to the back of her white coat like she was clutching a lifeline.

"You're a good girl," Maddie said into her hair. "And I promise you'll get through this."

Chapter 19

"What on earth is all of this?" Syd asked Michael. He was systematically unloading a tray containing five different appetizers.

"Nadine ordered me to bring these out here to you, and I obey her orders."

Syd gave him a questioning look, and he tipped his head toward the kitchen and kept unloading.

"You wanna go back there and argue with her—be my guest. But let me forewarn you . . . Raymond backed over her pansy bed this morning when he was out there spreading gravel, and it ain't pretty."

Syd looked down at the platters of food. "So her revenge is to put *me* into an early grave?"

"Not entirely. She knows about your lunch date, and I think she wants to make sure you have something to do if the conversation lags."

"*Lags?* With Doris?" Syd rolled her eyes. "That's about as likely as David having nothing to say during *American Idol*."

Michael laughed and looked at the front entrance to the café. "Where is your lunch date, anyway?"

Syd sighed. "Fashionably late, of course. With her, it's always about power dynamics. The longer she makes me wait, the more subservient I become."

"She sounds terribly charming."

"Imagine Joan Crawford on an estrogen patch."

"*Ouch.* Want me to join you?"

Syd shook her head. "I promise to scream if she starts making the furniture levitate." She waved a hand over the plates of food. "Want to tell me what all we have here?"

"Sure." Michael ticked off the items. "This is Nadine's famous butter bean spread—a.k.a. hummus. This is a vat of spicy pimento cheese—and it's truly fabulous today because I added a hefty shot of cayenne. Here is a basket of Nadine's signature cheese biscuits—rife with Henry's fairy sprinkles. This is a zesty bowl of hot collard green, bacon, and bleu cheese dip. And last, but never least—a succulent tomato pie."

"Good god."

"Now." Michael tucked the serving tray up under his arm. "Will you be needing menus, madam?"

Syd looked up at him. "I don't think so, but if we manage to eat all of this, you might need to scare up a couple of body bags."

Michael laughed.

The bell over the entrance door dinged, and he looked toward the sound. The smile evaporated from his face. "Oh. My. *God.*"

"What is it?" she asked.

"Don't look now," he muttered. "But either your mother-in-law just arrived, or Calista Gingrich is here for lunch."

Syd took a deep breath. "Once more unto the breach, dear friends . . ."

Michael clucked his tongue. "You got that shit right, sister." He patted her on the shoulder. "Here she comes. Call me if you need me."

Syd pushed back her chair and stood up. "Count on it."

Michael beat a hasty path to the kitchen as Doris approached Syd's table.

Three years and a helluva lot more Botox made Doris look . . . tighter than ever. She was impeccably dressed, as usual, in some inevitable Oscar de la Renta creation. Perfect for an informal lunch in a country café . . . *not.*

Each platinum hair was carefully coiled into place. Syd recognized her necklace—a double-strand emerald creation that Howard had bought her at Christie's one year for their anniversary. Of course, Doris picked out the "gift" herself.

She did not look pleased to be there.

She stopped just short of the table and looked down with disgust at the array of food items on display. "I see you decided not to wait for me."

"Hello, Doris. It's lovely to see you as well."

Doris met her eyes. Syd had a premonition that she might just turn into a pillar of salt if she dared to look back at her mother-in-law for too long.

"Let's dispense with the pleasantries. You know why I'm here." Doris dropped her Marc Jacobs bag onto a vacant chair and picked up a napkin to dust off her seat before claiming it.

Syd sighed and sat down. "Frankly, Doris, I don't have the least idea why you're here—unless it's some newfound desire to experience the best in low-country cuisine."

Doris glanced down at the table. "I'd hardly call *this* cuisine."

"I'd hardly call you an authority."

Doris fixed her with an icy glare. "You always did have a taste for the common things in life."

Syd smiled at her. "Which goes a long way toward explaining why I once found your son attractive."

"I would agree that you certainly would qualify as the most common thing about him."

"Really?" Syd refused to concede the point. "I'm sure there are half a dozen waitresses at Sonic Drive-In who would disagree with your assessment."

Doris colored. "I regard *you* as my son's only lapse in judgment. I think it's clear that any diminution of his sensibilities is entirely due to your influence."

"You mistake me, Doris. I was referring to your son's fondness for the *waitresses* at Sonic, not the food they served."

Doris leaned forward. "Let's not mince any more words."

Syd imitated her gesture and leaned forward, too. "I'm only too happy to expedite this conversation Doris. Why not cut to the chase and tell me why you're here."

"Don't play coy with me. You know what I want."

"I assumed you were making a sweep through southwest Virginia to raise money for the D.A.R., but apparently, I was mistaken?"

Doris reached into her handbag and withdrew a fat envelope. "This is an amended copy of your prenuptial contract with Jeff." She unfolded the pages and placed the document down on the only unoccupied spot on their table—between the bowls of hummus and pimento cheese. "I'd like you to initial each page, and sign it where indicated."

Syd didn't even glance down at it. "Doris, I've already signed this document once—remember? You insisted that I do so before Jeff and I could marry. Why do you need me to do this again?"

"Because by signing it, you will forfeit your right to invoke the provision that this agreement is nullified if either party commits infidelity."

Syd wasn't certain she'd heard her correctly. "What?"

"You heard me."

"I heard you, all right," Syd explained. "But I don't think I *follow* you."

"Don't make me spell it out. You're already fully aware that citing adultery as your grounds for divorce neatly positions you to walk away from this marriage with half of Jeff's assets."

Syd was stunned. "What?"

"You heard me. And don't try and tell me that you knew nothing about this fine print when your carefully scripted aloofness pushed my son into those other . . . dalliances."

Syd's head was spinning. *Half of Jeff's fortune?* This had to be a ruse of some kind. There was no way this could really be the case. Jeff was worth millions . . . *tens* of millions.

"I honestly don't know what you're talking about," she said.

Doris scoffed at her. "Of *course* you don't. That's why you had that barracuda of an attorney of yours contact us, demanding a copy of the prenup and stating that you were one hundred percent determined to prove your allegations of infidelity in court."

"Look, Doris . . . I've *never* wanted Jeff's money. I ended our marriage and walked away from him with little more than the clothes on my back. This is the first I've ever heard about *any* infidelity clause in our prenup agreement—I never read the fine print." She shook her head in frustration. "I signed the damn thing on the steps of Durham City Hall, for god's sake."

Doris took a deep breath. "If that's truly the case, then you'll have no objection to signing this document now," she said, in a softer tone. She uncapped a shiny, gold fountain pen.

Syd looked at her, and then looked down at the document that lay on the table between them. "Just out of curiosity. Why did you put a clause like that into our prenup?"

Doris lowered the pen. "Isn't that obvious?"

"Apparently not."

"It was insurance."

"Insurance against *what?* Against Jeff's proclivity for cheating?"

Doris gave her a contemptuous look. "No. Against *yours.*"

"*Mine?*" Syd was aghast. "What the hell are you talking about?"

"Oh, please. You can't expect anyone to believe that the perverted tryst which you currently call a relationship is your first foray into sexually deviant behavior."

"How dare you . . ."

"Jeff suspected that you had aberrant proclivities almost from the start of your marriage. Thank god I had the foresight to plan for such an outcome."

"I never looked *twice* at another person the entire time I was with Jeff. Unfortunately for you and your precious bank balance, he can't say the same thing."

Doris raised an index finger. "I find your choice of pronoun especially revealing . . . don't you?"

"You can rot in hell," Syd hissed.

"Oh, no, my dear. Nothing or no one related to me will *ever* rot in hell. Too bad I can't say the same thing about your lesbian lover's sainted reputation."

"What are you suggesting?"

"You're a smart girl. I think you know what I'm suggesting. In addition, I don't think it takes a rocket scientist to figure out that self-respecting parents in *this* county don't want a pervert teaching their children . . . or *raising* them, for that matter."

"That's *blackmail*, Doris."

"Is it? Oh, dear . . . I guess it is." She sighed. "Too bad you'd never be able to prove it."

"Would eyewitness testimony count?"

They both looked up in surprise. Celine was standing beside their table, and neither of them had noticed her approach.

"Hello, Dee Dee." Celine's voice dripped sarcasm. "Fancy meeting you here."

Doris was speechless. Syd could tell that she was having a hard time making sense of who was standing before her. Syd wasn't far behind her. Celine looked fantastic—dressed to the nines in a stunning black suit that gave her an almost imperial air. She was carrying a small canvas bag.

Syd couldn't believe she was there, and that she had managed to creep up on them without detection.

Across the table from her, Doris was sputtering. "*Celine?* How . . . what are *you* doing here?"

"It's the funniest thing, Dee Dee. I was on my way to the drugstore to exchange a piece of defective merchandise, and I thought I'd just pop in here for a bite to eat. When I noticed you sitting here in such earnest conversation with Syd, I just had to come over and renew old acquaintance." She smiled brightly at Doris.

"It's . . . this is not a good time."

Syd had never seen Doris so flustered.

"Oh, don't say that, Dee Dee." Celine pulled out a chair and sat down. "In fact, you might be just the person to help me out with this thing." She rummaged around inside her canvas tote and withdrew a flexible plastic bag equipped with a long, funnel-shaped tube. She swung it back and forth in front of Doris like a hypnotist's medallion. "I think you have some experience with these . . . don't you, Dee Dee?"

Doris was turning five shades of red. Syd was actually afraid for a moment that she had stopped breathing.

"What the hell *is* this?" she asked looking from Celine to Syd. "Some kind of shakedown?"

"I guess you'd be the judge of that, wouldn't you Dorrie?" The words dropped from Celine's mouth like chips of ice.

Doris pointed at the douchebag. "Take that disgusting thing and get out of here, Celine." She was starting to recover her composure. "This matter doesn't concern you."

"Oh, I beg to differ, Dorrie." Celine leaned over the table and dropped her voice to a near whisper. "Nobody threatens the sainted reputation of *my* little girl."

"Back off, Celine. This isn't prep school, and you're way out of your league."

"Again, I beg to differ. Experience is a hard teacher, Dorrie. Believe me when I tell you that I eat homegrown, new-money bitches like you for lunch."

"*Fuck you* and your Upper East Side pedigree." Doris boiled over. "You always thought you were better than everyone else—and your parents were nothing more than dried-up hunks of wetback Euro trash."

Celine was unfazed. "Is that the best you've got Dorrie?" She tsked. "I guess all those years you spent running from the family business finally paid off. Wouldn't your Brahmin buddies love to know that your family's real fortune came from all those toxic vaginal powders your granddaddy hawked to unsuspecting hillbillies in Tennessee?"

Syd was stupefied. She'd never seen Celine in action before. No wonder Maddie had been so terrified of her mother growing up. She slowly looked back and forth between them as their face-off continued. She had a feeling that she was about to be ringside for the cage fight of the century.

Doris took up the gauntlet. "I'm not surprised that your 'little girl' turned out to be such a disappointment, Celine. But then, it could hardly be a surprise when her father was a first-class *faggot*."

Syd stared at Doris with an open mouth. *My god . . .*

Beside her, Celine sat in silence for a moment. The only sign of discomposure was a tiny vein, visibly throbbing on the side of her forehead.

"You know, Dorrie. I'm a scientist, and I've devoted my life to solving problems," Celine said. Her voice was eerily controlled. "But there's *one* equation that just never comes out right." She tented her fingertips like a professor leading a seminar discussion. "You left school one month before the end of our senior year, citing a family emergency. Of course, we all knew what that meant. Your prom night fumble in the backseat of Carmine Fazzoli's Plymouth resulted in a little spring surprise, didn't it?"

Doris's lips were stretched thin—pursed so tight they were nearly translucent. She was taking deep breaths. Her eyes looked like hot coals.

Celine took advantage of her silence.

"I say that because barely two months later, you were the blushing bride of that poor little rich schmoe, Howard Simon." She dropped her voice. "But here's the part that just won't add up, Dorrie. Your precious philandering son was born only *six* months after that."

Doris was furious. "This is *pathetic*—even for *you*. You're making slanderous allegations that you can't possibly prove."

Celine raised an eyebrow. "Oh, really?" She sighed. "All my years, mentoring med students at Hopkins certainly came in handy. Last night, I made a phone call to a *very* reliable source in the medical records department at Beth Israel. Turns out that your pride and joy was a *big* baby—nearly eight pounds."

Doris gasped. "Violating HIPAA laws is a felony . . ."

"And I'm sure that's *exactly* the first thought Howard will have, too. Won't he, Dorrie?"

"Fuck you!"

"I'm glad you appreciate my quandary." Celine picked up a triangle of pita bread and bit off its tip. "The numbers just don't add up, do they?" She smiled. "You might say it's a spot of *Fazzoli* math."

Doris picked up a sweating glass and flung its contents across the table at Celine. "You bitch!" she screamed.

The liquid went everyplace. Celine jerked back and jumped to her feet, knocking her chair over. Sweet tea and chunks of melted ice dropped from her face and chest like an amber waterfall.

Syd couldn't take in what was happening. Time seemed to speed up—like someone had pressed a fast-forward button. Two men seated behind their table got to their feet, too.

"Hey!" one of the men, yelled. "What the hell?"

Celine ran a hand across her face, then picked up the tomato pie. "I think you'll like this Dorrie—it goes with your outfit."

Syd saw what was coming and reached out a hand to try and stop Celine, but she threw the pie with pinpoint accuracy and hit Doris right in the center of her silicone-enhanced bodice. An organic sash of chunky tomato magma spread out across her ample chest. Red splatters dotted her face and neck.

Syd stared at Doris with disbelief. *She looks like she has the measles . . .*

Doris stared down at her ruined couture and exploded with rage. "You *bitch*!" she shrieked. She shoved her hand into the bowl of hummus and scooped up a soggy handful. Celine ducked, and the gloppy mass flew past her and hit the same man who had already been doused with the iced tea.

"Goddamn it!" he yelled. "I've had about enough of this bull-shit. You two bitches need to take this shit *outside*."

Things went from bad to worse when Nadine exploded from the kitchen like one of the Four Horsemen of the Apocalypse. She made a beeline for their table, shoving bystanders out of her way with all the grace of a fullback busting through a goal line defense.

"Just what in the *hell* is going on out here?" she demanded.

Doris looked at her with a murderous gaze. "Stay out of this. It's none of your *fucking* business." She picked up a cheese biscuit and hurled it at Nadine.

Uh oh, Syd thought. *Not a good move, Doris . . .*

Nadine caught the incoming biscuit . . . in one hand. She stopped dead in her tracks and looked from Doris to the biscuit, then back to Doris.

Time stood still. Syd heard a collective gasp from the rest of the diners.

"*Oh, no.*" Nadine wagged a long, flour-covered index finger. "Somebody better *please* tell me that this skinny white woman did *not* just throw one of my own biscuits at me in *MY OWN DAMN ESTABLISHMENT!*"

Syd closed her eyes. *Hell was certainly out of its box now . . .* And that was pretty hard to imagine.

Nadine hurled the biscuit back at Doris and clocked her right in the center of the forehead. "Nobody throws my food but *me!*"

Doris staggered backward and slammed into the table behind her, sending three half-eaten bowls of chicken and dumplings crashing to the floor.

Nadine stormed to the table and stood over Doris, who was splayed across the floor in a most unladylike posture.

"Girl," she said, pointing down at her with all the umbrage of Jehovah on Judgment Day. "All I can say is you better have a *big* damn checkbook, because *somebody* is going to pay to clean up this mess."

Doris was too overcome to speak, but Celine stepped forward.

"Let me get that process started for you, Nadine."

She pointed the nozzle of the douche at Doris and gave the bag a good, big squeeze. A hefty stream of clear liquid shot out. Celine carefully doused her from head to toe.

A pleasing scent of Country Flowers filled the air.

Nervous titters of laughter started from someplace within the crowd of onlookers. Before long, it erupted into a full-blown chorus of whoops and whistles.

The noise was so loud that Syd didn't notice the sirens until all three of the sheriff's cars skidded to a stop out front on Raymond's fresh bed of gravel.

David was pouring them each a splash of champagne. He said they had something big to celebrate, and he couldn't wait around any longer for the rest of the crew to show up. Besides . . . he'd opened the bottle an hour ago, and there was only about one full glass left.

It was nearly four-thirty, and Syd wasn't home yet, but Maddie just assumed that she had stopped by the school to turn in her final grades, or gone on into town to run some errands on her way home. Maddie was very anxious to hear how Syd's meeting with Doris went, but she assumed that no news was good news. She was certain that she would've heard something if the encounter had gone south in any truly dramatic ways.

Celine wasn't at home either. David said she had asked to borrow his car around lunchtime, but he didn't think anything about it. She had been looking around the area at some vacation cottages, thinking she might invest in something more permanent, since she now was spending so much time back East. They all were encouraging her in this enterprise—Maddie especially.

David handed her a glass.

"What time did you say Mom left?" she asked.

David glanced at his watch. "I think it was noon, or shortly after." He took a sip of the champagne. "I guess it was more like twelve-thirty, because it was right before Isobel came to pick up Henry."

Henry was celebrating the end of the school year with his best friends, Gabriel and Héctor Sanchez. Isobel was taking the boys to pick strawberries, and then they were going to make ice cream and watch videos.

"Care to tell me what we're celebrating?" Maddie asked. "And *where* did you get this?" She held her glass up to the light. The straw-colored liquid looked familiar.

"It's that last bottle of De Margerie you've been hoarding."

Maddie lowered her flute. "I thought so. Where did you find it?"

David impatiently fluttered a hand. "On the third shelf in the barn refrigerator, behind four fridge packs of Diet Coke . . . you know . . . where you hid it."

"So much for *that* brilliant idea." Maddie took a sip of the champagne. The Grand Cru Brut was her favorite, and she had been saving it for . . . something to be determined. "I hope you enjoyed it," she added.

"Are you kidding? This stuff is *great*." He took another sip. "We're going to have to start stocking this at the Inn. It totally kicks The Widow's ass." He looked at Maddie. "Got any more of it hidden around this joint?"

"No."

"I so do not believe you. You're doing that thing you do when you lie."

"What thing?"

He pointed at her face. "That thing . . . you know . . . with the eyebrow and the convulsive blinking."

"Convulsive blinking? What the hell are you talking about?"

"See. You just did it again." He slowly shook his head. "You totally should get that checked out, Cinderella. It could be early onset blepharospasm."

Maddie sighed. "How do you come up with this crap, and where in the hell did you hear about blepharospasm?"

"It happens to be a serious and underreported condition that affects nearly one in every twenty-thousand people."

"Have you been watching *Nurse Jackie* marathons again?"

"*No.*" David was offended. "For your information, I *read* about it."

"You read about it?"

"I do happen to read, you know."

"Sure you do."

"For your information, wise guy—not only am I erudite and well-read, I'll soon be a published author."

Maddie raised an eyebrow, then realized what she was doing and reached up to smooth it with her fingertips.

David smiled brightly at her.

"Shut up," she said. "Tell me about your . . . book?"

"It's actually a story collection. I'm the editor and co-translator."

"*Translator?* You?"

"Yes, *me*. Why is that so hard to believe?"

Maddie sighed. "David. You're the only person I know who needs subtitles for operas that are sung in English."

He humphed.

"Okay, okay . . . I apologize. Now tell me. What are these stories, and what language were they written in originally?"

David continued to pout.

It was time to haul out the big guns.

"If you talk with me, I'll tell you where there's another bottle of De Margerie . . ."

That got his attention. He sat forward on his chair. "It's this incredible series of German stories—fan fiction, written by an amateur author in Düsseldorf. He posted them for free on the Internet, but they weren't available in English. I read about them in a random blog post comment at *Gawker*, so I contacted him."

"What on earth is fan fiction?"

"Are you seriously asking me this question?"

"Am I to infer from your response that I should already know this?"

He looked toward the ceiling. "You *might* say that."

She sighed. "Enlighten me, please."

"Really, Cinderella. You might want to consider joining this century."

"I'll take it under advisement."

"Fan fiction—also called, alternatively, fanfic, slash fiction, femslash, het, and gen—is fiction written about characters who were not created by the amateur authors. These stories are generally posted for free on various Internet sites that host the works and categorize them by subject or type."

"And these German stories are examples of genre work that spins off other, preexisting characters?"

David nodded.

Maddie was confused. "Don't you run into copyright issues with the creators of the original works?"

"Not if you're careful and change enough detail—including names—before publication so it isn't a clear rip-off."

"But if you do that, how do people know what the real subject is?"

David dropped his chin to his chest. "Do you live under a rock?"

"Come on . . . I'm really trying to be supportive here."

He gave a dramatic sigh. "Fine. Let me try to simplify this for you. Let's suppose, for the sake of discussion, that you and Syd are actually fictional characters patterned after other, preexisting and supremely popular cultural icons, and that I created you to loosely imitate them and make a tidy profit in the process."

"Cultural icons?"

He shrugged. "Sure. Like, say, Cagney and Lacey."

"Syd and I would be rip-offs of Cagney and Lacey?"

"It could happen . . . you're dark and brooding . . . she's light and hot. You're butch, she's femme . . . it's that whole yin and yang thing. Get it?"

"No. Weren't Cagney and Lacey straight?"

David slapped his palm against his forehead. "Duh. That's the whole point of fanfic, Cinderella. I get to make you anything I want, and fulfill the fantasies of zillions of baby dykes in the process. All of them, I might add, with credit cards and access to eReaders."

Maddie thought about that. Then she looked at him. "Do we have to be Cagney and Lacey?"

"*Good god.* Do you always have to be so damn *literal?* Pick any pair of popular Vagitarian wannabes you want."

Maddie finished her champagne. "How about Xena and Gabrielle?"

"Xena? *Seriously?* Can you say, 'welcome to 1995'? How about something for people who aren't on life support?"

"Um . . . Rizzoli and Isles?"

David raised his hands to the heavens. "I think she's got it."

"All right, all right. So this is what you're publishing? A collection of German fan fiction stories that spin off some cultural icons, but don't compromise any copyright restrictions?"

"Precisely."

"Who is your publisher?"

"MaleStrum Press."

"Maelstrom? Like the storm?"

"No . . . Male-Strum, like strum a male." He pretended to strum an imaginary guitar.

"I'm not familiar with that one."

"That's because I just created it. I also like the double entendre in the name—you know . . . homage to the tornado?"

"I'm confused."

"Ever heard of self-publishing? It's all the rage these days."

"Oh. You're putting this out on your own?"

"Did you overdose on Benadryl or something? Yes . . . I'm self-publishing. And why not? Even some of the top-selling authors are going this route now. The profits are astronomical."

"Don't you need an editor—at least for the German translation?"

David rolled his eyes. "I *have* an editor, thankyouverymuch. *And* she's an accomplished scholar with serious street cred."

Maddie was dubious. "Who? If you don't mind my asking."

"She's using a pseudonym—Stanford Hopkins."

"Stanford Hopkins?" Maddie pondered that for a moment, then she stared at David with wide-eyed disbelief. "*Mom?*"

He gave her a smug smile.

"You have *got* to be kidding me."

He shook his head.

"You got *Mom* to translate a bunch of German pulp fiction?"

"She's truly amazing, Cinderella. She knocked them all out in a fraction of the time we thought it might take. I think she has unsung talents. She should seriously consider ditching the med school gig and wading into this full time."

Maddie was staring at him with an open mouth.

"What's the matter with you? You look just like you did when you found out that *Little House on the Prairie* got canceled."

"You . . . and *Mom*? Really?"

"Yes, *really*. That's part of what we're celebrating. The first e-books went live at amazon.com last night."

"Oh, god . . ."

"Hey . . . before you try to rain on my parade, let me just tell you that the book is a *smash*."

"I'll bet."

"I'm not kidding. It debuted at *number one* at amazon.de, and in the U.S. alone, we've already sold more than twenty-five hundred e-books."

"I'm going out on a limb here and guessing that's good?"

"Good? No. It's not *good*, it's effing phenomenal."

Maddie was still in a semi-state of shock. "How much do these things cost?"

David brushed the fingers of his hand across his chest. "Seven ninety-five each."

Maddie did a quick calculation. "That's nearly twenty thousand dollars."

"No shit, Sherlock. And that's just the U.S. sales."

"What's the name of this book?"

"*The Tales of Rolf and Tobi*."

Maddie shook her head. "I need another drink."

"Now you know why your mom is out window shopping. Well," he took a deep breath, "at least it's safe to say that between this and the calendar sales, I finally met my fundraising goal."

"I'll say."

David set his glass down. "Now . . . where's that other bottle stashed? We have more good news to celebrate."

Maddie looked at him morosely. "I honestly don't think I can take any more good news."

"Trust me . . . this you want to hear."

She sighed. "All right."

He stood up. "So . . . where's the hooch?"

She jerked a thumb toward the big Sub-Zero. "In the back of the vegetable drawer, behind the broccolini and chard."

He stared at her. "Gross."

"That's precisely why I put it there."

"Whatever." He retrieved the champagne and a bar towel, then he reclaimed his seat and passed both across the table to Maddie. "You do the honors this time."

She opened the bottle and refilled both of their flutes. David reached for his glass, and she slid it just out of his reach. "Not so fast. There's something I want to ask you about."

He looked suspicious. "What is it?"

"You didn't, by chance, have a conversation with Tom Greene today, did you?"

"I most certainly did *not*. Why? Did something happen?"

Maddie narrowed her eyes. "You might say that. Tom called Lizzy and renewed her contract for another two years."

David clapped his hands together. "Score. That didn't take very long." He seemed to think better of his dramatic response to the news and quickly adopted a sober expression. "What a surprising turnaround," he said, with forced calm. "What do you think changed his mind?"

"Nice try," Maddie said. She pushed the glass across the table toward him. "David, you *promised* me that you wouldn't confront Tom about his . . . hobby."

"I most certainly did *not* promise any such thing. If memory serves, you blackmailed me, and I capitulated under duress."

"So you admit it?"

"I admit to nothing."

"Do you mean to tell me that you had *no* involvement in Tom's sudden turnaround with regard to the funding for Lizzy's position?"

"I didn't say that."

"I knew it."

"For your information, I did *not* speak with Tom."

"You didn't?"

"No." He took a healthy sip of champagne. "It was Muriel."

Maddie raised a hand to her eyes. "Oh, Jesus."

"She was very interested in the documentary evidence of your night of debauchery in Charlotte. I got the sense that she shared my concern about some of those photos being made public on Facebook."

Maddie dropped her jaw. "You *blackmailed* her?"

David rolled his eyes. "Of *course* not. She agreed with me that *you* wouldn't want people to know what kinds of questionable things you and Syd do when you're out of town."

"What Syd and I do?"

He sighed. "Work with me here, Dr. Strangelove."

Maddie started to get a clue. "You mean, you never told Muriel that you knew those were pictures of the two of them? And she actually *bought* that?"

David rolled his eyes. "Of course she didn't *buy* it. It was just a way for her to dodge the obvious bullet headed her way." He reached for the champagne bottle so he could top off his glass. "I told her that you'd plainly had a lapse in judgment, since you were so distressed about losing the funding for Lizzy's position. That's why you and Syd ended up giving in to such an uncharacteristically reckless impulse and went to a drag show in Charlotte." He smiled. "She seemed to commiserate right away—once she started breathing again."

"Oh, god."

"You're welcome, by the way."

She sighed. "I guess I do owe you some thanks."

"Well, eureka. It's about damn time I got some credit for something around here."

"And while we're on the subject . . . I recall that I deleted those photos from my cell phone. How did you get copies of them?"

"Duh. I emailed them all to myself as soon as I found them."

Maddie closed her eyes. "Of course you did."

"My mama didn't raise no Luddite. Unlike *you*, I have a healthy respect for the efficacious applications of technology."

"I really need to stop underestimating you."

"I'll say. You can repay me by making certain that the hunky Mr. Murphy drives down to attend our grand reopening soirée next weekend."

Maddie nodded. "I'll see what I can do."

"In the meantime, you'll never guess what *else* happened at Junior's this morning."

"Illuminate me."

"Well . . . I was actually out there to take care of a special little somethin' somethin' I've got planned for the party, and Junior mentioned how far behind he was because of all the body work that came his way after the storm. Seems that he and Cletus just can't keep up with it all, and people are getting frustrated with how long it's taking to get their rides back."

"I'm sure there's a point lurking in here someplace," Maddie said.

"Hold your horses and quit interrupting, Missy. You're about it hear it."

"Sorry."

"Well . . . shortly after Muriel watched my little slideshow, Junior came out give her the box containing whateverinthehell it was she ordered . . . probably chain lube or something. And I noticed his tattoo when he handed it to her."

"His tattoo?"

David nodded. "He has a big ole U.S. Army Infantry symbol— the one with the crossed rifles? Turns out that Junior is a Vietnam vet, and very involved in the local VFW post. We started talking about all of that, and I asked if he'd heard about what happened to Henry's dad."

Maddie was intrigued. "Had he?"

"Nope. But he was all over it—especially when I told him that James was reputed to be some kind of whiz kid at fixing cars."

Maddie could hardly believe what she was hearing. "What did he say when you told him about that?"

"He said that, if he wants it, James has a job, and that's not all. Cletus and Evelyn are moving out of the apartment and into town, so they can be closer to Azalea's doctor in Galax. That means their apartment out there will be available, and Junior said he'd let James live there for free until he got back on his feet . . . so to speak." He looked at Maddie apologetically. "I didn't mean that the way it came out."

She smiled at him. "I know what you meant."

"So," he said. "What do you think?"

Maddie didn't know what to say. If James took Junior up on

his offer, that would mean that Henry would still be nearby—close enough that maybe they could still see him often.

On the other hand, she really had no idea how James might feel about relocating to an area where he had no history and no attachments. He might prefer to take his son and make a fresh start someplace else—someplace far away from Jericho.

And there'd be nothing they could do about that.

There were just too many unknowns, and too much potential for disappointed hopes.

She looked at David. "Do me a favor, okay? Don't mention anything about this to Syd until we have a chance to find out if it's even something James is interested in considering."

David looked confused. "I thought you'd be ecstatic about this. I don't get it."

"David, I'm about as ecstatic as I could be about any scenario that involves losing Henry."

He dropped his eyes. "I know . . . I'm really sad about that, too. I just thought this was a way to make the best of a bad situation."

She reached across the table and took hold of his hand. "It is, and I appreciate this more than you know. I really do. And believe me, I'm going to call James tonight and see what he thinks about the idea. I just don't want to get Syd's hopes up until we know it's a real possibility."

"I understand."

Maddie squeezed his hand. "Thank you, David. I mean that."

David looked away. Maddie could tell that he was close to tears.

"It'll be okay," she said.

He nodded without speaking.

Outside from his customary perch on the front porch, Pete started barking like crazy. They heard him jump down from his glider and thunder off the porch—barking all the way.

Maddie heard the unmistakable sound of an approaching car. "I bet that's Mom or Syd. Grab another glass, and I'll meet you outside." She gave David's hand a final squeeze before getting to her feet.

He nodded and got up, too. Then he squinted and peered out the window behind her.

"That's not Syd or Celine," he said. "It's the sheriff."

Maddie whipped her head around. "What?"

David was right. The car rolled to a stop, and Charlie Davis climbed out. Maddie felt her heart lurch inside her chest. *What happened?*

Pete was dancing around Charlie's feet, and she stopped to scrub him behind the ears.

Maddie's panic subsided as she watched Charlie bending over to interact with the dog. *Whatever it is, it can't be too serious, or she wouldn't be playing with Pete. Right?*

She took a deep breath and walked out onto the porch. David followed on her heels.

"Hi there, Charlie," she called out. "What brings you out here?"

Charlie straightened up at once and brushed off her trouser legs. "Hi there, Dr. Stevenson—Mr. Jenkins. I'm sorry to show up like this . . . but Sheriff Martin sent me out here to ask you to come into town."

"He did?" Maddie was confused. "Why didn't he just call me?"

Charlie looked embarrassed. "It's . . . well . . . He, um, needs you to come make bail."

"Bail?" David blurted out.

Maddie held up a hand to shush him. "What happened?"

"Well, ma'am, there was some kind of fracas at the café, and . . . um . . . your, um . . . well . . . She got arrested."

"Arrested?" David was beside himself with excitement. "Syd got arrested? I *knew* this would happen . . . I *so* should've gone along. That pompous windbag mother-in-law of hers did this, didn't she?"

Maddie turned and glared at him.

"Sorry," he said.

Maddie faced Charlie. "Who got arrested, Charlie?"

Charlie looked down at the ground. "Well . . ."

"Was it Syd?" Maddie asked.

Her mind was racing ahead. She *never* should have agreed to let Syd meet Doris by herself. Syd was far too angry about the divorce, and far too fragile because of everything related to Henry and James.

"No, ma'am. It wasn't Miss Murphy."

Maddie was confused. "Then who was it?"

Charlie took a deep breath. "It was Dr. Heller."

"*What?*" Maddie was incredulous.

She jumped about a foot into the air when something loud crashed behind her.

She swung around to see that David—who had just knocked over half a dozen clay pots—had collapsed into a chair, convulsing with laughter.

"Ohmygod," he said between guffaws. "Stanford Hopkins is in the hoosegow . . ."

Maddie couldn't remember when it had ever taken this long to drive into town.

She decided to ride in with Charlie, since she'd had two glasses of champagne, thinking it was in everyone's best interest if only *one* member of the family ended up behind bars today.

It was a struggle, but she convinced David to remain behind.

He was furious at Michael for not calling to let him know what all had transpired, until he realized that the ringer on his cell phone had somehow gotten turned off. He found five voice messages and seventeen texts—all escalating in intensity—from the distraught chef. Furthermore, when he finally checked, there were even two messages on the house phone—a clear indication that Michael had tried to call while David was out in the barn conducting his hooch hunt.

Charlie was mostly silent during the ride downtown, but Maddie was able to extract some additional information from her about what had happened at the café.

As it turned out, Syd, Celine, and Doris had all been picked up and taken to jail by the sheriff's deputies, but only Celine and Doris were being held for bond. As near as Maddie could tell,

Doris was pressing charges against Celine for assault, and Nadine was pressing charges against Doris for the destruction of personal property that ensued in the . . . food fight?

Jesus.

Apparently, Syd had just got caught in the crossfire.

Good god. This whole thing's surreal.

Of all the experiences Maddie never thought she'd have with her mother, heading to the county jail to post bail for her *had* to top the list.

What on earth was her mother even *doing* at the café? And how did she get so entangled with Doris Simon?

Assault? Celine?

The woman was a poster child for self-control. Her maddening inability to express strong emotion had always been one of the hallmarks of her character. It used to drive Maddie's father *nuts.*

It just made no sense.

Maddie rubbed her forehead. She never should have had champagne so early in the day. Now she was getting a headache.

"Are you okay, Dr. Stevenson?"

Maddie raised her head and looked at Charlie. The young deputy had both hands gripping the steering wheel, and her eyes were fixed on the road ahead. They were now about three miles from the sheriff's office.

"I'm okay, Charlie," she replied. "I'm sure you can imagine that all of this is a pretty big shock."

"Yes, ma'am," Charlie said. "I was worried about coming out there to tell you about what happened, but Sheriff Martin said he really wanted me to be the one to do it."

"Why do you think he sent you?"

Charlie shrugged. "Maybe he thinks I know you better because of Henry and . . . um . . ."

"Roma Jean?" Maddie offered.

Charlie seemed embarrassed. "Yes, ma'am."

"It's okay. I'm glad Byron sent you out to the house."

Charlie glanced at her. Her blue-gray eyes looked surprised. "You are?"

Maddie nodded. "Sure. I know that you and Roma Jean are close, and she's like family to us."

Charlie nodded, but didn't say anything.

Maddie gave in to an impulse and pressed her point. "Charlie? I am right that you and Roma Jean are close, aren't I?"

"I hope so," Charlie replied. After a moment, she added, "I like her a lot."

"I do, too," Maddie agreed. "And I'm sure you know that I care a lot about what happens to her."

Charlie looked at her again. "So do I, Dr. Stevenson."

Maddie thought her tone was defiant, but in an appropriate way.

"That's good," she said. "That tells me that I can trust you not to take advantage of her friendship, or to push her into things she might not be ready for."

"I'd *never* do something like that." Charlie's expression was so earnest and open that Maddie had no doubt of her sincerity.

Maddie smiled at her to try and put her at ease. "I'm sure you never would, Charlie."

They reached the edge of town, and Charlie turned right onto the road that would take them to the county courthouse and jail. They pulled into the parking lot, and Maddie could see Michael standing outside the building next his Rover and talking on his cell phone—to David, no doubt. He waved when he saw her and walked toward the car.

Maddie unfastened her seatbelt and turned to her chauffeur. "I can't thank you enough for the sensitive way you handled this, Charlie. I'll always be grateful to you for that. I think Byron knew what he was doing when he picked you to be the one to fetch me. I think you're a person of integrity."

Charlie seemed to understand that Maddie was thanking her for more than the ride into town. "I'll do my best not to ever let you down."

In the few seconds that elapsed before Michael reached them and yanked open her car door, Maddie became convinced that Charlie would always live up to her promise.

◊ ◊ ◊

Maddie added a third teaspoon of sugar to her coffee, feeling confident that neither of her companions would have the temerity to protest. They were finally back at home, seated around the big kitchen table. Maddie had asked Michael to keep David corralled so she could talk with her two felons in private.

"Okay," she said. "Which one of you wants to go first?"

Syd and Celine both started talking at once.

Maddie quickly held up a hand. "One at a time, if you please. I already have a headache, and I just shelled out five hundred bucks for the privilege of getting to tell you both what to do."

Her mother grumbled something under her breath.

Maddie cupped an ear and bent toward her. "Did you say something, Laverne?"

Syd chuckled.

Maddie glared at her. "Don't think you're off the hook either, Shirley."

"*Me?*" Syd pointed a finger at her own chest. "What the hell did I do?"

"Ever heard the phrase 'guilt by association'?"

"That's ridiculous. Doris was the architect of this whole thing. Wasn't she, Celine?"

Syd looked at her accomplice. Celine was uncharacteristically slumped down in her seat. Maddie assumed her poor posture was as much an attempt to conceal the dried food stains on the front of her suit, as it was an expression of weariness.

"As tempting as that is, Syd," Celine began, "I can't really blame all of this on Dorrie. I showed up there, intending to bait her, and it worked with a vengeance."

"You think?" Maddie asked. "The arrest of the august Dr. Heller on charges of aggravated assault is going to make quite a salacious headline in this week's *Gazette*, Mom."

Celine waved a tired hand. "Oh, don't get your panties in a wad. Dorrie would never let it go that far."

Maddie looked at her mother with amazement. "You're in the joint for less than two hours, and you start talking like Lorraine Bracco?"

Syd stifled a laugh. Maddie shot her a dirty look and focused her attention back on her mother. "What makes you so certain that Doris will drop her charges?"

"Because the only thing she still hates worse than *me*, or tomato pie," Celine chuckled, "is having her precious name associated with *any* kind of scandal."

"That's true," Syd agreed. "She'd pay big money to keep this out of the news."

Maddie sighed. "Well, according to Nadine, she's going to have to pay big money to clean up the mess you all made at the café."

"How much were the damages?" Syd asked, with genuine-sounding concern.

Maddie shrugged. "I'm not sure about the final tally. Michael said Nadine was thinking about suing her for a couple thousand. That's as much for lost revenue as it is for actual cleanup and repair."

"A couple thousand?" Syd waved her hand. "Are you kidding me? Doris spends more than that on *brunch*."

"That's hardly a comfort, sweetheart."

"Well, it's a moot point, anyway," Celine said. "I already heard from Dorrie's attorney." She held up her cell phone. "She's offering to drop all charges and forget the entire thing happened."

Syd brightened up at once. "Really? Will she pay Nadine?"

Celine nodded. "She's *already* paid Nadine. But," she raised a finger, "she has a condition for you, Syd."

Syd slumped back against her chair. "Of course she does."

Maddie was wary. "What is it?"

Celine took a deep breath. "Apparently, she's willing to drop her son's contest of the divorce, *if* Syd will drop her allegation of infidelity. This would allow the marriage to be dissolved without prejudice on either side."

Syd appeared stunned by the offer. "Why would she agree to do that?"

"Because you and I would both sign affidavits, swearing that we will never make mention of anything that transpired today—especially my allegations about her son's premature birth."

Maddie looked back and forth between them. "Do I even want to know what you're talking about?"

"No," Celine and Syd replied in unison.

Syd sat quietly for a moment, then looked at Celine. "What does this mean about the prenup?"

Celine gave her a long, slow smile. "I think it means you just got your ten percent severance package."

Syd's jaw dropped. "You mean I still get the money?"

Maddie was really confused now. "What money?"

Syd looked at her. "Our prenup specified that if we ever divorced without prejudice, I'd get ten percent of Jeff's net worth."

"Oh," Maddie said. "And Jeff's net worth is?"

"Roughly twenty-five million dollars—give or take," Celine said.

Maddie was speechless.

Syd patted the top of Maddie's hand. "Don't worry, honey . . . I promise not to let it change me." She laughed merrily.

Celine slowly shook her head. "Poor Dorrie. She took all that punishment just to try and hang on to a paltry few million."

Maddie was still feeling shell-shocked. She looked at Syd. "Honey," she said in a quiet voice. "That's two and a half million dollars."

"Tax-free," Celine added.

Syd just smiled. "I've always wanted to invest in livestock."

Chapter 20

The day of the Inn's grand reopening was the warmest they'd had yet. The mercury had climbed steadily all day, and by three o'clock, it was pushing seventy-two degrees—perfect for an outdoor event of this magnitude.

Everyone in town was invited, and nearly everyone showed up. David had outdone himself with the preparations. He and Michael had actually moved back into their rebuilt bungalow the night before the party, and it was on the open-house tour, too, along with the grandly refurbished main facility.

The Riverside Inn and its grounds were better, bolder, and more perfectly appointed than ever. Four dozen tables dotted the big front lawn, and food and beverage stations were scattered about at precisely the right intervals. There were games for the kids and roomy Adirondack chairs for the folks who just wanted to sit and share stories about The Storm that Changed Everything.

Today was the day that David and Michael engineered to give their friends and neighbors a chance to celebrate how much they all had survived, and how hard they each had worked to rebuild their town and their lives. Nowhere was that resiliency more apparent than in the faces of the men and women who had participated in the rebuilding of the inn. They were special guests of honor—those carpenters, electricians, plumbers, painters, landscapers, gardeners, and cleanup crews who had worked so tirelessly to make today's celebration possible.

There were other guests of honor, too—people who had lost things that couldn't be replaced. Deb Carlson was there, and she made a valiant effort to join in the general air of celebration—even though it was clear that her heart just wasn't in it. More than once, Jocelyn had to go and fetch her when she wandered off down the path that led to the river.

Gladys Pitzer was there, too, and David had made sure of that by going to pick her up himself. He arranged a special seat for her at their table—right near the steps that led to the big front porch. She was antsy and nervous, but that wasn't really a change from her normal demeanor. She distracted herself by wandering from table to table, pulling the cattails out of every arrangement.

She'd already told David that it was the wrong time of year to be including those, but he did it anyway.

Azalea Freemantle actually showed up, but insisted that she was going to sit in the truck until Edna left. Once Cletus managed to convince her that Edna wasn't going to be leaving anytime soon, she consented to get out of the truck, but she would only sit on a folding chair near the food kiosk that was serving Nadine's fried chicken.

David later commented that every time he passed her chair, he noticed more leg bones piled up on the ground beside it. Astrid actually left the sanctuary of her dog bed beneath the porch and toddled over to take up residence on the ground at Azalea's feet. It was hard to tell whether she was guarding Azalea, or the pyramid of chicken bones, but whenever anyone got too close, she growled and bared her tiny fangs.

Charlie Davis came wearing her Sunday best, and David punched Maddie in the ribs when he saw Edna invite her to sit down at the Freemantles' table. He noted that Charlie was careful not to sit beside Roma Jean, and it was lucky for her that she didn't, because it only took Roma Jean about two seconds to knock over their pitcher of iced tea. Everyone laughed, though—including Edna—and Charlie just smiled, picked up the pitcher, and walked off to see about getting it refilled.

David supposed that Charlie might just be resourceful enough to survive as a companion for Roma Jean. When he said as much to Maddie, she did not disagree.

All in all, it had been a wonderful afternoon.

Syd and Henry were tasked with getting sticks and marshmallows ready for the big bonfire David had planned for after dinner. But first, he had a special announcement to make. He looked around to make sure that everyone he needed was in place—and that the "package" had been delivered.

He looked toward the big outbuilding where they stored all of their outdoor furnishings and lawn equipment during the winter months. Junior was leaning against the freshly painted bay door. David caught his eye, and Junior gave him a clandestine thumbs-up sign.

It was time.

David walked up the big front steps and went to where they'd set up the sound system. He picked up a microphone. Michael followed him and turned off the bluegrass music they'd been playing all afternoon, then went back down to reclaim his seat.

David faced the crowd with all the ease and panache of a sideshow barker. "Hey, y'all. Hey, there . . . Gimme your attention for just a minute or two. I promise it won't take long. Come on . . . come on . . . stop gabbing. Azalea, put down that chicken leg. Cletus . . . you and Evelyn wanna grab her knitting bag—just to be on the safe side? Thanks."

He waited for the titter of conversation to die down. "That's right . . . that's right. It's me. With a microphone. Be *very* afraid . . ."

There was a smattering of laughter, then it quieted down enough for him to continue.

"We're so very happy and grateful to see so many of you here today," David said. "Michael and I owe so much to all of you, and we wanted to say thank you for all you've done to help us stand here and realize our dream . . . once again. The Riverside Inn— like the town of Jericho—has been reborn. And that's because we all understand that the things that bind us together are more than bricks and mortar. We will endure, and we will persevere because we are part of a family—and families will always reach out, dig down, roll up their sleeves, and lift each other up whenever they fall. That's what we do because that's who we are."

Someone in the crowd started clapping. Soon, it spread across the lawn like wildfire, and the whole place erupted in cheers.

David looked out over the sea of faces that he'd known most of his life. They were all there. His mama and Celine. Nelda Rae Black and the Lear Twins. Nadine, Nicorette, and Raymond. Sonny and Harold Nicks. Bert Townsend. Byron Martin. Rita, from the bowling alley. The Buford brothers. The Wives. The Sanchez family.

Lizzy Mayes had even shown up with Syd's handsome brother in tow.

Finally, of course, he looked at the table where Maddie, Syd, and Henry sat with Michael. They were his family of choice.

The whooping and hollering continued. David let the celebration go on for another minute, then he shushed the crowd. He had something else to say.

"As much as we all lost—or nearly lost—three months ago, one of us stands out as the person who sacrificed the most. And I don't think it's hard to figure out who I mean." He saw the object of his remarks, walked to the top of the steps, and pointed at her. "Deb Carlson. Come on up here."

The crowd parted like a fork in the New River as Deb slowly and warily made her way to the porch. She was short and wiry with gray-streaked hair, but she looked hard as iron. She stopped short at the bottom of the steps and looked up at David with a mixture of fear and suspicion. David knew not to press her. Deb was small but feisty, and she was famous for her ability to bench-press an Oldsmobile.

"Deb, you lost something you loved in the storm, and we all bore witness to that. In fact," David looked out at the crush of townspeople, "how many of us here have pieces of Deb's beloved Camaro? Let's see a show of hands."

So many arms waved in the air, it looked like Sunday night at the Pentecostal Holiness Church.

"Look around you, Deb. These are your friends and neighbors, and your great loss became the bridge that brought us all back together. It unified us. It made us laugh. It filled us with excitement and hope, and it became an icon for our drive to endure."

He walked down the steps and stood just beside her.

"So we want to say thank you, Deb. Thank you for your great sacrifice, and thank you for giving us so many bright spots in the midst of so much loss and so much hard work."

He looked down the wide, open path the crowd had made, and gave the high sign. Everyone stood quietly, waiting. Deb was taking anxious looks at David, then back at the crowd. Behind her, Jocelyn was wearing about the biggest smile David had ever seen on a human being's face.

Then, they all heard it . . . the sound of a car starting. Every head in the crowd swung toward the shed. The next sound they heard was the unmistakable rumble of a 350-horsepower, big block V-8 engine. It was backed up by the sheer poetry of a four-barrel, Holley carburetor.

Deb turned pale and started to shake.

Zeke Dawkins and Bert Townsend rolled back the big bay door on the shed. Inside the dark interior, two headlights glowed like tractor beams.

Behind the wheel, Junior gunned the big engine a few times for effect before he shifted the four-speed Muncie transmission into gear and took the perfectly reconditioned, blazing red 1968 Chevy Camaro SS for the shortest, but most important, drive of its life.

Tears streamed down Deb's face. David turned to her and held out a duplicate set of keys.

"Miss Carlson," he said. "I think your ride is here."

And the crowd went wild . . .

◊   ◊   ◊

How fast things started to happen after she put James Lawrence in contact with Junior made Maddie's head spin. She felt like she was ten years old again, riding the Tilt-a-Whirl at Pacific Park in Santa Monica. Only now, it was time that was spinning faster and faster outside her control. She couldn't make it stop—any more than she could slow it down.

James Lawrence jumped at the chance to take a position as an auto mechanic at Junior's. Maddie really didn't know what kind of reaction to expect when she told him about Junior's offer, but James quickly expressed interest in relocating to Troutdale and taking the job. He explained that he didn't really have any ties anyplace else. He couldn't return to California to live, and since his mother was now in full-time nursing care, he didn't have a home in Kannapolis to return to. He was also realistic enough to know that he'd have an easier time managing Henry in an area where his son had so many close connections—especially with Maddie and Syd.

He eagerly accepted Junior's offer of the apartment, too, even though he knew that living out there would mean that Henry would have to change schools. The apartment wasn't furnished, but Junior was connecting James with a local chapter of the Vietnam Vets, and they were going to get him started with the bare necessities. Maddie had to fight an impulse to tell James that she would furnish the damn place herself, but she knew that wasn't the right thing to do. After so much time away, James wanted the chance to make a life with Henry on his own. She did make it clear, however, that she and Syd were available to help out in any way they could.

Walter Reed was discharging James on Thursday. He was traveling first to Kannapolis to see his mother and to pick up his car, then his plan was to drive himself to Jericho to spend time getting reacquainted with Henry and spend a couple of days getting situated in the apartment near Junior's.

James had already made contacts in the area. The Bureau of Veterans Affairs had a community-based outreach clinic in Wytheville, where he could continue his outpatient therapy. The

VA Medical Center in Salem, which was about an hour north of there, would be his primary resource, should he require any more serious care.

James would start his new job at Junior's a week after arriving. He would work a few hours each day—just to see how things went and to be sure he had enough stamina to manage the demands of the job.

He was confident that he would soon be able to resume a full-time work schedule—he was strong and healthy, and he'd worked very hard to adjust to life with an artificial limb. He admitted that he sometimes had bouts of what he called depression, but he was certain that these would diminish once he was able to resume a more normal life out of the hospital and away from the regular Army. And he was determined to have things as squared away as possible before taking Henry on a more permanent basis. He told Maddie that if things proceeded according to plan, he thought he should be ready to have Henry join him in Troutdale as early as the following Wednesday.

This meant that Maddie and Syd had fewer than seven days left with the boy who had been the nexus of their lives for the past year and a half.

That left them in a quandary. They needed to explain to Henry that his father was coming home, but that Henry would be living with him someplace else. They both understood that, all along, Henry had indulged a fantasy that his daddy would one day live with all of them on the farm. After all . . . it was big enough. There were enough bedrooms—even when Uncle David and Uncle Michael still lived there.

No matter how many times they each tried, gently, to explain to him that a different outcome was likelier, Henry clung to his idealized view that everyone would continue to live together in the big white house.

Maddie and Syd struggled with what to say, and how much to tell him. He needed to know the truth, and he needed, as much as he was able, to prepare for his impending separation from them, and from everything that defined his sense of the familiar.

In the end, they decided that less was more, and it was better to stick to simple, unvarnished facts—avoiding a lot of overlay that might confuse or scare him. He was already dealing with the loss of David, Michael, and Astrid—who had moved back to the Inn the night before the party. They didn't want to overload him with more than he could be expected to handle.

They finished dinner and walked with him to the pond so he could feed the catfish. Henry stood with his red coffee can near the edge, and Pete sat at his heels, hoping for any dropped morsels. Henry tossed small handfuls of feed onto the surface of the water, and so many fat fish competed to retrieve it that the pond soon resembled a pot of boiling water.

"I talked to your daddy today, sport," Maddie began.

Henry looked at her with an excited expression.

"He had some really good news. He's getting out of the hospital in just a few days."

"He is?" Henry's eyes were like saucers. "Are we going to go and get him?"

Maddie shook her head. "We don't have to. He's going to come here on his own—right after he goes to Kannapolis to see your gramma and pick up his car."

Henry had a big smile on his face. "Daddy has a fast car, and it's red like the Camaro." He looked at Syd. "You'll like it, and so will Uncle David. I only rode in it once, but I had to sit on the backseat." He looked up at Maddie. "But I bet I'm tall enough now to ride in the front—aren't I, Maddie?"

"I don't know, sport. We'll have to wait and see."

"Is Daddy going to stay here with us?" Henry asked.

Syd took a deep breath, but didn't speak.

"Not at first, Henry." Maddie knelt down beside him. "Your daddy got a job fixing cars at Mr. Junior's garage, in Troutdale, and he's going to live there."

"He is?" Henry looked bewildered. "Why can't he live here with us?"

"Because Mr. Junior is letting him use the apartment over the Esso station, so he can be closer to his job."

"But we have room for him here . . . especially since Uncle David and Uncle Michael went back to their house."

"I know, sport, but this is what your daddy wants to do, and it's important for us all to help him out as much as we can."

"Will he come and see me?" He sounded confused.

Maddie ran a hand through his hair. "Of course he will. And Henry? Once he gets all set up in his new apartment, he wants you to come and live with him."

Henry looked excited, then he looked at Syd, and his face fell. "But then I won't be here with you."

Maddie shook her head.

"Who will feed Before and my fish?" he asked.

Maddie squeezed his small shoulder. "You will, sport. Every time you come to visit us."

"But I don't want to go away. I want to stay here with you."

Maddie had no idea how she was managing to hold it together. "We want that, too, Henry. More than anything. But you love your daddy, and your daddy loves you. He fought very hard to come back to you from the war, and we're all just so happy and grateful that he found a place for both of you to live that's so close to us." She smiled at him. "We'll still be together a lot, and you'll always have your room here—just like it is now."

He looked down at the ground, where Pete was sniffing around, looking for stray pellets of fish food.

"Can Pete come with me?"

Maddie opened her mouth, but couldn't come up with any words to say. How could she tell him that the apartment was right on a county road, and there'd be no place safe for Pete to roam—much less for Henry to play?

"Honey." Syd knelt next to Henry and Maddie. Her eyes were puffy. "Pete needs to stay here so he can do his job, watching over the farm." She wiped some dirt off the corner of Henry's forehead with her thumb. "You know how hard he works, and how much we all depend on him to take care of us."

Henry nodded. Maddie thought he looked . . . resigned. Just like he had nearly two years ago when she first met him flying solo on a cross-country flight to live with a grandmother he'd only met once before. How was it possible for so much pragmatism to reside in such a small package? She had only an inkling of what that suggested about Henry's understanding of how life worked, and she didn't like it one bit. It made her think too much of her own childhood, and her angry tantrums in protest of her mother's taking her to live three thousand miles away from everything she loved. Away from the *same* place Henry would now be leaving in just a few days' time.

"Okay." Henry set his coffee can down on the ground and looked at Syd with his big blue eyes. "Can Daddy and I still come for taco night?"

Syd gave Henry a watery smile and pulled him into her arms.

"Of course you can," she said into his hair.

Maddie understood that Henry was already more focused on being reunited with his daddy than he was on any of the more disturbing details related to the impending changes in his everyday life. He loved her, and he loved Syd—but he was still a child. And for him, life was made up of a loosely connected sequence of moments—not events. And those moments came and went with a relatively finite set of emotions. Sometimes anger. Sometimes excitement. Sometimes anticipation. But never angst—and rarely, if ever, fear.

He was a loving and sweet—splendidly normal—kid. A kid, who in this mixed-up mash of the best and most unfortunate circumstances, just happened not to be theirs.

After their conversation, Syd cried for a solid two hours.

Maddie just tried to keep herself busy.

That's what she was doing today.

For too long, she'd neglected the blenders, toaster ovens, and vacuum cleaners that sat collecting dust in the barn. It was like the Island of Misfit Toys out there, and Syd kept complaining that trying to park her car was like navigating a motorcycle obstacle course.

It had been a long day.

Celine had left early that morning. Michael came by to collect her shortly before dawn so they could make the two-hour drive to the Charlotte airport in time for her eight o'clock flight back to L.A. Maddie and Syd remained behind because graduation services were taking place at the local high school just a few hours later.

Maddie teased her mother for leaving at such an ungodly hour, alleging it was nothing more than a flimsy attempt to avoid the paparazzi, who were certain to be dogging her in the aftermath of her arrest for assault. Celine replied that she was just jealous. But when they hugged goodbye, Celine held her more tightly than usual and whispered that it was okay for her to let down her guard and feel all the things she was fighting to hold back.

Celine had said her private goodbye to Henry the night before, and promised to be back for another long visit during his summer vacation. They even talked about the possibility of having Henry visit her in California—if his father agreed to the idea.

Henry, of course, was one hundred percent confident that he would.

The house had seemed so empty at breakfast that morning— like an inn during the off-season. No guests. No chatter. No complaints about the organic cereal. No Astrid competing with Pete for the inevitable scraps of—something—that Henry would "accidentally" drop. And the kitchen table seemed cavernous with just the three of them. The empty chairs mocked Maddie. She was halfway tempted to move them someplace out of view—in the same way she wanted to move her own cascading emotions to a more benign location.

Fortunately, they'd had graduation services to attend that morning, so they didn't have the luxury of overanalyzing the dramatic changes to their home environment.

The weather was good enough that the high school could hold its commencement ceremony outside on the football field. It was a poignant experience for parents and family members to sit on folding chairs set up just several hundred yards away from the spot where the school gymnasium had collapsed during the tornado. That site had been mostly cleared, and construction on a new facility was slated to begin in another week.

Graduation was an especially significant experience for Syd and Roma Jean—who had managed to escape serious injury after being trapped for several hours beneath the building's rubble. There were several commemorative speeches that made mention of the storm. And there was a special musical tribute, courtesy of the Oak Hill Academy Pep Band—on loan while Syd's marching band continued with fundraising efforts to replace storm-damaged instruments.

There were 164 students in the Class of 2012. This year's Valedictorian honors went to Jessie Rayburn, and Nicorette Jackson was named class Salutatorian.

There was one other special honor announced that day. An anonymous donor established a one hundred and fifty thousand-dollar endowment for the Jericho Public Library and instituted a merit scholarship program that would pay full, in-state college tuition and expenses for one enterprising student, renewable for four years. The inaugural recipient of the Gladys Pitzer Community Spirit Scholarship was Roma Jean Freemantle.

When the announcement was made, the audience sat in stunned silence before exploding into earsplitting applause. Nobody seemed more surprised than Roma Jean, who somehow managed to endure the barrage of public scrutiny without falling off the stage or knocking over the sound system.

It had been a day for the record books in more ways than one.

Maddie smiled when she thought about how happy Roma Jean had looked. The whole world was opening up for her in ways the teenager could never have been able to imagine. The irony of it all was hard to miss. Roma Jean's world was expanding by leaps and bounds, but Maddie's world was contracting and growing smaller.

Just like an aging heart muscle.

She shook her head and tried for the umpteenth time to concentrate on Edna's blender. The damn setscrews that anchored the heat shield to the motor housing were rusted into place and wouldn't budge—no matter what she tried. She was about ready to go at the thing with a ball pein hammer.

She stood back and remembered how her father had always told her to use all of her senses when she confronted a problem. "Sometimes," he'd say, "you can get further with a good dose of common sense than you can with conventional wisdom. The right tool for a job might not be a tool at all."

Okay. So tools aren't working, here. What are my alternatives?

She looked around her workbench. *Phillips screwdriver? Nope. Socket wrench? Nope. Vise grip pliers? Nope. Pry bar? Tempting— but, no. Hydrogen peroxide?* She stared at the brown bottle with a faded label. *Why in the hell is that out here?*

Then she remembered. Her father once used it to loosen the rusted head of a lawnmower screw when he ran out of Liquid Wrench—and it worked like a charm.

Why not give it a try?

She walked to her toolbox to get a bulb syringe, but the damn drawer wouldn't budge. Something inside the drawer was stuck and kept catching inside the opening. The more she pulled, the harder it stuck.

Use all your senses, Maddie.

Fuck that. She pulled harder. The bright red cabinet shook and rattled, but the drawer didn't give an inch.

She'd had it. There was *no* way this thing was going to best her.

She braced her foot against the base of the tool chest and yanked as hard as she could on the drawer pulls. They snapped off like dry twigs and sent her sprawling backward into a low storage bin. It toppled over, and half a dozen bags of birdseed spilled out across the barn floor. She ended up flat on her back in a sea of cracked corn, sunflower seeds, and thistle—still holding the drawer pulls in both hands.

She sat up and waited for her breathing to return to normal. Then she saw them. Little red-and-white-striped candies wrapped in cellophane. They were everyplace. The breath mints Henry fed to that damn, rogue heifer, B4.

It was too much. It was *all* too much. Too much loss. Too much change. Too many people who came and went before she was ready to lose them.

Her emotions boiled over and pulled her temper right along in their wake.

She hurled the drawer pulls across the barn. They hit an old kerosene lantern hanging from a support post and shattered its globe. Her rage gained momentum, and she threw anything she could get her hands on: bins, buckets, garden trowels—even a small weed whacker. It didn't matter. Anything within reach was fair game.

Then she started to cry. Gut-wrenching sobs shook her frame and rose up into her throat like hot bile. She hugged her knees to her chest and rocked back and forth on her bed of birdseed and peppermints, wrapped up in a cloak of torment like a modernized version of Job—the beleaguered ancient Hebrew who mourned his losses by scratching at his boils in a pit of ashes.

"Dr. Stevenson?"

Maddie froze when she heard the voice. She hadn't heard anyone drive up, but that wasn't surprising, given the volatility of her tantrum.

She hastily rubbed a hand beneath her nose and tried to wipe the tears from her face.

"I'm sorry to bother you, but I heard the noise in here from up on the porch, and it worried me."

It was Roma Jean. Maddie turned toward her, but made no effort to get up. She could tell by the look on Roma Jean's face that she must've scared the shit out of her.

"I'm sorry," she said. Her voice was husky.

Roma Jean stood rooted to the spot in the center of the doorway. A beam of sunlight was hitting the top of her head, and it radiated off her hair like fire. She was still wearing her dress clothes from the morning graduation ceremony.

"I came out here to see Miss Murphy," she said. "I knocked on the door, but nobody answered."

"No." Maddie cleared her throat. "She's not at home. She took Henry into town to run some errands."

"You've got birdseed in your hair," Roma Jean said. "I'm really sorry for bothering you. I'll come back later."

"No. It's okay, Roma Jean. You don't have to go. I was just . . ." Maddie struggled with how to explain her meltdown.

Roma Jean was looking at her intently. "You don't have to say anything, Dr. Stevenson. It's really okay."

"Is it?"

Roma Jean nodded.

"Henry is leaving us on Wednesday." Maddie made an oblique gesture toward the mess on the barn floor. "I guess I just hit critical mass with everything. I mean . . . it's not like I didn't always know it would happen—of *course* I did." She didn't know where on earth the words were coming from, but once they started, she didn't try to stop them. "Somehow, when James gave us an actual date, I just fell apart—on the *inside*. I couldn't even tell Syd . . . I didn't want her to see how weak I was . . . how weak I *am*. How much I'm hurting." She wiped at her nose again. "I didn't want to make this harder for her."

Roma Jean knelt down to clear off a spot in the carpet of birdseed. Maddie started to protest, but Roma Jean just ignored her and continued—as if sitting down on a dirty barn floor in her best outfit was the most natural thing in the world for her to be doing.

"You'll ruin your clothes," Maddie said.

Roma Jean shrugged. "I never really liked this dress all that much. Mama made me buy it because I had shoes it would match."

"That's very sensible."

"It would be if I liked the shoes."

Maddie had to smile at that.

"I know it was you and Miss Murphy," Roma Jean said, quietly. "It had to be you."

Maddie looked at her. "What do you mean?"

"My scholarship."

"Oh." Maddie looked out across the barn. The mess she made would take the rest of the afternoon to set to rights. She didn't want to slip up now and create an even bigger one for Syd to have to deal with. "I promise you, Roma Jean, as happy as I am for you, I had nothing to do with it."

"Nothing?"

Maddie shook her head.

Roma Jean sighed. "Okay, then. I'll just wait to thank Miss Murphy."

Maddie was curious about what led Roma Jean to be so confident in her supposition. "What makes you think Syd was involved?"

"Well, I know that Mrs. Pitzer couldn't do it, and nobody else in Jericho cares that much about the library."

"Those things are true, but they don't necessarily add up to Syd's being your benefactor," Maddie pointed out.

"No," Roma Jean agreed. "But Nicorette was at the café the day of the food fight, and she found some papers on the floor when she was helping her mama clean up the mess."

Maddie had a bad feeling about this. "Papers?"

Roma Jean nodded. "It was Miss Murphy's prenup. But don't worry. She gave it to Sheriff Martin."

"After she read it?" Maddie asked.

Roma Jean shrugged.

Maddie sighed and held up a palm. "I will neither confirm nor deny any knowledge of these events."

"It's okay. If she doesn't want people to know, I won't say anything." She looked at Maddie. "Even though I want to tell her how grateful I am."

"I think she already knows that."

"I'm grateful to you, too, Dr. Stevenson."

"Me?" Maddie was surprised. "Why?"

"Because you never judged me—even when I was a kid with a stupid crush on you. You always made me feel smart and special— like I could do anything . . . be anything. Now—because of you and Miss Murphy—I have a chance to try."

Maddie didn't know what to say.

Roma Jean didn't wait for a response. "Why don't we clean all of this up before Miss Murphy and Henry get back? It looks like another tornado rolled through here."

Maddie smiled at her. "You don't have to help me. I'm pretty good at cleaning up after myself."

"I know, but the other day you said we were friends. Did you mean that?"

"Of course I did."

"Then this is what friends do, isn't it? They help each other out when things get hard."

Maddie couldn't disagree with that, so she didn't try.

"It won't be forever," Roma Jean said.

Maddie looked at her.

"He'll be back. Even if it's not to live here—he'll be back, and you'll still have him in your life. He loves you both, and he'll always want that. I know it."

"Maybe . . . but it won't be the same."

"You're right. But nothing ever stays the same, does it? I mean . . . two months ago, I was dating those freak-show Lear twins. Now?" She thought about it. "Now I'm going out with a *girl*. Yesterday, I was planning to go to community college part-time because that's all my family could afford. Today, it looks like I might be going to Radford."

She climbed to her feet and extended a hand to Maddie. "Let's get started."

Maddie sat staring up at her for a moment, then reached out and took hold of her hand.

Epilogue

It rained all day on Tuesday—a steady, soaking rain that swelled streams and pushed ponds up over their spillways.

Maddie had been hoping to take the entire afternoon off, but an emergency called her back into the office after lunch. She ended up having to see two additional walk-in patients while she was there, and it was nearly four-thirty before she could head out for home.

Tuesday night was taco night—Henry's favorite. And David and Michael were coming over to join them for their last meal at home as a family.

Maddie didn't mind that one bit. James was coming to get Henry tomorrow morning, and she was grateful for any distraction that would help them lighten the pall that had settled over their lives. As much as humanly possible, Maddie and Syd worked to conceal their escalating sadness from the little boy who had filled their lives with so much hope and happiness.

But Maddie resolved never again to hide her emotions from Syd—or herself.

That had been the biggest revelation of all for her ... the discovery that baring her pain and insecurity to someone she loved and trusted didn't make her more vulnerable, it made her more human. It restored her sense of balance and equilibrium. It put the pieces of her fractured center back together and gave her the strength and courage she needed to keep moving forward. More than anything, it taught her that, together, they could weather any kind of storm.

She turned off Route 58 and started the long climb up the

county road that led to the turnoff for their farm. She couldn't even count the number of times she'd made this same trip, and she knew every dip and sag in the worn blacktop. But today, everything looked foreign. And it wasn't just because the rain clouds had settled down over the rolling hills and pastures like a misty shroud.

She rounded the curve where the Cox barn had been, before the tornado carried it off into history. Grass had grown up and nearly covered the remaining few stones of its foundation. In the next pasture, a few fat cows huddled together beneath a cluster of bigtooth aspen trees. Someone in a bright yellow rain slicker was out walking among them.

Maddie slowed down and did a double-take. It was Syd.

What on earth was Syd doing out in the middle of Joe Baxter's pasture during a rainstorm?

She stopped the car and climbed out.

She tried calling out her name, but the wind just carried the sound right back to her. So she pulled up her hood and made her way across the same deep ditch where she'd taken refuge with Henry while the tornado passed over them. She ducked under the split-rail fence and entered the soggy pasture.

It was raining harder now. It took her a few minutes to catch up with Syd, who was leading one of the cows along by a rope. Just when Maddie got close enough to touch her on the back of the arm, she realized the cow was Henry's beloved Before.

Syd jumped and nearly slipped on the wet grass when she realized someone was behind her, but she quickly recovered when she saw it was Maddie.

"Great," she said. "You can help me with her."

"What in the hell are you doing out here?" Maddie asked. Rain pelted her in the face and ran down the inside of her jacket. Her shoes and socks were soaked and covered with mud.

"I'm taking Before home." Syd cinched up her hold on the rope that was tied around the heifer's neck.

Maddie was confused, but just assumed that Before had broken out again and shown up at their place.

"Why didn't you just call Joe to come and get her?"

"Because I'm taking her home."

"I can see that honey . . . but you're going the wrong way." Maddie pointed a finger behind them toward Joe's barn.

Syd shook her head. "*Our* home."

"What?" Maddie was confused.

"I bought her for Henry."

Maddie looked from Syd to the cow and back again.

"Oh," she said.

It was crazy and ridiculous, but it made perfect sense. She wished she'd thought of it.

She linked her arm with Syd's, and they continued walking on toward home.

"What about the car?" Syd asked. Maddie was still driving her Volvo.

Maddie squeezed her arm. "Maybe we'll get lucky and someone will steal it."

Syd laughed. "Fat chance."

A big, white-faced Hereford lumbered out from beneath a tree as they passed and mooed at them with displeasure.

"I don't think she's very happy with us," Syd observed.

They walked on in silence for a few moments.

"Maybe we should buy her, too?" Maddie suggested.

Syd looked at her strangely.

Maddie shrugged. "We could name her After."

It was hard for Maddie to tell whether there were more raindrops or tears running down Syd's face as they slowly walked the rest of the way home. But once they topped the last rise that led to their own land, the rain seemed to taper off, and the heavy clouds that had hugged the tops of the ridges all day retreated just enough to reveal a bright blue sliver of sky.

About the Author

ANN McMAN is the author of seven novels and two short story collections. She is a recipient of both the Alice B. Lavender Certificate for Outstanding Debut Novel (*Jericho*) and the 2017 Alice B. Medal for Outstanding Body of Work. Her novel *Hoosier Daddy* was a Lambda Literary Award finalist. Her books *Sidecar* and *Three* won Golden Crown Literary Society Awards for Best Short Story Collection, and *Backcast* was awarded the Silver Medal for Fiction in the Independent Publisher Awards (IPPYs) for the Northeast Region. *Backcast* also received the Rainbow Award for Best Lesbian Book of 2016. A career graphic designer, Ann is a two-time recipient of the Tee Corinne Award for Outstanding Cover Design.

Ann and her wife, Bywater Books Publisher Salem West, live in Winston-Salem, North Carolina, with two dogs, two cats, and an exhaustive supply of vacuum cleaner bags.

Acknowledgments

Sometimes, the effort it took for me to write this book was as taxing as attempting to run a marathon in lead boots. In the short space of a year, I lost my sister and my father—and experienced other life changes that were nearly as volatile, and continue to be as far-reaching in their effects. *Aftermath* is a book about how a big storm changes everything. On a personal level, it is the companion volume to how a few more modest storms changed my life while I was writing it. For the Herculean effort it took to finish this book, I am deeply grateful to my real life cast of characters. Dee Dee, Luke, Jess, Trent, Jason, Domina, Winnie, and Georgia—you all know what your support means to me.

Jenny, Cap'n, Midway, and Montine—fond memories of our shared lives will always abide in the warmest place of my heart. Thank you for your friendship—and for ready access to your glossaries of great Southern names.

Jeanne Magill was a godsend for helping me arrive at accurate depictions of medical procedures. Any errors or inconsistencies in that realm should, therefore, be directed her way. (I know she'll be thrilled to read this.)

Deb Fazzina provided the impetus and the inspiration for the epic flight of *The Camaro That Will Live In*

Infamy. To her, I say thank you from the bottom of my heart—and I hope I did you proud.

I will always be grateful to my friends and followers at the Athenaeum and the Academy of Bards—thank you for believing in me, and for offering me such unbridled support.

I owe special thanks to Stephanie Tyson and Vivian Joiner, amazing women and co-owners of Sweet Potatoes Restaurant in downtown Winston-Salem, North Carolina. They serve up the best Southern cuisine on this side of the Mason-Dixon Line—and they (unknowingly) were the inspiration for the Midway Café, and for most of the recipes Nadine Odell cooks there.

Heartfelt expressions of gratitude go to *all* the wonderful women who work and write for Bywater Books—you all are family, and I love having a home here.

Charlie Redmond and Pam Sloss are two women who have generously contributed to nonprofit efforts in support of lesbian literature. Thank you for all the good you do. It was an honor for me to partner with you in the writing of this book.

Thanks, as always, to the Fraternal Order of Wood Huskies, Lodge 251. I'm proud to be among you.

Salem West, you are, and will always be, the still point of my turning world. Your love and companionship give everything in my life a depth and richness beyond imagining. (And I want to go on record here, and declare that I would have said this even *before* I tasted your meat loaf.)

I am most sincerely indebted to you all.

Goldenrod
— a Jericho novel —

"Goldenrod takes us back to Jericho, where its hardscrabble characters invoke Dorothy Allison, and its provocative humor, Rita Mae Brown. In other words—it's pure Ann McMan."

–KG MACGREGOR, Lambda Literary Award-winning author

Goldenrod

Paperback   978-1-61294-083-0
eBook   978-1-61294-084-7

Goldenrod is also available in audiobook and MP3 CD formats via *audible.com.*

www.bywaterbooks.com

At Bywater Books we love good books about lesbians just like you do, and we're committed to bringing the best of contemporary lesbian writing to our avid readers. Our editorial team is dedicated to finding and developing outstanding writers who create books you won't want to put down.

We sponsor the Bywater Prize for Fiction to help with this quest. Each prizewinner receives $1,000 and publication of their novel. We have already discovered amazing writers like Jill Malone, Sally Bellerose, and Hilary Sloin through the Bywater Prize. Which exciting new writer will we find next?

For more information about Bywater Books and the annual Bywater Prize for Fiction, please visit our website.

www.bywaterbooks.com

www.ingramcontent.com/pod-product-compliance
Lightning Source LLC
Chambersburg PA
CBHW031955130726
47904CB00013B/1719